Call Waiting

By Michelle Cunnah

CALL WAITING
32AA

Call Waiting

MICHELLE CUNNAH

AVON
TRADE

An Imprint of HarperCollins*Publishers*

HarperCollins books may be purchased for education, business, or sales promotional use. For information please write: Special Markets Department, HarperCollins Publishers Inc., 10 East 53rd Street, New York, NY 10022.

FIRST EDITION

Designed by Elizabeth M. Glover

Library of Congress Cataloging-in-Publication Data

Cunnah, Michelle.
   Call waiting / by Michelle Cunnah.—1st. ed.
      p. cm.
ISBN 0-06-056036-3
I. Title.

PR6103.U5C35 2004
823'.92—dc22

2003021471

04 05 06 07 08 JTC/RRD 10 9 8 7 6 5 4 3 2 1

For Kevin, Rhiannon, and Gareth

••••••••••••

Acknowledgments

I was so dazed and bemused first time around with *32AA* that I completely omitted to acknowledge anyone. So I'm making up for it now (but won't go on for too long).

My profuse apologies to all of my family and friends, whom I neglected shamefully during the writing of *32AA* and *Call Waiting*.

A gazillion thanks to my daughter, Rhiannon, for the ionic bonding theory; my son, Gareth, for mastering the freezer and the microwave; and my husband Kevin, for being such a pillar of support over the years. I am completely in debt to him for the waiters behind the potted plants, and because he gave me the voice of Aunt Alice.

Huge thanks also to my fabulous critique partners Leigh Raffaele, Kate Lutter, and Sue Kass. You're the best, girlies!

I also need to thank my friend Yvette M. Feliciano, for my author photograph, and my wonderful agent, Paige Wheeler, for the "To Do" lists and for her great insight.

And finally, my complete and utter admiration to my gods-among-men Led Zeppelin for all of their fabulous music. Keep on rambling, lads . . .

....

Prologue

ASSESSMENT OF PAST YEAR
Emma Taylor
Age 31 (just)

Accomplishments:
1. Have accepted self for Who I Am (i.e., small-breasted and skinny). After all, bigger boobs would only make me front-heavy, which is a *bad* thing because (apart from possibility of curvature of spine problem, or implants exploding on airplane due to air pressure problem) bigger boobs would only make me prone to falling on my face. Or not *exactly* on my face on account of surgically enhanced boobs breaking my fall—image of me bouncing along sidewalk on stiff implants is not attractive . . . However, have gained three more pounds thanks to disgusting bodybuilding shakes and am now well within personal body mass indicator. Excellent progress!
2. Have become A Couple! But not only this, have also been with lovely, caring, boyfriend Jack for eight

whole months, so is now officially a long-term, grown-up, covalently bonded relationship. *Y-e-s!* See, best friend Rachel (with her Texas-sized brain) has a really great atomic chemistry theory about men. They are either (a) ionic bonders, i.e., they bond with another atom (make you fall for them), dispel their extra electron (have sex with you) then leave fully charged; (b) noble gasses, i.e., don't bond with anyone; or (c) covalent bonders, i.e., permanently bond with another atom (fall in love with you), share electrons and create totally stable partnership. The perfect man! The perfect relationship! Very good progress so far . . .

3. Have pleased both parents and stepmom with my choice of Life Partner. Although (obviously) is more important to please self than others when falling in love, is very nice that Dad, Peri and Julia approve. Dad (plastic surgeon), because Jack is not in need of plastic-surgery procedures, plus Jack is up-and-coming architect with great future prospects (to support possible future offspring and me). Peri, my stepmom, because Jack is her younger brother and therefore perfection personified. Julia, politically correct, Human Rights-lawyer mother, also approves because Jack is in touch with his feminine side—see, Jack has no masculine/feminine identity problem when driving my daffodil yellow, painted-with-flowers Beetle. Plus, when Julia cross-examined him as to exact locations of female erogenous zones, he passed with flying colors. Although all she had to do was to ask *me* . . . Honestly, I'm the one sleeping with him so have insider information!

4. Have made progress on Career Front. Kind of . . . Although I thought that being promoted to Junior Account Manager, Advertising, would involve more

creative work with Vietnamese potbellied pigs and cellulite creams, or similar, and less typing and coffee making . . . Not *bad* progress . . . but not great, either. Hmmm . . .

5. Have become A Woman of Means! At least, have become A Woman With Savings Account . . . promotion to Junior Account Manager, Advertising, means more money, and have so far saved nearly three thousand dollars (possibly toward Jack's new roof when he asks me to marry him?). Very good progress—need to continue good work.

6. Have become A Philanthropist. At least, have committed self to monthly fifteen-dollar donations to assist children in Third World. Excellent progress!

7. Have retained Personal Friends despite being half of A Couple. Because is important to retain friends, and not to lose sight of them just because one has fulfilling personal relationship.

8. Have met personal Gods Among Men, Robert Plant, Jimmy Page and John Paul Jones! Crowning personal achievement! Y-e-s! (Apart from relationship with Jack, obviously.) Well, didn't actually *meet* Led Zeppelin . . . but was only few feet away from them at launch of new DVD movie, so at least have breathed the same air . . . could almost have reached out to touch Robert Plant's lovely blond hair.

Still to Accomplish:
1. Subtly indicate to Jack that am ready to take next step with mature, covalently-bonded relationship, i.e., move in properly (e.g. next week?).

2. Get engaged (but in fullness of time—Tiffany ring is definitely not a prerequisite, though. Definitely not).

3. Get married (also in fullness of time—sooner would be nice, but possibly next spring?).

4. Purchase more Manolo Blahnik shoes (possibly for wedding?).
5. Expand philanthropic works. Look into details of purchasing livestock for third-world villages in near future (possibly goats or chickens).
6. *Do* something positive about career. But what? Need to give this more thought . . .

All in all, not a bad year . . . but still room for improvement . . .

1

············

Déjà Vu

TO DO

1. Stay in bed with Jack allll mooorning looong (is my birthday, after all).
2. Have romantic sex (or deliciously wanton sex—both are equally acceptable), repeatedly, and at length, allll moorning looong. With Jack.
3. Choose exactly right outfit for tonight's birthday (and possible engagement) celebration!
4. Be stunned and enthusiastic tonight when Jack surprises me with emerald engagement ring. Even though ring is too big. Even though am not fond of emeralds . . .

Saturday, June 28.
7:30 A.M.

Happy, happy thirty-first birthday to me, I think, as I snuggle sleepily into the comforter, and Jack spoons me closer.

Mmm. Although it's only early morning and my birthday's still young, it's already my best one yet. Definitely.

And Jack says I owe it to myself to spend at least half of the day in bed on account of it being my day to be pampered. But also on account of him wanting to spend time in bed *with* me! Y-e-s! This is definitely one of the pluses of having such a gorgeous, loving boyfriend—sex on demand!

Twice so far this morning . . . in fact, the second time Jack did this really great thing with—No. I'm not going there. Let's just say that Jack has a great imagination and is full of surprises. Let's just leave it there. But it was *truly* sublime . . . Actually I'm already feeling ready for a bit more birthday loving . . . wonder if Jack does, too?

I snuggle closer into his warmth, but although his arm tightens around me, I can feel his even breath on the back of my neck. Best to let him doze for a bit to regain his strength. Over the past couple of months he's been really busy with his latest architectural project in Boston—something to do with the harbor, I think. I don't really know, because Jack doesn't usually bring work home. Actually, he does bring quite a lot of work home these days—he spends a lot of time closeted in the dining room with his computer and his blueprints . . .

Anyway, because he's been soooo busy and tired, our sex life hasn't exactly been overactive recently. So today we're just making up for lost time. See?

As I try to drift back to sleep, I can't help but think about today and how wonderful it's going to be. This is our plan:

1. Stay in bed until at least noon, then take a leisurely (and naughty) shower. Together.
2. Amble down to the waterfront and have lunch in the fabulous new seafood restaurant. Together.
3. Amble back here to Jack's house. Go back to bed for the rest of the afternoon. Together (but not to sleep, obviously).

4. Get ready for my party, tonight. Together. Best friends Sylvester and David are hosting it at their restaurant, even though it is Saturday night—their busiest time of the week. How lovely is that? They insisted, because although thirty-one isn't a milestone age, my thirtieth birthday was a complete disaster . . .

Oh, togetherness is wonderful . . .

Wish we could be together more permanently, though. Like me moving in with Jack properly, instead of just spending most of my time here . . . Of course, it is *important* to maintain one's individual identity within a relationship. But I just want to maintain my identity while actually *living* with Jack.

Wonder if Jack will ever get around to asking me to move in? No, I'm not going to think about that now. After all, we've only been together for eight months . . .

And anyway, look what happened with Bastard Adam, my previous boyfriend. I moved in with *him* and we broke up three months later. And where did that leave *me?* Boyfriend-less, homeless . . . Yes, maintaining separate homes is *definitely* the right thing to do for now. I'm definitely going back to sleep.

7:40 A.M.

It's no good, I'm just not sleepy. It's this living together thing—I've really been giving it a lot of thought recently.

Okay, so things didn't work out with Adam. Okay, so Adam forgot my birthday, used me for sex, cheated on me with a much older, well-endowed woman, and screwed me at work by ruthlessly stealing my ideas. But Adam, according to best friend Rachel, was a total bastard ionic bonder.

Jack, on the other hand, is a wonderful, kind, covalent bonder. But he does have commitment issues . . . I mean, he has this private area of his past that he keeps separate from me. When I've tried to broach the subject of his ex-fiancée sleeping with his best friend, or about our long-term future, he kind of gets quiet and defensive, and so I change the subject.

But despite his commitment issues, Covalent Bonder Jack is so lovely in other areas of our personal life. I mean, Bastard Ionic Bonder Adam would *never* have made a public fool of himself for me. He was always very conscious of appearances—particularly his own.

Jack, on the other hand, is not a self-obsessed jerk and did make a *complete* fool of himself for me. Oh, but it was the most romantic thing in the world when he did the karaoke-complete-with-long-blond-wig Robert Plant impersonation thing at my friend's birthday party. Just so he could apologize to me, and to make me see how much I mean to him.

Adam would never have requested a Led Zeppelin song for me on the radio, or accompanied me to the Led Zeppelin DVD launch, because he assumed that I only liked classical music, like him.

Now Jack *knows* that I love Led Zeppelin—hence his Robert Plant ("Bob" to me, his number one fan) impersonation, and his cheerful willingness to spend Memorial weekend helping me dial the radio station to win those tickets.

But you know, I especially couldn't resist Jack after he rescued Betty the Beauty. I mean, how *could* I resist a man who rescues a hit-and-run dog, hands out wads of money for emergency animal-hospital treatment, and then adopts the dog? Even if the dog only has three legs . . .

So you see, Adam and Jack are two completely different types of men. So I shouldn't worry about me not-yet living with Jack. I'm sure he'll open up to me when he's ready. I think he just needs time . . .

And Betty the Beauty manages exceptionally well with three legs, I think, as she trot-hops across the bedroom and scrambles up onto the bed beside me. I was wondering where she'd gone—it's about time for her breakfast. She's such a sweet, clever little dog, but I think she gets embarrassed when me and Jack have sex—she usually yowls a bit, then takes refuge in one of the spare bedrooms.

We called her Beauty at first, but then we changed it. Although *we* think she's beautiful, it's in a *nontraditional,* beautiful-ugly, scrawny-mongrel kind of way. Because when we take her for walks people tend to notice her missing leg, and they always ask, "What's your dog's name?" When we used to say, "Beauty," they generally grinned, or even worse, laughed aloud. I mean *really*. How *rude*. Didn't they realize how damaging that could be for Betty's self-esteem?

Of course, I know all about the stressful demands of an inappropriate name. My mother named me for Emmeline Pankhurst, the famous British suffragette. Trust me, it took me years to quit worrying that I just wasn't cut out to be a letterbox-burning radical . . . Although, obviously, I *do* strongly believe in the women's suffrage movement. And World Peace and Human Rights.

Betty licks my nose and curls into a small ball of black fur, and I'm instantly flooded with love for her. As I cuddle her closer, I wonder if she misses me when I'm not here? I wonder if Jack and me not living together is stressful for her? See, that would be another good reason for me to move in—we're probably scarring poor Betty for life!

7:45 A.M.

Oh, telephone. Wonder if I should answer it? I mean, it's technically Jack's phone, so it's not really down to me to answer it . . . But who would call at this time of the morning apart from a bastard telemarketer in a bid to extricate cash from us? On the other hand it could be my mother calling from London. She forgets sometimes about the five-hour time difference. But it *is* Jack's phone, so I should just leave it.

That's the third ring. I don't know how Jack can sleep through it. Wonder if I should wake him up? No, he needs his sleep . . .

I try to ignore the strong urge to grab for the receiver. If it rings twice more, the voicemail will pick it up, so whoever is calling will leave a message. We can always call them back later . . . But what if it's urgent?

Betty scrambles to full three-legged alert, and howls at the ringing phone. See—it's a sign! Someone needs to answer that call right now.

"Go on," Jack rumbles in my ear, and I can hear the smile in his voice. "You know you want to pick up. It's probably for you—one of your multitude of friends, desperate for your advice. Or your mother."

See—this is another reason I love Jack—he totally understands me!

As I slip out of his arms and reach for the receiver, Jack moves with me and nuzzles my neck, and his hands are—well, I won't tell you where his hands are . . . Betty is not impressed—she yowls, flashes me a disgusted look, then trot-hops off the bed and out of the bedroom.

"Hello," I burble down the cordless telephone just a bit breathlessly. Thank God the person on the other end can't see what we're doing!

"Emma." Oh. It's Claire, Jack's boss. "I need to speak to Jack."

This is a *baaad* sign! Why is she calling him on a Saturday morning? On my birthday?

"Finish up quick," Jack whispers in my ear. "I have more plans for you and they don't involve conversation."

I wish I *could* just hang up and disconnect the telephone

from the wall, but I don't, because the Boston project is very important to Jack. Oh, but his hands make it very hard for me to think straight, and I am tempted, briefly, to throw the phone (and Claire, but only in a metaphorical sense) across the bedroom. But I don't.

"Oh, hi," I say cheerfully to Claire instead, because although I can barely breathe on account of Jack and his wonderful hands, and what they're doing to me, I'm also getting a very bad feeling that my birthday is about to be ruined. And anyway, it's rude to call someone and not say "hi" isn't it?

Actually, I don't think that Claire likes me, because on the few occasions I've met her she hasn't made much effort to disguise the fact that she thinks I'm an empty-headed idiot. And she does have this habit of making sly little remarks . . . Okay, so I do tend to sound a bit dumb when I speak to her, but that's because she makes me nervous. Plus, my feminine instincts bristle whenever she's around. I'm *sure* she wants to be more to Jack than just his boss.

"How *are* you?" I add, because I want to rub in her rudeness just a bit more.

"Fine," Claire says curtly. And then, "Emma, it's urgent that I speak with Jack."

"Hurry, hurry," Jack whispers in my ear again. "If you don't finish up your conversation right now, whoever is on the other end is gonna get very, very embarrassed."

"It's Claire," I tell him, reluctant to let her interfere with our day together. And he immediately stops kissing my neck and removes his hands from my person as he takes the phone.

"Claire, hi." Jack rolls over to his side of the bed, and I am instantly cold. But not just from the lack of Jack's body heat. "What's the problem?" Jack climbs out of bed and starts pacing the bedroom, and icy fingers of dread clutch at my stomach. "I specifically told them not to cut corners on—" Jack pushes a hand through his hair and frowns.

As Betty (who is smart enough to figure out that the sex is now a nonhappening event) joins me on the bed again, we both watch Jack pace. Our heads follow him back and forth; our synchronicity is impeccable. Betty is wearing the same "Oh boy, this is bad news" expression as me. As I said, Betty is very smart. Plus, she doesn't like Claire. Betty is also an excellent judge of character.

"Today?" Jack stops in his tracks. He is truly magnificent in his nakedness. "I can't go to Boston toda—" He begins pacing again as he listens intently to whatever bad news Claire is imparting. But how lovely is that? Saying "no" to Claire, because he wants to spend my birthday with me.

"How about tomorro—" He pinches the bridge of his nose. "Yes, I understand how important this project is to—"

How selfish am I?

Poor Jack is between a rock and a hard place. If he refuses to go to Boston, his project could be in serious trouble. If he goes to Boston, he'll be letting me down.

I look at Betty, who licks my hand and gazes at me with complete understanding. We know what I have to do.

"Jack," I say, my voice trembling just a bit.

"Yes, Claire, I know it's—"

"Jack," I say again, this time with conviction.

Jack looks across at me, shakes his head, and mouths "Don't worry." But I am worried.

I jump out of bed and pad over to him, taking his free hand in mine.

"Let me put you on hold a moment, Claire," Jack tells her.

"If you need to go to Boston, don't worry about hurting my feelings." There. I said it. I feel like shit, but I can see the relief on Jack's face. "We can do the birthday thing tomorrow, instead." God, I feel like Mother Teresa. Or at least how Mother Teresa *used* to feel. When she was still with us, instead of in Heaven. I should give my halo a bit of a polish.

"No," Jack tells me, his hand hovering over the mute button, but I can see he's tempted. "We've made plans. You're far more important than work." Oh, that's one of the nicest things anyone has ever said to me.

"But I'll still be here when you get back." I squeeze his arm and smile reassuringly. Even though I don't want him to go.

"You really mean it?"

"Absolutely." *Nonononono.* But I don't say that, obviously.

"You are amazing." He plants a quick kiss on my mouth. I don't feel very amazing. I feel amazingly horrible and empty. "Okay, Claire, what time's the flight?"

And as they discuss the ins and outs of whatever problem is going on, I climb back into bed with Betty.

"I'll see you in an hour." Jack clicks off the phone as my brain clicks into gear.

Of course he'll see Claire in an hour; it makes perfect sense for Claire to go with him. The fact that Claire is tall, blond, intelligent, and wears a C cup is a nonissue for me, because as Jack has told me on many occasions, my 32AAs are perfect, and that more than a mouthful is a waste. No, I'm not worried about Jack being alone with Claire. Call me suspicious if you like, but I'm not so sure about Claire making a play for Jack . . .

"You sure about this?" Jack asks, pulling me into his arms, and I sigh as I rest my head against his chest. "Because if you're not, I can call her right back and—"

"It's totally fine," I lie, as I link my arms around his neck. "Betty and me will be so busy hanging out and doing girly things we'll hardly notice you're gone."

"Try to miss me just a little." Jack pulls me even closer. "I'll be back for your party, I swear." And then he whispers in my ear, "How about a real fast quickie?"

Exactly what I had in mind . . . Mmm.

Betty marks her departure with a disgusted yowl.

8:10 A.M.

It's not the same—spending the morning in bed if you're on your own. Think I'll get up and make some coffee.

"Yes, I know," I tell the now-impatient Betty, who is tugging at the comforter in a way that implies "Feed me now." "It's past your breakfast time, and you're hungry, poor baby."

Don't think Jack will mind if I borrow a pair of his boxer shorts. It's hot, and the boxers are so comfy for lounging around the house . . .

"Jack," I shout through to the adjoining bathroom, but he can't hear me on account of the shower and him singing. I'll just help myself, I think, as I rummage through his underwear drawer. I have to say it, Jack is not the most melodious of people—Oh, what's this?

It's a small jeweler's box. A ring-sized box. Hidden away at the back of Jack's underwear. It's not Tiffany's but . . .

My God!

My engagement ring!

Jack's going to propose to me! And after all my worrying about not living with him, and his commitment issues . . .

My heart pounds right into my mouth as I finger the smooth velvet. Should I take a peek? Or will that spoil the surprise? I glance across at the bathroom, but Jack is still singing along in his own special way.

Betty raises an ear and snuffles in what I think is a very encouraging manner. I feel a bit sneaky, though, rummaging through Jack's personal stuff . . .

Okay—just a small peek.

I glance again at the bathroom, take a deep breath, and open the box.

Ohmigoditsanemeraldring. *Breathe,* I tell myself.

Itstoobigforme. *In-out, in-out.*

The shower and singing shut off abruptly, and I hear the

swish of the shower curtain. So I shut the box, carefully (but quickly) replace it exactly where I accidentally found it, and leap back into bed.

Now call me a bit ungrateful if you like, bearing in mind that my loving boyfriend has bought me an engagement ring in order to make a lifelong commitment to me. But an emerald is not my stone of choice. And the thing *is.* The thing *is* that Jack *knows* this, because I have mentioned it to him on several occasions. You know—on the odd occasion we've passed a jeweler's store together, I've made the rare, nonchalant comment about how I think that diamonds are so much prettier than colored stones . . . not as a hint or anything, but it's better to get these things out into the open. Also, Jack knows my ring size. Because I've mentioned *this* once or twice, too . . . actually, quite a lot more than once or twice . . .

"You okay?" He flashes me a concerned glance as he dries himself with the towel.

"Yes. I'm fine," I squeak, and Jack looks puzzled.

"But you don't look okay. You're flushed."

"Oh, I'm just a bit—you know—excited about my party."

"I almost forgot. Do you want your gifts now or later, birthday girl?"

Oh God. Do I want him to propose to me now? Or later, when we can celebrate properly?

"Oh, tonight will be just fine," I squeak at him again, because my vocal cords are not responding to orders from my brain.

"You look like you're worrying about something. Or getting sick." Jack frowns at me.

"No, no. Never felt better."

"Okay." Jack, not convinced, checks my forehead with his hand. "Give it up. What's bothering you?"

Jack knows me too well, sometimes.

"Really, everything's fine," I babble. "I think I just need to eat—you know, low blood sugar from all that exercise—do you have time for breakfast? Only breakfast is really, really important, because—"

"Emma, sweetheart," Jack interrupts me. "Quit worrying about whatever the hell it is you *are* worrying about." He kisses my forehead. "Okay?"

"Okay."

"And the answer's yes."

"Hmm?"

"Breakfast—go take a look in the refrigerator."

8:30 a.m.

Jack got strawberries and croissants for my birthday breakfast! How lovely is he!

So this is the puzzle, I think, as I pour coffee into two mugs and carry them to the kitchen table. Jack, who knows me so well that he can tell something is worrying me; Jack, who knows that I love strawberries, and warm croissants, and Robert Plant, has bought me an engagement ring that I will hate.

How did that happen?

"Hey, where have you gone?" Jack gives me a puzzled little smile, midchew.

"Just thinking about—you know—" I say, looking at Betty for inspiration. "—things. How they can change in such a short time." Like from not actually living with someone to being engaged, in one fell swoop. But I don't say this.

"Yeah. Betty sure settled in quick. Can't believe she's the same dog as the nervy little thing I brought back from the animal hospital."

Right on cue, Betty begs for another bite of croissant, because apart from the fact that she is greedy, she is a dog of excellent culinary taste.

"You are such a fraud," I laugh. "Croissants are not doggie food." But I give in to her and feed her a small chunk.

"And you," Jack tells me, feeding me a strawberry, "are a completely softhearted sweetheart. You'd better get that," he adds, as the phone rings.

Caller ID says "out of area," but I swallow my strawberry and pick up, because although it could be (a) a bastard telemarketer, it could also be (b) my mother.

"Hi, this is Scot. May I please speak with Jack?"

This is a cunning ploy on Scot's part to make me think that he is personally acquainted with Jack. But I can just tell that this is yet another telemarketing tactic to lull me into a false sense of security. I know for a fact that Jack doesn't know anyone called Scot. I quickly decide on my strategy for Scot evasion.

"Hi, Scot," I greet him like a long-lost friend. "Jack's indisposed in a priapismically difficult way at the moment." I grin as Jack chokes on his coffee. I have just told the hapless Scot that Jack is suffering from a prolonged (and probably painful) erection.

"I'm sorry to hear that," Scot tells me, not sounding sorry at all. "Is this Mrs. Brown?"

Hmm. Mrs. Brown. Mrs. Emma Brown. That has a nice ring to it. Or should I be Mrs. Emmeline Beaufort Taylor-Brown? No, that's a bit of a mouthful. I think I like the simple option.

"Mrs. Brown?" Oh, I forgot about Scot . . .

"No, definitely not," I say in my mother's Mrs. Thatcher voice. "I'm Jack's wanton sex slave, and we're right in the middle of an extended bondage session. Did you want to leave a message, Scot? Only he'll be tied up for a while. You know, it's amazing what you can do with a pair of handcuffs, a tub of chocolate sauce, and nine-and-a-half inches of pulsating, penile muscle."

Jack has now given up trying to drink his coffee and is clutching his stomach.

"Thanks for your time, ma'am," Scot gasps. Click.

"You are *baaad*." Jack grabs me and kisses me. And then, a bit faintly, "Nine-and-a-half inches?"

"Well, it was the first measurement that sprang to mind."

"I'm flattered, but I think you might be off by an inch or so."

"Maybe we should—you know—find out for sure with a ruler," I say, pressing myself against him. Mmm.

"Not a chance—there are some measurements a man likes to keep to himself. But I love the idea of the handcuffs and the chocolate sauce. Sounds . . . intriguing," he says, between kisses. And then his taxi honks from the street.

"You'd better go." I release him and straighten his tie, not wanting him to leave.

"See you tonight. Torture many telemarketers." He smiles his wolfish smile and my heart pittypats. And then to Betty, "Be good." And then he's gone.

8:45 A.M.

So what will I do with myself all day? It's still a bit early to call my friends. Besides, I must keep my mouth firmly shut about the ring. The ring . . .

I can't help it. A vision of The One Ring from *The Lord of the Rings* flashes before my eyes in an orangey-greeny blur (on account of the emerald). I mean, I love the *idea* of the ring, but not the actuality of its greenness. I hear Gandalf whispering in my ear, "Is it secret? Is it safe?" Oh, God, this is too much . . . Maybe I *should* go and take another peek at it—maybe it will grow on me (but not in a bad, all-consuming *Lord of the Rings* kind of way, obviously).

No. I'm going to be strong. I'm going to wait until tonight . . .

8:55 A.M.

Okay, so I'm going to take just one more little peek . . .

Maybe if I try it on, it will look better. And I *should* practice in front of the mirror, just so I don't show any signs of distaste when Jack surprises me later.

8:57 A.M.

The ring is not here.

Jack has taken it to Boston with him!

I am instantly filled with horrid feelings of déjà vu.

You see, last year I thought I was getting a ring from Bastard Adam, but it wasn't for me . . . It was for his mistress.

The emerald ring is too big and just too . . . green.

Has Jack bought it for someone else?

2

....

The Twilight Zone

TO DO

1. Remind self that am a mature, reasoning adult and must not jump to incorrect conclusions re: The One Ring.
2. Remind self that as a mature, reasoning adult, only sensible thing to do is keep mouth firmly shut until Jack's return. Discuss concerns with Jack in mature, reasonable fashion.
3. Avoid telephones for entire day! (Else will be tempted to confide in friends about ring issue and nonliving-with-Jack issue. Not mature—see [1] and [2] above.) Easy, see!

Of *course* Jack hasn't bought the ring for someone else, I tell myself, as I check through his underwear one last time. The idea of it is completely unthinkable.

Betty plunks herself on the floor next to me and whines, then licks my hand.

"Am I obsessing?" I ask her, and she tilts her head and whines again. "You're right, I think I am just obsessing."

I *must* stop comparing last year with Bastard Adam to this year with completely lovely, Nonbastard Jack. I *trust* Jack. But then, I trusted Adam until he cheated on me . . .

Oh, it's so hard not to draw parallels . . .

But Jack and I had sex three times this morning. I mean, you don't have sex with someone three times in two hours if you're planning on ditching them, do you? And after all, I didn't have sex with Adam at all for *weeks* before we broke up, on account of him having no sexual energy left for me because, of course, by then he was dispelling his extra electron with Stella.

But Jack *has* been tired and not so interested in sex recently. And he does work with the beautiful, intelligent Claire of the C cups . . .

No.

Jack wouldn't do that to me. He just wouldn't.

There is a perfectly reasonable explanation for the ring, and I am not going to worry about it. Not at all. I will talk to Jack about it in a mature, reasonable fashion when he gets back from Boston tonight.

Back from Boston with Claire . . .

Oh, telephone . . .

Oh, God.

I don't want it to be one of my friends. Of course, I do so love to chat with my friends, but if it's Tish, or Rachel, or Katy, I will immediately *spill all,* and then will instantly hate myself for doubting Jack. No, wrong word choice. It's not *Jack* I doubt, but myself.

Gingerly, I check the Caller ID. "Out of area." Not one of my friends, after all . . .

But this is a *good* thing, I tell myself. Doing battle with a telemarketer will be good therapy—it will release my pent-up angst. Or I could even tell the telemarketer my worries—I mean, it would be better than telling one of my nearest and dearest, wouldn't it?

And they do say that it helps to talk to a complete stranger, because they're completely noninvolved in your situation, so are not invested in being on your side. They just want to keep you on the phone long enough to extract cash from you; they have a vested interest in maintaining a conversation with you . . .

Therefore, I reason, discussing the situation with a complete telemarketer stranger has its advantages. They will *have* to listen to me, because they live in hope of a minimum fifteen-dollar bronze donation.

And so I pick up, ready to tell "Hello ma'am, this is Suzie," all about my totally stupid insecurities. I will feel better, and will probably make that bronze donation out of a burst of gratitude. A win-win situation, see?

"Happy birthday, darling." Oh, not a telemarketer. My mother.

"Julia," I say, comforted to hear her voice from so far away. It's at times like these that a girl needs her mother. Even a no-nonsense kind of mother, who will tell me to stop worrying, and to think about World Peace instead. Or will quote famous feminists to me. So I won't mention The One Ring.

Wonder what she's bought me this year? Last birthday, it was a herd of goats for a village in Uganda, because Julia nearly always gets me presents that are not actually *for* me, but *from* me. For a good cause. Which is completely admirable.

"You've made a donation to help the village of Elmina in Ghana," she tells me. "Darling, those poor canoe fishermen are losing their little red yeki fish because of the greedy trawlers illegally depleting the waters. You wouldn't believe how critical the situation's become. The fishermen are taking their children out of school because they can't afford to keep them there. I've put the information in the mail to you."

"That's great, Julia," I say, because it is. I mean, I really love the Manolo Blahnik shoes she bought me one year, but depleted yeki stocks and child education are far more important than designer shoes. This is a good way to expand my philanthropical interests, after all . . .

"God, it's raining again over here—what's it like over there? Ruin my day—I expect it's beautifully sunny and hot."

My mother's so *English,* chatting about the weather. It's to be expected, seeing as she is actually English. I suddenly get a strong urge to drop everything and just dash over to London to see her.

"It's too hot," I tell her, without adding that it is, in fact, a gorgeous summer's day—why make her feel worse?

"We could do with some heat over here, but at least the crap weather means that George can't grumble about how lovely it would be if we were in Devon or Cornwall for a minibreak."

"But a minibreak sounds romantic," I tell her, because it does. Although they haven't been married long, they've been living together for years, and it's nice that George still has romance in his soul, isn't it? I wonder if I should plan a minibreak for me and Jack? It would help Jack to relax and then maybe he'd open up to me some more . . .

"I think George is sweet to suggest it," I say to Julia.

"Don't *you* start," Julia tells me darkly. "It's bad enough with George complaining about spending the day making banners for tomorrow's march." And then, as I hear a low, masculine rumbling in the background, "Look, we'll go at the end of the month. Will that suit you?"

"What?"

"Not you, Emmeline—I've just promised the idiot man we'll go on the blasted minibreak." More rumbling in the background from George. "Honestly, George, we are not attached at the hip—of course it's a promise. Yes, I'll tell her." And to me, "George says happy birthday and sends his love. Speaking of which, what are you and Jack up to today?"

"Nothing," I tell her glumly. "Jack had to go to Boston—something urgent with a project."

"Do remember, darling, sometimes one *has* to work on the weekends." This is obviously a touchy subject for Julia, and I get the distinct impression that her words are more for George's benefit than mine. "Sometimes"—Julia continues—"it's unavoidable. One just has to get on with it. Stiff upper lip, darling."

"But he'll be back for my party tonight," I tell her soothingly.

"George, I can't have a three-way conversation," she says. "No, Jack will be back for her party."

I'm starting to feel excluded from this conversation. I hope Mum and George aren't having problems . . . You see, she wasn't that keen on getting married—once (very briefly to my dad) was enough—but it *was* important to George to have their relationship formalized.

I wonder, as I have done fairly frequently through my life, how my parents ever got together long enough to produce me.

Picture this. My dad: top tristate-area plastic surgeon (sometimes to The Stars). My mother: top London feminist lawyer (always to The Underdog). Mum, who was at Harvard on a student-exchange program, was married to my dad just long enough to get pregnant before taking herself (and embryonic me) back home across the Atlantic Ocean.

"Auntie Alice has donated a thousand pounds to the Elmina fishermen for you, too," Julia adds.

Dear, *dear* Auntie Alice. What a lovely thing to do!

Although Auntie Alice and me haven't been as close as we might have since I was younger, and lived with Julia, she is my *icon*.

I took Jack to meet her when we went to London last Christmas, because although I don't need her approval, I really wanted her and Jack to get on well. To tell the truth, I think Auntie Alice quite fancied Jack herself . . . I must write her a thank-you letter, because she's nearly deaf and can't chat easily on the phone . . . Oh, which reminds me, she must be on speaking terms with Mum again . . .

"So—you and she are talking again, then?" I ask tentatively, because Julia also completely admires Auntie Alice, and The Rift has caused Julia a lot of pain.

You see Auntie Alice is vehemently opposed to marriage, and refused to speak to Julia after she and George tied the knot. Marriage, according to Auntie Alice, is a bastion of the blatant male enslavement of the female sex. Which is a very unusual opinion for a woman of her age . . . but then everything about my great-great-aunt Alice, Baroness Beaufort, age one hundred and six, is unusual.

"Oh, that's all water under the bridge now," Julia tells me in her matter-of-fact way. "We just don't mention the 'M' word. To tell the truth, I think she's conveniently forgotten about the wedding certificate, and talks about George as if I'm just using him for sex."

On the other hand, Auntie Alice is totally pro having a great sex life, and (rather embarrassingly) quizzed Jack at length about his techniques (which no doubt is where Julia got this habit from). Auntie Alice even gave Jack some rather explicit advice . . . Julia and me are used to her very direct manner, but after his initial shock Jack took it all in good part. After all, it's very nice of her to be so concerned about my orgasms!

Back in the early part of the twentieth century she was the toast (notoriously so) of London. Beautiful, intelligent, well-connected, rich . . . She had a string of admirers and lovers, but she wouldn't marry any of the eligible men her parents paraded before her on account of not wanting to be someone's chattel.

I just don't *see* her as chattel fodder—formidable Auntie Alice bows to no one . . . except to the Queen, of course. And to other royal family members—at least, *female* royal family members. Not that Auntie Alice can bow at all these days, on account of not being able to walk. But she's had a new lease on life (to the horror of her carers) since she got the super deluxe electronic wheelchair.

"If all I have to worry about at her age is an occasional memory lapse, I shall be very content," I say to Julia.

"Oh, I doubt she's forgotten," Julia says. "When I said she'd conveniently forgotten about my marriage to George, I meant that it suited her to forget. The Elmina fishermen are her latest project, and she wanted to get me on board."

As I said, Auntie Alice is formidable (but we wouldn't have her any other way).

"We're doing a march tomorrow," Julia continues, "to the Houses of Parliament. She's very passionate about the fishermen, and the adverse effects it's having on the women and children."

Imagine living that long. Imagine being part of the suffrage movement. When I was little, she used to tell me all her tales of Emmeline Pankhurst (my mother's other idol, hence my name). Auntie Alice, along with Mrs. Pankhurst, chained herself to iron railings, got thrown in prison on occasion, and went on hunger strikes. It's all completely true!

In view of such selfless womanhood, I feel rather guilty about worrying about Jack and the ring. I mean, what have I ever done to further the women's suffrage movement? When I depart this mortal coil, what will I leave behind except for an emerald ring and a pair of Manolo Blahnik shoes?

"Anyway, darling, I have to go and check with the various committee leaders about tomorrow. Have a lovely birthday. Bye."

10:00 A.M.

Actually, I feel a lot better now that I've had a chat with Mum. Although I didn't touch on my worries re: the ring thing, and the living-together thing, just talking about Auntie Alice has really made me see things from a different perspective.

You see, there are far more important things in life than obsessing about your perfectly nice, covalent-bonding boyfriend—there's *bound* to be a perfectly logical explanation for the hideous engagement ring.

No, instead of obsessing, I'm going to make some tea, and read the *New York Times* to enhance my all-round knowledge of world affairs. Also, I will check the atlas for the exact location of Elmina, and Ghana, so that I am more knowledgeable about the worthy causes I am (indirectly) supporting. I need to be more proactive!

Yes, I am an intelligent, mature woman of the world, and I'm going to model myself on Auntie Alice . . . except for the part about marriage being a bastion of the blatant male enslavement of the female sex . . .

Talking about male enslavement, wonder if I should get some handcuffs and chocolate sauce for when Jack gets back? Hmm . . .

Wonder what Jack and Claire are doing in Boston . . .

10:15 A.M.

Oh, telephone . . .

Caller ID shows it's best friend Tish, so I don't pick up. I *cannot* speak to Tish right now because she is such a kind, sympathetic friend that I will immediately crumble and blurt out my Jack/Claire worries. Besides, she *lives* with *her* boyfriend, Rufus, and they've only been together a little while longer than Jack and me . . .

10:30 A.M.

Telephone again. This time the Caller ID shows it's scarily clever best friend Rachel . . .

She will only tell me to pull myself together, and to stop being such a wimp. And she'd be right, but I don't want to expose myself to one of her rants right now. Plus, she's getting married to Hugh in a few weeks' time. And they've only been together a bit longer than Jack and me, too . . .

10:36 A.M.

Tish again . . .

Nope. I mustn't pick up . . .

10:42 A.M.

Rachel again . . .

Who knew this would be so hard?

10:47 A.M.

Other happily-married-forever best friend Katy . . .

10:51 A.M.

Caller ID now shows Sylvester/David's number—my other happily-living-together best friends.

This is unbearable!

Think about Auntie Alice, I tell myself firmly.

"Come on," I say to Betty, because I am desperate to escape telephone temptation. "Let's go for a trot-hop."

Yes, this is the life, I think, as Betty and me stroll down to the river. It's a beautiful day, it's my birthday, and I'm spending it with woman's best three-legged friend.

I am wearing khaki cargo pants and a simple white T-shirt (Donna Karen, of course, because Donna is a queen among designers), and black, backless sneakers from Kenneth Cole. On my back I have my small, black, Kate Spade (also a designer goddess) backpack that Jack bought for me as a surprise Christmas present. My pixie hair is gleaming with blond highlights, thanks to a visit to my hairdresser friend Jason yesterday, and my makeup is simple, clean, and fresh.

This is a *great* look for me, and although I don't *feel* particularly great, it is important to at least look one's best on one's birthday. Plus, looking good boosts my wavering morale.

Betty is attracting a lot of attention, and not just because of her three-leggedness, but because I have tied a little blue ribbon in her straggly coat, just between her ears. I've also fastened a smart blue bow to her collar.

"This is a great look for you, honey," I tell her, bending to give her a pat, and she lolls her tongue appreciatively. At least, I think it's appreciatively. "You are a babe among dogs."

I mean, if people are going to stare at her, they might as well have something other than her missing leg, or the fact that her body is a bit too big for her remaining spindly legs, to comment about. How would they feel if I said, "Yes it's a shame about her missing leg, but then again isn't it a shame about your fat, ugly nose?" Plus, I want Betty to feel comfortable and well adjusted to her imperfections.

You see, I am totally familiar with physical imperfections

myself, so know how important this kind of thing is. I used to be a bit (a lot) self-conscious about my lack of cup size. A bit torn in two.

I mean, if I truly felt that implants would complete my life, my father could arrange it in an instant. He wouldn't do it himself, of course, on account of that not being ethical. But either "Uncle" Derek or Norbert, Dad's partners, would do it in a flash. It would be *hey presto!* Goodbye 32AAs—*hel-lo* 32Cs. Not that I'd let Uncle Derek or Norbert anywhere near my boobs . . .

No. Last year, I finally made my peace with them.

And my lack of artificial enhancement has nothing to do with my mother being totally anti plastic surgery. I *choose* not to have implants, or take breast-enhancing pills, because I am happy just the way I am.

And I want Betty to be happy with herself, and not to worry needlessly about artificial legs, or being too barrel-like. Not that she would. I mean, I do *realize* that she's a dog, and probably doesn't give two hoots about beauty—but still . . . who knows what dogs worry about, apart from the next meal?

As we stroll along the promenade, it seems that the whole of Hoboken is also making the most of the lovely June day. And I can't help but notice that nearly everyone else is part of a couple. Everywhere I look there are couples holding hands, laughing together, eating ice cream together . . . no offense to Betty, but I wish Jack were here . . .

I wonder what my friends are all doing today?

I wonder if there's something wrong? I mean, they did call me a lot of times. I'm sure it was just to say happy birthday to me, but what if something serious is going on?

I'm just borrowing trouble.

Oh no! My cell phone's ringing. After all, it's totally necessary to have my cell phone with me at all times, just in case of emergency. Maybe I should just answer it, because if I don't, my friends will worry about my telephone silence. Especially on my birthday . . .

Particularly since that time I disappeared for the weekend, and none of them knew that I was safely at Jack's house. They nearly called the state police, the lifeguard, and were seriously considering dredging the Hudson River for my lifeless body . . . Actually, Jack was very discreet about that— he's totally kept quiet about my temporarily homeless and nearly-sleeping-in-car episode. See, another good point in Jack's favor.

My God, they probably think that Jack and me have had some kind of horribly fatal accident . . . I can't leave them in limbo!

I fumble to take off the backpack, and then fumble even more as I try to find the cell phone. Success!

"Hello?"

"Emma, where have you been?" It's Tish. "We've been calling and calling."

"I'm fine. Jack's fine," I tell her soothingly.

"What are you talking about?"

Oh, she's *not* worried about Jack and me.

"What's wrong?" I grip the cell phone tightly, instantly cold, despite the heat of the day, because I know that this is going to be bad. Betty, picking up my mood, whines and rubs herself against my legs.

"Can you come over to Rachel's apartment right now?" Tish sounds very insistent.

This could be really bad. What if Jack *is* having an affair? What if my wonderful friends know all about it, and are going to gently break the news to me?

"But what's going on?" I ask her, all the while conjuring up even *worse* possibilities than a Jack/Claire affair. What if Jack's had an accident in Boston? What if his plane developed engine trouble? Or what if he drowned in the harbor when a freak gust of wind blew him off the scaffolding . . .

"I can't say over the phone. Just come."

This is *really* bad. Instant visions of me standing over Jack's open grave, as I tearfully wave a last good-bye. I didn't even tell him I loved him this morning. Who gives a flying fuck about the emerald engagement ring now?

"I'm on my way."

3

....

Trouble in Paradise

TO DO

1. Stop listening to my English half. Is bad for my stress levels.
2. Stop being subtle with friends. Subtlety only causes misunderstanding and mayhem.

By the time I reach Rachel's apartment, as well as being scared half out of my wits due to impending, possibly (probably) awful Jack news, I am also, (a) disheveled and dripping wet, because of running all the way from the waterfront, and (b) dog tired.

When I say dog tired I mean *literally* dog tired. I had to carry Betty for most of the journey. You see, although Betty tries hard, she cannot run very fast on account of her three-leggedness making her a bit lopsided. And although she is small, and can't weigh more than fifteen pounds, it's a lot of extra weight to carry when you're trying to break the world record for the mile run in eighty-degree-plus heat.

And let's face it, I'm only four feet eleven. And although

I'm barely within the bottom end of the normal range of my body mass indicator, I'm not exactly built like a pentathlon-competing athlete.

As we reach Rachel and Hugh's rather posh converted warehouse apartment block, I plop poor Betty onto her three feet and jab the doorbell. Hurry, hurry, hurry . . .

"Hello." Finally!

"Hugh, it's me," I gasp into the intercom, barely able to breathe.

"Ah, the Fourth Element," Hugh, Rachel's soon-to-be husband says rather cryptically. "We were all beginning to worry about you. Come on up." And then he buzzes open the door.

He doesn't sound very worried, though . . .

As Betty and me ride the elevator to Rachel's floor, I wonder what Hugh meant about me being the fourth element . . . Is it something to do with biochemistry? (Rachel and Hugh are both scientists and often talk in biochemically incomprehensible riddles.) Or is it an obscure reference to the movie *The Fifth Element,* and that somehow I'm needed to help save the planet from an evil, manmade asteroid? Or even worse, that I have to fly immediately to Boston to Jack's hospital bedside . . .

Oh no! *Jack, grievously and horribly wounded, is in a coma, and only the sound of my beloved voice will coax him back from traveling toward the light!*

I wish I hadn't had such horrid thoughts about Jack and Claire! This is what I get for doubting my poor, wonderful Jack . . . This is what I get for being such an ungrateful, petty Emma and hating the emerald ring.

As we reach Hugh and Rachel's front door, I've already made a silent bargain with all the gods from every religion I can think of (after all, it's only prudent to cover one's bases, just in case).

If only Jack can be spared, I'll devote myself to his

months—no *years*—of painstaking recovery, selflessly sacrificing my own needs to nurture Jack back to full health, in the manner of Christopher Reeve's wife . . . even if Jack has amnesia and has forgotten who I am. Even if he *never* remembers me, or that he ever loved me! Even if he thinks he's in love with Claire . . .

Oh God, Buddha, Shiva, Krishna, Jehovah, Allah, and all you other omnipotent beings whose names I cannot remember, *please* let Jack recover (plus, please let him love *me* instead of Claire).

"Hugh—what's going on?" I pant, before the door is fully open.

"Happy birthday, Emma," Hugh smiles, leaning forward to kiss me on the cheek.

Happy birthday? Is that all he can say at a time like this? What about Jack? And why is Hugh smiling?

"My God, you look hot and flushed," he says. "Are you coming down with something?"

He's very calm and collected. Not at all worried about Jack. Must be his scientific training . . .

"I came as soon as I could. Is it Jack? It *is* Jack, isn't it? I just know—"

"Whoa." Hugh holds up his hands. "Everything's fine. I think there's been a crossed wire somewhere along the line."

"But Tish said it was urgent—"

"I think you'd better go through to the living room, and all will be revealed."

"But—"

"Relax. Come on." He grasps my elbow and leads me to the living-room door.

Relax? Oh *Buddha,* the Jack news is so bad that Hugh can't bring himself to tell me!

"Here she is," Hugh announces to Rachel, Tish, and Katy. Who are all comfortably seated on Rachel's funky sofa, and are also all smiling in a nonworried kind of way.

And then I notice the ice bucket, complete with two bottles of champagne.

"Surprise," Rachel, Tish, and Katy say to me, jumping to their feet as Katy pops the top off one of the bottles.

Oh . . .

Okay. I'm good. Jack's alive! I am most certainly not going to faint with relief. I can breathe again. Not bad news, then, if we're celebrating . . .

And then their mouths fall open as they actually take in my rather bedraggled appearance.

I feel like an idiot. Because I've obviously let my English half jump to the wrong conclusion. Rachel says that my English half is insecure, and that it worries compulsively—I think she might have a point.

"Here—drink this, you look like you need it." Katy, bemused, hands me a glass. I down the champagne immediately, to calm myself.

"What the hell happened to you?" Rachel, ever one for getting straight to the point. "You're drenched. You getting sick?"

"That's what I thought," Hugh says, retreating to the kitchen. Wise man. "I'll leave you girls to it."

I sneeze, although not to add weight to Rachel's question. I'm not sure if it's from the champagne bubbles, or from the hairs from Rachel's three cats (who are fortunately absent—because they somehow know that they will cause maximum allergy pain to me and always, *always* make a beeline for my ankles when I'm here). It's odd that I'm not allergic to Betty . . . maybe it's on account of Betty not having much actual hair—she's kind of shorthaired, but with long tufts in between. A kind of punk-rocker dog . . . but Rachel's cats cause me immediate red-eye problems.

"Happy birthday, sweetie. I hope you're not contagious." That's a bit callous of Rachel. She's supposed to be my friend.

She retreats from me, and I'm a bit hurt because if I had

something nasty and contagious, I would take good care to keep it to myself.

"She's right, you do look sick, honey," Tish tells me, pressing a hand to my forehead. That's more like it! A concerned friend! But then I remind myself *why* I'm so hot and bothered . . . I need an excuse. I don't want to sound all pathetic and obsessive!

"Who, me?" I say, trying for an innocent expression. "Hahahaha." I am not going to tell them about the stupid conclusions I jumped to after Tish's call. "Not at all sick." I'm still wheezing a bit from the exertion. "Just thought I'd take Betty for a bit of a . . . run . . ."

I stop, because all three of my lovely friends are not buying my excuse. They look from me and down to Betty (who is definitely not gasping from exertion) . . . and back to me, again.

"What have you done to that dog?" Rachel asks sourly. "I can't believe you made the poor mutt wear blue ribbons."

"Betty," I say rather prissily, in an attempt to divert their attention elsewhere, "is not a mutt. She is a very interesting crossbreed—a mix of—"

"I told you she'd worry," Rachel says to Tish. "You shouldn't have been so vague on the telephone—you know how she jumps to the wrong conclusion."

Okay, my lame plan to transfer attention has failed. How to explain my appearance . . . Hmmm . . .

"Here." Rachel hands me another glass of champagne, braving my airspace now that she knows she won't catch something nasty from me. "Drink this—all of it."

I oblige, of course, because Rachel has a doctorate in something scientific, therefore she knows about the calming effects of alcohol.

"I didn't want to spoil the surprise," Tish says, her lip drooping just a bit. "I'm sorry, honey." Tish guides me to the sofa and gently pushes me onto it. "But Jack called us on his

way to the airport—he told us about his emergency. He
didn't want your birthday to be completely ruined, like last
year."

Oh! *Lovely* Jack!

And thank *Krishna* he's not dying or even comatose! He's
fine, after all. He didn't want to ruin my birthday! Everything's fine, just like I knew it was in my heart of hearts.

"It's okay," I tell my lovely friends. Because it *is* okay, isn't
it? All is well . . . whew. And bless them for not wanting me
to spend my birthday on my own. "I'm fine." I smile cheerfully, because the champagne is kicking in very nicely.

"We just want you to have a special girly day," Katy says,
patting my hand.

"Although why Jack couldn't wait until Monday to go to
Boston beats me." Rachel sips her orange juice. Which is
odd, because Rachel is very partial to champagne, and I
wonder, fleetingly, why she isn't partaking like the rest of us.
Come to think of it, she does look a bit peaky . . .

"If Hugh told me he had to work on a weekend, especially
my *birthday* weekend," she says, warming up for a rant, "I
wouldn't be very pleased about it. I mean, I have a demanding job, too, and what about all the weekend chores? Who
gets to do them? I mean, who goes to their deathbed wishing
they'd spent more fucking time at work?"

I think Rachel has something on her mind.

"Sweetie, quit ranting," Katy calmly tells Rachel, and I
hold my breath as I wait for Rachel's temper to flair. "At least
Hugh knows how to operate the vacuum cleaner."

Katy can be a bit touchy sometimes when it comes to divi-
sion of labor around the house. Because of being the stay-at-
home mom, she gets to do most of the cleaning and laundry.
Not that there's anything wrong with that, because I think it
shows what a selfless, nurturing person she is to sacrifice her
career in favor of rearing her child, and creating a loving envi-
ronment for her husband. And Tom *does* work long hours . . .

"We can't all inhabit a perfect world, much as we'd like to," Katy continues, although she's gazing into space and it seems as if she's talking more to herself than to us. "Sometimes, to quote the great John Wayne, 'a man's gotta do what a man's gotta do'—especially if he wants to keep his job."

Tom's company on Wall Street has been gradually downsizing over the past year or so. Just hope that Tom isn't going to be downsized, too . . . Hope that Rachel isn't about to explode, too . . .

"I know, I know, I'm a fucking grouch these days," Rachel says, surprising us with her about turn. "I can't seem to open my mouth without sticking my foot in it."

It's true. She has been very grouchy just recently . . .

"Anyway," Tish, ever the peacemaker, brightly changes the subject. "Let's forget about housework and overtime for now. We've got the day all planned. First, the beauty salon—facials, massages, manicures and pedicures."

Heavenly! A whole day of girly pampering.

"The torture chamber." Rachel grimaces.

"Don't be such a killjoy." Tish takes a gulp of champagne. "It's good practice for your wedding—it'll be relaxing and fun."

"Fun? Pah. Who cares whether we have roses or dandelions in the church?" Rachel asks, but her question is rhetorical, and I worry that all is not well with her. And *why* isn't she drinking champagne? That is very odd . . .

"At least you're *getting* married." Tish picks up one of the bride magazines from the rack, and starts flicking through the pages. "I think Rufus is happy for us to live together forever."

Rufus, deli owner and delicious muffin maker, is not renowned for making the first move. Or for being overly chatty. Tish loved him from afar for three whole years before she finally took the plunge and seduced him, then moved in with him before he knew what was happening. She sighs, and we all sigh along with her. That is, except for Rachel.

"I just want it to be over," she says. "Ever since we announced the engagement, my mother's been driving me nuts with guest lists and orchestral selections—did I tell you a regular band isn't good enough for her little girl? God, I wouldn't be surprised if she changed the venue at the last minute. I can see it now—Carnegie Hall, with a full orchestra!"

Ah—now we're getting to the bottom of Rachel's bad mood!

"I'd love a big wedding." Tish smiles blissfully.

"And my dad's been driving my mother *nuts* about the cost of everything. I can't blame him. She'll bankrupt him before she's finished with this."

"Carnegie Hall." Tish's eyes are shining at the thought. She and Rachel should swap places . . . Tish would truly love and appreciate a lavish wedding, with all the bells and whistles. Unlike Rachel, who hates all the fuss and rigmarole. Actually, I quite fancy the idea of Carnegie Hall, myself . . .

"And Hugh isn't any help," Rachel tells us. "Whenever he speaks to my mother, he just goes along with whatever she wants. Fuck, I just want to elope!"

"Oh, you'll regret it if you elope," Katy says, because while she and Tom didn't exactly elope, they did have a quickie wedding at a tacky wedding chapel, with two witnesses dragged in off the street. They were young, they had no money—they just wanted to be together. Actually, that's very romantic in its own special way, isn't it? I'd marry Jack in a tacky wedding chapel . . . if he ever gets around to asking me, of course.

"It's a special day just for you," Katy says. "You have to make the most of it, because once you start a family, and you're spending twenty-four/seven looking after other people's needs, that *one* day you were a princess will be a precious memory."

I wonder if Katy ever gets fed up of being just someone's wife and mother? Not that she *is* just someone's wife and mother, because she's a terrific, independent person with her own life—she's chairman of the PPPTA (Pre-Preschool PTA) and her bake sales and Chinese auctions are legendary.

"More like a black nightmare," Rachel says, bleakly. "And I don't want kids."

You know, she can be a bit of a pain at times, but she's not usually horrible. At least not to us, her nearest and dearest . . . My birthday treat is beginning to sound more like an *endurance test*.

"Anyway." Tish forges womanfully ahead to dissipate the tension. "After the beauty salon, which we will all enjoy—" she pauses and flashes Rachel a meaningful look. "We're going outletting."

Oh, shopping! Goody. There's nothing I like more than a trip to the outlets! Definitely not hard to endure a little trip to Donna Karan . . .

"We," Tish says, "are going to be frivolous and girly, and we're going to have fun. And while we're there we can check out the shoes," Tish adds. "We need to find just the right ones to go with the darling bridesmaid dresses."

Although Rachel's mother is in charge of the wedding, Tish is in charge of dressing the bride, bridesmaids (Tish and me) and the matron of honor (Katy). Which is a relief, because Tish is an interior designer with an infallible eye, and won't make us wear something yucky and vomit colored.

"Look," Rachel pins us all down with her gimlet glare. "Can we please have one day when we don't talk about my fucking wedding?" And then, because the room isn't exactly filled with party cheer, "I'm sorry, okay? Just ignore my foul mood—finish the fucking champagne and let's go have some fucking birthday fun."

2:30 P.M.

Bliss! I've been exfoliated, pummeled, kneaded and de-free-radicalized (or is it the other way around? I can never figure out if free radicals are good or bad), and I feel like a new woman.

Hugh, the dear man, offered to take care of Betty, because a beauty salon isn't a good place for a dog, and Betty is used to having company most of the time—Jack even takes her to work—so I couldn't just leave her home alone for hours on end, could I?

Katy and Tish are still having their radicals liberated, and Rachel and me are relaxing in the sauna. I can almost feel my pores cheering.

But I'm still a bit concerned about Jack's tiredness and lack of interest in sex just recently. I know I shouldn't, but I can't help it . . .

You know what? I shouldn't brood, because I will only make a mountain out of a molehill.

"This was a really great idea." Rachel leans back and closes her eyes. "I know I'm not the easiest of people these days—it's this wedding thing—I didn't realize how stressful it would be."

And Rachel (who is obviously in a much better mood than earlier) is a doctor, after all. Although not a medical doctor, she *is* scientific and is therefore the obvious person with whom to discuss such a delicate matter. But I don't want to sound *too* obvious. I don't want her to know that it's actually Jack and me we're talking about . . .

"Do you . . ." How to phrase this with diplomacy and tact? Hmmm . . . "Do you think it's—you know—normal, to go off sex for a bit. I mean, in a long-term relationship. Even if you really, really think the love of your life is gorgeous and sexy and everything?" There, that was very diplomatic, I think. "Only I read this article in a magazine and it said that—"

"Has Hugh been talking to Jack?" Rachel jumps in. "He *has* said something to Jack, hasn't he?"

"No—" I think I've just ruined her good mood—Rachel is very defensive.

"Why do men worry so much about sex? I mean, okay, so I've been a little tired and washed-out, is all."

Oh. So Rachel's off sex, then. Which is odd, because Rachel loves sex, but in a non-nymphomaniac way, obviously. Wonder why she's gone off sex . . .

"Hugh will suffer for this," she says, warming up for another rant. "He will truly understand the meaning of no sex by the time I've finished with him."

"Rachel, I didn't mean you," I blurt. "I meant Jack and me." Oh God, I didn't mean to say that.

"Oh."

We sit in silence for a couple of minutes. Me, because I'm embarrassed. I don't want her to think less of Jack. I feel, somehow, that I've betrayed him.

"It's perfectly normal to go off sex for a while," Rachel says, decisively.

"Completely," I agree with her.

"So we won't mention this little chat to anyone."

"Absolutely not."

What was I worried about? I mean, if Rachel can go off sex for a bit, then it must be okay. Besides, Jack and me did have great sex this morning. Three times.

3:45 P.M.

I love outletting! The thrill of finding a bargain can't be beaten, I think, as I sign my credit-card slip for the new pants and jacket that I have just acquired from the bargain rack in Donna Karan.

"It seems like ages—it is ages—since we did this," I say to

Katy as we step outside into the heat. Tish and Rachel are in Jones New York, just around the corner.

"I can't remember the last time," Katy says, peeking into her bag. "Much as I love Tom and Alex, it's great to get away from them for some retail therapy. We must do this again. Soon."

"Mmm," I sigh in agreement, wondering if I could get Jack to come with me next weekend—that leather jacket would look gorgeous on him.

Thinking of Jack, I wonder what he's doing now . . .

I'm sure he's working. Just working. Not flirting, or anything, with Claire . . . Okay, call me a bit of a worrier, but is it normal to spend so much time at work? I mean, he *is* doing well, and Rachel *did* have a point when she said that the problem in Boston could possibly wait until Monday . . .

Now, I'm not going to worry, needlessly. Because look at Katy and Tom—Tom's working a lot of overtime, and their marriage is solid as a rock. Actually, she would be a good person to consult about long working hours, and my worries about Claire having a bit of a crush on Jack . . .

"Can I ask you something?" I ask her. "Only I've had something on my mind—just a bit—in fact, not on my mind much at all, hahaha—you know how I like to worry—"

"Emma." Katy interrupts me gently, but firmly. "Just spit it out."

"W-e-l-l . . ." Here goes. I take a deep breath. "You know when you've been with someone . . . you know, for quite a while . . . and your relationship is established, got a daily routine going, everything is great—"

"Y-e-s."

"Do you think it means something when the other person is suddenly working all the hours God sends, and doesn't have as much time for you as they did before?" I say in a rush. "I mean, you wouldn't assume that just because their coworker was gorgeous and sexy that they were working longer hours because they were—you know—romantically involved with that coworker."

Katy looks at me for what feels like an age, the color draining from her face.

What have I done? What have I said to upset her?

"Why didn't I see it? Why didn't I recognize the signs?" she wails, putting her hand over her mouth. "I mean, I just thought Tom was working late because of all the pressure on him and all this time he was—oh, I can't take this—Alex is going to have a single-parent family—he'll be emotionally scarred for life."

Ohmishiva! Is Tom having an affair? No, surely not. I've never seen a more suited couple than Katy and Tom. He can't *do* this to her and Alex.

"Oh God, Katy, I'm so sorry," I tell her. And then, because I just can't see it, I mean I really can't see Tom having an affair. And I certainly can't see him keeping a secret of this magnitude for long, either. "Are you sure? How long has this been going on?"

"You tell *me*. How did you find out? Did he say something to Jack? He *did* say something to Jack, didn't he?"

Oh. I think she's got the wrong end of the stick.

"No," I say, quickly. "I didn't mean you and Tom. Not Tom. He'd never do anything to hurt you or Alex. I meant Jack."

"Jack's having an affair?" Her eyes widen to saucers.

"No . . ." *Buddha!* I'm just not good at this subtle stuff. "He's just working long hours, is all. Forget it. I'm just being a worrywart."

As Rachel and Tish come out of Jones New York, Katy turns to me and says very firmly, "I definitely don't think long working hours means that someone's having an affair."

"Okay," I say, gratefully.

"So we'll forget all about this conversation, yes?"

"What conversation?"

See? I was right all along. Jack's not having an affair, which I knew, but it's good to consult with friends about such matters.

That's a huge weight off my mind.

4:15 P.M.

But I do think it's time that Jack and me moved forward with our relationship . . . time that I move in with him.

And let's face it, Tish knows all about reticent men (one reticent man—Rufus) and she managed to move in with him! Look how well that's turned out. She would be a *great* person to consult about this, I think, as we sip our cappuccinos. Katy and Rachel have gone to the restroom, so now would be the perfect time to have a little chat about it . . .

"Do you think—" Now I must choose my words carefully.

"Do I what?"

"Do you think that men find it harder to commit to a relationship than women? Do you think they accept the status quo, and are happy to leave a—you know—a relationship to . . . well, stagnate for a bit?"

"Oh, God, you're right." Tish puts her hand over her mouth. "I just didn't want to push him too hard. I know he loves me, but he's never been the loudest or most willing-to-take-a-risk kind of person. And I *do* want to have a family— I mean, I'm thirty-six now, I'm not exactly a spring chicken. You're so right. I have to take matters into my own hands. I'm going to propose to Rufus."

9:00 P.M.

I think I'm going to give up trying to be diplomatic. So far, today, I have:

1. Unintentionally upset Rachel by worrying her about her lack of interest in sex.
2. Unintentionally upset Katy by hinting that Tom is having an extramarital affair.
3. Unintentionally suggested that Tish propose marriage to Rufus, on account of their stagnating relationship.

And all in vain after all, it seems . . .
Jack isn't back from Boston. He isn't back for my party.

4

....

Party Animal

TO DO

1. Smile a lot, but not in a rictus-death mask kind of way. Is my party, after all. (Plus, it worries people in a scary kind of way.)
2. Laugh a lot, but not in a hysterical kind of way. Even though don't feel much like laughing, must keep reminding self is *my* party.
3. Chat gaily to all my friends and family, but not in a desperately-missing-Jack kind of way. Copious amounts of wine may help with this, because after all, is *my* party.

By nine-thirty my party is in full swing.

When I say full swing, I don't mean in a wife-swapping-swing kind of way, I mean that all of my nearest and dearest are here to celebrate, and to generally enjoy themselves—Katy and Tom, Tish and Rufus, Rachel and Hugh, my dad and Peri, my stepmother. And, of course, our hosts David and Sylvester. And Betty and me . . .

Jack hasn't made it back from Boston yet, so Betty is my

stand-in date. As dogs aren't strictly allowed in restaurants, Betty is upstairs in Sylvester and David's apartment, so she's not even a proper stand-in date. But I keep popping up to check on her, and I must say—she's very taken with the video of *The Lord of the Rings*. Every time Viggo Mortensen appears on screen, she trot-hops from the faux-suede sofa and peers at him on the screen, her tongue hanging out to one side. Obviously she knows a hot man when she sees one. Or it could be that she's just incredibly nearsighted.

But I'm having a good time. I really am. Despite being the only person here who is not part of a couple . . . But I shan't worry about that now. After all, Julia has a good point. She and George are not joined at the hip. And Jack and me are not joined at the hip, either. And it is *so* important to maintain one's identity within a relationship.

Actually, I think the battery in Jack's cell phone must be flat because when I called him a little while ago I got switched straight through to voicemail . . . Or maybe he had to turn it off, because he's on a plane and on his way home right now. So that's a *good* sign. Right?

I will not think insecure thoughts about Jack or The One Ring. Instead, I will be positive, and concentrate on my wonderful friends and family. And one very positive aspect of the evening is that this glass of Chardonnay is positively excellent. See—it is important to appreciate the simple (yet of an expensive vintage) pleasures of life, rather than worry about something intangible.

I retune myself back into the conversation at the table. And immediately wish that I hadn't . . .

"I was in labor with her for *thirty hours*," Peri gleefully tells Tish. Tish is all ears, and is lapping up Peri's every labor twinge.

We're doing the baby thing. Again. I love Peri, but I really feel I've lived the birthing experience right along with her. I mean, I could have *been* there cutting the umbilical cord!

I tune out again as I wonder if it's occurred to Peri that naming her offspring for her favorite musical icon might cause the poor child a hefty bout of expectation-induced angst? Living up to a high-achiever namesake is not easy, as I know all too well. Especially if baby Britney follows in the tradition of her mom and her Uncle Jack, neither of whom can hold a note . . .

Mind you, if I had a baby boy, I'd be tempted to call him Robert James Brown. Not because I totally love Robert Plant and Jimmy Page, of course, but because I think they're just great names . . .

Hmmm. Robert James Brown . . . I really like the sound of that. But not James Robert Brown, because that would only lead to a nickname of Jim Bob, and all the horrid kids at school would torment him with phrases such as "Good night, Jim Bob," and sing *The Waltons* theme tune every time he walked into class! (Even though I *did* used to have a bit of a crush on John Boy.)

And let's face it, Robert and James aren't quite such definitive names as, say, Elvis. Or Madonna. Or Britney. Plus, adding James as a middle name would be inspired, because that's Jack's proper name. (Apparently, Jack and Peri's parent's had a deep, abiding love for the music of James Brown—naming kids for musicians must run in Peri and Jack's family!) So, see? I could name my baby for my gods among men *and* for my husband, at the same time. Perfect.

Well it would be perfect . . . in the future, after lots more non-living-togetherness, of course . . .

"I like, really wanted to do it natural and all in a birthing pool." Peri's voice breaks insistently into my Jack daydream. "But after all those hours you get kinda tired and wrinkled. You know, it wasn't so bad after I got the epidural."

I know exactly what she's going to say next. It's time for the part where she nearly gets paralyzed for life! I pin a grin to my face and try to look interested.

"Are you okay, sweetie?" Peri asks me. "You have, like, a strange smile on your face."

"Who me? I'm totally fine," I say, then laugh just a bit hysterically.

"Good," Peri says, then immediately switches back to her favorite subject. "I was, like, so worried that I'd flinch while the doctor was inserting that huge needle directly into my spinal cord—you know, what would happen if I jerked, and then my spinal cord got severed? I'd be, like, in a wheelchair for life."

Peri's seven-weeks-ago labor has become her major topic of conversation. On the phone to her the other day, I casually asked how my four-year-old half brothers were adapting to having a new baby sister. Dad's a bit concerned about what they might try to do to the new baby—not that they'd intentionally hurt her, but they don't really have that great a grasp of "no," or the phrase "stop that, it's dangerous."

Actually, *I* was worried about what they might do to little Britney, too, because Peri's version of parenthood is that you should let your kids explore their boundaries by doing exactly what they like, whenever they fancy doing it, and "discipline" is a ten-letter word.

But at least she has Mary to help her now. Mary, the new nanny, is great—she's really getting a handle on the boys. They're nowhere near as . . . as unintentionally naughty as they used to be.

Anyway, when I asked how she was coping with baby Britney, Peri immediately went into the pros and cons of giving birth in a birthing pool of warm water, and how she read in a magazine that Baby feels it's a natural progression from the mother's womb. So Baby won't be psychologically scarred by being thrust headfirst into a dry, bright, maternity ward, see? And did I think that baby Britney would suffer in future life because she, Peri, didn't give birth to her in the birthing pool on account of the epidural?

Julia gave birth to me in a maternity ward, and I have to say I don't think it did anything to *my* psyche.

And when I tried to change the subject to something more general (i.e., did she feel like getting away from the house for a bit to go on a girly shopping trip? Dad was a bit concerned that she's too involved in the birth thing, and thought it might do her good to get a change of scenery), she got onto the subject of her stitches and how one had to be careful about infection.

So I've heard every gory detail of the birth of my half sister at least a million times already. But Peri assumes that the whole world takes great delight in the gruesome minutiae of labor, and even made dad film the whole thing from start to finish.

"Oh, but it sounds so painful." Tish is very interested in the details of Peri's labor. Because Tish, of course, is very interested in starting her own family.

"Yeah, it's excruciating," Peri says happily. "How long were you in labor with Alex?" she asks Katy.

"Only sixteen hours," Katy tells her. Then adds, almost proudly, "But there were complications so I had to have a C-section."

"A C-section!" Peri squeaks with glee. "Like, what happened? How many stitches did you get? Was it harder to get your figure back afterwards? I heard that you don't recover so quick after a C-section."

"Oh, it wasn't so bad," Katy tells her airily. "I'd do it all over again in a New York minute." She sighs and smiles wistfully, and I wonder if Katy wants another baby? She's a completely great mom to little Alex. I can see her with another baby or two . . . Actually, I quite fancy the idea of two babies, myself. A little sister for Robert James would be nice. Wonder what I should call her? Hmmm . . .

"Why do they do this?" Rachel says very quietly in my ear, breaking my baby fantasy. Actually, she looks a bit sick. A bit green. Although she is a scientist, Rachel does not like anything to do with blood or gore. She can't even donate blood because she's puking before they get the needle into her arm.

"I know—it's a bit yucky, isn't it?" I whisper back.

"Why do mothers feel compelled to compare their labor horror stories? Don't they realize that they're putting off a whole generation of possible mothers-to-be? They're in danger of making the human race extinct."

Rachel has a good point. I mean, I like the idea of a new, tiny human being (or two), but don't really want to think about contractions, and stitches, and hemorrhoids . . .

"I think it's, you know, a badge of honor thing," I whisper. "Woman the Life Giver, and what She has to endure."

"Ugh. If I ever complain about my mother and her wedding arrangements again, just bite me," Rachel tells me under her breath. "Remind me to send her some fucking flowers." And then, "What's with the rictus smile? You're not letting your English half worry needlessly again, are you?"

"Of course not," I lie. I must try to smile more naturally. Before Rachel can say another word, Peri takes center stage again.

"But don't worry," Peri laughs loudly. "After the birth, you really, like, forget about the pain. Jeez, if I'd remembered the pain of giving birth to the twins, four years ago, I'd have given up sex forever! Wouldn't I Joe?" she calls across to my Dad. Who looks a bit embarrassed. "But don't be put off all you childless girls," Peri says. "After the birth, you know, after a time of healing, the sex is just as great as before."

"Honey, I don't think you should—" Dad begins, a bit red faced.

"Oh, Joe, you're so old-fashioned." Peri bubbles.

Actually, I'm with Dad on this one. I *do* get a bit uncomfortable when Peri talks about sex. I mean, it's a bit icky, isn't it, being presented with snippets about your dad's sex life?

God, I *wish* someone would change the subject to something other than sex or babies.

"Talking of babies," Peri adds. "Have you heard from that baby brother of mine yet, Emma? What time is he due back from Boston?"

But not to the Jack subject, obviously.

My wonderful friends have been trying to reassure me all evening about Jack's absence. They are doing this by pointing out the obvious differences with last year's party and this year's party. That Jack is wonderful and fabulous, unlike Bastard Adam. This is sweet of them, but don't they realize they're just making me feel even worse? I wish we could talk about childbirth again.

"Er, his cell phone's dead," I say, taking a gulp of my wine. And then, as nonchalantly as possible, just to show that I'm really not worried about him. "This project's really important to him. He'll be here when he can."

"Well, I can't think why he needs to work on a weekend. It's just not right," Peri says, shaking her head. And then, "Hey, did I tell you about the problem with my placenta?"

Oh yes—at length and in great detail, but I don't say this to her. Euch! I excuse myself from the table and wander over to Sylvester and David at the bar, in search of more wine. White wine. On account of red wine reminding me of blood and gore.

"Poor Jack," David says, refilling my glass with Chardonnay. "What a crock having to work on your birthday. He must be really pissed. He was so looking forward to it."

David, a huge Jack fan, is trying to placate me. This is sweet, but I don't want my friends to think that I'm in the least bit concerned. I wish we could talk about something else.

"So how's the restaurant business?" I ask, pointedly changing the subject.

"Such dedication to his work. Zis, I understand." Sylvester, another huge Jack fan, reassures me. "Look at David and me. We start out wiz nozing, and now we have zis restaurant. It is ze same wiz Jack. He's just trying to build his career."

"I know," I tell them, pinning a huge smile to my face.

"And you two are made for each ozzer," Sylvester says.

"So when are you going to take the plunge and move in with him?" David asks.

"We are all wondering why you are not yet taking ze next step, *chérie*. We zink zis is a great idea."

So do I. But I don't say this, because I don't want to be disloyal to Jack. Instead, I fix my smile more firmly on my face.

"Are you okay, hon?" David peers at me. "Your smile looks like a rictus death mask."

"I'm fine, I'm good," I say, too cheerfully. "We'll, you know—hahahaha—get around to it. In the fullness of time."

I think I'll just escape to the ladies' room for a minute or two by myself. Just to give my face muscles a rest. But my attempts at solitude are foiled.

"Remember—Jack's a total covalent bonder," Tish says, as she follows me into the bathroom.

"I know." It's sweet that everyone's so concerned. It really is.

"This is nothing like last year. Jack isn't anything like Bastard Ionic Bonder Adam."

"I know," I tell her as brightly as I can. And then, as she follows me to the cubicle. "I'm totally fine." Oh my God, I think she's going to follow me *into* the cubicle. Just in case I do myself some damage. But she *knows* that I'm allergic to pain in any shape or form.

"I've been giving our conversation this afternoon a lot of thought," Tish tells me, as I pause at the cubicle door. "When we get home, I'm gonna follow that advice you gave me last year," she says, as I start to close the door in her face. "I'm gonna seduce Rufus, and just tell him that we're getting married. I mean, it worked when I wanted to date him and move in with him, so why not use the same plan again?"

"Tish, I think that's great," I tell her. Because it is, isn't it? I mean, Rufus does need a push in the right direction. God, I'm getting a bit desperate here, I wonder how long I can cross my legs. "Look, I really need to close the door now."

"Oh sorry, honey, you go ahead and pee. And don't worry about Jack."

I'm so not worried about Jack. "I won't," I tell her.

Fifteen minutes later, after Tom and Hugh (also huge Jack fans) descend on me and spin me the spiel about what a great guy Jack is, I decide to go and check on Betty. Although concerned that the movie may have finished and she may be waiting for me to restart it, I also need to give my facial muscles another little rest. I am foiled when Rachel decides to come with me.

I wonder if she's worried about her lack of interest in sex and wants a little girl-to-girl chat about it? Obviously I won't mention it until *she* does, because that would be insensitive of me. But I'm sure it's *completely normal* to go off sex occasionally, so I will do my best as wise-counselor friend to reassure her.

"I just wanted to say sorry, sweetie," she says, as we reach the top step, and I'm a bit taken aback. Rachel is one of the most kindhearted people I know, but she covers it with a veneer of hard-as-nails toughness. For her, sorry really is the hardest word.

"I was a bitch earlier—I've had this upset stomach and it's really turned me into a bear with a sore head."

"Don't worry," I tell her. "We didn't take you seriously." But she does look rough, though. And it hasn't passed my notice that she's still avoiding alcohol. And rich food. I wonder if she should go and see a doctor. Wonder if I should suggest it to her . . . in a diplomatic way, obviously.

"I have to say it—your mutt has great taste in men," she says, before I can utter my pearls of wisdom. She bends to scratch Betty's head just behind the little blue bow. Betty woofs with appreciation, and as I restart the movie I wonder where this conversation is going.

Rachel, although kind to animals, is more the pure pedigree type of pet owner (her cats are Persian Blues), than the mongrel from all backgrounds kind of person.

"She's completely wild about Jack."

Aha! So that's why she followed me up here! So that she, too, can give me the "Jack is great" speech.

"I know," I say for the millionth time tonight.

"So don't you go putting two and two together and making ten from it, kiddo." Rachel touches my arm. "I *know* you, Emma Taylor."

Rachel's unaccustomed display of concern is almost my undoing, and I feel the lump in my throat expand to the size of a football. I need to talk about something else . . .

"So how are *you* feeling?" I ask her. "Only you look a bit—you know—off color. Have you seen a doctor yet?"

Rachel immediately launches into a detailed yet incomprehensible account about stomach acids, and enzymes, and complicated digestive processes, and I relax with this. I don't understand her, but Rachel is a scientist and she obviously knows her stuff. But I *do* notice that she doesn't mention whether or not she's actually *planning* to see a doctor. And I am just about to casually, yet diplomatically, point this out when we are interrupted.

"Hey, girls," David calls up the stairs to us. "Come on—time to give the birthday girl her birthday gifts."

"Sure—we're coming right now," Rachel shouts down to him and heads for the door.

Maybe I should have a quiet word with Hugh about her stomach problems?

I love birthday gifts! I've been wondering about the gaily-wrapped (yet huge) boxes in the corner all evening . . .

Ah, my friends and family are so lovely, I think, fifteen minutes later. They obviously pay attention to me and to my likes and dislikes! This is what they got me.

1. Katy and Tom. A standard lamp from Tish's store. The stand is all intricately wrought iron, with a neutral (but not cold) shade, complete with little amber jewels hanging from it. It's very retro—very "in" according to Tish. It's part of the new line of beautiful objets she's ordered in. She's a bit worried, actually, that she might be expanding her stock too much, but I fell in love with it the minute I saw it. I told her it would get snapped up, and I was right! It's a bit (a lot) too big for my tiny apartment, but it would look really lovely in Jack's living room . . .

2. Tish and Rufus. A large, ceramic, greeny-bluey urn from Tish's interior design store that I also waxed lyrical about . . .

3. Sylvester and David. The quirky (yet six-foot tall) metal giraffe from Tish's store that I thought would look perfect in the corner of Jack's living room—he has too many empty corners . . . This is so nice of them, but I must make a mental note to myself. Next year I will wax lyrical about Donna Karan and Kate Spade, instead of lovely objets . . .

4. Rachel and Hugh. Led Zeppelin's new double DVD set! Out of all my dear friends, I love Rachel and Hugh the most at this point in time—they are the voices of Led Zeppelin reason amidst beautiful (yet large) objets paranoia. Although, it has to be said, I don't actually *own* a DVD machine . . . I shall have to watch it at Jack's house.

5. Dad and Peri. Something book shaped. As I open the packet I hold my breath because Peri, like my great-great-aunt Alice, is very interested in ensuring

I have a great sex life. Last year, she bought me *How to Rekindle Your Sex Life,* which was a bit de trop at the time, on account of not having a sex life back then . . . Maybe I should dig it out of the storage box and have a look at it. Maybe it would prove interesting in terms of getting Jack to be more interested in regular sex . . . Oh, but I really want to save this gift to open later, when I'm by myself, just in case it's something really, really embarrassing. "Come on, honey, open it," Peri bubbles at me. "I can't *wait* for you to see what Daddy and me got for you." I am a horrid person for not wanting to open Peri's gift. I'm among friends, who cares if it's embarrassing or not? Oh. "This is great," I tell Peri with far more enthusiasm than I feel. It's *Living Together: How to Transcendentally Compromise with your Loved One* by Dr. Padvi Choyne. "This will come in handy in the future," I tell her.

11:30 P.M.

Still no sign of Jack . . .

"Friends," Rufus calls from the front of the restaurant. "If I could just have your attention for a minute or two, there's something I'd like to say."

I wonder what's going on? Rufus isn't into speeches. I glance across at Tish, who is equally perplexed, and she shakes her head. Tom, Hugh, Sylvester and David, however, are giving Rufus the thumbs up. They obviously have insider information.

"As you all know, I'm not one fer makin' speeches—"

"That's the understatement of the year," Katy murmurs to me.

"So I'm going to make this quick. I feel it's time to make

me intentions known to me lovely Tish. And I wanted to do it in front of yer all, just to make it special, and to make her realize how much I love her, like."

Oh, God, I think he's going to propose . . . this is so romantic.

"Fuck, he's going to propose," Rachel tells me. "I didn't think he had it in him." But I know that she is not unmoved by emotion, because her eyes are shining suspiciously. As are mine.

"Tish, me darlin', can you come up here?"

Tish, hand on her mouth, looks around at us and we all smile encouragingly. And as she reaches Rufus, he takes her hand in his and *gets down on one knee!*

"In front of all our friends as witnesses, I wanted to tell you that you are the jewel in the crown of me life. Please take *this* jewel as a lifelong sign of me love for you," he says, pulling a box out of his pocket.

Oh, but this is the most lovely gesture I've ever seen. Peri hands Katy, Rachel and me a tissue to dab at our eyes. And then she hands one to Sylvester and Dad, too.

"Patricia Maria Visconti. Will you marry me?"

With trembling fingers, Tish takes the small box and opens it. And gasps.

"Oh, Rufus. It's beautiful. Of course I'll marry you," she says between tears, and we all cheer as Rufus carefully takes the ring out of the box and slips it onto her engagement finger.

And then I gasp, too.

It's The One Ring.

5

....

All For Love

TO DO

1. Remind self am not fond of emeralds. Is very bad dog-in-manger attitude to still want emerald ring, even though I hate bloody emeralds.
2. Cut out own tongue when am next in position to be goaded to make stupid life statements. Especially after overindulging in Chardonnay and champagne.
3. Think positive thoughts re: padded bras and long working hours.

11:55 P.M.

The things one does for love!

I mean, who knew that Rufus, of all people, had it in him to make such a beautiful, poetic, public declaration of his love for Tish?

Since his wonderful proposal, the last twenty-five minutes have featured many toasts to the happy couple (and many glasses of champagne), many speeches of congratulations and many hugs. The last twenty-five minutes have also featured much eye dabbing with tissues, and much repairing of mascara . . . there wasn't a dry eye left in the place!

"Oh, sweetie, I'm so happy for you," I tell Tish for the umpteenth time, as I hug her again. And I am. I truly am. She's wanted this for so long . . . She deserves it!

But there is a teeny little part of me that still covets the emerald ring . . . but not in a horrid, jealous kind of way. More in a wanting-to-progress-relationship-with-Jack kind of way . . . At least the mystery of the ring is now clear—Jack was just keeping it safe for Rufus, so that he could completely take Tish by surprise.

There's still no word from Jack.

In a few minutes, it won't be my birthday anymore . . .

"It will be your turn, soon," Tish says in my ear, before Rachel pulls her away and hugs her again.

But will it?

"Now that you have your very own wedding to plan, honey," Rachel tells Tish, her voice cracking. "I want you to talk about it as much as you want—I promise I won't complain."

That's rather a hasty promise from Rachel—must be the emotion of the moment.

"I'll remind you about that," Tish laughs, "when you get pissed when I dither over what flowers to have in church."

"If I say one bad word just smack me, but don't ask me to help choose the dress," Rachel says. And then, "I've been such a grouch. Sometimes I wonder why you're all still talking to me. Even *I* don't like me much at the moment."

"Of course we're talking to you—we love you," Katy says, her eyes filling with emotion-of-the-moment tears again.

Oh, now *my* eyes are filling with tears again. I feel a group-hug moment coming over me.

"Group hug," Peri commands us. "You too, Rachel."

"Let's not get too carried away," Rachel says, but she's smiling in a pale, wan kind of way.

And we're all hugging and bawling like babies.

Wonder if I should, you know, do what Tish did with Rufus. You know, just kind of Zen myself into Jack's house? Hmmm . . . maybe I should, you know, just move myself in without mentioning it and see if he notices? A kind of gradual movement of my stuff (especially the giant-sized birthday gifts) from my place to his place—after all, I *already* have a lot of my stuff at his house so a bit more won't make much difference. Then in a few months from now, it will be like Jack and me have been living together forever. And then Jack will feel comfortable enough to confide in me, to open up to me . . . This could be a good plan . . .

12:01 A.M.

Or maybe not . . .

It's official. I have spent another birthday without my significant other in attendance. To tell the truth, I'm getting more than a bit upset with Jack, now. I mean, he could have *called* or something. If *I* were going to completely miss *his* birthday party after promising to be there, I'd *definitely* call . . . unless my cell phone was dead and I couldn't get to another telephone . . .

Anyway, the girls and me are all sitting around the table, and we're all a bit more subdued due to the lateness of the hour and too much champagne. Apart from Peri, because of breastfeeding. And Rachel.

The guys are all doing the bonding thing at the bar, and it involves much laughter, many slaps on the back for Rufus, and many shots of whiskey. It's a good thing that tomorrow is Sunday. But we're all a bit the worse for wear, and I'm getting tired, as well as more antsy and pissed off about Jack-the-absent.

"Joe, honey," Peri says to my dad, stifling a yawn and get-ting to her feet. "I hate to break up the party, but we've got to, like, go home now—I only left enough expressed milk for one feed and it's nearly time for Britney's next one."

"Yeah, we gotta leave, too—we told the baby-sitter we'd be back by midnight and we're late already," Tom says to Katy. "Come on, woman." He puts his arms around her and rests his head on her shoulder. "Carry me home and take me to Paradise."

"Sounds like a good proposition." Katy snuggles up to him.

"Ah, you temptress." Tom kisses her cheek, then yawns. "If I can stay awake long enough. I'm beat."

See? I *knew* he couldn't be cheating on her.

And as we're all doing our good-byes, and kisses, and hugs, Dad suddenly decides to show his support for the missing Jack, too.

"Emma, sweetheart," he says rather loudly, wobbling just a bit. I'm glad that Peri will be driving them home. "You tell that young man of yours that any time he wants to ask your old dad for permission for your hand in marriage, just to come and spit it right out."

It's lovely of Dad to say that, but I rather wish he hadn't. Or quite so loudly. Or in such a way that assumes it's a given fact we'll get engaged, rather than just a future possibility.

"You're not old," Peri tells him, patting his hand affec-tionately. "You're a man in your prime." How sweet and loyal is that? Dad and Peri were made for each other. And then Peri adds to me, "That brother of mine needs, like, a good wake-up call. It's time he made a commitment to you. You two should be living together by now, and I'm gonna tell him that when I call him tomorrow."

Oh, no. That would be terrible!

I mean, I do agree with Peri, but how to subtly yet nicely

keep her out of this? Because if I make even the slightest comment that I think it's a good idea, too, Peri will put her mouth in it, swiftly followed by her foot. And she will continue to nag Jack until he gives in and asks me to move in, just for a quiet life. And I don't want that—I want him to want me for *myself.*

But I *do* feel like shit.

And I don't think it's just my overactive imagination at work here due to my Jack worries, but because I'm sensitive to the pitying glances, and head shakes, and pep talks I've been getting all evening. Where *is* Jack? *Why* hasn't he called? How can I transform myself from Object of Pity to Strong, Independent Woman?

"Jack and me are fine," I tell Dad and Peri firmly. "We're just taking our time," I add, carefully choosing the right words. Well, as carefully as someone can when they are full of Chardonnay and champagne, anyway. "You know, just one step at a time. We're not joined at the hip, or anything. And it *is* important to maintain one's independence within a relationship."

Oh, God. I sound just like my mother. But this is a good thing. I *must* try to be more like her. And like Auntie Alice . . .

"For a minute there you sounded like Julia," Dad tells me, shaking his head.

"Well, maybe, just maybe I want my freedom for a bit longer. Plus I have a career to concentrate on." And then, because I feel very bad about Jack and also because I'm getting into the Independent Woman thing, "I mean, Jack and me don't have to *live* together to prove anything to anyone. I *like* having my own space."

And Jack missed my birthday after he promised to be here.

And he couldn't even take the time to call me.

I have every *right* to be angry with him.

"But I thought you *wanted* to move in with him," Tish says, obviously perplexed. Because let's face it, I've already chosen my wedding list and she knows this.

"Living together is not mandatory," Rachel starts a half-hearted rant. "I think that maintaining separate apartments has its own merits—at least you don't have to wait to use the bathroom."

"This, from the woman who has two bathrooms," Katy says. "The bathroom issue is not a good example, hon."

"Well, I'm just trying to be supportive."

"It's obvious that Emma wants to move in with Jack," Peri bubbles. "You can see it just by looking at her sweet little face. Poor, poor Emma." Peri engulfs me in a bear hug, almost in tears on my behalf.

But pride and alcohol in the name of saving face fuel my mouth, and instead of succumbing to the threatened bout of self-pity, I fan the flames of my anger.

"Actually, I might even get a mortgage on my *own* place," I say just a bit too loudly, because I'm warming to my theme now, and my mouth is running full steam ahead. "I've been thinking about it a lot recently. You know, it's always good to have the security of one's own home, plus it's a good investment. After all, there are no guarantees in this life and even if I do move in with Jack, and then later if we split up or something, where the hell does that leave *me?*"

Where the hell did that all *come* from?

There is a sudden hush.

What? Did I say something that terrible? Why are they all looking behind me?

"Guys, look who I just found at the kitchen door," David says from behind me.

"Jack, old buddy." Tom moves swiftly into the breach. "Here, have a glass of champagne. Rufus did it. He proposed—he was great."

"You'd have been proud of me," Rufus slurs cheerfully. "You know, I got down on me knee and everythin'."

"He was magnificent," Tish tells Jack, holding out her

hand, and The One Ring. "I never guessed what he was going to do."

"We saved you some food." Sylvester bustles into action.

"In case you were hungry after your trip . . ." David trails off.

Oh, God. I have just announced to the whole room that I have no intention of settling down or moving in with Jack. What's worse, I have a sneaky suspicion that Jack heard every word, because Rachel is rolling her eyes heavenwards, Tish shakes her head very slightly, and Katy has her face in Tom's chest.

This is terrible. How could I be so stupid? But then I remind myself that I am pissed with Jack. I am hurt by Jack.

I close my eyes and swallow, wishing I could rewind the clock to this morning when everything was right with the world. Well, right with my world, at least. What do I say? What do I do?

"Jack, I can't believe you missed Emma's birthday." Peri dives in feet first, and this is not helpful. "The poor girl's, like, been really worried about you. You should have called. If Joe missed my birthday and didn't even call, I'd be really angry with him."

"Now, Peri, let's not be too hasty, here," my dad tells her, and I remember to breathe again, because hopefully Peri won't now mention Jack and me living together. And then I cringe at Dad's next words. "I'm sure Jack had his reasons for standing up my little girl on her birthday. Very *good* reasons."

"I'm sorry," Jack says tiredly, and I finally pluck up the courage to turn to look at him.

Oh, but he *does* look exhausted.

My anger dissipates just a bit, but not completely, as my eyes eat up his beloved face. He is also a bit crumpled and harried. He's obviously had a terrible day, and all I can do is fret about my own needs.

"My flight got delayed," Jack tells the room, but he's looking directly at me. "We sat on the tarmac for four hours while the engineers checked out the problem. And my cell phone died. By the time I got off the flight, I just wanted to get here as quick as possible."

"That sucks, honey," David says to him. "That happened to us when we went to Québec to spend New Year with your mom, didn't it Sylvester?"

"*Oui.*"

And then the room is filled with conversation as everyone compares travel horror stories to give Jack and me some space. In that instant, I love my friends even more for trying to smooth over the awkwardness of the moment.

And I love Jack even more as he stumbles over his next words, like a child making a public speech for the first time.

"I—I should have called. I should have, you know, made the time to let you know I was thinking about you. Because I *was* thinking about you. And I didn't call. And I'm sorry."

"I was worried," I say to him, softly. But I don't mention that I worried about Claire making a pass at him, too.

"It's been a day of playing catch-up," he tells me, moving closer as he pushes his hand through his hair. "I so didn't want this to be a repeat of your last disaster birthday."

My bad temper vanishes completely.

After all, he worried enough about me to call my friends this morning so that I wouldn't be on my own. And I want to smooth his furrowed brow and make it all better. I want to kiss all his troubles away.

"It's not," I say, anxious for all to be well between us. Anxious that he realizes how much I love him—and that I didn't mean a word of that stupid speech. "How was Boston?"

"All the worse for the lack of you, Emmeline Beaufort Taylor. Boston doesn't know what it's missing. *I* missed you," he whispers, very quietly, and I almost want to cry at the depth of emotion in his voice. "A lot."

"Me too," I whisper back, as he rests his forehead against mine.

"Jack, Emma, we really have to go." Peri interrupts the moment, just as I'm about to try and explain the stupid speech. "We'll see you on Independence Day." And then, very pointedly, "That is, if Jack's not working and can fit in the time to see his own family."

"We'll be there, Peri," Jack tells her as he takes my hand, and I feel much better. "It's a promise," he adds, as his eyes search mine, and the butterflies flap in my stomach, because his promise is to me alone.

And then everyone is leaving again.

"Don't go doing anything stupid," Rachel says to me at the door. "That man loves you, but I know you, Emma Taylor."

"I won't. I hope you feel better tomorrow."

"God, so do I. This stomach thing is really the pits. But I feel a lot better already," she adds, before I can mention that I think it would be a good idea if she saw a doctor.

And finally it's just Jack and me. And Sylvester and David.

"You must *eat*, Jack," Sylvester fusses around like an old mother hen.

"Stop fussing, sweetie," David tells him. "They're tired—they just want to go home." David stops, then changes his words. "I mean back to *Jack's* place, of course."

There is an awkward little pause.

"What about your birthday gifts?" Sylvester reminds me. "Zey are too heavy to carry. You leave zem here overnight and come get zem tomorrow wiz your car." Sylvester kisses me, then adds rather pointedly, "You will love zem, Jack."

"Beautiful objets from Emma's favorite store," David tells him, fondly stroking the huge metal giraffe. "But then, Emma has such exquisite taste in everything."

"*Absolument*," Sylvester nods wisely. "Zey will look great in *Jack's* house, *n'est-ce pas?*"

I know that they mean well, but I wish they wouldn't be so heavy-handed with their hints.

"Oh, they'd look—you know—beautiful anywhere, ha-haha," I say. And then into the awkward silence, "Talking of beautiful, better go get Betty the Beauty."

Before we leave, I grab Peri and Dad's birthday book, because I think I may need advice about compromising within a relationship. I also take my new Led Zeppelin DVD, because Bob and Jimmy can always be counted on when one is feeling a bit low.

As Jack and me walk back to his house, and as Betty trot-hops along with us, we don't say anything.

I worry that David and Sylvester went too far with their hints, because the silence is loaded with awkwardness and expectation.

"So—what did you and Betty do today?" Jack asks me quietly, as he links his fingers through mine and gives my hand a bit of a reassuring squeeze.

"Oh, girly things." I grasp the subject and his hand with relief, and launch into a chatty, almost too-happy account of the beauty parlor, the outlets, and Peri's obsession with labor, carefully skimming the part where I get obsessive and worried, and the part where I declare my independence. I just want things to go back to the way they were. And we'll both feel better after a good night's sleep.

"I love Betty's new bows," Jack says, smiling down at me in the darkness, and I smile back. "Only you would think of that." He raises my knuckles to his mouth and kisses them, and I melt with love.

"Betty had a great day, too, didn't you baby? She stayed with Hugh and he spoiled her rotten."

"But do you think the bows are helping with her positive self-image?" I love it when Jack speaks to me like this. See—

most of the time he really understands where I'm coming from. Most of the time . . .

"Oh, definitely," I laugh. "She even flirted with a cute shih tzu in the park."

"That's the way to do it, babe." Jack bends to stroke her. "Aim high." And then, just as we get to the steps to his house, he comes to a stop and turns me to face him.

"Emma," he sighs, and I hold my breath. "You know, I'm not great at mushy stuff."

Nervous butterflies flutter in my stomach. Because he *is* bad at mushy stuff. He's not that great at talking about the deep, relationship stuff. He *does* skirt around the more important issues.

I mean, he's not immune to the odd tear when we're watching a sad movie. And let's face it, when it comes to sex he's not shy about suggesting stuff . . . It's just discussing us and our future that he's not good at. Or saying "I love you" to me. But I don't say this. Because I, too, am guilty of the same thing.

"Look—we haven't really talked about it—this living together thing—" He pauses, and sighs.

"Er, no, we haven't." Oh. He's going to do it. He's going to ask me to move in. Or not.

"If you like, you could—you know, move in." But although he has said the words that I want to hear, my heart sinks into my pumps. Because he's obviously not enthusiastic with the idea. "I mean, we did it before and it worked out okay, didn't it?"

"Yes, it did," I say, as a lump forms in my throat, because I think this is more to convince himself than me.

Actually, it did kind of work out well that time we lived together. But that was before we were actually a couple. We were just sharing for convenience—me, because I had to move out of Bastard Ionic Bonder Adam's apartment when

I split up with him, and for Jack, the convenience of the extra rent money to help remodel his house.

But that time Jack was kind of pressured by Peri, because we're kind of family. And we weren't actually "living together" living together.

"We had fun," he grins, and sits down on the steps, pulling me with him. "Apart from that time Peri and the twins moved in for a week."

"Wasn't that terrible?" I giggle, as Betty jumps up into my lap. I love Peri and my half brothers, but I don't think I could ever live with them . . .

"And we didn't get in each other's way, did we?" Jack asks.

"Nah," I say, trying to find Ursa Major in the night sky. I'm not good at star constellations, but it's a good way to hide my concern that he's in need of such reassurance. Reassurance that it would work out okay. If I moved in. I mean, he's obviously worried that it *wouldn't* work out, and it *is* a big step, after all . . .

Because on the other hand, living together *didn't* turn out that well at the end. Just as Jack and me were about to get it together, Bastard Adam appeared on the doorstep and Jack misunderstood my reasons to want to speak with him. Jack didn't get it, at the time, that I needed to have closure with Adam before I could move on to a relationship with him. He took it so badly that he went out in search of another woman. Result: we both ran from the truth of our situation. We had a fight, and I moved out.

"But if you're serious, you know, about getting your own place, then don't feel pressured to move in here," he says, and the lump in my throat gets even bigger.

I look down at Betty instead of at Jack, because she is the safer option. I am a coward. I should just come out and tell him how I truly feel, but I don't.

Because *he's* obviously feeling pressured, and is uncomfortable with the idea. Which is why he's asking me. This is exactly what I didn't want.

"Well, it was just, you know, a thought," he says.

Convince me to move in with you, I want to say, as I readjust Betty's hair bow, but I don't.

"You could, you know, think about it . . ."

"Yeah." I nod, and shift my attention to the moon. Anything but look at Jack. Anything but let him see that I'm trying not to cry. I'm just being sensitive. I just want too much too soon.

And, I reason with myself, all relationships go through their ups and downs. Look at Tish and Rufus. They loved each other from afar for three years before they even had one date. So based on their timescale, eight months of dating is nothing. No time at all.

I can deal with this, I tell myself firmly. No point borrowing trouble. And things are generally pretty great between Jack and me. And just as I've nearly convinced myself that I'm happy with the current state of our relationship, he adds another worry to my growing list.

"You know," he says, then clears his throat as he slides his arm around my shoulders, "I'm gonna be pretty busy for the next few months. With work and all . . ."

"Oh?" How so? More busy than he's been recently?

"I'm not going to be around so much. Claire wants to push the business and we're going to be aggressively bidding for new projects. That will mean longer hours, maybe even more business trips."

"You're a fabulous architect," I say, trying to be upbeat. Because he needs a new roof for his house, and they don't come cheap. It's just an investment for our future.

"So—are you okay with that? It means I'll be spending a lot of time at work, or away, so I won't be home so much. So if you were to move in, you might be here on your own a lot . . . but only if you really want to . . . move in . . ."

"Hmmm . . ." I nod, furiously studying the heart-shaped stain on the concrete step. He's so desperate for me not to live with him.

"But if you really want to get your own place . . ."

"Hmmm . . ."

For a few minutes we just sit, as Jack watches the night sky, and as I wonder about the heart-shaped stain on the step. Is the crack running through the center of it symbolic of a broken heart? Is this a sign?

Is Jack really sending me subliminal messages that he wants to back off from me for a while? Or is he really just telling me that he's not ready to take the next step in our relationship. And just as I'm about to explode with anxiety, he tells me something.

"Hey, birthday girl," he says in an upbeat voice. "I haven't given you my gifts yet. They're upstairs—in the bedroom."

"It had better not be from Tish's new collection," I grin halfheartedly.

"Not a lamp or animal in sight. They're just for you," he smiles his wolfish smile, and I shiver. "*And* for me. Which reminds me," he says, rummaging in his briefcase. "I got you another present in the airport store. Couldn't get any handcuffs, but I'm sure we can . . . improvise."

And then Jack hands me a tub of chocolate sauce.

"You are *baaad,*" I tell him, as he gently takes Betty from my lap and pulls me to my feet.

"Just wait until you see the rest of your gifts."

1:15 A.M.

I am in the master bathroom trying not to read between the lines, instead of in bed, asleep, like normal people.

For my birthday, apart from the chocolate sauce, Jack got me a really lovely black lace bra-and-panty set. It is beautiful, truly a work of art, and it looks great against my skin. When I modeled it for Jack half an hour ago, he told me that it is truly a lovely look for me. So that's good, isn't it?

The bra also has gel padding, and transforms me instantaneously from 32AA to 32C.

And Jack just fell asleep while we were having sex . . .

This does not mean that he's bored with me, or the smallness of my breasts.

It just means he's tired.

Doesn't it?

6

....

Chocolate Sex and Death

TO DO

1. Carefully study great advice of Dr. Padvi Choyne re: relationships. After all, Dr. Padvi has a doctorate in the psychology of relationships, therefore must know what she/he is talking about.
2. Try to put grief behind self and think positively re: new heiress status. Concentrate not on monetary gain, but on possible worthy charities to support.
3. Think positively (or in fact, *at all*,) re: next meeting with Prime Minister Blair! (If, in fact, ever get to meet him again. Possibly to discuss donations to worthy charities?)

Sunday, 1:15 P.M.

All I can say is that chocolate sauce is a completely fabulous look for Jack! (And for me . . .)

It's true. We tried it this morning. Twice. Y-e-s!

And you know what? That old phrase "things will look better in the morning" is completely true.

Parts of Jack *certainly* looked much better this morning when I awoke to the rather erotic sensation of him pouring chocolate sauce into my navel . . . and on other areas of my body . . .

Hmmm . . .

It's odd, isn't it, how relationship situations can sometimes seem depressing when you're tired or overstressed? Or if you have an overobsessive nature.

Not that *I* have an overobsessive nature, of course . . . it's just that sometimes, very occasionally, I'm a glass-half-empty kind of gal instead of a glass-half-full type. But, as Dr. Padvi says, at least I can admit to this character flaw and am therefore *unenclosed* and *willing to work on my positivity*.

I mean, if I hadn't decided to take a look at my birthday book from Dad and Peri last night after Jack fell asleep while we were having sex, I'd have spent the night stupidly obsessing. Instead of recognizing that Jack was just tired, I might have spent the whole night worrying about my sex appeal. And obviously the chocolate sauce-sex episode this morning put an end to that stupid worry!

But the gel bra is a bit of a mystery . . . something which I will address when I get to the relevant chapter in the book . . .

Anyway, according to Dr. Padvi Choyne, relationship guru, I can change my approach to life and relationships by taking a step back and reevaluating the situation. Dr. Padvi really *speaks* to me . . .

Not that I usually put much store by self-help books, because there are just so many of them. It's hard to select just the right one. And frankly, I wonder if people choose them because that particular book is just going to agree with whatever is their own philosophy on life. For vindication. But ob-

viously that's not why *I* like *this* particular self-help book . . .
This is a completely fantastic book!

Yes, I'm definitely thinking that *Living Together: How to
Transcendentally Compromise with Your Loved One* could really
help me to understand my questions about my relationship
with Jack. (See, Dr. Padvi says "understand questions" rather
than "face fears" or "challenge worries"—positive words re-
flect a positive mind.)

I mean, it makes complete sense to take a step back from
a situation and to allow for a cooling-off period before con-
fronting your partner.

But let's face it, confrontation isn't, strictly speaking, my
forte: Not that I *can't* confront, because I definitely can.

Oh, telephone. Caller ID shows "out of area," so I pick up.
See, I *choose* to confront the telemarketer.

"Hi, Emma? This is Pete. How are you doing today?"

Very impressive pitch. This guy has just the right amount
of friendly enthusiasm in his voice. The kind of "I'm a nice
guy calling for a friendly chat, and at the same time will either sell you something you don't want, or extract a promise
of fifteen dollars for my very worthy whatever." But I'm not
swayed.

"You don't need to pretend with me Pete," I tell him, as I
decide on my telemarketer-torture tactics for today. "I'm here
to *help* you," I add in my best "I am a caring person" voice.

"Pardon me, ma'am?"

"Don't be coy," I tell poor Pete, who sounds thoroughly
confused. "Impotence or premature ejaculation are nothing
to be ashamed of. Or perhaps you're worried about your . . .
size . . ."

Click.

I somehow feel I won't be hearing from Pete again.

"How was I?" I ask Betty, as she snuggles closer to me on
the sofa. "I was pretty good, don't you think?"

Betty's better off with me this afternoon, because Jack and Claire are working on some new project or other. ...

True to his promise, Jack really tried to make up for missing my birthday. Yes, after the chocolate sauce episode this morning we had a lovely shower (to destickify) followed by brunch at Johnny Rocket's. But he needs to get on in his chosen profession, so if he has to spend Sunday afternoon poring over boring plans, rather than having fun with me, then I'm totally fine with this.

Yes, according to Dr. Padvi, you have to choose that perfect period in time when you're both ready to have a frank and open discussion. Jack and I will have a frank and open discussion once our relationship reaches a *higher transcendental plane of togetherness*. Dr. Padvi says, I will *recognize the tranquility signs* in Jack.

So we're going to have that chat tonight because I think it's time we reached our higher transcendental plane of togetherness.

In the meantime I'm expanding my mind a bit with important reading, because (apart from the fact that Dr. Padvi says it is essential to my sense of self and well-being, and apart from the fact that I've already called my friends and they're all busy, apart from Rachel, who is still grumpy on account of feeling shitty) it's very important to be aware of greater issues in the world at large.

God, I hope I don't get reincarnated as a freshwater pearl mussel . . . who knew they had such tragically nonexistent sex lives?

It's true! I mean, how sad is it that the poor mussels in England and Wales have no hope of sex ever again! The poor things have all somehow got separated from each other. I got the brochure from Julia in the mail, along with the details of my birthday donation re: the dreadful plight of the little red yeki fish in Ghana . . .

Inexplicably, the sex life of mussels makes me think of Jack . . .

Oh, telephone again. I check the Caller ID and grab the receiver.

"What color panties are you wearing?" Jack breathes heavily down the receiver.

"I'm not . . . wearing any panties," I breathe back at him. "It's just . . . too hot for clothes." Yes, this is a bit naughty. It's a little game we play sometimes.

Betty, who until now has spent the afternoon snoozing on the sofa, immediately yowls at me, gives me an embarrassed look, and trot-hops to the kitchen in search of food.

"What are you . . . doing?" Jack's voice goes down another notch, and I shiver and close my eyes.

"I'm . . . squeezing a sponge of cold water over my naked body . . ."

"You are a *baaad* girl."

"Maybe you should come over and . . . punish me."

"I wish," Jack says in his normal voice. "I just called to say we'll be a while longer, here." And then I hear Claire's voice in the background.

"Oh, tell me Claire didn't just hear that."

"Not the good part," Jack laughs. "Look, I gotta go—I'll meet you at Chez Nous later. Okay?"

"Okay," I tell him, a bit disappointed I won't be seeing him sooner. And then, "I'll bring my wet, dripping sponge with me . . . for later."

"That sounds . . . intriguing," he says, then lowers his voice. "Bring more chocolate sauce, too."

Can't wait until later . . .

Oh. Telephone again. I am more than a little disappointed when the caller ID says "out of area," because there's only so much time one can spend on mind-expansion, and I feel like a chat. But I don't pick up. Voicemail will deal with it.

See, I choose not to confront the telemarketer on this occasion. Just because I am bored is no reason to torture the poor person.

And then it rings again . . . the bastard telemarketer is just trying to catch me out. I bet he's thinking "let's dial Emma Taylor's number again, just to trick her." But I'm not buying that.

When it rings for a third time, and Betty howls at me, I pick up. Because I figure that by now, whoever is calling me *knows* that I am here and will not stop ringing until I speak to them.

"Emma, love, it's me." It's George. My mother's husband.

George *never* calls me unless he really has to. George never calls *anyone*. He doesn't *like* telephones and usually passes messages to me via Julia. This is not good. This can only mean one thing—something terrible has happened to Julia!

"George," I gasp, barely able to speak as I imagine all kinds of dreadful accidents. "What happened? Where's Julia?"

"Julia's fine," George says immediately, and I close my eyes with relief. And before I can open my mouth to ask why he's actually calling, George adds, "It's Auntie Alice, love. I'm very sorry but she's gone. Passed away."

"But—but she *can't* be gone. She's as healthy as an ox. The doctor said so when she had her checkup last month. Julia told me." *Was* as healthy as an ox, I should have said, but I'm still thinking about her in the present tense. I can't take this in.

"Oh, it were nothin' to do with her health, love," George tells me in his northern accent. "It were being struck by lightning that did it. A freak accident, like."

"What? *When?*" One-hundred-and-six-year-old aunts just *don't* get struck by lightning. They don't *have* freak accidents.

"It were earlier this afternoon, on the Elmina yeki-fish demonstration. We were right outside the Houses of Parliament, just across from Westminster Bridge," George continues, "and the march were going well, it really were. But Auntie Alice got a bit, you know, involved with making her point and wouldn't listen when we told her a storm were coming."

Auntie Alice always does . . . did . . . exactly what she liked, despite her years. I can't believe I'll never see her again.

"She were great," George tells me. "You'd have been proud. When the police arrived and asked us to move on, she were up in arms, telling them about her rights, and how hard the suffragette movement fought for them, and did they know that she weren't scared by some young upstart bobbies telling *her* what was what."

I smile at this, although tears are streaming down my face. I'm trying to imagine a world without Auntie Alice in it . . .

"Anyway, this thunderstorm had been brewing for a while, like, and you know Auntie Alice. Said a bit of rain had never hurt her in all these years on the planet, and it weren't going to start now. It were her finial, see."

Finial? Finial . . . What on earth is George talking about?

"You know—on the end of her walking stick," George says.

Oh, the lily-shaped iron bit that looked like the top of a railing. In fact, it *did* used to be a railing . . . Auntie Alice told me the tale often enough. It's from an actual railing to which Mrs. Pankhurst and Auntie Alice chained themselves during a victorious protest in 1913.

"Yes, but *what* does the finial have to do with this?" I prompt George.

"See, if there hadn't been a metal rod running from the finial and right through the middle of the wood, it would have been all right," George says.

"I don't see what difference that made," I say, because this whole thing is about as clear as mud to me.

"Just as she were zooming up and down on her wheel-chair, brandishing her walking stick, a bolt of lightning struck it—it acted like a lightning rod, ye see."

But I don't see. I don't want this to be true.

"It seemed right appropriate that we were just across from

that statue of Queen Boudicca going to war on her chariot. Auntie Alice would have liked that, she would."

George is right. Through my tears, I smile at the image of Auntie Alice zooming to war on her wheelchair, walking stick waving imperiously, just like Boudicca, Icini Queen, riding to war on her chariot, hair flying out behind her imperiously . . . but call me unrealistic if you like, I just haven't given any thought to the possibility of Auntie Alice dying.

I mean, I know that she's been on this planet for over a century, which is extremely good by anyone's standards, isn't it? But because she's been around so long, she's practically an institution. I just assumed she'd go on forever. And so did Julia.

Oh, *poor* Julia. She must be taking this very badly.

"Julia's taking it right badly," George says, reading my mind. "We've just got back from the hospital—you know—to sort out all the paperwork and that. I've put her to bed with a herbal sleeping tablet. I don't think she's up to all the arrangements. Can you come?"

"Of course I'll come," I tell George, wiping away my tears.

Friday, July 4th

Independence Day somehow seems appropriate for Auntie Alice's funeral. Because you don't get any more independent than Auntie Alice. Yes, a fiercely independent woman who campaigned for women's rights, amongst other things, for her whole life.

Oddly enough, despite the fact that it has been gray and rainy since I first set foot on British soil on Monday morning, today it is a gorgeous summer's day. And I'm glad, because sunshine is a very positive way to celebrate Auntie Alice's tremendous life.

I'm trying to be happy, you see. I'm trying really hard to

put a positive spin on this, but it's difficult. I miss Alice so much, especially since being back in London . . .

And the central-London church is packed to capacity as evidence of the many people Auntie Alice touched during her time on the planet. Lords, Ladies and Members of Parliament from all parties rub shoulders with equal rights campaigners and representatives from the many charities she supported.

Julia even got a message of condolence from the Queen! Imagine that, being so well thought of that the Queen takes the time out of her busy schedule to send a telegram.

Two of Auntie Alice's surviving lovers even came to pay their last respects—Eddie (eighty-nine) and Charles (a spring chick of eighty-six). They knew her way back when. When I say knew, I mean in the biblical sense, because Auntie didn't have any hang-ups about age—and me and Mum have obviously inherited that from her. After all, George is ten years younger than Julia (although we don't mention it), and Jack is two years younger than me . . . yes, the women in my family *prefer* younger men . . .

Jack couldn't come with me. And I'm fine with that. He even had to break his promise to spend today with Dad and Peri. Apart from work, and not being able to take vacation time, he hardly *knew* Auntie Alice. He only met her once, after all . . . I'm so glad he *did* get to meet her, though. But he's been great, he really has.

Obviously, he was the first person I called last Sunday when I got the news from George, and you know what? He came straight over and took charge. He was lovely. He called my boss and organized my flight, and everything. And put me on the plane.

But Auntie would have been delighted to see such a good turn out of people . . . Especially Tony and Cherie Blair, unless grief is doing strange things to my eyes . . .

Oh my God—that's—*that really is Tony and Cherie Blair coming toward us*. They're actually here!

Tony (who looks great, considering he just turned fifty) shakes George's hand like they're old friends. And now he's shaking Julia's hand. And now Cherie kisses her on the cheek and is murmuring condolences. My mother is on cheek-kissing terms with Cherie!

And then they turn to me and *they shake hands with me!* I can't wait to tell everyone about this. Can you imagine it? The next time Claire Palmer says something sly to me, I will be able to say, "Of course, but Tony's thoughts on this are . . ."

My mind, of course, goes completely blank as I try to ransack it for something brilliant to say. And as Cherie Blair tells me that my aunt was an inspiration to all women, my tongue takes on a life of its own.

"Thank you, Mrs. Blair," I tell her, grasping for something to say. "Er, your suit is very nice. Is it Chanel?"

And as Tony tells me how proud of Auntie Alice I should be, I grin like an idiot and say the first thing that pops into my mind.

"Thank you, Prime Minister," I say. I may never wash my hand again! "Of course, er, we're very concerned about the sex-starved mussels," I add, digging an even bigger hole for myself. "I do hope you'll find time to look into it—er, in between all the other important political things, of course."

Tony gives me a vague smile—you know—the one you save for lunatics who sit next to you on the train, and you just want to get rid of them without being rude.

"Such nice people, the Blairs," Julia tells me, as we're limousine-driven to the Ritz for the postfuneral tea. "But darling," Julia adds, "did you have to stand there and ask the Prime Minister of Britain about mussel sex? Hardly appropriate at any time."

"Well, I wasn't exactly expecting to meet them," I tell her. "If I had, I'd have read the newspapers this morning to get up to speed on what's happening over here."

"They're just people." George, as well as being a fantastic landscape gardener, is a very practical northern man. "And right nice, too."

"Talking of reading," Julia says morosely as we drive alongside Hyde Park and down Park Lane, "I've arranged for the will to be read this afternoon. I just want to get it out of the way."

"I know what you mean." I squeeze her hand. It's so final, isn't it? I mean, after Auntie Alice's stuff is dispersed (probably all to charity) then Auntie Alice will be gone. This is a depressing thought, and I reach for my hanky as my eyes fill with water again.

None of us feel like the Ritz, but we have to—apart from the fact that Auntie Alice used to love to come here in her younger years, people expect at least a sandwich and a cup of tea after a funeral. It's kind of a relief mechanism, isn't it? It affords everyone the chance to talk a lot about Auntie Alice—to laugh about her exploits, to cry about the fact that she's gone, and start the grieving process.

"I expect Alice sorted everything out," George rumbles. "Always one for tidying loose ends, that woman."

"She's been sorted for years," Julia says. "The house, the money, everything, to avoid death taxes." Julia's voice breaks and she reaches for her hanky, too. "I have to get my will updated," she announces suddenly. "Just in case something happens to me. After all, I'm a woman past my prime, now."

Auntie Alice passing has had a very strange effect on Julia. It's like she's suddenly aware of her own mortality. But death does that, doesn't it? It brings it home to us how fragile we are.

"I hope you're not going to start on about that age rubbish again," George tells her. "You will *never* be past your prime, lass."

"It's easy for you to say." Julia blows her nose. "After all, you're a whole decade younger than I."

Now a less sensitive man might take this as a rebuttal. But George, although a man of not too many words, is definitely sensitive to Julia. Especially with this age thing—it's just not like Julia to worry about it. I mean, I know she's fifty-four but she looks at least ten years younger. And acts it.

"I'm a lucky man, getting the benefit of your extra experience," he tells her, taking her chin in his hand. "Look what I'd have missed out on if I hadn't come to cut your grass and trim your bushes all those years ago. I'd be like a barren garden."

"Oh, George, that's the most poetic thing anyone's ever said to me." Julia gives him a watery smile just as the car pulls up outside the hotel.

And you know, it *is* poetic, isn't it?

And in that moment, I miss Jack desperately as I ponder George's words. If I hadn't lost my vile-green bikini top last year at Dad and Peri's, Jack would never have seen my nonexistent boobs. And I'd be that barren garden . . .

"Come on now, lasses," George tells us. "Let's see Auntie Alice off in style."

And, surprisingly, we do.

After all the tea is drunk, and all the cucumber sandwiches are eaten, and everyone has departed, we meet with the lawyer in a very nice, private function room.

"Let's get this over and done with," Julia tells Auntie Alice's lawyer. "At least there won't be any surprises."

But Auntie Alice, it seems, didn't share every detail of her will with Julia . . .

I'm an official heiress.

It's true!

I can't wait to tell Jack and everyone back home in Hoboken . . . Of course, I'd rather have Auntie Alice than any old inheritance, any day . . .

But at least she left me something totally unique. I mean, normal aunts leave you their porcelain collection, or their memorabilia from a royal wedding or the Queen's Golden Jubilee.

Auntie Alice, on the other hand, has left me her penis-shaped finial. Penis-shaped, on account of the lightning melting it and changing its shape.

But there's more to the will. Auntie Alice has left me a letter that explains everything. Julia says I shouldn't count my chickens before they've hatched. I mean, I *do* have the conditions to fulfill before I qualify for the rest of the bequest . . .

7

....

Lethal Weapon

TO DO

1. ~~Chain self to railings outside Number Ten Downing Street and demand equal rights for women.~~ But Prime Minister Blair *believes* in equal rights for women. After all, Cherie is mother of four, plus is also top judge. You don't get any more equal-rights-for-women than *that.*

2. ~~Chain self to railings outside Buckingham~~ Palace ~~and demand equal rights for women.~~ Remind self that Queen Elizabeth is *female* Head of State. Remind self that Queen Elizabeth is also one's cousin, but only in a distant kind of way . . .

3. ~~Chain self to railings outside White House and demand equal rights for women.~~ Maybe not. After all, White House officials will only quote Condoleezza Rice as shining example of female equality.

Sunday, July 6
12:35 P.M.
Greenwich Mean Time

Who knew this would be so embarrassing?

Or so difficult to explain?

The luggage X-ray machine has, of course, identified my penis-shaped inheritance as a potentially lethal weapon and instead of being on the plane awaiting takeoff, I am being detained in a small cell-like cubicle with two very horrible airport officials.

"I've already explained. It's my inheritance," I tell the two airport officials grumpily, as one of them brandishes my nine-and-a-half-inch iron vibrator.

"It's a very odd shape, miss," the shorter of the officials tells me with a smirk. "Very—missile shaped." He's dying to say penile shaped. I can just see it in his face, along with what his dirty mind *thinks* I'm going to do with it.

I've had enough of this.

"Actually, it's not a vibrator if that's what you were thinking," I stare him squarely in the eye. "It's a historic piece of railing." I am *so* not in the mood for this. All I want to do is to get on my plane and go home.

At least, I console myself, Auntie Alice didn't leave me her early-to-mid-nineteenth-century collection of female sex aids . . . just imagine the fun these bozos would have with that. She left that to Julia, fortunately. My, was that an eye opener. I didn't realize vibrators even went back that far in time. Those Victorians were obviously not as repressed as they made out . . . George was very interested in it . . .

"It's a bit of a strange thing to inherit, miss," the taller official tells me, trying to keep a straight face. He had a *very* good time checking through my underwear when they searched my case, so I scowl at him. "I think we'd better get our superior officer to verify it—we have to be careful what we let people transport on airplanes these days."

"Look, it's not like I packed it in my hand luggage, is it?" I say, trying to reason with him. I really want to get on my plane. "I mean, I do *know* that possession of a possibly lethal instrument while airborne is not a good idea, which is exactly why I put the bloody thing in my suitcase," I add, building up for a rant.

But at least it isn't a *real* vibrator.

You know, I read somewhere that a women was forced to open her suitcase in front of all her fellow passengers because she forgot to take the batteries out of her vibrator. It's true. The airport staff noticed that her case was making an odd noise, and *everyone* watched as she unpacked the offending article and took out the batteries. Now that truly was an embarrassing, nonKodak moment . . .

As the airport official leaves to get his manager (yet another person who can have a good laugh at my expense—or arrest me for possession of a lethal object), his dirty-minded partner leans against the wall, arms folded across his chest.

I sigh and sit down on the uncomfortable metal chair, as I try not to lose the shreds of my temper. I just hope we can clear this up quickly—my flight is due to leave in fifty-five minutes and the plane is already boarding.

The small, harshly lit cubicle is windowless and cell-like, and reminds me of prison, but despite the stuffy heat, I shiver. I wonder if I *have* broken the law? What if I get charged with smuggling a historic relic, or something, and thrown into prison?

Actually, prison could be a *good* thing. Surely it would qualify as one of the things I have to do to get the rest of my inheritance? I mean, I'm sure the press would love my human-interest story . . .

I can just see the headline, now: FAMOUS SUFFRAGETTE'S NIECE ARRESTED FOR POSSESSION OF LETHAL PHALLIC WEAPON.

I could go on a hunger strike, just like Auntie Alice did back in 1913! I could make a stand for women across the world. Newspapers will vie for my story, and will throw huge wads of cash at me . . .

But, of course, I will not be swayed by money and will choose only a politically correct publication in which to tell my tale. And, obviously, I will donate the cash to women's rights! See—I would be making my stand, doing something positive and good for others!

Picture this: me, doing time in prison, just like Auntie Alice. Me, skeletal and weak due to being on a hunger strike, just like Auntie Alice . . . I haven't eaten for weeks and cannot even lift my frail head from the lumpy prison pillow.

But at least the cell isn't cold and dirty. And force-feeding, thankfully, is a thing of the past. Auntie Alice was force-fed. She told me that several prison wardens had to hold her down, while the doctor pushed tubes down her nose and into her stomach . . . euw! And if the terrible nausea wasn't enough, some of the liquid got into her lungs and she got a nasty case of pleurisy . . .

"I'm fighting for my heritage," I say almost inaudibly to the imaginary reporter, because *I* now have a nasty imaginary case of prison pleurisy.

"But what is it, exactly, that you want to prove to the world?" the reporter asks me. "What is your message?"

My message? Hmmm . . . good question.

"Women of the world, unite!" I tell the reporter, coughing feebly. "We must fight against chauvinistic airport officials for our right to . . . to . . . transport historic, phallic, iron railings—or vibrators—across the globe in our luggage . . ." Oh, this is weak, and even my imaginary reporter does not look impressed. I must work on this . . .

I check my watch again—only forty-five minutes until takeoff. The gate will be closed soon.

"Just how much longer is this going to take?" I snap at

Shorty. "If I miss my flight on account of this stupidity, I will be pressing charges for harassment. I will *so* sue your asses—"

And, as I'm building up for a rant, the door opens and the taller guard, plus an older, gray-haired, stern-looking woman enter the room.

"Miss Taylor?" She's all businesslike and not at all smiley. "I understand there's a question about your luggage. Let's get to the bottom of this, shall we?"

"I explained it already to these two bozos," I tell her, throwing my hands up in the air. "And frankly, I'm not at all impressed with your security measures. You should be out there arresting the *real* criminals, not entertaining yourselves with innocent peoples' underwear and penis-shaped finials.

"Here," I hand her my railing. "Knock yourself out. Have a good laugh. It belonged to my auntie, Baroness Beaufort, okay? She chained herself to this very railing in 1913 and I inherited it. Now either charge me with something so I can call my attorney, who is a top human-rights lawyer I might add, and has a very high win record in court, or let me get on my bloody flight."

God, I'm kicking ass. This is great! Just like Auntie Alice and Julia.

"You're related to *the* Baroness Beaufort?" she asks, a few moments later, and I am shocked (and relieved) to see that she's impressed.

"She was my great-great aunt."

"A wonderful woman," she says. "I've admired her all my life—I was very sorry to read her obituary in *The Times.* If it hadn't been for women like your aunt who took such an active role, we might never have got the vote. And I wouldn't be where I am today," she says.

And then, to emphasize just exactly *where* she is today (i.e., in charge) she adds, "Gentlemen, I've got more important things to occupy my time, and frankly, we will speak about this later."

Shorty and his partner are no longer smiling.

"Come, Miss Taylor, let's get you on your flight."
Whew.

4:00 P.M.
Eastern Standard Time

That airport official must *really* admire Auntie Alice because not only do I make the flight (I was escorted on at the last minute like a famous person), I also get upgraded to first class! I never realized how much nicer it is than coach.

And the flight attendants can't do enough for me (possibly due to my now-famous status) and keep offering me nice food (on real plates, not the plastic trays you get in coach) and champagne. And after all, it would be churlish to refuse the champagne, because it's already been poured and will go to waste if I don't drink it.

So while I am drinking the champagne, and generally feeling very pleased with myself for being so firm with those officials, I reread Auntie Alice's letter again and ponder what it *is*, exactly, I'm supposed to do to get my inheritance. Only she's a bit vague . . .

My Dearest Emmeline,

If you are reading this then I am dead and will have confirmed my suspicion that God is, in fact, female. If this is not the case then I expect I shall find myself fully occupied in furthering The Cause on the Other Side.

Now, my dear, much as I love you (or should one say "loved" in this context?), a few home truths are in order and I shall speak my mind.

Not that I can recall Auntie Alice ever speaking any other way . . .

Frankly, your mother has done very well, apart from an unfortunate tendency to marry, and has been a credit to the family name.

However, it has to be said that you, Emmeline, have been far too flighty in your ways. It is a distressing tendency that I have noted is all too common amongst young girls these days.

Of course, I blame your father. A plastic surgeon! Whatever was your mother thinking? But blood will tell in the end and the Beaufort blood runs through your veins, as surely as it ~~does~~ did through my own. The same blood that has flowed through the veins of our family for five hundred years.

Euch . . . how icky! Surely not the same blood? Auntie Alice, it seems, despite being all egalitarian, recently traced our family tree back to Margaret Beaufort, Mother of Henry VII . . . (just like the Queen—but I expect a lot of people can claim bloodkin to Her Majesty if you go back that far . . .).

In order to encourage you to find a purpose in life I have made arrangements for a bequest. However, my girl, this bequest will have to be earned. Far too much in life is taken for granted these days, I feel.

My beloved finial you already have

I'm glad she can't see what the lightning did to it . . . although she might actually approve, knowing Aunt Alice. She would probably think it was poetic justice.

—as inspiration. But I assure you that there is much more at stake. The administration of the bequest will be handled by Mr. Stoat of Stoat, Ferny and Willow, whose services I have retained for a number of years. He has always given satisfaction. He has my strictest instructions as to the manner in which the terms of the bequest are to be executed.

Now, my dear, to the nub of the matter. Not to put too fine a point on it, you need to make something of yourself. Should you do so by satisfying the conditions I shall list below then you will receive the remainder of your inheritance, but they must be observed scrupulously, mark you.

It is my most earnest wish that you prove yourself worthy of the Beaufort name and I have therefore determined that you should be required to demonstrate the following qualities:

1. The courage of your convictions.

Do I *need* more convictions? I'm completely committed to Human Rights and World Peace, after all. . .

2. Commitment to others, world or otherwise. Take note, my dear, Deeds not Words. And donations most certainly do not count. And even the smallest amongst us can make a difference.

I have it! I will travel to the village of Elmina in Ghana (showing courage of my conviction to the yeki-fish situation—I need to see how my thousand pounds is being spent). I haven't thought about Africa in the sense of actually going there . . . Would I have to live in a mud hut? (Of course, it *is* noble to make sacrifices for one's Cause.)

3. Triumph in the face of adversity.

I wonder if winning tickets to attend premiere of favorite rock band's new DVD release counts. I did spend all weekend calling the radio station, and I did triumph in the adversity of a gazillion other fans calling in at the same time!

This to be demonstrated in support of points 1 and 2.

So it obviously doesn't count, then. Back to the yeki plan . . . Africa's really hot, isn't it? (Must make a note to pack highest SPF sunscreen.) So the sun would be an adversary, wouldn't it? Therefore I would be showing triumph against . . . sunburn.

Maybe not . . .

I make no conditions as to what form precisely your actions should take to enact the above. I only advise you that a theme of service would be appropriate and that your actions must be reported in the media.

You have sixteen weeks (the duration of my incarceration in prison) from the date on which you receive this letter to fulfill its terms. On completion Mr. Stoat will handle all the particulars.

Now, show me some spirit! Show me some backbone! I know you have it in you.

I do have backbone and spirit. I just displayed it with the airport officials, after all . . .

Good Luck!
Much love as always,

Aunt Alice

P.S. There is one final thing. Under no circumstances should you marry. Your Jack seems a decent enough sort and I have always thought architecture a very worthy profession, in the tradition of Sir Christopher Wren, but even so. Keep him for sex and companionship, my dear.

I don't like that last part about not marrying Jack, though. Does it mean forever? Or does it just mean I can't marry him for the next sixteen weeks? Which isn't likely anyway, in view of his disinclination to discuss personal matters—must give it some more thought . . .

I wish that the lawyer, Mr. Stoat, had given me a clearer idea of what it is I'm supposed to do. Although Auntie Alice left *him* specific instructions, she also left specific instructions that he *wasn't* to share them with me. I mean, how unfair is that? How am I supposed to know what to do if he can't tell me?

But I don't think Auntie Alice expects me to carry out wanton acts of violence . . . I mean, I just can't *see* me on a golf course, burning the grass with acid to make my point (whatever that point might be). Or cutting telegraph wires . . . or breaking into the Jewel Room at the Tower of London to smash the showcases . . . I don't think the Queen (my cousin) would like that very much, and let's face it, it will crush the bud of my friendship with Tony and Cherie . . .

I wonder what the actual bequest is . . . I mean, if the first part of it is a finial, then maybe the second part is the entire railing itself. Historic or not, what will I do with an iron railing?

But just supposing, though, that it *is* money? If I had some kind of nest egg, then I could rethink my career plan. I could leave Cougan & Cray and . . . what *would* I do instead?

But surely quitting would be admitting defeat? I think that's what Alice means about me being committed. That's it!

This is going to be great. I will commit myself thoroughly to my work. If I land a really terrific account, then surely I will get media interest? You know—JUNIOR ACCOUNT MANAGER STEALS LUCRATIVE ACCOUNT FROM MAJOR COMPETITOR kind of thing.

I wonder if Bill Gates is happy with *his* advertising team . . . after all, I might as well aim high. Oh, but why stop there . . .

Just as I am coming through customs, just as I am planning my pitch for Robert Plant to advertise his next tour and CD, just as I am getting really excited about seeing Jack, I am stopped by an airport official.

"Ma'am, please come with me."

I do not believe this.

4:30 P.M.

By the time the airport officials stop laughing at the phallic railing, and after I explain all about the will *again,* I am finally on my way through to the arrivals lobby. And to Jack . . . I'm dying to tell him all about my inheritance . . . but not the no marriage part, obviously.

4:35 P.M.

Jack is not here . . .

He must have been delayed . . .

4:50 P.M.

Still no Jack. Which is odd, because when I spoke to him on the phone last night, he wrote down my flight number and the arrival time. I've just called his house and there's no answer. No answer from his cell phone, either . . .

I don't panic, because I'm sure there is a logical explanation for his absence. Nor am I going to allow my overactive imagination to conjure up possible accident scenarios involving him. Because Auntie Alice and Dr. Padvi wouldn't panic.

I'm going to take the initiative. I'm going to call around to my friends and find out if something's happened . . .

5:10 P.M.

I think it's just a coincidence that none of my friends are answering their home phones. Or their cell phones . . . I'm a bit surprised that Sylvester or David didn't pick up at Chez Nous, though, because of it being a restaurant. There's always someone around . . .

Except for Sunday nights, on account of Sunday night being quiet and the staff always has the night off . . . Okay. I'm going to give it five more minutes and then I'm going to get a cab.

5:14 P.M.

"Emma, *chérie,* I am so sorry to be late." Sylvester swoops on me, kissing me on both cheeks. "Ze turnpike is a mess. Zis week is a *mess.* Zis week is ze week from hell," he says, taking control of my cart. "Come. We have no time." He strides off with my baggage. "*Vite.* I tell you everyzing in ze car."

What does he *mean* by everything? This does not sound good. But Sylvester can be a drama queen, so I try to quell the queasy bubbles of dread that are forming in my stomach.

"But what about *Jack?*" I pant. I am running to keep up with Sylvester. I think he forgets sometimes that his legs are over a foot longer than mine. "Exactly *why* isn't he here? Everything was fine when I spoke to him on the phone last night."

"Jack is okay." Sylvester slows down, grabs my case from the cart, and climbs onto the escalator. "He is ze *only* one who is okay," he adds darkly, raising his eyes to the ceiling. "He had to go to Boston again, *chérie.* He couldn't call you to tell you himself, because already you are on ze plane. He says he will call you tonight."

Tonight? Does that mean he's not coming home later? I

try not to be too disappointed. I mean, he's only doing his job . . . but I haven't seen him in nearly a week. And I don't ask the obvious question. The "Did Claire go too?" question, because I expect that she did.

I ruthlessly squash my jealously and step onto the escalator. And then I remember Sylvester's cryptic little comment about Jack being the only one who is fine . . .

Before I can extricate any information from him, we reach the bottom of the escalator and he strides even more quickly toward the parking lot.

I can't take all of this in. After a seven-hour flight my brain isn't exactly up to speed, here.

"What's going on?" I ask, as I finally catch up and climb into the passenger seat. "Why are we in such a hurry? Why is this the week from hell?"

Sylvester raises his hands to the ceiling, then slips into a stream of complicated, ever faster French curses as he starts the engine. His voice gets higher and higher as he reaches his crescendo, and I wish I could speak French.

Sylvester is now highly agitated, and because I love him dearly (but also because I do not want to die young—he's not the best driver in the world, even when he's calm), I reach across and pull out the car key, placing my hand on his arm.

"Calm down," I tell him. "Take deep breaths, sweetie. I'm sure it's not as bad as it seems." At least, I hope it's not. "Just start from the beginning."

"Oh, Emma, it is so good zat you are home," he says, leaning across the shift stick to hug me. "I missed you. You will know what to do."

I might, if I ever find out what *it* is. But Sylvester is squeezing me so tightly I can hardly breathe, never mind speak. Although it's nice that my friends have such faith in my advice . . .

"Okay, I start from ze beginning. *C'est bien compliqué.*

First, David, he is in Florida wiz his *mère*," he says, releasing me. "She says she is sick, she has ze palpitations, she has ze pains in her left arm, and she needs him zere. And I don't know how long he will be zere. Pah," he says, pausing to draw breath. "She is not even in ze hospital. Sick? *Non*, she just wants to keep him away from me."

"David loves you." I pat his arm. "I'm sure he'll be back just as soon as he can." David really has to tell his mother about Sylvester. I mean, if Jack's mother were still alive, I'd be terribly hurt if he didn't tell her about me.

"Second, on Wednesday poor Tom he lose his job. And now he is desolate. He is feeling like a failure and poor Katy, she does not know what to say to make him better. He didn't even tell her about it until yesterday morning."

"Oh God." That's terrible. How will they manage? How will they pay the humongous mortgage on their house? But I don't say this, because it will only make Sylvester worse. "Tom will find something," I say, with more conviction than I feel. "He's a clever man with years of experience. I bet he won't be out of work for long."

"Zat is what Katy tells him. She is so strong . . . so brave . . . and now Tish and Rufus, zey are not speaking. Zey have had a fight because of Rufus's *mère*—oh, all zese mozzers interfering in ze lives of zeir children. It is not good."

I can't believe it. I go away for a week, and everything happens. At least Rachel's okay.

"At least they have their health," I say to Sylvester. This is one of Julia's phrases, and sounds a bit prissy.

"I have not finished," Sylvester pauses. I'm sure he can't help it, but I wish he wouldn't be so dramatic sometimes. "It's Rachel," he wails dramatically. "Today she is even more sick. She cannot eat, she cannot drink. Everyzing makes her vomit."

Instantly nauseous at his words, my stomach heaves with fear and threatens to dislodge the first-class food I ate on the flight. My heartbeat accelerates and I rub my hands with the sudden cold chill.

"And when she fainted zis afternoon, Hugh wants to take her to ze hospital. And she is so sick zat she *let* him take her to ze hospital."

Rachel fainted? Rachel in the hospital? It *must* be serious; she must be really worried, if she actually agreed to go.

I berate myself for being so wrapped up in my own concerns. I have failed my friend. I should have made her see a doctor last week. What if she's got something incurable? Rachel's been my best friend since high school—I just can't bear the thought of losing her . . .

"Have the doctors said anything yet?" I finally ask Sylvester, dreading his answer. "Are they running tests?"

"We are all zere in ze hospital waiting for ze doctor to see her, and zen Hugh remembers zat *you* are here waiting for Jack."

"Hurry." I hand Sylvester the car key, touched by the fact that Hugh remembered my flight, despite his worry for Rachel. "And put your foot down."

Never. Again. Will I voluntarily. Be driven. By Sylvester.

I should *never* say things like "hurry," or "put your foot down" to him. I should know better. Because he takes me literally, and the minute we hit the turnpike he turns into a Grand Prix race driver. And the state police don't approve of people who travel at eighty miles an hour in a fifty-five-mile-an-hour zone. They don't like drivers who tailgate and lane hop, either.

One ticket and a fine for speeding, and a possible charge for dangerous driving later, and after I explain the situation to the nice officers (and promise to drive the rest of the way), we finally arrive at the hospital just after six. (I think the officers were distracted by the sight of Sylvester sobbing inconsolably.)

And when the unhelpful receptionist finally decides to check Rachel's whereabouts for us, we discover that she's been admitted to the hospital.

She's actually been admitted.

It must be so serious that the doctors can't just prescribe the appropriate drugs and send her home (as I was hoping). And when Sylvester and me finally arrive in the ward's waiting room, my friends' worried faces do not offer solace.

Tish and Katy are huddled together on the sofa. Rufus is pacing the room like a dark, brooding, Heathcliff. All huddling and pacing cease as we enter, and when they see that it is only Sylvester and me, they sigh collectively.

"We don't have any news yet. Hugh's in with her now," Katy tells me immediately. Although her face is white with fear, her voice is calm and even. "We should know something soon."

"I should have done something," Tish wails from the sofa. "I haven't seen her all week—I've been so wrapped up in my wedding plans, I totally neglected her."

"I wasn't much help, either." Katy frets. "She called and left a message for me on Thursday, and I didn't get around to calling her back . . ."

"I could have pushed the doctor issue with her more forcefully," I say. "I *should* have."

"How important is checking out wedding venues when your best friend is ill?" Tish says.

"I wish I'd called her back . . ." Katy trails off.

"Yer know what she's like," Rufus says, unexpectedly. "Rachel don't listen to anyone. Even Hugh. So there's not much use all blamin' yerselves, is there?"

He has a point.

"She's not the only one who doesn't listen," Tish tells him pointedly.

"Rufus is right." Sylvester shakes his head. "Rachel, she is just like a French woman. Stubborn, strong."

We all shake our heads and revert to silence as we wait. And then I notice that Tom isn't here.

"How's Tom doing?" I whisper to Katy. I don't know why I'm whispering, it's just something about hospital waiting rooms.

"We'll work it out." She gives me a weak smile. "He's taken Alex home for a while. Hospital waiting rooms are no place for kids. He's got Betty with him."

As I am about to make reassuring noises to her the waiting-room door opens, and it is Hugh.

"She's fine," he says holding up his hands. "She's just tired, but that's understandable since her endocrine glands are working overtime."

Hugh is a scientist. And although he is without question a lovely man, he has a habit of talking to us as if we are all scientists, too.

"So it's all entirely normal. They just want to keep her overnight for observation, since this is a difficult initiation to parturiency," he adds, which makes the whole thing about as clear as mud.

And then we're all talking at once.

"Do they know what's wrong?" Me, because I don't know what parturiency actually is. It sounds nasty . . .

"What did the doctors say?" Tish.

"Have they decided on a course of treatment?" Katy.

"Why don't you let her tell you herself." Hugh's face breaks inexplicably into an enormous grin. Which is odd. And then he pulls his features into a somber expression. "Although it may take a little getting used to the idea."

Rachel is gray and shrunken and small against the hospital pillow. Her arm is connected to an IV drip, which adds to her air of fragility.

She is also good and angry.

"I don't fucking *believe* it," is her opening gambit. "I don't fucking understand how this *happened*. This is a fucking *nightmare*."

"Sweetie," I say, taking her hand. "Whatever the problem is, you can pull through it." I just hope I sound more reassuring than I feel.

"They make incredible breakthroughs in medicine every day," Katy says.

"Is it an ulcer?" Tish asks her. "It *is* an ulcer—I *knew* it. But what did the doctor actually say?"

"I'll tell you what the doctor said." Rachel, despite being tired and washed out, is building up for a major rant. "I'm fucking *pregnant*."

8

....

Mother-to-Be

TO DO

1. Buy dog food.
2. Choose better moment to tell Jack that Claire Palmer is trying to steal him away from me.
3. Choose better moment to ask Jack if he has sexual thoughts about Claire Palmer.

If Rachel had just announced that she'd found the cure to a horrible, life-threatening disease, and had injected herself with a dose of said horrible, life-threatening disease just to prove to the scientific community that her antidote worked, I wouldn't be half so shocked.

But pregnant?

Rachel, a mother?

Unbelievable.

I can see I am not alone in this thought, because Tish and Katy are also stunned into silence.

On the bright side, at least Rachel's not dying . . .

"But how the fuck did this happen?" Rachel asks us rhetorically. "Of course I *know* how it happened, I'm a fucking scientist, for God's sake. I *understand* about contraception. I'm always so fucking careful about it."

Rachel, as we know (because she mentions it quite frequently), does not want children. She never has. She is a career scientist and she's fairly high up at work, I think. So this pregnancy is obviously far from a joyous event for her.

I try to think of something soothing to say. Something along the lines of "these things are sent to try us" or "worse things happen at sea."

"And don't anyone tell me 'these things happen,' or I will explode," Rachel snaps, so I close my mouth.

Katy and Tish glance at me ominously. They obviously expect me, in my role as wise-counselor goddess, to utter words of wisdom.

"Will someone please say something?" Rachel's voice wobbles just a bit as she covers her face with her hands. "Will someone just tell me what I'm supposed to do here? I'm . . . scared."

And we're all even more stunned, because being unsure about anything, or being scared about anything, is just not Rachel. She always knows exactly what she wants and goes after it. And let's face it, if she truly can't face the thought of having a baby, then there is a solution . . . although I really don't want to think about that . . .

And then Rachel does something else. She bursts into un-Rachel-like tears.

"Oh sweetie, thank God it's not terminal stomach cancer," I say, trying to infuse a note of optimism in my voice as I put my arm around her shoulder. Rachel's not really big on hugs, but this is an emergency. A crisis situation. "We all thought you'd gotten something really horrid," I add. "So on the positive side, at least you're not dying."

"Thank you, hon," Rachel sniffles and gives me a weak smile as I hand her a tissue. "I sure feel like I'm dying, though. It just never occurred to me I might be pregnant."

She dries her tears, then looks around at us, her eyes as large as saucers. "What the fuck am I going to do?"

I'm damned if I know. I mean, it's not like you should really give advice about these things, is it? It's very personal.

"Whatever is right for you," Katy tells her firmly. "Only *you* can know what that is. And while motherhood can be a wonderful thing," she continues, as she perches on the end of Rachel's bed and pats her leg. "It's not the end of the world if you decide otherwise. You do have . . . choices. Options."

"And whatever you do, we'll support you, honey," Tish chimes in from the other side of the bed as she also places an arm around Rachel's shoulders. "How far along are you?"

"Five weeks," Rachel says glumly. "Although I would argue with the unscientific way that the doctor calculated those five weeks."

This is good. Although I don't understand what she means, at least she's thinking scientifically again. And she's arguing, which is also a good sign.

"Did you know that your progress is calculated from the beginning of your last period? I mean, how strange is that?" she rants. "Women are fertile mid-cycle. My last period is only one week late. Therefore I calculate that I'm only three weeks pregnant. Oh god . . . pregnant." She bursts into tears again.

"You have plenty of time to think it through," Tish tells her soothingly. "Just take your time. You don't have to make a decision yet."

"And this *is* the twenty-first century," I say, trying to think of something intelligent yet noninfluential. "It's your body, your choice," I add, because it's a good line. I think I heard it in a movie, somewhere.

"What does Hugh think?" Katy asks.

"We haven't exactly had time to discuss it yet. But he said it was totally up to me."

"Well, that's good, isn't it?" Because it is. Hugh is such a nice, uncontrolling kind of man. I have to say that when I first met him, I was a bit surprised Rachel went for him because although he is super intelligent like Rachel, he is also very nice looking in a cuddly-teddy-bear kind of way. But not in a handsome kind of way. On the other hand, although Rachel is also super intelligent and doesn't give two figs for what society deems the handsome qualities a man ought to have, she is also one of the most stunning women you could imagine. Think Miss USA, then double it.

You see, Hugh is not overpowered by Rachel, which is excellent because Rachel (although I love her) can be pretty overpowering. Plus, Rachel adores him. Until she met Hugh, she considered men good only for sex . . .

I remember, once, when we asked Hugh how he knew that Rachel was The One, he said something about how it was all to do with diffusion. Something about how their particles mixed and merged. So you see, he *understands* Rachel, he speaks the same *language* . . .

"Then he added that, if I wanted, it *could* be a prime opportunity to *merge our respective DNA and formulate a unique life.*" Rachel's eyes sprout tears again.

Oh. He obviously wants the baby . . .

Rachel leans back against the pillow. "I just don't know if I can stand months of vomiting, feeling tired, and swelling, after which I will suffer horrible agonies giving birth to an ugly, pukey little gnome to whom I will then be enslaved for the rest of my life."

Put like that it doesn't sound terribly attractive. I wonder why we women go through such agonies to procreate? I mean, like Peri, each and every mother I know has at some point told me at great length how yucky and messy it is—the pain, the sleepless nights . . .

But I'd still *love* to have Jack's babies . . . Obviously in the fullness of time, after I've shown my commitment to something and got Auntie Alice's bequest. After all, Auntie Alice didn't say anything about having children.

"I'm sure Hugh doesn't want you to have a baby just because *he* wants one," Katy says, though she doesn't sound very sure. "I mean, *if* he actually wants one. Haven't you guys discussed this? You're getting married in a few weeks' time."

"He knows I don't want kids. But now that the deed is done, it changes everything." Rachel sighs glumly, and we all sigh along with her.

"Thinking positively, you might just suffer terrible morning sickness and not have any of the other symptoms," Tish says. "But only if you decide to go ahead. Because it's totally up to you . . ."

"Absolutely up to you." I squeeze her hand.

"No one else can tell you what to do." Katy nods, folding her arms across her chest.

"But . . ." Tish says, a trifle tentatively. "If you *do* choose to go ahead, this awful sickness will pass, honey—probably by the middle of your second trimester. Or sooner, if you're lucky. It's just your body producing hormones to accommodate the fetus . . ." Tish trails off as we all look at her in surprise. "I'm just trying to give her a balanced view," she says. "After all, it's better to have all the relevant information before making such a life-altering decision, isn't it?"

It sounds like Tish has been reading pregnancy magazines. Oddly, this makes us all smile and lightens the doom and gloom in the room.

"You've been reading pregnancy magazines, haven't you?" I say.

"Well—" Tish has the grace to blush.

"You definitely *sound* like you've been reading pregnancy magazines," Rachel adds with a weak smile. "That's so like you, Miss Tish."

"It doesn't hurt to know about these things . . . for the future . . . Information is power." Tish blushes even more. "I'm sorry, sweetie," she says, squeezing Rachel's shoulder. "I didn't mean to sound like I was trying to influence you. It was thoughtless of me."

"You know, I'm too tired to think about it right now," Rachel says, closing her eyes. "Please can we just drop the subject and talk about something else? Something cheerful? What's going on with you guys?"

Katy flashes me a worried glance. Well, we could discuss Tom losing his job, but that's hardly cheerful, is it? Or we could discuss Sylvester's worries about David. Or Tish and Rufus's disagreement . . .

"Em, Rufus's family are coming across from Ireland for a visit next month," Tish says. "They want to meet me."

"Well, that's great," I say. Because it is. "They must be thrilled about the engagement."

"His mother didn't sound too happy about it when I spoke to her on the telephone." Tish bites her lip. "She wants him to marry a nice Irish girl."

"At least he's marrying a nice Italian girl, who also happens to be Catholic," Rachel tells her firmly. "Stop worrying about it. They should thank their lucky stars."

"I'm sure they'll love you once they meet you," Katy says.

"Which will be sooner than I expected," Tish says unhappily. "Next month is too soon—we have Rachel's wedding coming up, and other stuff. Fuck, I'm not asking him to tell her she can't come—I just want him to tell her to come another time. That's not unreasonable, is it?"

"Honey, you have to make a stand. Hell, I'll call her for you," Rachel says, sounding more like her old self. "After my mother, Rufus's mom'll be a piece of cake."

"Talking of making a stand," I say, because I'd forgotten all about my own news until now. "*I* have to make a stand with my iron penis."

"Rewind that statement," Katy says as they all stare at me with amazement. "Iron penises I want to hear about."

"Ohmigod. And Tony and Cherie Blair came to Auntie Alice's funeral."

And so I launch into my "Emma meets the Blairs" episode, but omit the part where I ask Tony about the sex-starved mussels, and Cherie about Chanel. And then I give them a determinedly upbeat account of Auntie Alice's collection of vibrators, my phallic iron railing, and my trouble at the airport.

By the time I tell them about Auntie Alice's letter (minus the no marriage part), they are all laughing.

"This could only happen to you, Emma," Katy gasps between laughs.

"But what can I do?" I ask. "What do you suppose it all means? What have I got to prove and how do I prove it?"

And after pondering my situation, my three friends come up with three possibilities.

"You could help with the bake sale I'm planning," Katy says, clutching her stomach. "You could make a commitment to school computers."

"You could use Betty," Tish giggles. "You know—to encourage people to adopt less-than-perfect pets in the face of adversity."

"Why don't you ask your cousin, Queen Elizabeth?" is Rachel's suggestion, and they all immediately fall about laughing again.

Honestly, doesn't anyone take me seriously?

By the time we leave the hospital, it is nearly ten in the evening and obviously too late for our regular Sunday-night dinner at Chez Nous. It's odd, isn't it, how everything can change in just a week?

But although my body clock is still running on UK time, which means that it is really the early hours of Monday morning for me, I don't feel tired.

I feel really positive and empowered. I really do.

"Auntie Alice is right," I tell Betty, who raises an ear. "I *need* a change."

This could really be a great turning point in my life.

A change of the good variety, rather than the bad variety, obviously.

Thinking of good things makes me think about Jack. I wonder if he left me any messages . . .

When I check my voicemail, there are seven messages.

Five of them are from telemarketers *and they are all recorded messages!* I mean, what is the state of telemarketing coming to? Not only do they have the audacity to invade my personal space, they can't even be bothered to *do it in person.* After all, if I'm going to get hassled, then it should at least be by a real human being and not a perkily happy recorded message inviting me to call a 1 800 number!

But I have two messages from Jack. Yes!

"Hi, sweetheart, it's seven in the evening. I've just called my place and you're not there, either, so I guess your flight was delayed. I'll try you again before we go to dinner. I miss you."

Despite the fact that his words are mundane, just the sound of his voice runs over me and I feel instantly better as I listen to his second message.

"It's me again. It's eight-thirty, and you're still not home. I tried Chez Nous but there was no answer. Where are you all? We're going out for dinner now so give me a call at the hotel or on my cell phone when you finally make it home. I'm sorry I had to leave—this Boston project is turning into a nightmare. I'm not sure when I'll be back home but hopefully soon."

I'm definitely not going to worry about the fact that he said "we're" going out to dinner, rather than "I'm" going out to dinner. After all, he has to eat, and I'm glad he's not eating on his own. Because that's mean and miserable of me, isn't it?

I settle myself on the sofa and dial Jack's cell phone. I

really need to hear the sound of his voice. I haven't even had
the chance to tell him about my inheritance, yet, because we
didn't really get a chance to talk properly while I was in London. But his cell phone switches me immediately to voicemail, so I call the hotel number instead and ask to be put
through to his room.

"Yes." Oh God. It's Claire.

What is she doing in Jack's room at, I check my watch,
ten-fifteen at night? I'm sure it's all perfectly innocent, and
so I will try to be nice to her.

"Hello, Claire, I'd like to speak with Jack please." Okay, so
polite and to the point, rather than nice, because that's better than rude, isn't it?

Betty growls, and I pat her to comfort her.

"He's in the bathroom," Claire tells me rather unhelpfully.
And rather rudely, too.

She doesn't elaborate on what she's doing in his room at
this time of night. She doesn't make polite conversation. She
doesn't even offer to take a message. Instead, she waits to
hear what I have to say.

"Could you ask him to call me back, please?" My voice is
stiff and formal, and I am not happy that I have to even ask.
But I don't say anything, because there's no point borrowing trouble, is there? Besides, Jack's *expecting* me to call.
Therefore Claire's presence in his room must be completely
aboveboard.

"It's very late. Is it urgent?" she asks, and I bite my tongue.

Betty's growls intensify, and I cuddle her closer for
warmth. It's none of bloody Claire's business whether or not
it's urgent. I'm Jack's girlfriend, for God's sake. And if I want
to speak to my own boyfriend, late at night, in his own hotel
room, then what right does she have to cross-question me? I
mean, I could be calling late at night to engage in a bit of
naughty phone sex . . . but she is his boss, so I don't say any
of this.

"Yes," I say instead.

"Okay." Click.

Okay and click? That's it?

I seethe as I glare disbelievingly at the telephone handset.

Now, I don't know if it's just a combination of Auntie Alice's letter, and empowerment, and making a stand, and everything feeling a bit surreal after the long flight and the worry about my friends, or my near-death experience with Sylvester's erratic driving, but I am definitely suspicious about Claire Palmer.

I'm *sure* I'm not just overreacting and obsessing.

I will make tea. I will read what Dr. Padvi Choyne has to say about jealousy. I will also make a list.

REASONS WHY I THINK THAT CLAIRE WANTS TO GET RID OF ME AND HAVE JACK FOR HERSELF

1. She is always horrible to me (but in a covert, clever kind of way when other people are around).
2. Betty hates her.
3. She is in Jack's hotel room at ten-fifteen at night.

It's true. Claire *is* always horrible to me. It's just really, really hard to pinpoint, because it's not *what* she says to me, exactly, but *how* she says it. And why would she even waste time being horrible to me unless I have something that she wants, i.e., Jack?

Last month, for example, I met Jack at his work because we had plans to go to the movies. He had a few things to finish up, so I just pop into the restroom to tidy myself. I wish I hadn't, because Claire is also in there. And as she's drying her hands and fluffing her hair, and as I'm applying lipstick, I try to be nice to her. Because you can hardly ignore someone in the close confines of a restroom, can you?

This is what happened.

"Hi, Claire," I say. "How are you?"

"Hi, Emma, I'm great," she says, giving me the benefit of her perfect teeth and full lips. "That's a nice shirt you're wearing."

Well knock me down with a feather . . .

I mean, this *is* a nice top—I got it from H&M on Fifth Avenue last week, and although it is body molding (and let's face it, I don't exactly have much cleavage to mold) it *does* show my nicely firm abs and my delicate shoulders. But I'm shocked that Claire even bothered to notice it.

And just as I'm thinking that I'm wrong about her and that I just haven't given her a proper chance, and that she *can* be nice, she delivers her underhand blow.

"You know," she says, as she readjusts her bra cups under *her* cleavage-revealing top. "A woman owes it to herself to make the most of what she's got. Or not," she sniggers, scathingly eyeing my 32AAs.

Innocent words, but her meaning is completely clear.

Now I could at this point either (a) just swallow her nastiness and slink away like some sad, victim-like person, or (b) be nasty back, but in a falsely nice-sounding kind of way. I think (b).

"I know," I tell her, my voice oozing with artificial sympathy as I eye her 34Cs. "It must be so hard being so . . . abundant . . . I expect it's difficult to get men to take you seriously in the workplace, when they're leering at your boobs. Well, gotta dash," I tell her, grabbing my purse. "Jack's waiting for me."

Jack's boss or not, I couldn't let her get away with that, could I?

I wish Jack would call me . . .

Fifteen minutes later Jack still hasn't called me back . . .

I chew on my pen as I consider my options. I can either

(a) assume that Claire didn't pass on my message (for her own nefarious reasons) and call him back, or (b) obsess about it all night long.

Although Dr. Padvi advises caution and to wait until one's partner is on the same tranquility page, Auntie Alice wouldn't worry about higher transcendental planes of togetherness. Auntie Alice would just say what she thinks and have done. I'm sure I can combine the best parts of their mutual advice.

I think (a).

Take deep breaths, I tell myself. *I am a mature woman; I am not going to get all hysterical and silly. I can deal with Claire Palmer.*

I dial the number.

"Hello."

"Jack." I immediately forget to be calm, so relieved and happy am I when he picks up. "I'm so glad it's *you.*"

"I'm glad it's me, too," he teases, and I can hear the smile in his voice. "I was getting kinda worried that you'd met a rich lord in England and decided he's a better bet than a struggling architect."

"No chance," I laugh. And then, because I'm nervous and my mouth is running away with me, "I was getting a bit worried about you, too, because when I called fifteen minutes ago and spoke to Claire, I asked her to tell you to call me back, and then you didn't, so I was anxious that she hadn't passed on my message because she really, really doesn't like me." Oh. I didn't mean to say that.

"What are you talking about? Sure she likes you," Jack says, obviously puzzled. "She's always asking about you. She must have forgotten to pass on the message."

"How could she forget? Especially when I told her it was urgent. Not that it *is* urgent, because we're all fine, kind of, but I just wanted to make sure she actually told you I'd called."

"I'm sure there's a reasonable explanation," Jack tells me. "I think you're overreacting. She has a lot on her mind, is all. This project is really getting to us."

Us. Him and Claire. He obviously hasn't reached the point where he can project his tranquility signs to me, yet. He just can't see what she's like, yet.

But I have to make my feelings known.

"I'm not overreacting," I tell him, because I'm definitely never going to feel tranquil until I get this out of my system. "Claire *doesn't* like me. In fact, I think she's after you. Even Betty doesn't like her, and dog's know about these things."

"Oh Emma," Jack laughs. "That's too funny. And dumb. She is *so* not chasing me. I can't believe you're worried about that. She knows I'm with you."

"What difference does *that* make?"

"It's not like that between us. Honey, you're overreacting."

Well I'm obviously not going to get very far with this train of thought. But I do think he could trust my instincts more. And I'm *not* dumb . . .

I wonder if he *has* ever thought about what it would be like—you know—to have sex with her. She's beautiful, she's built, and guys do that, don't they? Fantasize a lot about other women.

"So you've never thought about her in a sexual way, then?" I ask, before I can bite off my tongue. Fuck, I shouldn't have said that. But the question is out there and I can't do anything about it.

"What *is* this?" Jack asks, obviously puzzled.

"Well have you?" Yes, I know I'm pushing it. And I don't think I truly want to know the answer. "Oh, it was just this thing I read somewhere—that all guys think about sex with every woman they meet."

There is a silence, and then Jack sighs. "I'm not even going there. I am not having this conversation because it's just too stupid. Emma, don't you trust me?"

Oh God, his sheer refusal to answer means that he *has* thought about having sex with her. I *never* think about sex with other men! Because, pop stars, actors, and other famous male personalities just don't count, do they?

"Of course I trust you," I say primly. And I mean it. I do. I just don't trust Claire.

"What's eating at you? Come on, spit it out."

"Nothing. So how long will you be away?" I ask, abruptly changing the subject. I should never have started this in the first place.

"Are you mad at me?"

Yes. Although I don't really understand why. He's just being nice, normal, straight Jack. But men can be so blind about these things.

"No," I lie. "Not at all."

"Well, you sound pissed at me."

"I'm just tired. It's been a long day." And then, because I really don't want to finish this phone call on bad terms with him, "Call it worry over Tom losing his job, David being in Florida, Tish and the dreaded mother-in-law, and Rachel being pregnant."

"Oh my God. All this happened since I left this morning?"

Back on safe ground, I fill him in on the details and when I have nothing more to say, there is a silence. I'm tired and depressed, and I don't want to think about anything.

"You must be beat," Jack says finally. "You need to get some sleep."

"Yes," I sigh, wishing he were here, instead of in Boston.

"Emma?" I can almost see him running a hand through his hair. "Don't worry about—you know—anything."

I wish he would explain what he means when he says "anything," even though I know he means him and me.

"I won't," I say finally. "Good . . . good luck sorting out the Boston problems."

"Thanks," he says, his voice curiously tender. "Oh," he adds.

"I had to leave Betty with Katy this morning—will you take care of her while I'm away? You know she hates to be alone."

"She's here with me now. We'll be fine."

Silence stretches between us as I try to think of a way to bridge the widening gap. But the words stick in my throat. I need reassurance. I need to know that this relationship is going somewhere, but I know that Jack doesn't want to discuss it now. I'm not sure *I* even want to discuss it now, despite being empowered and wanting to make a stand.

"I—I miss you," he tells me quietly.

I love you, I want to say, but don't. "I miss you too," I say instead.

After I hang up the telephone I have a nasty taste in my mouth and a queasy, unsettled, nervous anxiety in my stomach. It is as if Jack is drifting away from me, and the closer I try to get to him, the further away I push him. I really don't mean to do this, but his unwillingness to talk in depth about our long-term relationship is unsettling.

And as I pull Betty closer for comfort, I realize that Jack hasn't said just *where* I should keep Betty company.

His place or mine?

9

....

Stylish Success

TO DO

1. Begin first day of new attitude to career and relationships With Style. (Auntie Alice always used to say that one should do everything With Style.)
2. Think positively re: Prince of Pads incontinence products. After all, twenty-five million Americans are depending on me.
3. Become a HUSSI (but a good kind of HUSSI). My mission awaits me!

Monday
8:35 A.M.

The wakeup song on my favorite classic rock FM station this morning was Led Zeppelin's "Good Times Bad Times," and you know what? It was a sign!

Jack and me are *bound* to have our bad times, as well as our good times, so I'm just going to take each day as it comes . . . And I'm bound to have bad times and good times at work. And with my friends.

You know, I just don't have enough outside interests.

When I say outside interests, I mean interests that are *separate* from Jack and my friends. I just have too much free time to worry about things that might never happen.

Yes, Auntie Alice's letter has really made me assess my life. My problem (apart from figuring out what I need to do to get my inheritance) is that I am too *insular*. I need more *diversity* in my life.

After my conversation with Jack last night, I got to thinking about it, you see. And after I put Auntie Alice's phallic finial on my bedside table for inspiration (spiritual rather than sexual), I read a few chapters of Dr. Padvi's book. And do you know what? I didn't get much sleep, but surprisingly, I feel positive, I really do.

Over the past year, all of our lifestyles have shifted and our patterns have changed.

In the old days (apart from the three months I lived with Bastard Adam), I shared an apartment with Tish. In the old days, Rachel, Tish and me were the Three Musketeers, single girls being hip and having fun. No long, lonely weeknights stretched out in front of us because we had each other.

Of course, we *do* still have each other. But our weeknights are now spent with our partners instead of each other. Which is good, because life is all about change, isn't it?

But now that Jack's working longer hours, I can't just assume that he'll be around for me. And I can't just assume that my girlfriends will just drop everything and come out with me, because they have their own men to spend time with.

I need to be positive and take action.

The first point on my list is my career, because we spend such a lot of our time at work that it should be rewarding and interesting. And if I have a more interesting, demanding job, then maybe *I'll* have to work longer hours, too . . . not that I *want* to spend *too* much time at work, but it certainly couldn't hurt. I'm going to give it my best shot. I'm going to take *affirmative action.*

And I'm certainly dressed for affirmative action. I chose my outfit very carefully this morning, to present my new go-getter image at work. This black power suit from Jones New York sends out just the right signals.

This is a great, career-minded look for me.

And Betty, sporting black-and-white-striped ribbons, is ultra businesslike for *her* first day at work . . . Actually, I'm a bit nervous about the reaction to a dog at work, but I can hardly leave her alone at home for hours, can I? I don't think anyone will even *notice* her. She's a very good little dog and she fits perfectly inside my oversized bag (black, of course) . . .

"Emma, tell me that's not a dog in your tote bag," Grady Thomas, my boss, says to me as I reach my cubicle.

"Morning Grady," I say brightly. "It's not a dog in my tote bag." How did he know? I mean, the bag is big, but it doesn't look dog shaped . . . please let him not make a fuss about this.

"Oh, good. Because if it were a dog, then I'd have to tell you that pets aren't allowed at work due to the disruption they cause, and because people have allergies." And then he reaches under the blanket, pats Betty's head, and carefully replaces the blanket. "Make sure your nondog is discreet."

I like Grady. He's been with Cougan & Cray forever and is known to be one of the nicest senior managers in the company. He expects us to work hard, of course, but he's always fair and willing to compromise.

"You won't even know she's not here," I smile, relieved. "It's only for a couple of days."

And then after he asks about my trip to England, and sympathizes about Auntie Alice (I give him the abridged version minus the phallic finial and meeting the Blairs), he hands me a folder with my new account. I can't wait to get started!

"I know this is hardly the cutting edge of advertising, but give it your best shot," he sighs as my telephone rings.

"Be assured, I'm aiming for the top," I tell him with a wink. "That'll be the CEO of McDonalds calling to ask me to design his new advertising campaign. Better see what we can do for him," I say airily, desperate for Grady to go in case it's one of my friends.

"The Emma Taylor hotline." He nods at my phone. "Right on cue."

"We're all aware that William Cougan doesn't approve of personal calls at work," I tell him, just a bit primly. How does he know it's a personal call? "Good morning, Cougan and Cray, Emma Taylor speaking," I say in what I think is a very professional manner, as I carefully slide my tote bag containing Betty under my desk.

Grady sighs and turns back to his office.

"It's me." It's Tish. "It's nothing, I just called for a chat—we didn't get a chance last night with everything going on and I haven't seen you for a week."

This is how my morning usually goes. I like to start my day with a chat with Rachel, Tish, and Katy, just to touch base with them before beginning work. But maybe that's what Auntie Alice means by me being a bit flighty . . .

"Can we chat later on the way to the hospital?"

"Oh."

"Only I'm really busy because it's my first day back," I add, because I don't want her to feel like I'm blowing her off.

"Sure, er, fine."

"But I'm sure no one will miss me for a few minutes," I say, feeling guilty. "I'll call you back from the restroom in five."

Besides, Betty will be able to stretch her legs for a few minutes.

9:45 A.M.

Finally, time to start my new project! I open my folder and start reading . . .

Who knew that so many people in this country suffer from incontinence? It's true. We spend four-point-five billion dollars every year on incontinence pads alone . . .

It's going to be hard to get excited about incontinence pads . . . though I expect I'd get rather excited about them if *I* suffered from incontinence . . .

Mmm. But how to come up with a fresh, new, positive spin on the actual pads themselves? How?

I can't make it humorous, because let's face it, incontinence is nothing to be laughed at. And I can't make it sexy, because, well . . . it's just not sexy, is it? How about sophisticated? The James Bond among pads . . . hmmm . . . Licensed Not To Spill? Definitely a no.

10:10 A.M.

Positive Life Change kind of theme might work, though.

Oh, telephone . . .

"Emma, I need you to call David in Florida and tell him how much he is hurting me," Sylvester wails in his melodramatic way.

"Sylvester. Can we talk about this later? I'll call around on my way back from the hospital."

"Oh. You are too busy for me, zen? Too wrapped up in your career to help an old friend?"

"No, of course not," I sigh. "I'll call you back from my cell in five." Honestly, at this rate I'm not going to get any work done.

10:50 A.M.

Picture this: Rich banker type, mid-forties, the image of good health, saying, "Prince of Pads really changed my life. Now I can bungee jump and sky dive without a care," as per glamorous tampon adverts featuring beautiful girls in white bikinis, or on roller blades, dressed in white shorts? Also definitely a no . . .

I really *am* trying to put a positive spin on these pads. When my telephone rings again, and it's Katy, I promise to call her back on my cell.

11:20 A.M.

Who knew this would be so hard?

Maybe some kind of patriotic theme might be good. Something involving the flag . . .

Picture this: The client loves my idea. I get a great review, and then I get another promotion, and before you know it I'll be single-handedly running the department.

That will show my convictions and triumph in the face of adversity!

Emma Taylor, Director of Advertising . . . that sounds completely fabulous. I can just see it now . . . Jack and me, the golden yuppie couple of Manhattan, obviously doing good deeds . . .

But Emma Taylor, Junior Account Manager and General Dogsbody (which is what I am), *is* at least a step up from Emma Taylor, Administrator and General Dogsbody (which is what I used to be).

It's stupid, you know, but when I got promoted to actually *being* a junior account manager, I thought it would involve a lot more than it actually does. I'm not complaining or anything, but although my ideas are taken more seriously these days, and although I got a pay raise, I do still end up doing a lot of the boring, mundane stuff . . . like any account (e.g., incontinence pads) that no one else wants. Like research and admin for the other, much more senior account managers—

"Emma, can you organize coffee and lunch for the department meeting next week?" Grady asks me.

"Absolutely," I tell him, patting Betty's head under my desk.

—like making the coffee for my boss's meetings. I mean I do *like* Grady. He's very easy to work for, and always has time if I want to discuss something with him. And he always (unlike Bastard Adam) credits me with ideas if he uses them. But arranging for coffee is just not what I had in mind when I got promoted.

But after all, Angie (assistant to the Director of Advertising) can't do everything. Apart from the fact that she's my friend, I used to do her job so I know how heavy her workload is. Even more so since one of the other secretaries in our department left, and hasn't been replaced . . .

And the coffee is important, I suppose. It's for the meeting with William Cougan, CEO of our esteemed company, Cougan & Cray. All the account managers have to attend, and although I'm not senior, I expect they need someone to pour the coffee and pass round the food . . .

It's something to do with Mr. Cougan's vision about the future of the company, which (according to Tracey in Human Resources) isn't doing as well as it used to. Actually, that's a bit of a worry because a few other staff members have left recently and haven't been replaced . . .

I bet Claire Palmer doesn't make coffee for meetings. I bet she asks the most junior architect to make the coffee for meetings— *Stop it,* I tell myself. I am not going to even try to compete with Claire, because in the words of Dr. Padvi (and in the words of the song), I, Emma Taylor, am my own special creation. I am who I am. And it's just a way of getting my inheritance, after all . . .

I *do* wonder sometimes though if I'm in the right career . . .

I wonder if I should become an architect, because that's very creative, isn't it? Hmmm . . .

And immediately I fall into daydream mode imagining the Emma Taylor-designed museum, the Emma Taylor-designed theatre, the Emma Taylor-designed opera house, the Emma Taylor-designed annex at Buckingham Palace . . .

Before I can stop myself, I imagine I'm at the main architect awards ceremony with Jack. He's all tall and gorgeous in a black Armani tux, and I'm wearing that gorgeous, pink Carolina Herrera dress I saw in *Vogue*. Everyone who is anyone is there, including (naturally) Robert Plant, Jimmy Page, and John Paul Jones (they've agreed to perform together just for the night). And also present is my cousin, Her Majesty the Queen (she's going to make me a dame of the British Empire). The nominees are announced—Claire Palmer and me.

And the winner is . . . *me!*

And just as the gathered throng are thunderously clapping and cheering (except for Claire, who storms out of the building with a bad case of sour grapes), just as the Queen gives me a regal nod, just as I am about to receive my award and qualify for Auntie Alice's bequest, my telephone rings.

"Emma." It's Tracey, the secretary from Human Resources. "You'll never believe what I just heard," she whispers conspiratorially down the line. Tracey, oh font of all knowledge, is the office grapevine.

"What happened?" I whisper back, after glancing around to make sure no one is close enough to me to overhear. This sounds like it might be juicy (and will thereby alleviate the need to reconcentrate on incontinence pads for a few minutes).

"This is too hot for the telephone," Tracey tells me. "All I can say is that it's about Babette Cray. I'll meet you in the ladies' room on your floor in five."

Oh, it *must* be good and juicy for Tracey to come down to our floor. I bet it's to do with the paternity test!

"I'll bring Angie with me," I say, hanging up.

Babette Cray (twenty-something ex-cheerleader) was married to Johnny Cray (octogenarian), my old boss before Bastard Adam and Grady.

When I say Babette was married to Johnny, I mean only for a day. Johnny died mid-orgasm on his wedding night. Which was sad . . . And although Babette *did* get the lovely apartment overlooking Central Park, plus five million bucks, what she *didn't* get were Johnny's shares in the company.

You see, William Cougan had an agreement with good old Johnny. Because William Cougan's father and Johnny were the original founders of the company, they made a pact to keep their shares *within* the company. As Johnny didn't have any offspring when he died, his shares automatically reverted to William.

Only snag for William is that Babette got pregnant on her wedding night (allegedly) and is now the proud mother of Johnny Junior, age ten months. How fortunate was that? Talk about a lucky shot. But how difficult for William Cougan. If baby Johnny is truly dear old Johnny's son, he gets to inherit his dad's considerable shares in Cougan & Cray.

"You are never going to guess what I just found out," Tracey tells us breathlessly a few minutes later, anxiously checking the cubicles for eavesdroppers. "This is hot, so come close girls," she says in a *Deep Throat* kind of way. She always starts her stories like this—she likes to build the anticipation.

"Don't tell me, William Cougan tapped the telephone lines of our major competitors, and last night a hand-selected group of spies broke into their offices to steal their best ideas," Angie says, rather dryly.

I don't know why she bothers—Tracey and irony are not a match made in heaven. But Tracey can be a bit annoying sometimes—she does tend to push peoples' irritation buttons. Especially Angie's irritation buttons.

"Really? How come I didn't hear about it?" Tracey asks.

"They got caught by the night security team, and now William Cougan's been arrested," Angie pushes on regardless.

"Has he?" Tracey's eyes pop wider.

"It's bigger than Watergate. Important names are implicated and it goes all the way to the top." Angie is really getting into her stride, now.

"Really?"

"No, she's just teasing," I say. Honestly, Tracey takes things so literally.

"I've lost my thread, now." Tracey glares at Angie, then continues. "You just won't believe it—this is big. This is huge—" She pauses and takes a deep breath.

"Baby Johnny's paternity test came in positive," Angie says flatly.

"Baby Johnny's paternity test is positive," Traccy announces, and then stops short and glares at Angie. "How did you know? Who told you?"

"I have my sources," Angie says, tapping the side of her nose.

This is what *Tracey* always tells *us* when we ask her how she knows, well, everything that is going on within the company. Come to think of it, I never did get a straight answer when I asked her how she found out about me sleeping with Bastard Adam. We were very careful not to be seen together at work . . .

"I guess you know the whole story so I won't bore you with the details," Tracey says sullenly, and turns as if to leave. "I'll take my *old* news someplace else."

"What whole story? Come on, give us the dirt." I give Angie a warning glance. I know Tracey gets on her nerves a bit sometimes, because she gets on mine. But I really want to know. And I know that Tracey will be easily persuaded to share the hot news. Because there's nothing on this earth she loves more.

"I'm sorry—I was just teasing," Angie tells her, not sounding sorry at all. "Call it a wild guess."

"Okay. So the paternity test *is* positive." Tracey, happy to be back in her role as imparter of new gossip, is easily appeased. "So are the second and third tests Mr. Cougan insisted on. Bet you didn't know that," she says triumphantly.

"Typical tyrant. Trust him to insist on two more tests." Angie isn't terribly fond of Mr. Cougan.

"And Babette says that as she's baby Johnny's mother, she wants an active role in the company so's she can protect baby Johnny's inheritance."

Oh. I wonder if that's what the department meeting is about? The new world order of our company, with a baby and an ex-cheerleader at the helm. But I *love* the idea of Babette Cray being equal to William Cougan. It has to be said, Cougan & Cray is very old-fashioned. Very testosterone biased, despite the strict equal opportunities mandate.

"This could be *great*," I tell Angie and Tracey (and Betty who is happily skitting around the floor). "Imagine it. A woman at the top of the food chain."

This is a sign! I mean, Babette's *bound* to want to encourage her female workers to get on in the company.

I feel my backbone stiffening, already!

By the time I get back from visiting Rachel (who is being released tomorrow morning, much to her annoyance—she was hoping to go home tonight but they want to keep her just a bit longer to make sure her rehydration is complete), my jet lag has caught up with me and all I want to do is fall into bed.

God, it's tiring trying to be convicted (or is it convictive?) and triumphant . . .

But at least Rachel looks better. She still hasn't decided what she wants to do about being pregnant, but it's early days . . .

Talking of early days, I think I need an early night. But

when the telephone rings, and Caller ID says "out of area" I pick up. Because it might be Jack from his Boston hotel, or Julia, who might want to chat about Auntie Alice.

"Hello?"

"Hi!! Am I speaking with Human Being Emma?"

"Er, yes," I say, stunned to be addressed in such a fashion.

"Congratulations on your Life Force, Human Being Emma!! My name is Human Being Stacey!! How are *you* today?"

"I'm, er . . ." Perplexed. And just a bit curious. But I don't say that, because I don't get a chance to say another word before Human Being Stacey burbles more of her Life Force at me.

"It's a beautiful life, Human Being Emma!!" This girl is so happy and peppy she could have exclamation points tattooed on her vocal cords. "Especially so for you, Human Being Emma!! For you have been specially selected by the Hoboken United Sisters Suffragette Institution to receive our weekly newsletter free for one whole year!! Isn't that *wonderful?*"

"Er, fantastic!" I say, getting into the spirit of her joy.

"Oh, I'm so happy to hear that!! Because we Human Beings at the Hoboken United Sisters Suffragette Institution—HUSSI for short—are dedicated to the fight against the male-person subjugation of the female-person sex at all levels!!"

"That's terrific!!" I'm really getting into this now. What a *great* acronym.

"Maybe you've heard of us!!"

"I don't think—"

"We meet every Wednesday night to discuss positive issues, and we'd just love to have you join us Human Being Emma!!"

Actually, that's *fabulous*. I mean, that's exactly what I need. Positive issues, making a difference within the community.

"You know, I—" 'd love to come to the meeting, I nearly say, but don't quite manage because Human Being Stacey is in full flow with her script.

"But because we know that you are a busy, fulfilled person, Human Being Emma, you may assist our worthy cause by pledging one hundred dollars to our Anthropoid Allotment!!"

"That's—" I *knew* it. I just knew there'd be a catch, because I should know by now that there is no such thing as a "free" newsletter.

"Alternately, we offer the Homo Sapiens Handout, which is seventy-five dollars, or the Creature Contribution which is fifty dollars!! Whichever you feel most comfortable with!!"

Actually, this is great. They're obviously a committed community group if their donations are that high. The language is a bit strange, but then it's to do with making members feel as if they fit, as if they're all equal. Equality for all. I *love* it!

"Human Being Stacey!!" I say, because I'm really getting into this now. "I'd love to come to a meeting!!"

"You would?"

Poor Human Being Stacey. She's obviously so used to being given the brushoff, she's lost her exclamation points.

"Absolutely!!"

And after she recovers from her shock at my interest in HUSSI, she tells me where to be and when.

"This is a really positive move in the right direction, isn't it?" I tell Betty after hanging up with Human Being Stacey.

10

. . . .

Human Being Emma

TO DO

1. Become Spokes Human Being for physically challenged people the world over!
2. Apply to Nobel Foundation for consideration for Peace Prize (or does someone have to nominate you? Must check, but only after HUSSI newsletter is printed).
3. Send copy of HUSSI newsletter to Mr. Stoat of Stoat, Ferny and Willow in London.

Wednesday, July 9
11:00 P.M.

I really think my backbone is getting stronger by the minute! Yes, this life change thing and getting outside interests is really taking off well.

So many things to do, so little time to do them in . . .

Betty and me have just been out for a bit of a trot-hop before bedtime, and now we're just couch potatoing on the sofa for a bit. We're watching a really interesting show about the rescue of mistreated pets. After all, I can get my daily half hour of enlightenment and mind expansion (as per Dr. Padvi's advice) from TV if I want, can't I?

It's very sad. And depressing. The ASPCA has just rescued some tragic pit bulls from a basement in Chicago. They have to be put to sleep because they've been illegally bred just for fighting, and apparently that's what they have to do with the poor creatures . . .

I just can't believe the things that people do to poor, defenseless animals. But then I don't believe the things people do to other people most of the time . . . Truth be told, I think Betty's finding it rather depressing, too, because she's buried her head under my arm.

"I think we've enlightened ourselves enough for one evening," I tell her. "Let's cheer ourselves up and watch a bit of Viggo shall we?"

Betty woofs her assent. I could swear sometimes that she understands what I'm saying . . .

I love the opening scenes of *The Fellowship of the Ring,* where all the Baggins hobbits get together for Bilbo's birthday. They're all having such a good time; they're such a close-knit, friendly community . . .

Thinking of close-knit, friendly communities makes me think of my first HUSSI meeting earlier this evening. I think it went exceptionally well, I really do . . .

When I say exceptionally well, I mean mostly well. But HUSSI seems like a nice group . . . apart from the more radical members . . . and especially apart from Marion Lacy, Chair Human Being (who is rather more of an orc than a hobbit).

But, I remind myself, I've only actually *attended* one meeting, so I don't have the full feel for it yet. I must give it a chance, because this could be a good outside interest for me. And they're certainly enthusiastic—the HUSSI newsletter editor was very keen to interview me about how I cope with small breasts in today's society . . .

This is what happened.

I'm a bit nervous as I arrive at the community hall, because I'm not sure what to expect. But at least I *look* confident. I'm hoping that this group will be full of strong, independent, intelligent women (or rather, strong, independent, intelligent Human Beings), so I have chosen my outfit with care.

I am wearing white, loose-fitting pants (Emporio Armani) with a cropped white-with-thin-black-stripes casual jacket (also Emporio Armani). Elegant, summery, yet casually smart. My face is dusted with powder to give me a sun-kissed glow, without actually having spent time in the sun, and my lips are glistening with clear lip gloss.

This is a great look for the meeting! A career-human-being-yet-not-afraid-of-my-feminine-side kind of look.

As I approach the entrance, I see a woman in casual khakis and a shapeless, black T-shirt just ahead of me, and I feel instantly overdressed. I think I'll just go home and change. Or better still, I could just come back next week, instead. After all, it doesn't have to be tonight . . .

"Hi!!" The woman in the khakis and black T-shirt spots me as she pauses at the door. "You must be Human Being Emma!! I've been waiting for you!! I'm Human Being Stacey!!" she beams at me, vigorously shaking my hand. "It's so great you could make it!!"

Her face is cleanly scrubbed without a trace of makeup, and I wonder if my clear lip gloss is also a bit over the top.

"Er, fantastic to meet you," I smile back rather tentatively as I try to suck it off.

"Be welcome, fellow Homo Sapiens!! Come on in, Human Being Emma!! Hey, this is great—you can be my initiate!! Because I've never had an initiate training under me before and Chair Human Being Marion thinks I'm ready for more responsibility!!"

Be welcome, fellow Homo Sapiens? I'm her *initiate?*

I somehow feel like I've stepped into a *Star Trek* episode and at any moment Mr. Spock will leap out from behind a door and flash me the Vulcan peace sign, and tell me that the good of the many is more important than the good of the one. Or something like that.

And before I can think up even a remotely pathetic excuse along the lines of either (a) "Sorry, Human Being Stacey, the dilithium crystals in the main engine need my attention," or (b) "I have to zap the Klingons on the starboard bow," she links arms with me.

"You're going to love the group!!" She pulls me along into the entrance with the sheer zeal of her enthusiasm, thereby cutting off all means of escape.

"Oh," I say, as I see at least twenty khaki-pants-and-shapeless-black-T-shirt-clad women sitting in a circle in the large room. Obviously this *is* some kind of secret society, where everyone except me knows the dress code. I wonder if they have a special handshake . . .

As they see Human Being Stacey and me, they pause their conversations to call out "Be welcome, Homo Sapiens all."

This gets weirder by the second.

"Let's get you some Human Sustenance, then we'll introduce you to everyone!!"

I don't really want Human Sustenance (i.e., coffee and a nasty-looking doughnut), but feel it would be churlish to refuse. I don't have to actually *eat* the doughnut—I can just kind of nibble the edge of it . . .

"Because this is your first visit," Human Being Stacey tells me as she adds a five-dollar bill to the collection cup, "your Human Nourishment is free!! At future meetings we encourage you to make a minimum five-dollar donation to help our cause!! You don't have to, but it shows that you are committed to sharing the burden of cost, and playing an equal role in society!!"

I like the idea of playing an equal role in society though (as would Auntie Alice). Maybe I'm just jumping to conclusions too quickly . . .

Human Being Stacey leads me to two empty seats and we take our place in the circle. I furtively place the coffee and the doughnut under my chair, and smile genially around the room.

"One of the first things you need to learn is that we refuse to be labeled by society's definitions!! We are all human beings, regardless of class, color, sexual orientation or gender!! And so to remove our labels, we all add the prefix Human Being to our name!!"

"That's very equalizing," I say, still a bit (a lot) stunned. But that's good—removing labels is important.

"Everyone, we have a new member!! This is Human Being Emma!! My new initiate," Stacey announces.

And as the room reverberates yet again with "Be welcome," someone new enters. The room is instantly quiet.

"Be welcome, Homo Sapiens, all," barks the middle-aged, stocky woman with the bundle of papers. "Human Being Kim, please distribute tonight's agenda."

"Chair Human Being Marion is in the Leadership Chair," announces Human Being Kim, and everyone claps.

I clap, too. Although I'm completely stunned.

Chair Human Being Marion is none other than Katy's old arch-nemesis from the Pre-Preschool PTA.

Marion bloody Lacy. I don't believe it.

Marion used to run the PPPTA with a rod of iron and a tongue like a whip, causing mass mayhem and upset wherever she went. The same Marion Lacy caused poor Katy all that stress when she tried to hijack Katy's life and forced her to get e-mail for Alex (then age two), enroll the poor kid in all kinds of educationally beneficial classes (as I said, Alex was only two), and spend her weekends telemarketing to raise funds for the PPPTA.

I once got involved (to give Katy moral support) with one rather unmemorable campaign which, apart from driving up and down the New Jersey Turnpike in search of drunk drivers, also involved being cross-examined about my life, my career, my family and my sex life by Marion. Honestly, I only met her twice and yet I felt as if she'd wrung every last shred of information from me.

I wonder if I can just sneak out now . . . no, everyone would notice, especially as I stick out like a sore thumb in my nonHUSSI clothes . . .

I hope Marion doesn't remember me . . .

When someone hands me tonight's agenda, I scrutinize it closely to keep my head down (and to keep attention from myself). I focus carefully on the words as the meeting gets into full swing.

This agenda doesn't really, you know, indicate anything that we can get properly adversarial about or triumph over . . .

I glance around furtively at the other Human Beings. Surely someone will laugh in a minute? I mean, I thought we were supposed to be making a stand for women's rights, not wasting time debating whether or not fat-free cookies should come with a health warning, on account of the fact that although they don't contain fat, they still contain high quantities of sugar, and can therefore make you fat if you eat too many . . .

I mean, the sugar issue *is* important, of course . . . but I just envisaged, you know, weightier issues, such as the importance of teaching young women about birth control to lower the incidence of disease and unwanted teenage pregnancies . . .

But all of the Human Beings are studying the document quite seriously. Not a smile or a raised eyebrow to be seen.

"Fellow Human Beings," Marion Lacy booms. "This meeting of HUSSI is officially open."

For the next hour, as they seriously debate the inappropriately breast-shaped Hershey's Kiss and the unacceptably phallic connotations of the baguette, I keep a low profile and try not to snort.

And when they switch to fund-raising, and the effectiveness of telemarketing, I phase it out and drink my free coffee (now cold) and I nibble unenthusiastically on my free (but stale) doughnut. And I'm a bit depressed as I feel my inheritance slipping away from me. I wonder how soon I'll be able to excuse myself and head back home to Betty . . . Actually, it's quite warm in here on account of no air conditioning and the summer heat, and I am so sleepy I begin to doze off . . .

"Are we all agreed on this?" Marion booms, making me jump. "Show of hands in favor of the proposed action."

Every single woman in the room raises an arm, so I do, too. And then Marion's beady eyes descend on me.

"I see that we have a new member in the room," Marion says, pinning me to my seat with her gimlet eyes.

"Chair Human Being Marion!!" My new buddy Stacey jumps to her feet. "This is my new initiate, Human Being Emma!!"

"Human Being Stacey," Marion barks at her. "The correct procedure is to introduce new Human Beings at the beginning of the meeting, so that they can be properly informed of their obligations and sign the Human Being Contract."

Marion hasn't changed, then . . . still a pain in the ass . . .

"I'm sorry, Marion." Stacey loses her exclamation points as she bows her head, and I feel my temper rising.

"*Chair Human Being* Marion," Marion chastises her, and my face flushes with the heat of my anger.

"Yes, Chair Human Being Marion, I—"

"I'll let it pass this time, but if you're training a new initiate, you mustn't forget the basic principles of our group."

"No, Chair Human Being Marion."

As poor Stacey sits down, I clench my fists. Really, Marion is insufferable.

"I remember *you,* Human Being Emma," Marion says as she forgets about poor Stacey and focuses on me, making it sound more like a threat than a welcome. But then, after Katy's verbal fight with her last year, and after Katy took over the PPPTA and ousted Marion, she probably has me down as The Enemy. "Everyone—Human Being Emma's father is a *plastic surgeon,*" Marion says, making Dad sound like the Devil Incarnate, rather than a mild-mannered physician. "One of the top, plutocratic, gluttonous plastic surgeons in the tristate area."

"I object to that," I protest in my mother's best Mrs. Thatcher voice as I jump to my feet. Really, Marion might be scary, but she's not getting away with insulting my father. Only Auntie Alice could get away with that kind of thing.

"My father is a Human Being, too. He's a good person, providing a service for those women who . . . who feel that plastic surgery would enhance their lives. I mean, it's all a matter of supply and demand, isn't it?" I say, getting into my stride.

"But this very demand is created by men's preconceptions of the perfect woman," Marion jumps straight in.

"It's a matter of individual choice," I insist, because this is one of those unavoidable confrontational moments Dr. Padvi talks about. I mean, really. My dad is a complete pussycat.

"If men didn't demand perfection, plastic surgery would be obsolete. *Should* be obsolete." There are murmurs of assent at Marion's statement, but I ignore them.

"It's totally down to the woman to choose for herself. After all," I push on, as a lightbulb comes on in my head. "I'm the daughter of a plastic surgeon and I *obviously* haven't had breast implants.

"If my dad was so terrible, like you're making him out to be, then surely I'd have succumbed to men's preconceptions of the perfect woman by now. But I haven't." I pause for dramatic effect as every pair of eyes in the room is focused on my chest. "I'm small . . . and proud of it," I finish with a flourish.

That's a point in my favor! *Stick that in your mouth and chew on it Marion Lacy,* I think, as silence descends on the room.

As my fellow Human Beings glance at each other for inspiration, and as Marion glares at me as if she wants to savage me with her bare teeth, I wonder if I'll get out of here alive. But at least I've rendered Marion speechless. Y-e-s!

"Ahem, Chair Human Being Marion," says the woman who handed out the agendas. "I have an idea. I think I see how Human Being Emma could make an immediate contribution to our cause."

Marion switches her ferocity from me to her assistant. "Where are you going with this, Human Being Kim?"

"Well, ahem, it seems to me that we could do an article about Human Being Emma in the HUSSI newsletter," Human Being Kim says, her eyes lighting with fervor. "About her decision not to have implants, despite the large-breasted perfection foisted on her every day of her life via her peers and the media."

Maybe I'm judging HUSSI too hastily—this is a great idea! Plus, Human Being Kim would be totally sensitive to the story, in view of her own lack of cup size . . .

"Hey, that's so cool!!" Human Being Stacey squeaks. "My first initiate doing an interview!! I'll help you all I can, Human Being Emma!!"

Stacey is so happy and bubbly again, I'm going to feel terrible when I say no, and tell her I'm never ever coming to another HUSSI meeting.

"We could slant it to how disgusting it is that women are indoctrinated with the idea that to fit in, they need to have bigger breasts," Human Being Kim says. "Human Being Emma could counter that, she could be our antiestablishment mascot, I can see it now . . ."

Actually, so can I. I could do something *positive* and show my conviction to my small boobs. Although I'm not sure about the antiestablishment part . . .

"It would be great, Human Being Emma!! Just think of the women you'd be helping!!" Stacey pipes up.

And, of course, I slip immediately into daydream mode . . .

I could actually impact *millions* of women around the world . . . well at least several hundred women in the Hoboken area, depending on HUSSI's print run and distribution. I could share with them my views on how unimportant is the size of one's breasts in the grand scheme of things.

I, Emmeline Beaufort Taylor, could make a difference, just like my namesake, Emmeline Pankhurst. I could change lives for the better. I can just see the headline now: HOW I CONQUERED MY FEELINGS OF SMALL-BREASTED INADEQUACY.

Auntie Alice would love it.

Except Marion doesn't like me, and will not let me anywhere near her HUSSI newspaper. Marion glares at me as if I'm something nasty she trod on, and I glare back because my English half might be a bit wimpy sometimes, but I have Beaufort blood in my veins, after all!

"It could be a really good article," Human Being Kim insists. "It could really, like, speak to the Human Beings of Hoboken."

"Well done, Human Being Kim," Marion says, surprising me as she does an about turn. "I can see your point. Welcome, Human Being Emma. Human Being Kim, if I could have ten minutes of your time alone, you can go ahead and do the interview tonight."

"Now?" I'm a bit alarmed by this. I thought I'd have time to get my thoughts together. You know, plan out what I'm going to say so that there's no room for misunderstandings.

"Fantastic," Human Being Kim tells me. "It would make great front-page copy for next week's edition."

Fifteen minutes later Human Being Kim and me are ensconced at the back of the room with a notebook and a tape recorder . . .

11:45 P.M.

Yes, I think the interview went very well. Kim, or should I say Human Being Kim, was a bit nervous when I asked for a copy of the transcript, just for my records. But I think I made some valid points . . .

HB Kim: "So, Human Being Emma (lowering voice). When did you first realize that you weren't like other girls?"

Me: "Well, it wasn't exactly a case of realizing I was different to other girls, hahaha, I mean, we come in all shapes and sizes don't we? But I suppose I got a bit sensitive about, you know, the smallness of my boobs when I was sixteen and Chris Stevenson asked Susan Grayson to the senior prom instead of me."

HB Kim: "Did Human Being Susan have bigger breasts than you? Do you think that's why Human Being Chris invited her to the prom instead of you?"

Me: "Well, I'm not completely sure . . . he might just have fancied her more than he fancied me . . . maybe he liked her because she was taller than me . . . It might not have been the breast thing at all. I mean, she *was* the head cheerleader . . ."

HB Kim: "Tell us about your early years, Human Being Emma. It must have been distressing and totally demoralizing for you to realize that by society's warped standards, you were deficient. You were lacking. How did you cope?"

Me: "Well, maybe just a bit distressing . . . er . . . but that's a strong a way of putting it. See, until I was fourteen I lived with my mother in London, and she's great. It was just never an issue. I mean, apart from the fact that we don't all develop by fourteen—and some of us not at all, hahaha . . ."

Human Being Kim does not return my laugh, and is obviously sensitive about her own diminutive cup size. I wonder, briefly, if she has a sense of humor . . . better not crack any more small-boobs jokes.

Me: (making a swift recovery) "Er, but back to Mum. Julia really stressed the point that World Peace and Human Rights are far, far more important than one's cup size. And after all, she should know, being a top Human Rights lawyer."

HB Kim: "But what about your father? How did you come to live with him when you were fourteen?"

Me: "Well, Mum's an equal-opportunities parent, so she thought it was vital for me to spend equal time living with my dad. So I went to high school in New Jersey."

HB Kim: "I understand that he's a top plastic surgeon. Wasn't he determined that you should have implants?"

Me: "Oh, no. I don't think determination comes into it, actually. He was more concerned about me being happy, but of course, he always made it clear that if I truly wanted implants, then he'd arrange it for me."

HB Kim: "So he actively encouraged you in this did he?"

Me: "Well, I wouldn't say actively encouraged, exactly—"

HB Kim: "I understand that you had a devastating blow last year when your live-in boyfriend cheated on you and dumped you for an older, bigger-breasted woman. How did that feel?"

At this point in the interview I'm floored.

Where on earth did Human Being Kim learn about Bastard Ionic Bonder Adam and me? I mean, that's all ancient history now . . .

Of course! Marion bloody Chair Human Being Lacy . . . I

bet she extracted the details from Katy . . . I try to refocus on my interview and the positive spin I want to emphasize.

Me: "Obviously I was shattered at the time. But once I realized how shallow my ex-boyfriend was—"

HB Kim: "What about your new boyfriend. Does he have issues with your lack of cup size?"

Me: "Oh, no. Hahahaha. Not at all."

HB Kim: "So you haven't caught him looking at other women. Other, full-breasted women?"

Me: "Well, no . . . (pause in recording as the gel bra springs to mind). I mean, all men look at women, whether they're in a solid relationship or not, don't they? Just as women look at other—"

HB Kim: "So what is your message to the Human Beings of Hoboken?"

Me: "My message is this. Breast size, height, weight, and all other issues we might have with our own bodies are just that. Our *personal* issues. We have to overcome them, to accept ourselves for who we are. We should worry about doing good works instead of our physical attributes. And as the famous British suffragette Emmeline Pankhurst said, it's all about 'Deeds not words.' "

Yes, I think that sounds pretty definitive.

I think Human Being Kim was very impressed with my message, especially when I told her about my connection to Emmeline Pankhurst.

Oh, I can just see it now—the media around America will pick up on my interview and I'll be a national success! The Nobel Foundation will beg me to accept the Peace Prize for my efforts for the Women's Movement. Kofi Anan will invite me to dinner to discuss problems in the Third World . . . I can't *wait* until Saturday to get a copy of the newsletter.

Only blot on the evening is that I missed Jack's call, but he's coming home on Friday! Only two more days until I see him. And besides, I can't just wait at home by the telephone on the off chance that he'll call, can I? It will do him good to miss me, and wonder what I'm doing and who I'm doing it with.

Must get an extra copy of the newsletter for Jack. And for friends and family, of course.

I think Auntie Alice would be proud of me.

11

....

Cell-Phone Sex

TO DO

1. Become new, sexually committed me! (After all, Dr. Padvi suggests subtle changes to routine to ensure one keeps one's partner intrigued.)
2. Possibly check with Mr. Stoat to see if cell-phone sex from office bathroom counts as carrying out one's convictions.
3. Make detailed plans re: filling one's quiet, empty evenings as old friends are obviously too busy to even talk to one.

Thursday
3:50 P.M.

Nothing can pierce my euphoric glow today, I think, as I try to concentrate on my Prince of Pads account. I feel I can safely say I have my inheritance in the bag. Just as I nearly have the Prince of Pads account in the bag . . .

Picture this: Independence Day. Four generations of an

all-American family in an all-American yard, having an all-American barbecue. Hugging each other and smiling at the camera, the caption underneath reads: "Prince of Pads—For All Generations of American Freedom."

This is *inspired*. I think the American flag is a nice touch, and people always respond well to cute babies . . .

And the fact that my friends all have lives of their own and haven't called me today is a *good* thing. I mean, we can't live in each other's pockets all the time, can we?

When I say my friends haven't called me, I mean everyone except for Sylvester.

He called me on my cell phone on the way to work.

"David, he says he doesn't know when he can leave his *mère*. He is never coming back to me, Emma. I am going to sell Chez Nous and move back to Québec."

"I'm sure he—"

"It is ze end," he says, slipping into a stream of agitated French. "After all, I am not getting younger."

"Sylvester, you're not ol—"

"David, he is a chicken wiz all his life before him."

I sigh and just listen, because Sylvester really wants someone to talk *at* rather than talk *to*.

Sylvester worries too much about the eight-year age difference between them since he turned forty, last year.

"I'm on the PATH train," I interrupt him as he's telling me about his cellulite, and how he thinks he's getting arthritis. "We're going under the Hudson River right . . . now."

And my cell phone dies.

When I arrive at work twenty minutes later, my desk telephone is ringing.

"It'll be Sylvester again," Grady tells me from his office door. "This is the third time in ten minutes."

"Sorry, Grady, he's having a bit of a crisis," I explain.

"Please try to make him have it somewhere else. William Cougan is on the warpath, so be warned." And as he turns to go back to his desk, "I thought you were only looking after Betty for a couple of days." He gives my tote a pointed look.

"It's just until tomorrow. I promise."

"Make sure you keep it. This stress I do not need."

Oh, that doesn't sound very promising. I wonder if it means more downsizing . . .

"I just cannot live in zis limbo," Sylvester announces as soon as I get the receiver to my ear.

"Sylvester, calm down, I—" think you're overreacting a bit, I don't manage to say because, of course, Sylvester dives straight back in.

"I call him while you are on ze train," Sylvester announces dramatically. "I tell him exactly what I have said to you. And if he isn't here by ze weekend, we are *fini*."

"You didn't!" My God, this is serious. They've been together practically forever, and I can't imagine how one would survive without the other.

"*Non*, of course I don't say zis. I am a Frenchman. I have more finesse zan zis. I simply tell him to take his time wiz his *mère*, and not to worry about me, and zat ze restaurant is doing well," Sylvester says without drawing breath. "And zen I tell him all about ze cute, fabulously talented chef I have hired to take his place until he can bear to be parted from his *pauvre mère*."

"That was a masterstroke," I tell him, impressed by his ploy. "Very sneaky."

"Yes, I know zis." Sylvester is rather smug.

Despite being an absolute drama queen, Sylvester is also very astute. And it has to be said that while the temporary chef is definitely attractive, it also has to be said that said chef is a woman. I think, somehow, that David will be back soon . . .

And I haven't heard another peep out of Sylvester since this morning, so I guess he's okay.

I think I worry too much about my friends, sometimes . . .

So I'm not going to worry about today's silence. If they need me, they will call.

And anyway, I have a busy, successful career to get on with. I hope Prince of Pads likes my ideas . . . Wonder what I should do now, because it has to be said that actual account work is a bit thin on the ground at the moment.

Oh God, William Cougan's heading toward me. I have to project a confident, career-minded image.

"Hello, sir," I say, shuffling some papers. Thank goodness Angie's taken Betty for a walk.

"Hmm," he grunts, as he heads into Grady's office and closes the door.

The business with Babette Cray is really getting to him, according to Tracey. This is great. But not so great if he's come to talk to Grady about natural wastage, obviously . . . But I'm sure I'm not going to be natural wastage, because I'm too valuable to the company (i.e., Prince of Pads).

Oh, telephone.

"Good afternoon, Cougan and Cray, Emma Taylor speaking," I say very efficiently.

"I love it when you sound all professional and . . . in control," Jack breathes down the phone line at me and my heart starts to bump. "It sounds so . . . dominant."

"A girl likes to be in . . . control," I purr back at him, happy to hear his voice, even though we spoke when he called me this morning before I left for work. I'm so happy that things between us are back to normal—he hasn't mentioned our conversation last Sunday night at all, and neither have I.

"What are you doing?"

"Oh, you know, just plotting my strategy for world domination in the incontinence pads market before I leave for the day," I say.

"Sounds like more fun than I'm having. Another evening of wining and dining fractious clients lies ahead of me. I wish I was home," he says, lowering his voice as he adds, "in bed . . . with you . . ."

"I wish you were, too . . . It seems like so long since we spent any, you know, time together." It's nearly two weeks since I saw him . . . nearly two weeks since we had sex . . .

"What color panties are you wearing?" Jack's voice goes down another notch and my body floods with heat. I quickly glance around the office for eavesdroppers. I mean, I don't want any of my coworkers thinking I play odd sexual games with my boyfriend, do I?

"They're black lace," I tease him. "High cut to reveal as much . . . of my soft, creamy flesh as possible."

"Tell me more . . ."

"The lace is so transparent, you can see . . . almost everything . . . there's an . . . opening in the crotch, and—"

"Emma." I nearly leap out of my skin as William Cougan appears at Grady's door.

"Yes, sir?" I ask, trying not to shudder or blush. I wonder if he heard me?

"Coffee," he barks at me.

"Certainly, sir," I say, feeling the color rush to my face.

"About those panties," Jack laughs down the phone at me, and then lowers his voice, "Tell me more about them . . . especially the slit-in-the-crotch part."

"Where are you?" I try to breathe normally.

Although this is a game we play, we never actually, you know, carry it through. It's a joke, you see, and usually ends up with me dashing to Jack's house, or Jack dashing to my apartment. But Boston is too far away for a quickie, isn't it?

"In my hotel room . . . alone . . . and naked," Jack tells me, and my pulse hums as my breathing quickens. I wonder if we should . . . wonder if I can . . . Actually, Auntie Alice was right about me dithering. And I know what I'm going to do. This is the new, sexually convicted me!

"Give me five minutes and I'll call you back on my cell phone."

"I'll be . . . waiting."

God, I hope this doesn't make me a pervert or anything . . .

4:15 P.M.

My God, *I did it. We* actually did it.

A lot hot and flushed from Jack's call, I slink back to my desk. I'm sure it's written all over my face. But I don't care. I can't think why we didn't try this sooner . . .

"What have *you* been doin?" Angie asks me as she slides my tote and Betty back under my desk. "You look hot and flushed."

"Oh, nothing, nothing," I say airily. After all, indulging in a furtive bit of phone sex with one's boyfriend is hardly something to discuss in an open-plan office, is it?

God, I really did it. And in the ladies' restroom. *At work.*

I think Jack was a bit stunned, too . . . but in a delighted, sexy kind of way.

4:30 P.M.

Wonder what I can do now to fill the next half hour?

I mean, I want to be committed and everything, but after the cell-phone experience I've just had it's hard to focus . . .

You know, it's *nice* to have a whole, quiet evening ahead of me. It really is. I mean, I'm really looking forward to some *me* time. To work on my triumphing-over-adversity attitude.

Or I should say Betty and me time. After all, there are plenty of things to do to fill the hours. *Plenty.* If I just break it down into segments, it won't seem so long. Now there's a good idea—I'm going to make a list. Let's see . . .

1. 5:00 P.M. Home time!
2. 5:45 P.M. Arrive home!
3. 6:00 P.M. Call Rachel to see how she's feeling (am a bit worried that we haven't spoken since yesterday morning).
4. Call Tish to check if she's talking to Rufus (haven't spoken to her since yesterday, either).
5. Call Katy to check on situation re: Tom (haven't spoken to her since Monday).
6. ~~Call Sylvester to see how he's managing alone at Chez Nous.~~ Move to later—Sylvester too busy with early dinner crowd.
7. 7:00 P.M. Head to gym for an hour. I've been neglecting my pilates and yoga recently, so this will be good for muscle tone. (And Betty will be fine for a couple of hours watching Viggo defeat many orcs.)
8. 8:30 P.M. After leisurely sauna and shower at gym, go to bookstore to find mind-enlightening magazine or book re: other worthy causes to get involved with.
9. 9:00 P.M. Arrive home. ~~Prepare light yet nourishing meal.~~ Add boiling water to cup of noodle, and spend an hour enlightening my mind.
10. 10:00 P.M. Call Sylvester before taking Betty for evening trot-hop.
11. 11:00 P.M. Watch news on television (mind enlightening).
12. 11:30 P.M. Bedtime.

I'll hardly have time to fit everything in. Oh, telephone. "Hugh's driving me fucking nuts. Call me back." It's Rachel.

"How are you feeling?" I ask her a few minutes later, as Betty makes her normal circuit of the restroom. This place is almost a second home to her, these days.

"Fucking terrible," Rachel says. "And Hugh won't even let me operate the fucking TV remote."

"Well, he's concerned about you," I soothe her. "You gave us all a nasty scare on Sunday."

I think it's sweet Hugh's so concerned about her. Rachel hasn't returned to work yet. She's hardly ever ill—she *deserves* to take the rest of the week off in her condition. It's sweet that Hugh took the week off, too, to look after her. And to help her reach a decision. Whatever it might be.

"I'm not a piece of fragile porcelain. Women get pregnant all the time. It's not like I'm gonna melt. Fuck, I can't even pee in peace. I went to the bathroom to call you for a rant earlier, but he followed me."

"At least you've got enough water in you to be able to pee," I remind her.

"There's nothing *wrong* with my fucking legs," she rants.

"I know," I soothe her.

"So you agree with me then?"

"Er, yes." I wonder what it is I'm agreeing to?

"So what are you doing tonight?"

"Not much," I confess. "Me and Betty are going to hang. Oh, I've got a call waiting. I'm just putting you on hold for a minute—"

"No need. I'll come around later and hang with you. If I stay home I will explode. See you at seven."

And before I have a chance to say anything else, she hangs up.

"Hi, it's me," Tish says. "Call me back in five from—"

"It's okay. I'm already in the bathroom. Rachel just called me for a rant."

"Well, that's good timing—I've called you for a Rufus rant, too. I didn't like to call earlier in case you were too busy. What are you doing tonight?"

"Actually, Rachel's coming around at about seven to hang with me and Betty."

"Good. I'll come too. It'll be just like old times."

"Great," I tell her happily, because it will be. Although I had plans, I can be flexible . . . Oh, I've got another call waiting. What it is to be popular! "Tish, I'm putting you on hold, sweetie, I've—"

"Don't worry—I've gotta run. A customer just came into the store. I'll catch up with you later," she tells me and hangs up.

"Emma, please say you're going to be home this evening, please," Katy pleads. "I know it's only been like a few days, but Tom's driving me insane, and . . . I need to run something by you—if I don't tell someone soon I'll bust."

"That's fantastic," I say happily, then hastily retract my words. "I don't mean it's fantastic about Tom, I mean it's fantastic because Rachel and Tish are coming around, too."

"You're a lifesaver, see you later."

I'll just save my list for tomorrow.

Katy, Tish, Rachel, Betty, and me are all squeezed into the tiny living room, made even tinier by the huge, yet lovely birthday gifts. We have a bountiful supply of wine, of which Katy, Tish and me are taking full advantage. Rachel (safely deposited by car by Hugh, although they only live five blocks away) is sipping soda—apparently the bubbles help to settle her stomach. We also have two large pizzas, but the smell has preempted an emergency visit to the bathroom by Rachel so we moved the boxes into the kitchen.

I have to admit no one else seems very hungry, apart from me. Even Betty can't seem to summon the enthusiasm to beg for scraps like she usually does. I think she's missing Jack. She is not the only one.

And despite our intention to have a girly good time doing girly things, the atmosphere is glum and everyone is preoccupied with her own thoughts. Although I did manage, briefly, to cheer them up with my phallic finial and my HUSSI interview.

Rachel is preoccupied with her impending wedding and impending (possible) motherhood.

Tish is preoccupied with her impending mother-in-law.

Katy is just preoccupied and hasn't said much yet.

"Tell me again how long I have to put up with feeling crappy," Rachel pleads as she languishes on my sofa. "I have to know that there's an end in sight."

"About two more months," Katy tells her absently. "I was the same when I was pregnant with Alex. Sick as a dog for the first trimester, then all of a sudden I felt great—I ate absolutely everything before me, my skin glowed, I was bursting with energy . . ."

"So this is definite? I'll really feel better if I can just stick this out for a few weeks?"

"Well, I can't give you a written guarantee," Katy adds, staring into space. "It's different for every woman."

"Does this mean what I think it means?" Tish jumps in. "Are you going ahead with it?"

"But I thought you didn't want a family," I say without thinking, because my mind is wandering back to cell-phone sex. I wish I'd bitten my tongue.

"I know, I know," Rachel sighs. "But I never thought I'd get married. It never occurred to me that I might actually meet a man I'd want spend my life with, so the motherhood thing wasn't really an issue. Not really *my* issue."

"Honey, that's great news," Tish enthuses, as she comes out of her mother-in-law induced trance. "Just think, in eight months' time you'll have a tiny Rachel or Hugh of your very own."

"I'm so happy for you," Katy smiles for the first time tonight. "And it's true what they tell you—it really is different when it's your own child."

"I'll baby-sit," I tell her, because the thought of a new baby is a lovely distraction. Although she's made a very quick decision. She only found out four days ago that she was pregnant . . .

"What does Hugh think? Is he delighted? I bet he *is* delighted." Her horrid future mother-in-law forgotten, Tish is beaming.

"Oh, Hugh's over the moon," Rachel says rather dryly as she rummages in her purse. "He bought me this, earlier, when he went out to buy me soda."

It is a sweet, tiny teddy bear wearing a yellow bow.

"Oh." I'm a bit surprised, and I know I am not the only one because Katy and Tish's mouths are also open in fly-catching mode. I mean, it *is* a lovely gesture, isn't it? But do you usually start buying baby presents this early?

And after an awkward silence, we're all talking at once.

"That's adorable," Katy says. "So Hugh really is happy about this, then. But you're happy, too, aren't you?"

"You have to want this," Tish says. "A baby isn't just for Christmas—it's forever."

"But you—you mustn't feel like you're being pushed into this . . . or . . . anything," I add a bit lamely.

"Hugh would never push me into something as important and life changing as this," Rachel says loyally, but she's frowning and we lapse into silence again.

"I, er, have some good news," Katy ventures, but she doesn't look very happy for someone with good news . . . I bet Tom got a job. I knew he wouldn't be out of work for long, but maybe he had to take a big pay cut. Maybe that's why she's miserable . . .

"Tom got a job," Tish jumps the gun. "He has, hasn't he? I knew it would all work out."

"I'm sorry, honey," Rachel says to Katy. "Hugh told me Tom's bad news but I've been so preoccupied with this baby thing I forgot. But wow—he found something else already? That's great."

"Tom hasn't found another job," Katy says rather miserably. "I have. I've been headhunted."

As we all absorb this rather remarkable news, Rachel leans forward. "Spill."

"Well, you know the PPPTA organized the Children's Day fund-raiser in March?"

"Sure," Rachel says, as Tish and me nod enthusiastically.

"It was fabulous," I tell her.

It was a tremendous success. Katy coordinated the whole thing—there were craft stalls, children's activities, live music from local musicians and local restaurants (including David and Sylvester) ran food stalls. The PPPTA raised ten thousand dollars for a children's charity.

"Well, I was talking to the Director of Children of the World this afternoon about another fund-raising event we've got planned for November, and when she said she could use someone like me on her permanent staff, I kinda jokingly told her to make me an offer. And she did. A really good offer."

"How amazing," I say. Because it is. This is really encouraging. Tom loses his job one day, and a few days later Katy gets offered a good job out of the blue.

"She obviously knows a good thing when she sees it," Rachel comments.

"It couldn't have come at a better time, could it?" Tish says. "This is fabulous."

"But I'm not sure if I should take it or not," Katy chews on her lip. "Tom needs to be free for interviews, and I always said I was happy to stay home with Alex. It would mean getting a baby-sitter . . ."

"Millions of women do it all the time," Rachel tells her firmly. "That's what I'll be doing after Junior makes an appearance. I told Hugh, just because I'm having a baby doesn't mean our lives are going to change completely. I still have a career to think about."

"And that's great," Katy says. "Really, it is. And I'm sure you and Hugh will work it out. But my point is this job is fairly high level. I'd be working long hours. I may even have to travel. And I just don't know how we'll manage once Tom's working again."

"But what did Tom *say* about it?"

"I haven't told him yet. I don't want to rub his nose in it . . . Do you think he'll be okay with it?"

"It will take the pressure off him a bit," I tell her.

"The money's nowhere near as high as he was earning, so it won't threaten his masculinity . . ."

"Honey." Rachel has a dangerous glint in her eye. "This is the twenty-first century. Threatening his masculinity is not an issue."

"It would sure help with the mortgage payments," Katy takes a gulp of her wine. "I'd make enough to cover that, and some living costs, but we'd still need to use some of our savings . . ."

"Stop fretting," I tell her. "Tom's a sweetheart. He'll be delighted." I hope I'm right about this. Tom really *is* a sweetheart, but he does take his role as the breadwinner very seriously.

"But I'll get all the medical benefits, and a pension package, and the Director told me that once I finish my probation period I'll get a significant pay raise."

It sounds more as if Katy is trying to convince herself, than us.

"It's not a question of who earns the most money," Tish tells her soothingly. "Just that *someone* earns the money."

"But I don't know how Tom will feel about leaving Alex with a stranger." Katy jumps to her feet and begins to pace. "Tom's mom worked full time when he was a kid, and he's always saying how great it is that I'm there for Alex. And I was totally happy to give up my career when I had Alex, really I was. But this . . . this is a real good opportunity."

"At least give it a trial period and see how it pans out," Tish tells her.

"Opportunities like this don't fall off trees," I say.

I catch Rachel's eye as she opens her mouth to speak, and I have a strong suspicion that she's building up to a rant about men's changing role in society, and equal rights. I shake my head and, surprisingly, she closes her mouth. And then she opens it again, and I cringe as I ready myself for her diatribe.

"Honey," she says. "If Tom feels so strongly about Alex being left with a baby-sitter, he could always stay home with Alex himself."

I think that was rather restrained of her.

By nine-thirty Betty and me have the apartment back to ourselves, and I feel oddly depressed and at a loose end.

I know that there are lots of things I could be doing, but I feel lonely, and more than a little apprehensive at all the changes taking place in our lives.

I mean, I know change is good, but does it have to happen so quickly? I think I'm just tired. It's probably just losing Auntie Alice so suddenly, then with all the rushing around of the past couple of weeks . . . I probably just need a good night's sleep.

I am about to get undressed when the telephone rings. I check the Caller ID and grab it, because it's Jack's cell-phone number.

"Where are you . . . touching yourself?" Jack's voice hums down the phone line at me, and I sigh, feeling instantly less lonely.

"Where would you . . . like me to . . . touch myself?" I try for sexy but can't help the giggle.

"I'd rather touch you myself," he says. "Why don't you come downstairs and open your front door?"

"What? Now?"

"Yes, now," he says, and then I hear the doorbell ring. "Unless you plan on leaving me outside all night."

Ohmigod! He's home a day early! I dash down the stairs, and fling open the front door.

"Surprise," says Jack, his eyes crinkling as he smiles and opens his arms.

"Jack, it's you," I say, launching myself at him. "I thought you were due back tomorrow. Oh, God, it's so lovely to *see* you." And it is. As I inhale the familiar smell of his skin mingled with his cologne, I forget everything. It's just so good to be held by him again.

"If this is the kind of welcome I can expect, I should go away more often," he says, kissing me. "Our truculent client got called away to his Washington office, so I'm playing hooky." And then, "How come you girls didn't hang at my place? There's much more room."

"Oh, you know," I say, not wanting to sound pleased that although he didn't make it *clear* I should stay at his place while he was away, it's the thought that counts. "I had—stuff to do, and all—but that doesn't matter, now. You're here."

He can see that I'm delighted, because I'm practically hanging from his neck and planting kisses all over his beloved face.

"God, I missed you," I say, pressing myself as closely as I can into his T-shirt.

"Come on, wanton phone-sex girl," he growls in my ear. "Let's go upstairs so I can show you how much *I* missed *you*."

"So you liked the cell-phone thing, then?" I tease him as I lead him up the stairs and into my apartment, and I'm just a bit coy that I actually had the guts to do it.

"Are you kidding me? It's every guy's secret fantasy. Why do you think I was in such a hurry to get back here? God, you smell good enough to eat," he says, burrowing his face into my neck.

"That sounds—delicious."

As soon as Betty sees Jack, she rouses herself from her favorite lying-down-snoozing position on the sofa and woofs excitedly.

"Hey, Beautiful Betty," Jack puts me back on my feet and lifts Betty into his arms, laughing as she licks madly at his face.

"She really missed you, too," I say. "She's even off her food."

"We can't have that," Jack tells me, plopping Betty back onto the sofa with a promise of "later," as he leads me to the bedroom.

"My God," Jack says, his eyes widening at the sight of my nine-and-a-half inch finial, in pride of place on my nightstand. "Alice was one hell of a formidable woman. Is this my competition?"

"No," I giggle, tugging impatiently at his zipper. "It's my inspiration."

"I can see why," he says, quickly pulling my T-shirt over my head. "I'm starting to feel a little inadequate, here."

"Oh, you're more than adequate," I breathe, as he pulls me onto the bed.

And then we don't say anything else for quite a long time . . .

12

....

In With the New?

TO DO

1. Give new, gel-padded bra a chance. Is a whole new silhouette for me, and change is sometimes as good as a rest. (Also, will show Jack that I am receptive to his courting rituals and the ever-changing nature of our relationship, as per Dr. Padvi's advice.)
2. Investigate other gyms in area. Current gym is not as good as it used to be, on account of Claire Palmer.
3. Repeat after me: "I am a Telemarketer—Ohm. This is a *good* thing—Ohm."

Sunday
7:30 P.M.

You know, they say a change is as good as a rest, but I'm glad to get back into a normal routine again.

On Friday night, Jack and me went back to our normal Friday-night routine: workout at the gym, followed by dinner at our favorite Thai restaurant. It's a tradition, see? Actually, that was our very first tradition together.

It was kind of how we got together in the first place . . . If I hadn't been killing time at the gym on that fateful Friday night last year, and if I hadn't bumped into Jack, he wouldn't have asked me for a nondate dinner . . .

It's our private joke, the fact that we started dating with a purely nondate—see, we didn't even *like* each other back then, but it's miserable eating on your own, isn't it?

And if we hadn't had our nondate, he'd never have insisted on walking me home, and he'd never have found out I was planning to sleep in my car, and he'd never have invited me to stay with him for a while . . .

Anyway as per another of our traditions, I've spent the weekend at Jack's place . . . a whole weekend of blissful sex and domesticity, just Jack and me. And Betty, obviously, because she's Jack's dog. I really missed taking her to work on Friday. That space under my desk seemed so—so empty.

But talking of normal, David is back from Florida . . .

It's true. Sylvester's ploy worked and David arrived home yesterday morning . . . so we're having our normal Sunday night at Chez Nous.

Anyway, I feel . . . booby . . . I really do.

But I can't decide if this is a good look for me or not.

I mean, I do love these cropped black trousers (Nine West from my birthday outletting trip), because they're very Madonna in her "Papa Don't Preach" phase. And I also love this black, form-fitting top with little white polka dots (also Nine West, from my birthday outletting trip), because it's very nineteen fifties. But I'm just not sure how I feel about the . . . cleavage. It's just so . . . prominent. In a Jayne Mansfield kind of way.

I'm wearing the new gel bra that Jack bought for me. Because it's important to show him how much I appreciate his gesture. I'm just trying it out to see what it feels like to have cleavage (feels a bit like I'm letting down my new HUSSI convictions). But after all, it's only a bit of an experiment. Just like the chocolate sauce and cell-phone sex . . .

Before I can change my mind and take off the wretched thing, I attach Betty's leash to her collar and we step out into the warmth of the fading summer evening. Betty (who I brought home with me this afternoon, because Jack and Claire have to have a conference about the Boston Crisis, as I am now calling it) is wearing black-and-white polka dot bows tonight (to match me), and is completely adorable.

I am fine with Jack working this afternoon. After all, when I get more thoroughly involved with HUSSI, I might have to spend more time planning our good deeds on the weekends . . .

As me and Betty stroll down the sidewalk toward Chez Nous, I push my chest proudly forward, shoulders back, and my boobs boldly go where they have never gone before (i.e., before me). I am *hot*. Marilyn Monroe and Madonna all rolled into one.

It does not escape my attention how many men smile and leer at me. This lifts my spirits and I sashay, and jauntily swing my overnight bag. I am a gorgeous, desirable woman with gorgeous, desirable gel boobs. And I'm comfortable with this, I really am. Until I step inside Chez Nous.

"Oh. My. God." Rachel, unsurprisingly, is the first to notice. "I thought we'd finished doing the 'my boobs are too small' thing." She hits her forehead with the base of her palm.

"I just felt like a change," I tell her. And then, because she still looks pale, plus I want to deflect her from the forthcoming rant about society's stereotypical values, "How's the stomach?"

"Still bothering her," Hugh says. "But the vomiting isn't quite as bad. She just needs to keep off her feet and rest."

"Hugh, will you stop!" Rachel turns back to me. "See what I mean about the fussing?"

"Okay." Hugh holds up his hands. "But you have to take care of yourself."

"I'll make you a bargain," she says to me. "Don't mention my vomiting, or being pregnant, or my wedding all evening and I won't mention that you're pandering to society's stereotypical values."

And then Hugh notices my boobs. "Here, have a glass of this delicious Shiraz," he says, his eyes on my cleavage. I think he's trying not to laugh. "I think *I* need another glass of this, too. Boy is Jack in for a surprise."

"That's a very . . . different look for you," Tish says diplomatically, her eyes pinned to my newly abundant chest.

Rufus says nothing, but his eyes are also pinned to my newly abundant chest as he takes a swallow of his Guinness.

They could be a bit more positive.

"Why do you do zis?" Sylvester raises his Gallic eyebrows at me as he comes from the kitchen. "You are already enough of a woman." He breaks into an incomprehensible stream of French and shakes his head.

"Come, Betty, upstairs to Viggo Mortensen for you. You are too young for all zis," he says, taking Betty's leash from me. "*Sacré bleu*, I cannot believe you do zis Emma. Now French women, zey know zey are sexy wizout shaving ze legs and armpits. Or wizout big bras. I may stay upstairs and watch Viggo wiz Betty," he adds, flouncing out of the room.

"Take no notice of him," David tells me, as he kisses me. "He's still pissed with me."

"How did your trip go?" I ask, delighted to see him. But what I am really asking is "Did you finally tell your mom about Sylvester?"

"Don't ask." David raises his hands and rolls his eyes. "It's just so hard," David says morosely. "Every time I try to broach the subject she spins me the spiel about how her time on this planet is drawing to a close, and how wonderful it would be if God saw fit to bless her with a grandchild before she dies."

"You didn't tell her about Sylvester, then?"

"So, enough about me." David changes the subject. "What about these babies? They're gorgeous. They look so lifelike."

"Well I'm glad someone likes the new, improved me," I say, sipping at my Shiraz. "It's my new gel bra."

"Can I touch them? Our friend Simon is getting a drag act together. This gel bra may be his own personal answer to boobs."

I smack away David's hand as he tries to squeeze my gel.

"Wow," Katy says as she and Tom step through the door. "Talk about breasts with attitude. Happy Birthday, Mr. President," she sings to me.

Tom says nothing, but I can see that he is also trying not to laugh.

"What did Rachel say?" Katy asks, as she pecks me on the cheek.

"Look, I don't care what *anyone* says. This is not a life statement," I tell her. "This is just a . . . a . . . an experiment. To see if the general male population react to me in a different way." I know this sounds lame. Don't think I'll mention that Jack bought it for me for my birthday. Rachel, for one, will only give him a hard time.

"It worked." Tom winks at me. He seems very cheerful. I wonder if it's because of Katy's new job? And then, "Hi Jack—we were all just admiring Emma's new cleavage."

Jack stops in the doorway, his eyes wide open as they focus on my chest.

"Wow. You look—er—great, Emma," he says, disbelief written on his face. But does he mean better-great or just great-for-a-change great? "But you always look fabulous, babe," he adds, crossing the room and planting a kiss on my lips. And before I have time to think through the "great" comment, I notice that he is not alone.

Claire Palmer is with him.

And she is to-die-for gorgeous.

She's been at Jack's house all afternoon looking like *that?*

Coolly elegant, her tanned legs go on forever in the chic, white dress, and four-inch heels. Her blond hair swings like a bell around her shoulders.

"Everyone, this is Claire—my boss."

"Oh, Jack, that sounds so formal." Claire smiles prettily. "I hope we're becoming good friends, too. Hi, everyone. I hope you don't mind me crashing your dinner party."

I *do* mind. What was Jack thinking, bringing her here?

"Not at all." David is the first to reach her, and shakes her hand in a very familiar way. He might be gay, but he just loves beautiful women. "Any friend of Jack's is a friend of ours. Welcome to Chez Nous."

"Thanks," she laughs into his face in a lovely, open, guileless way.

Surely David won't be taken in by her beach-babe friendliness?

"I kind of twisted Jack's arm," Claire continues, radiating confidence and niceness. "I don't really know anyone in the area yet, and he talks a lot about you guys."

"I couldn't leave her to go home to a cup of noodles and Sunday-night TV," Jack says. "That just seemed too cruel."

As Jack makes the introductions, I feel sick. How could he bring her here? This is for close friends only. It's a tradition.

"Where are you from?" Hugh seems to like her.

"I'm from California, originally, but I swapped coasts six months ago," she says, smiling charmingly. "I've been renting a place in Secaucus but I just bought an apartment in Hoboken. So I don't really know anyone here . . . ." Her voice is tinged with just the right amount of wistfulness. "Except for Jack, of course."

*   *   *

By ten-thirty, Claire Palmer is the life and soul of the party. Everyone loves her. All the men, because she just jumped right in and charmed them out of the trees . . .

Even Rachel, but then Claire got around her by knowing quite a lot about the current breakthroughs in DNA research. So, of course, Hugh thinks she's marvelous, too . . .

And Tish thinks she's the best thing since sliced bread, because Claire, it seems, has been into her store and wants Tish to help her choose some beautiful objets for the new apartment. Plus, Claire waxed lyrical about the emerald engagement ring.

Claire even won over Katy by enthusing about Alex, and how great it must be to be a mom, and how fantastic an opportunity her new job is, and tells Tom at every opportunity how lucky he is to have the chance to stay at home with his son, because so many men miss out on their children's early childhood.

But even though she speaks perfect, fluent French (naturally) and knows Québec like the back of her hand, I don't think Sylvester's keen. Because he's the only one not hanging onto her every word.

As for me, I really am *trying* to just ignore her. I don't think I'm being paranoid about her negative attitude to me at all, because earlier, when I lied to her and said "It's nice to see you again, Claire," she kind of gave me a snide little look and said, "Love the new boobs, Emma. I told Jack that you would."

So see? Jack didn't even choose my birthday gift by himself. He had Claire's help.

And now, just as I am catching up on telling David and Hugh about Auntie Alice's funeral, and about the sex-starved mussels, she jumps right in and *steals* my conversation.

"But isn't it tragic?" I say. "And now the mussels are all middle-aged or elderly and have no prospect of ever having sex again. And then they'll be extinct. How sad is that?"

"Don't worry your little head about the mussel problem—the scientists have it all worked out," Claire says, and I think her comment about my little head is completely bitchy. "They're planning to get the mussels together in a riverbed, Emma," she says, patting my arm in a very condescending way. "To encourage group sex sessions."

"Oh, to be a mussel," David laughs, rolling his eyes. He's completely charmed by her.

"Don't get too excited, darling," Claire tells him.

Darling? She's only known him five minutes and she's calling him darling already?

"I'm not worried about the mussels," I say, rather pointedly. "Tony Blair assured me he would check into it."

"My God, you met Tony Blair?" David asks, because I hadn't gotten to that part yet.

"You should never believe a word a politician tells you," Claire jumps straight back in again, giving me a condescending smile. "Everyone knows they mouth platitudes to keep their supporters happy. Even your Prime Minister."

And then she's off, telling everyone about bloody Julius Caesar, and how he only invaded Britain because he loved pearls, and let's face it, whatever else does that small, cold, wet, dreary island have to offer?

I take this as a personal insult to my English half and go upstairs to check on Betty. She is the only one with perfect character assessment skills.

Ten minutes later, just as Betty and me are watching Boromir getting tragically killed (again), Jack comes to find me.

"Hey," he says, slipping into the space next to me. "How are my two favorite girls?"

"We're good." I rest my head against his shoulder.

"You okay? You're very quiet tonight, and I'm worried about you."

How nice is that?

"Because it occurred to me that you might go reading something into that bra," he says, and I love him even more. "Don't go thinking I'm sending you subliminal suggestions or anything, Emma Taylor," he tells me, nestling me closer. "It just looked nice in the store, is all, and I thought you'd like it. Claire thought you might like it, too."

"Yeah, she told me that earlier."

"I thought it would be good to get some womanly advice. I'm a *guy*, I don't know about these things."

Jack *is* such a guy. Why can't guys see bitchiness when it's as plain as the nose on their faces? But at least the mystery of the bra is explained. And I am more certain than ever that Claire is after my man. But she's not going to get him. I snuggle even closer to Jack. He's so lovely.

"I hope it was okay to bring Claire tonight," he says, ruining the moment. "She's kinda lonely and I felt mean not asking her to come."

"Hmmm." Keep it vague, I tell myself.

"And I thought it would be good for you to get a chance to know her better."

"Hmmm."

"Are you sure you're okay?"

"Actually, I've got a bit of a headache and it's getting worse," I tell him. This is not a lie. It's been coming on from the minute Claire entered Chez Nous. "I think I just need to go home and sleep it off."

Friday, July 18
3:30 P.M.

"More personnel wastage is on its way," Tracey tells Angie and me in hushed tones as we huddle, yet again, in the ladies' restroom. "And it ain't all gonna be natural wastage—I heard William discussing it with Jacintha, earlier."

"Did he mention names?" Angie asks, obviously worried, because at forty-eight it's not going to be so easy for her to get another permanent job with good health benefits. "Fuck, I don't believe he's letting more staff go— after that huge pay increase he got himself voted at the last AGM."

I'm a bit shocked by Angie's un-Zen-like response. She usually takes these things in her stride . . .

Actually, it was a bit of a shock when William voted himself such a huge pay increase in March. After all, he pretty well had carte blanche, seeing as how he controls (or rather, controlled) sixty percent of the shares.

"Just think how many people his fifteen percent would save." Angie shakes her head, and Tracey and me shake our heads, too. Oh, the injustice of it all.

"Babette just found out about that doozy—I heard them fighting about it earlier," Tracey says. "Babette's demanding that he drop his salary to match hers."

"Good for her."

Babette, it seems, is making her presence known and is getting heavily into the running of the business. Bless her, being an ex-croupier and an ex-cheerleader isn't exactly the best background in the world for preparing one to co-run a business. I really admire her for her stand over the fifteen percent . . . and for protecting her son's interests . . .

I knew having a woman at our helm would be a great thing!

"You've gotta be our eyes and ears at this meeting," Angie tells me. "We need to know what's going on."

Babette Cray's name is not mentioned at the meeting.

"Our profit for the first quarter is down overall by eight-point-nine percent," Mr. Cougan tells us, and goes on to paint a bleak picture about what he thinks we're doing wrong. Everything, apparently.

"We are entering a period of natural wastage and downsizing," Mr. Cougan drones on, and I try to understand what this means for me personally. Does this mean that *I* will be downsized out of a job? From the worried expressions around the room, it looks like everyone else is worried about this, too.

And as I fix a very intelligent, enthusiastic expression to my face (to show him my commitment to the incontinence pads), he tells us what we've got to do to remedy the situation.

"We can't sit back on our reputation. We can't wait for recommendations from satisfied customers. We've got to get out there and proactively expand our current customer base," he booms. "I have therefore developed a strategy—each of you is listed within this twenty-page report, along with your new initiatives—Emma, pass these around."

Obviously my initiatives include report distribution. Can't wait to see what my others are . . .

But it's then, just at that moment, just as he's detailing his plans and I'm leafing anxiously through the document for my name, that I panic.

My name isn't in here!

I am *natural wastage.*

And Prince of Pads really liked my ideas. They called Grady to schedule a meeting, only yesterday . . .

Before the panic attack takes control, I remind myself that I would hardly have been included in the meeting if I was going to be fired, would I? After all, who will arrange coffee and hand out important papers?

Plus, the HUSSI newsletter comes out tomorrow. Maybe I'll qualify for my inheritance and won't have to worry about being employed. At least I won't if it's money, rather than a historic relic . . . God, I hope it's money . . .

I take a breath and scan the document again.

Ahh . . . here I am on page nineteen under "Junior Staff." Whew. Wonder what my new tasks are . . .

I am about to become a thing that I loathe.

A thing that I detest above practically all others.

Here it is. In black and white.

At thirty-one years of age, after putting myself to the trouble of taking a business studies degree at night, and after devoting four years of my working life to this company, I am about to become a—a—telemarketer!

A bloody *telemarketer!*

It doesn't actually *say* the word telemarketer, but it does say that I am expected to take a *verbal initiative* and cold call companies in a bid to persuade them to switch their advertising to our company.

This is *terrible.*

I can't do it.

I'd rather walk barefoot over broken glass. Or hot coals. Or hot, broken glass . . .

By the time I meet Rachel and Tish for our regular after-work Friday coffee, I am still trying to put a positive spin on my new job requirements. Actually, it might not be all that bad . . .

"Why the hell don't you just quit that place?" Rachel asks me when I've told them my tale.

"Because that's exactly what Auntie Alice meant in her letter," I tell them earnestly. "I have to stick to my convictions and triumph in the face of adversity."

"I don't think she had telemarketing in mind. It's not exactly a fight for Human Rights or World Peace, is it?" Tish shakes her head.

Rachel, who is still suffering with her stomach, is also still suffering with Hugh fussing, and from her mother and the obsessive wedding plans.

"Only eight fucking weeks to go," she says, sipping on her soda. "Then I'm free of this madness. If I don't die of Hugh's smothering, first."

"You won't," I say, crossing my fingers that I'm right. At least the soda's helping her stomach. "Have you told your mom about the baby yet?"

"Are you kidding me? Hugh's fucking Mother Hen routine is enough. The last thing I want is for my mom to decide that this is my Time of Need and move in with us."

I'm totally with Rachel on this. I mean, her mom is great, but she has a tendency to *over* mother—imagine a Norman Rockwellesque mom complete with immaculate hair, immaculate makeup, frilly apron and rubber gloves, maniacally cleaning the house, and there you have Rachel's mom.

Actually, now I come to think about it, Rachel tends to be a bit obsessive on the cleaning front—although she decries housework as a waste of time and energy since the place will only get dirty again—her baseboards are always dust free, and her kitchen is always surgically scrubbed . . .

"You're lucky she *likes* Hugh," says Tish, who is also still suffering from *Rufus's* mom. At least Rufus managed to put off his mom's visit for two months, I think. That will give Tish a bit of breathing room.

"I know, I know," Rachel says, holding up her hands. "I'm an ungrateful daughter. I just can't get excited about all the minutiae."

"At least you have minutiae to get unexcited about," Tish says a bit wistfully, extricating a list from her bag. "I don't want to take the focus away from your wedding, sweetie, but I need to tell you my date. I'm thinking October twenty-fifth."

"Why the hurry?" Rachel asks. "Is there something you're not telling us, Miss Tish?" she asks, pointedly checking out Tish's abdomen.

"I wish. A big wedding would be great, but—" Tish pauses, and takes a deep breath. "But Rufus's mom is like a steamroller. She hates me, I *know* she does. But since she's visiting in October, I thought we could kill two birds with one stone and present her with a fait accompli," Tish says in a rush.

Poor Tish. This should be the happiest day of her life. Instead, her wedding is almost going to be an afterthought.

"Rufus's mom can't be that bad," I say.

"Trust me, she is—which is exactly why we need to get married quick," she says, looking at The One Ring. "Before she can talk Rufus out of it." Tish's hand shakes as she picks up her coffee cup.

"Rufus loves you." I pat her arm encouragingly. "She doesn't have that kind of power."

"You don't know Concepta O'Leary," she says darkly.

"What is it with these men and their mothers! Honey, stop this," Rachel tells her firmly. "I can't believe you let the old battle axe wind you up so much. Hell, give me the number and I'll call her myself—who does she think she is?"

It's nice to see Rachel getting back to her old self.

"Thank you, honey," Tish smiles weakly. "I appreciate the support, but I think this is the best way."

"So when do we get to see the famous newsletter?" Rachel asks me.

"Tomorrow," I say, excited about my moment of fame.

"Well, just be careful." Rachel is a bit pensive. "Don't let Marion Lacy force you into anything."

"Remember what happened with Katy," Tish reminds me.

"Oh, no worries there," I smile happily. "I can manage Marion—you should have seen me when I stood up to her at the HUSSI meeting. I was great. This interview is going to be great. It's going to save me from a life of telemarketing."

I haven't actually told Jack about my triumph in the face of adversity yet, because I want it to be a surprise. I want to see his face when he reads it.

"Ohmigod, is that the time?" I jump to my feet and quickly peck Rachel and Tish on the cheek. It's time for our weekly tradition of the gym, followed by our Thai meal. "I gotta run." I'm late. "See you both at nine tomorrow morning for yoga?"

"Count me in," Rachel says. "Anything to escape Hugh's fussing for an hour. At least he agrees that gentle yoga is great for pregnant women."

"Me too," Tish nods. "I need to work off my Concepta stress."

That's our *girlie* tradition for Saturday mornings, see. Yoga followed by breakfast at Rufus's deli.

I *love* these girls.

I *love* our private little traditions.

"Oh," Tish adds. "I hope it's okay, but Claire came into my store earlier and I've asked her to join us."

Nononono.

They've known Claire less than a week and she's joining our yoga class? God, I wish Claire would move back to California. Or Venus. Pluto would be too close a planet for her to emigrate to. But I don't say this, obviously.

"Cool—she seems really nice," Rachel says.

"Sure," I lie, and make a quick exit.

And as I dash down Washington toward the gym, and Jack, I try not to obsess. I take deep breaths as I try to steady myself. *I'm spending the evening with my wonderful boyfriend,* I tell myself. So I'm not going to even think about Claire Palmer tonight.

The first thirty minutes of our Friday night proceed just as planned.

I'm on the Stairmaster increasing my stamina. And although I'm puffing and panting like a madwoman, at least I look cute. And sexy. I know this, because when I met Jack outside the changing-room door thirty minutes ago, he wolf whistled at my clingy, hot-pink workout shorts and matching top.

The memory makes me puff and pant even harder . . .

"That is one hot look for you Emma, babe," he grins his

wolfish grin as he slides his hand over my bottom. "Let's forget the gym and go home for a workout of a . . . different, more interesting kind."

"Later," I purr, enjoying my role as sex kitten. "We have to keep you in . . . good shape." And I press closer to him, teasing him, tempting him (but only after checking that there's no one around, obviously).

"Come on, woman," Jack groans, backing away from me and grabbing my hand, tugging me toward the gym. "Any more of that and I'll need a cold shower *before* my workout."

I can hardly wait until later!

Anyway, Jack is lifting weights, and my God does he look tasty in his tatty-old-sweats gym gear. I am not the only one who thinks so, because all of the female clientele have checked him out more than once, but he doesn't seem to notice. See, Jack only has eyes for me . . .

And as I only have eyes for Jack because his muscles are rippling gorgeously under the strain of the weights he's lifting, I can't resist another peek at him . . . and nearly fall off the Stairmaster with shock as he puts down the weights and smiles at the gorgeous, leggy blonde standing next to him.

I don't believe it.

I don't bloody *believe it.*

Claire Palmer is in *my* gym.

13

....

Table for Three

TO DO

1. Project image of pheromone-satiated goddess whenever Claire Palmer is near.
2. Procure and destroy all copies of latest HUSSI
   newsletter (but avoid getting arrested for tampering
   with U.S. Mail).

Oh, but she's stunning in white Lycra. Her tanned, mus-
cled body is gleaming and perfect. And I can't help but note
what a truly gorgeous couple they make. Jack, all tall and
darkly handsome. Claire, all tall and blondly beautiful. They
could be models in *Vogue* . . .

I quickly adjust the pace of my Stairmaster before I can do
myself some serious damage. And so that I can watch Jack
and Claire without being too obvious, of course . . .

As Jack smiles and chats to her, he points over to me.
Claire, two-faced bitch that she is, flashes me her loveliest
smile and waves. But even at this distance I can see that her
smile doesn't reach her eyes, which glitter greenly and ominously, unaccountably reminding me of The One Ring. She

is the embodiment of a female Sauron, her quest: world domination. Well, at least, Jack domination . . .

I give her a cool, I-know-what-you're-doing-but-you-won't-succeed smile, but am sure it looks more like a grimace. A hobbit smiling at an orc. A mouse grinning at the snake who is about to make it lunch. Obviously I don't have to bother waving back, on account of needing both hands for the Stairmaster.

And then they're not looking across at me anymore—Jack is showing her the weights and Claire is giggling at him in a very flirty fashion.

As Jack kindly helps Claire with the weight exercises, I seethe, and hike up my running speed again. As Claire commences with the leg weights, I bite back my annoyance as Jack helpfully arranges weights on her shapely ankles.

Can't you see that she's bluffing? I want to yell to him. Anyone in as good a shape as Claire must work out regularly therefore *knows* how to use the bloody weights. This is simply a feminine *ruse* to get Jack's hands on her legs.

I run faster and faster.

Because exercise relieves stress, and encourages endorphins, so will therefore make me feel better.

It doesn't work.

By the end of my workout, I'm exhausted. I'm completely soaked with sweat, and as Claire and Jack approach I note with envy and disgust that not one hair on Claire's head is out of place. She hasn't even got beads of moisture on her lovely, yet oddly snakelike face. How can she look that great after a workout? Has she no sweat glands? Is she really a reptile?

"Hi, Emma," she greets me like an old friend, but barely looks at me, and I wonder why I haven't noticed before that her eyes are so close together.

"What a coincidence," Jack grins at me. "Claire just joined our gym."

Did she, indeed?

"I didn't realize you guys were members," Claire smiles into Jack's face, totally ignoring me, and I feel my blood boil. I just *bet* she didn't. "Jack's been really great, helping me master the weights."

Yeah, right.

"Didn't Tish mention the name of the gym when she invited you to join our yoga class?" I inquire sweetly. Because how else would Claire know where to meet us tomorrow morning?

"She's totally sweet, isn't she?" Claire deftly avoids my question. "She's already given me some great ideas about refurbishing my new apartment. The place needs to be gutted and remodeled from scratch."

"Tell me about it—I've spent the last year working on my house," Jack says, rolling his eyes.

"That's architects for you," Claire grins at him conspiratorially. "They can't resist the urge to remodel."

She looks like she wants to remodel Jack, too.

"And Rachel's really great, too—in fact all your friends made me so welcome that night in Chez Nous," she adds just a bit wistfully, and I know she's angling for another invitation.

She's not getting it from me.

"Well, we've got to be going. It was nice seeing you, Claire," I lie. This is a cunning way to dismiss her and escape. And to Jack, "I'll meet you outside in, what, twenty minutes?"

"Sure." Jack nods.

"Yeah, nice seeing you both," Claire addresses her comments mainly to Jack. "I guess I'll hang here for a while— maybe I'll hit the Stairmaster. That's gotta be better than an evening alone with the TV for company." Her voice is pitched with just the right amount of pathos.

Honestly. She's completely transparent. I just hope that Jack doesn't fall for it . . .

And then he does it.

He says the words that Claire has primed him for, the question that I *know* he's going to ask because he is a Nice Guy.

"Hey, if you haven't anything better to do, you could always join Emma and me for dinner."

"Oh, but I couldn't," Claire refuses, but I can see in her snake eyes that she doesn't mean it. "You guys have barely seen each other for the past two weeks—Hell, Jack, I've seen more of you than your girlfriend has," she laughs, and I grimace politely as I resist the urge to push her perfect teeth down her perfect, swanlike neck.

"Aw, come on—you'll love it. Won't she, Emma?"

"Sure," I lie, and Jack gives me a puzzled little look.

"Well, it sounds like fun," Claire pauses, waiting to be convinced. She's not getting any encouragement from me.

"That's settled then," Jack says smiling at us both.

Oh, joy . . .

And from that point on, my evening goes even more downhill . . .

As we're showering and changing into our street clothes, I do not bother trying to make polite conversation and Claire ignores me completely. This is fine. At least we know where we stand.

I leave the changing room ahead of her because she is still fussing with her hair. No doubt because she wants to look great for Jack . . .

"This is okay with you, isn't it?" Jack asks, as I step out into the still-hot summer evening. "Claire joining us?"

"Sure," I tell him, not meeting his eyes.

"Hey." He gently grasps my chin and raises my face. "I know you, Emma Taylor—when you say sure you mean no. Look, I'm sorry—it just seemed mean to leave her to spend the evening by herself."

"Hmm," I say a bit miserably. I could point out that Claire hasn't spent many evenings by herself recently, on account of spending them with Jack in Boston. But that would sound mean and petty and jealous of me, so I don't.

"Hey, come here." Jack pulls me into his arms and I feel instantly better as I hear the familiar, even thudding of his heart against my ear. "I know you think she doesn't like you, I know you think she's coming on to me, but she's not like that. And you," he says, rubbing my back, "are more than enough woman for any one man."

"Hey, guys." Claire ruins the moment. "Sorry to keep you waiting," she says, and her eyes are fixed on Jack's arm around my shoulders, and then her eyes slide down to mine. Without missing a beat, or her meaning (i.e., her jealousy), I slip my arm firmly around Jack's waist as we start to walk, clearly sending out the message to her that this is my man, and she can keep her dirty paws to herself.

Dinner is horrible.

It features me pretending to eat my favorite spicy chicken. It also features Jack who is, as usual, vacuuming up all of the spare food as he talks animatedly. It also features Claire, who eats sparingly, but firmly takes center stage as she dominates the conversation with snippets about people who she and Jack know, but I don't, and architectural talk that I do not understand.

Oddly, *I* feel like the third wheel . . .

I am completely relieved when it's time to go home. Finally, *finally*, we can get rid of her . . .

I don't know how this happens, exactly, but as we three walk home along the narrow sidewalk, I become The Person Who Follows.

You know what I mean? There are three of you on a narrow sidewalk so you can't all walk together. Someone has to cede their position and follow the other two. The obvious person to cede would be Claire, so that Jack and me can walk together, as boyfriends and girlfriends do.

Claire, who still hasn't drawn breath and is (I have to

grudgingly admit) very entertaining, is walking alongside Jack, casually touching his arm at frequent intervals. Not blatantly flirting, not blatantly touching, but her intention is clear.

I follow behind . . .

"Hey, sweetie," Jack, my lovely man, stops in his tracks and looks back to me. "You're getting left behind." And then he reaches out his hand to me, and I grasp it, luxuriating in his warmth, in his strength.

This is lovely. This is thoughtful. This also foils Claire's opportunity to touch Jack, as I am now firmly sandwiched between them. Still a little behind, but *with* them. *With* Jack.

"This is me," Claire says, as we nearly reach Jack's road. I hadn't realized she lived so close to him . . .

"Good night," I say, more quickly than is polite.

"Tonight was fun," she says to Jack. "Thanks for asking me."

"No problem—we had a good time, didn't we Emma?"

"Sure," I lie, and Jack gives me a puzzled little look.

"I—I don't suppose you guys want to come in for coffee?" Claire pauses prettily, key in the lock. "I'd really love your opinion about the changes I'm planning, Jack."

"Well," Jack looks down at me for approval. But I'm too busy studying my shoes. "It's kinda late, and I think Emma's tired . . ."

"Surely not too tired for a quick cup of coffee?" Claire is insistent. "The caffeine will wake her up."

Really, this woman is too much. I might be a wimp, but I do know how to unsheathe my claws when the occasion demands it.

"Coffee will be lovely," I say brightly. "Claire's right," I look at Jack with what I hope is a very sexy smile. "The caffeine will wake me up so I won't be sleepy when we—you know—get home."

My meaning couldn't be more clear.

I have more or less announced to Claire that I have plans for Jack later that don't involve sleep.

Jack gives me another puzzled little smile. He's giving me a lot of those puzzled little smiles these days . . .

As we step into Claire's apartment, and as she serves us coffee and bubbles about her plans to Jack, and ignores me as much as possible, I know that I positively *exude* pheromones. Jack is *my* man. I'm getting lots of great sex. At least, I got a lot of sex last Sunday night . . .

But I am good and ready for a fight, should a fight be required.

Saturday
9:30 A.M.

"Yoga is such great exercise for pregnant women," Claire Palmer wisely tells Rachel as we stretch and raise our arms in the manner of Exulted Warriors. "It's so important not to lose sight of one's self."

"I'm determined not to let myself get out of shape," Rachel says. "Just because I'm having a baby doesn't mean I'm going to get fat and bloated, and out of condition."

"You're so right," Claire assures her as we move into Sun Salutations. "It's depressing to see what motherhood does to some women."

"I know—once they have babies, they lose all interest in themselves."

Actually, I think Rachel's worrying too much about it. I mean, pregnant women are *supposed* to get fat, aren't they? Not in an obese, health-threatening kind of way, but in a blossoming, fecund kind of way.

"It's disgusting—they lose all pride in their appearances." Claire wrinkles her elegant nose as we all perch on one leg in Dancer position. "Their lives are no longer their own. But you won't be like that, Rachel," she adds, with a winning smile.

"Katy's not like that, either," Tish points out, just before I can open my mouth to say the same thing. "She looks great. And she has a really full life."

"Does Katy come to yoga?" Claire asks, the picture of innocence as she elegantly brings her leg around and lifts it in front of her.

God, it's not fair. She says this is her first yoga lesson, but I think she's lying. I mean, *how can she be so well balanced*, I muse, as I wobble ungracefully, nearly toppling over.

"Well, no," Tish frowns in concentration as we move our arms into impossible positions. "But she has Tom and Alex at home—and she's Chairman of the PPPTA—that takes up a lot of her time. And she's just started her new job."

"That's my point." Claire grabs this tidbit of information. "Katy seems like an intelligent, independent woman—I bet she doesn't get enough time for herself because she's too busy with the demands others place on her."

Although I'm avoiding talking to Claire whenever possible, I don't like the way she's taking this conversation. And although she doesn't say it outright, she's making out that Katy's some kind of doormat. Which she isn't.

"You're right," Rachel agrees. "I'm going to make damn sure that Hugh doesn't expect me to give up my personal time when the baby comes along. I expect him to be a totally committed, equal-task-sharing parent."

"Oh, so doesn't Tom contribute his full share to the child-rearing process?" Claire asks mildly. "Is he one of those fathers who thinks he's finished for the day when he gets home from the office?"

"Tom can be marginally chauvinistic," Rachel agrees with her, unsurprisingly, because this is currently a topic close to her heart. "But he's a sweetie. And he's recently lost his job."

I'm glad Rachel said that, but although I know that Tom has some old-fashioned ideas, I wouldn't say that chauvinist is the right word.

"Poor Katy," Claire sighs and shakes her head. "She's having a tough time."

Claire's making her sound like a martyr, someone to be pitied. Which Katy definitely *isn't*.

"Katy," I say, rather pompously, "loves Tom just the way he is. And it was *her* choice to put her career on hold when she had Alex," I point out, carefully focusing on my balance as we stand on one leg in the manner of cross-legged storks. "And Katy knows that his demands on her time will lessen as he gets older. Plus she has a full and active life," I add, for good measure.

"Emma, sweetie, you're missing the point," Claire looks down her nose at me. "I'm not *criticizing* Katy for the choices she's made—I think she's completely admirable to have made those *sacrifices*."

"I don't think Katy regards her life as a series of *sacrifices*," I say, because Claire is putting my nose out of joint. "More a question of compromises. Because that's what marriage and parenthood are all about, aren't they? And she's just become a top fund-raising businesswoman for a huge charitable organization."

"And that's a wonderful opportunity for her," Claire tells me, as she looks at me with a mixture of pity and contempt. "But will Tom be as prepared to compromise for *her?*"

"Tom's lovely," I insist.

"I'm sure he is. But my point is Katy should get more free time for herself. I think we should persuade her to join us, don't you?" Claire looks to Rachel and Tish.

"That's a great idea," Rachel agrees, although I think she's referring to herself and her new situation, rather than Katy. "I'm not going to let marriage and motherhood change me or my life."

"You're right—Katy *should* have more time for herself," Tish agrees, too. "But only if she wants to."

And although obviously I agree with women having time

to themselves, and options, and not being male dominated and everything, I'm rather surprised Claire is so concerned about Katy. She's only met her once!

Later, as we're having breakfast in Rufus's deli, Claire strikes again.

"Tish, I really loved those fabric swatches you gave me," she gushes. "You have such a terrific eye for color and texture and I want you to come on board with me as my consultant for the makeover of my apartment."

"Claire, that's fabulous," Tish enthuses. "Thanks. I've put some bijoux objets to one side that I think you'll really love."

"I'm sure I will. But I want you to charge me the full price," Claire says. "Just because we're friends, I don't want you to think I expect a discount."

"I wouldn't dream of taking the full amount—"

"I insist," Claire takes a delicate bite of her banana-granola muffin. "My, but Rufus is talented. These muffins are delicious. You're a lucky woman, Tish, to be marrying a man who can actually cook."

And I know that this will mean a good deal of money for Tish, but I can't help the nausea in the pit of my stomach. Because it means that Tish will be spending quite a lot of time with Claire . . .

"I used to look forward to my Saturday muffin," Rachel says, miserably taking a sip of her sparkling mineral water. "I may never be able to eat one again." And just as I am about to sympathize with her and tell her that it will pass, Claire jumps in ahead of me.

"It's perfectly normal," Claire tells her, touching her hand in a very familiar way. "And look on the positive side. You won't gain weight if you can't eat."

But surely that's bad? She *needs* to eat. Not only for herself, but for the baby, too.

"Of course you do *need* to eat," Claire, the pregnancy expert, continues. "Because the fetus is basically a parasite. It's sucking all of the nutrients out of you, so you need to replenish them to keep yourself healthy. But I wouldn't worry about it for now. Are you taking your vitamins and folic acid?"

I don't believe it. Claire has known my friends for all of five minutes, and she's already making snap judgments about their lives and offering advice.

And as the conversation switches to Tish's dominant mother-in-law problem, and as I sit here playing with my banana-granola muffin because I've lost my appetite, I have a very bad thought.

I think that Claire Palmer is attempting to hijack my life.

"You must put your foot down with Concepta," Claire says to Tish, discreetly lowering her voice as she glances over to Rufus at the counter. "It's Rufus you're marrying, not his mother."

God, I've had enough of this. I'm going to see if my HUSSI newsletter has arrived. *Think triumph,* I tell myself.

"That's exactly what I said," Rachel tells them, as I get to my feet.

"I've gotta go guys." I place money on the table for my uneaten muffin and my untouched cappuccino.

"Can't you stay for a while longer?" It is very gratifying of Tish to ask me this, because it's nice to know I'll be missed.

"Oh, I've got things to do." I'm pretty vague, because I've already caught up with my laundry, and shopping, and all I'm going to do is hang around Jack's house with Jack . . . who is probably still asleep in bed, on account of being so tired from work . . . and from the sex, of course . . .

But at least we'll have some quiet time together—tonight we're staying home with a DVD—my new Led Zeppelin DVD, actually, which I'll finally get to see . . .

You know, since we left Claire's house last night, he's been really tender and gentle with me . . . so tender and gentle, I didn't want to ruin the mood and complain about Claire . . .

"But you've barely eaten anything," Rachel says, her face wrinkling with concern. It warms the cockles of my heart . . . "You must eat, Emma. You need to keep up your good work with your body mass indicator," she adds, and then to Claire, "Emma doesn't eat enough, sometimes, and we worry about her getting too thin."

"My God, don't you just *hate* women who don't have to worry about their weight?" Claire covers her dig with a laugh, and I wince. "It's just so hard to keep off the extra pounds," she says, running her hands down her perfect waist and over her perfect curves.

She is gorgeous, and she knows it.

"I'm *sooo* lucky," I say, smiling falsely as I let my eyes linger on her hips. "I can eat anything I like and not have to worry about extra fat around my hips."

Her eyes narrow and I know she hasn't missed my meaning.

"See you tomorrow night," I say kissing Rachel and Tish's cheeks. I do *not* kiss Claire.

And as I open the deli door, Claire's voice follows me.

"So you guys always meet for dinner at Chez Nous on Sundays. That's so cool, that you've been friends for so long . . ."

"It's kind of a tradition," Tish says.

"What are you doing tomorrow night?" Rachel asks.

I don't wait for Claire's response.

If this were any other Saturday night, it would be perfect and sublime. But not this Saturday night . . .

I am ensconced on Jack's sofa, snuggled up to Jack. Beautiful Betty is sandwiched between us, and is snoozing after her mini feast (i.e., my dinner).

We have pizza with extra pepperoni and cheese, which I usually love. We have Special Reserve Shiraz, which I also usually love. Jack, a romantic at heart, has dimmed the lights and the wonderful scent of cinnamon-apple candles fills the room.

We have watched the entire first DVD of my new Led

Zeppelin set, as the boys strutted their sublime stuff at the Royal Albert Hall.

We are about to embark on the second DVD, but for once, my gods among men fail to lift me from the gloom that has descended around me.

Surprisingly, it has nothing whatsoever to do with Claire Palmer and my new conviction that she is trying to ingratiate herself with everyone I love. Nor is it due to my new, forthcoming career as a telemarketer.

"Hey." Jack's arm tightens around me. "Are you gonna tell me about it?"

"Hmmm?" I panic. What does he know?

"Whatever it is that's got you so wound up." He sighs, and strokes my shoulder, then drops a kiss on the top of my head. "You've been quiet and distracted all day."

"I'm—fine," I lie, biting my lip. I may never be fine again . . .

"Yeah, right. You're so fine that you haven't eaten a bite of pizza—you love this pizza—and you've barely taken a sip of your wine."

"I'm just not hungry." I may never be hungry again, either . . .

"And you didn't eat last night in the restaurant. Hey, I'm worried about you. Are you getting sick?"

"I think you're right," I say, clutching at this ready-made excuse. "I haven't been feeling too great since yesterday." This is not a lie, because I do feel ill with the cumulative effect of Claire and the telemarketer thing . . . and my latest disaster. Although the cause is mental rather than physical . . .

"It's probably something I ate . . . Oh, I love this song," I say to distract Jack from quizzing me any further, as Bob sings "It's Nobody's Fault But Mine."

I pretend to settle and to concentrate on the movie, but I can't. You see, I think I may have just single-handedly ruined my father's livelihood . . .

And it really is nobody's fault but mine . . . and Marion Lacy's, of course.

It's true.

Oh, but I couldn't *wait* to get to my apartment this morning and settle down for a bout of self-congratulations at my one-woman crusade to help those as physically imperfect as myself.

The phone would begin ringing immediately as famous reporters across the land vied with each other to scoop my story.

A presidential aide would be on the phone to me in a matter of seconds to add his praise, or at least to invite me to tea at the White House to discuss my new role as Special Adviser for Women's Issues with the President—yes, I could be woman enough to put our political differences to one side . . .

Instead, the article is a blatant attack on my father, and on plastic surgeons in general. It is loaded with vitriol and half-truths. It is slanted to paint my father as an arrogant, self-serving megalomaniac . . .

And in that instant, I know whom I have to thank for this. If Marion Lacy wanted revenge for my having had the audacity to stand up to her the other night, she could not have accomplished it more thoroughly . . .

My Years of Small-Breasted Torment

Emmeline Beaufort Taylor, or Human Being Emma as she is known to HUSSI members and friends, bravely shares her story with Human Being Kim Stratton, editor.

"I always knew I was different from the other girls, but my mother made sure I had an idyllic childhood with her in London," Human Being Emma says, smiling at the fond memories of her icon mother, Human Being Julia Beaufort, Women's Rights lawyer and Human Rights activist. "Julia made me proud to be myself, despite my 32AAs."

Human Being Emma pauses at this point in the interview,

her distress obvious as she recollects the sudden change in her life when she left her mother, her friends, and all her familiar surroundings, to cross the Atlantic and live with her plastic-surgeon father in New Jersey.

Julia Beaufort and Joseph Taylor were married very briefly. Soon after their marriage she discovered that her new husband fully intended to pursue a plutocratic life of pandering to the debauched and their quest for physical perfection, instead of dedicating himself to saving lives. Julia plucked up the courage to flee this monster of a man to save her unborn baby from his megalomaniac madness.

Joseph Taylor, jealous of young Human Being Emma's relationship with her wonderful mother, forced Human Being Emma to abandon all that she loved so that he could take over her life and turn her into the perfect plastic surgeon's daughter. Her mother, faced with the possibility of Joseph Taylor's threat of an expensive custody court case, reluctantly parted with her daughter.

When asked about the unbearable pressure her father placed on her to submit to silicone, Human Being Emma said, "He [her father] made it clear that if I truly wanted implants, then he'd arrange it for me . . ."

Her wavering voice, full of unspoken implication, tells a thousand tales of sadness. Of peer-group pressure among the girls at school; of being jilted by the boy of her dreams when he selected a full-breasted senior to take to the high school prom; of a father's unrelenting, constant torment; of her father's partners who only added to the weight of Emma's guilt.

Imagine how mortified Joseph Taylor must have felt about his tarnished position within the plastic surgery community. The shame of having a daughter who didn't conform to either his or his clients' vision of physical perfection.

Imagine his constant threats and urgings, and those of his partners Derek Underwood and Norbert Boyle, that

Human Being Emma finally submit to the ignominy of their scalpel.

Despite this unbearable strain, Emma has remained implant free at much personal cost. Her mother has remained her staunch pillar of strength.

Last year, another blow was dealt Emma when her ex-boyfriend had an affair with a much larger-breasted woman and he ultimately deserted Emma in favor of his mistress.

Instead of returning to her father's spacious, luxurious five-bedroom home in New Jersey, such was her fear of her father and his new wife that Emma chose instead to move into her friend's tiny Hoboken apartment and to sleep on the sofa in the minute living room.

When quizzed about her current boyfriend's feelings about her diminutive mammary glands, Human Being Emma became quiet and reticent. When asked if her current boyfriend ever displayed interest in other women, Human Being Emma was strangely hesitant to discuss him.

And so it goes on. And on. And on.

It's completely awful, and gives the impression that my dad is some kind of dictatorial despot! That Jack is less than content with my small boobs, which is not true. I just didn't want to talk about him with bloody HUSSI.

And the most frustrating part is that it doesn't actually misquote me, but the editorial reading-between-the-lines totally slants the story in the opposite direction. And where is all the mention of Dad's voluntary work to help accident victims?

And, as I read the rest of the article, I thanked my lucky stars that this piece of crap would only be seen by a small number of people in Hoboken, probably the main readership would be HUSSI members. And then I started to panic.

What am I going to tell my friends?

What if Jack sees it?

What if Dad and Peri read this?

Or even worse, what if Claire Palmer gets her hands on a copy? Imagine the mileage she'd get out of humiliating me . . .

But, I console myself before I talk myself into a full-scale panic attack, I bet the circulation of such a small, wacky newsletter would be *tiny. Minute.* Hardly anyone would actually *read* it . . .

Even so I spent the rest of the afternoon skulking around people's mailboxes, illegally tampering with their HUSSI newsletters in my bid to control HUSSI-crap readership . . .

Actually, I covered quite a lot of ground.

I'm just glad that the police didn't see me . . .

"Hey," Jack says, pulling me back to the present. "Where did you go? You *love* Led Zeppelin but you're not even watching."

"Sorry," I say. "I'm feeling worse. I'm just going to head up to bed."

Oh, but guilt is such a miserable bedfellow.

Just hope the local press doesn't pick it up . . .

14

....

The Fourth Estate

TO DO

1. Become Warrior Queen telemarketer in manner of Queen Boudicca.
2. ~~Rise out of ashes in manner of Phoenix Reborn re: dreadful HUSSI article~~. Figure out way to apologize to Dad and Peri re: dreadful *New Jersey Times* article. Or emigrate.

Thursday
9:30 A.M.

I avoided my usual Chez Nous Sunday-evening dinner with friends, on account of being a coward (just in case of possible HUSSI newsletter mention).

Actually, it was on account of being ill and not feeling well enough, which was true, because by then I really had worked myself up into a state, and was only fit for a quiet night at home. Plus, Jack stayed home with me, therefore meant a lovely evening of no-Claire togetherness. Y-e-s!

But on Monday when I stopped by my place after work, there were two messages for me from Matt Jones of the *New Jersey Times*. Two! He wanted to speak to me about the HUSSI newsletter. So of course, I didn't call him back. After all, if I don't say anything to him then he can't run it. Can he . . . ?

Well, it wasn't in Tuesday morning's edition (and I know this because I got up early so I could pop to Mr. Patel's corner store and anxiously scour the paper from cover to cover— had to tell Jack a small white lie. I mean, we *were* nearly out of milk, so it was not completely a small white lie).

It wasn't in yesterday's edition, either, whew . . . (this time I visited Mr. Patel under the pretext of a bread emergency).

But you know, last night, while Jack was asleep, and I was tossing and turning on account of the HUSSI newsletter, and Matt Jones, and Claire, and my life as a telemarketer (fifth night in a row) I had a visitation . . .

From Auntie Alice . . .

When I say visitation, it was one of those dreams you have when you're lightly asleep, and are worrying about something, and then you dream about it and you have the answer to whatever it is you're worrying about.

Picture this: Auntie Alice, racing along like Boudicca in her chariot, phallic finial held high . . .

"Show me some backbone! Show me some spirit!" she tells me, brandishing her finial at me. "Royal blood flows through your veins, and even the smallest among us can make a difference!"

And you know what? I woke up this morning feeling a lot better. I think I might be safe . . . I mean, Saturday's news is *old* news by now, isn't it? After all, it's been *five days*.

So I'm going to forget about the stupid HUSSI newsletter. And the phone messages from Matt Jones. I'm going to commit myself to this telemarketing thing and really give it my best shot. See, if I get a great account from doing it, I will be triumphing in the face of adversity.

And instead of Queen Boudicca at our helm, Cougan & Cray now has Babette Cray . . . and William Cougan, of course, but I'm not going to let that stop me.

Still have to work out how to qualify for my bequest, though . . .

Anyway, here we go . . . my first ever telemarketer call . . . (after all, I was too stressed to begin on Monday, Tuesday or Wednesday—but I think Mr. Cougan might notice if I avoid it for any longer).

"Hi," I say, pleased at the professional tone of my voice. "My name is Emma Taylor calling on behalf of Cougan and Cray. May I please speak with Mr. Kemp?"

"What do you wanna speak to him about?" the bored-sounding woman asks me.

"A business matter between Mr. Kemp and myself," I say firmly. After all, one should never give anything away unless one has to. And if I tell her *why* I'm calling, I'll never get as far as Mr. Kemp, will I? Let's face it, I know how telemarketing works!

"I'm putting you on hold," she snaps, switching me to piped music.

See? My strategy is working. Y-e-s!

Twenty minutes later, as I am listening to a terrible, sanitized, instrumental cover version of "Stairway to Heaven," I can only admire her technique for avoiding me.

I hang up and dial the next number. Because I am not defeated, oh no. After all, one battle does not the war lose!

"Good morning, my name is Emma Taylor, may I please speak with Mr. Witherspoon?"

"What are you selling?"

"Oh, I'm not actually *selling* anything," I assure the hard-sounding woman. "More proposing an idea than selling something. I would like to discuss an advertising opportun—"

Click.

She hung up on me! She didn't even give me chance to explain. How rude is that? Okay, third time lucky . . . maybe I should try a different approach. After I answer my telephone.

"Good morning, Coug—" I begin in my assertive telephone voice.

"Call me back." It's Rachel.

"I just saw today's edition of the *New Jersey Times*," she tells me a few minutes later, when I (obviously) call her back from the restroom. "You're on page seven—human interest story."

"Oh," I say faintly as I clutch at my stomach. God this is *terrible*. Just when I thought I was safe, my horrid article comes back to bite me in the ass . . . How could Matt Jones do this to me? I feel sick as I wait for the flood of her scorn.

"This is why you were so fucking secretive about it."

"But I—" God, this might ruin Dad's reputation!

"That fucking Marion Lacy is a *maniac*," she rants loyally down the telephone line. "How else would Matt Jones have got his sticky paws on this story?" And then I hear the splintering of glass smashing against a hard surface. I hope it wasn't something dangerously lethal, and that I'm not about to become responsible for my best friend dying of some terrible, laboratory-created disease. As well as responsible for the downfall of my father's medical practice . . .

"What was that? What just broke? Are you okay?"

"Shit," she curses. "At this rate I'll have no glasses left. This pregnancy's turned me into a clumsy, forgetful idiot."

"But don't you think you should—you know—evacuate the lab or something?" Because I might be deep in the shit with the article, but my best friend's health is more important.

"I've already evacuated my lab of me," she tells me morosely. "It was just a water glass I dropped in the sink. And why am I at home?" she asks rhetorically. "Because I've got the beginnings of a summer cold, and Hugh thinks I'm made of fucking porcelain and insists that I stay off work."

Hugh is kind of her boss at work. Not exactly in charge of her, which obviously wouldn't be an ideal situation for domestic harmony, but he is technically her next superior up the line. Not that superior is the right word, because obviously Hugh and Rachel are equals, but he *is* one step above her in the scientific food chain.

"Anyway," she says, sneezing. "Stop distracting me. What was I saying?"

"Fucking Marion?" I prompt her, chewing on my lip. What am I going to *do?*

"I warned you what she was like. Tish warned you—we all warned you."

"I know," I agree, because I'm feeling like a complete idiot. Plus lead butterflies are flapping in my stomach.

"God, if it didn't mean life imprisonment, I'd strangle her myself. How are you? I bet this is why you didn't come for dinner on Sunday night, isn't it? I bet you've worked yourself into a fit of worry and panic."

"Yes," I wail. "What am I going to do? What if someone sees it?"

"The *New Jersey Times* isn't exactly the *New York Times*. Don't panic. I only bought it because I'm bored. It's going in the garbage disposal where it belongs."

"It totally misrepresented my point of view," I moan.

"And anyone who knows you will immediately understand what happened."

"But what will I do if Dad or Peri sees it? I don't even know if they subscribe to the *New Jersey Times.*"

"Peri is obsessed with babies and doesn't read newspapers," Rachel tells me in a no-nonsense voice. "And neither does her best friend Gracie, before you ask that one. As for Joe—come on Emma, you know your dad—he doesn't read anything if it doesn't relate to the latest treatment for cellulite or skin-grafting techniques. Stop. Borrowing. Trouble."

"You're right," I say, but I'm not convinced.

"Now, are you eating? I bet you've stopped eating. Emma—you have to take care of yourself."

"I will," I promise her. I think pregnancy has sparked her motherly instincts. How nice is that, worrying about my weight?

And after I assure Rachel that I'll come by on my way home, and after I tell her that "Yes, Hugh's overdoing the concern thing but only because he's wonderful and he loves you," I click the "off" button.

Buoyed by Rachel's support (and determined not to Borrow Trouble) I head back to my desk to conquer the telemarketing world. I'm going to try a different approach . . .

"Hi," I burble cheerfully, despite the fact that the lead butterflies are making a bid for freedom and have now traveled up to my throat. I think I might be sick. "Please tell . . . Stanley that Emma's on the line." This is a cunning ploy on my part to convince the person on the other end of the line that I am personally acquainted with Stanley, see? Plus, it is also a cunning ploy to distract myself from my own worries.

"What is the nature of your call?" she asks me politely.

"It's concerning a matter between myself and, er, Stanley." Wonder if I should leave early and scour Hoboken for all copies of the *New Jersey Ti*—. I hold that thought right there. I am not going to overobsess about this. Definitely not.

But I do have loads of *great* ideas for Stanley's pet-store chain, as it happens. His current advert on the PBS station is really tacky. I feel I could give Stanley's stores a whole new image . . .

"This is Lisa. His financée. He doesn't know any damn Emma," the now-indignant woman tells me. "Unless you're his latest piece of ass. Jesus, I knew he was up to his old tricks—all that crap about late-night meetings. Fuck, I shoulda listened to my mother—"

"No," I interrupt her quickly. Oh no. This is terrible. "You've got the wrong end of the stick."

"Sweetheart, I can beat up on him with either end of any damn stick—"

"I mean you're mistaken—"

"I don't think so. All those early breakfast meetings—I shoulda guessed he wasn't being straight with me—"

"I am *not* his mistress. I would never date an engaged man," I say emphatically. Because I wouldn't. "I'm—I'm—" God, I can hardly bear to admit it. "Look, I'm just a telemarketer," I say in a rush. "And I'm really sorry I gave you the wrong idea."

"Oh," Lisa says, and bursts into tears.

"Er, so are you alright?"

"How would *you* feel if your fiancé was a cheating, lying bastard?" Well obviously I know what it's like, on account of cheating, lying Bastard Adam. "You still there?"

"Er, yes?"

"Can I ask you something? It's not like we're ever gonna meet up, is it?"

"Er, sure," I say, a bit confused. "Go ahead."

"Did you ever have a guy cheat on you?"

"Did I *ever.*"

"What did you do when you found out?"

I feel somehow that I have a lot in common with Lisa. Plus, discussing Lisa's cheating Stanley will help me put my own problems into perspective . . .

"I can't believe you spent a half hour comforting that woman." Angie is laughing so hard that she nearly drops the pile of papers she's carrying. "You're supposed to be soliciting advertising business, not running an advice service."

"Well, I'm new to this, and at least I have three potential clients calling me back. And I couldn't just hang up on poor Lisa," I tell her as my phone rings. "See, I bet that's someone calling me back right now." Unless it's Dad to tell me that I've ruined his business . . .

It's Tish, so obviously another trip to the restroom is in order . . .

"Sweetie," Tish half whispers down the telephone. "Me and Rufus have closed our stores and we've bought up as many copies of the *New Jersey Times* as we could lay our hands on. Obviously it's a complete pile o' shite."

How lovely and loyal is that? To forgo profit margins for the sake of a friend . . .

And after I assure her that I'm okay (even though I am a complete bag of nerves), and after I tell her "yes," that an October wedding is perfectly grand (musing how much she sounds like Rufus these days—I wonder if she's adopting an Irish accent to encourage mother-in-lawly acceptance of her), I have a another call waiting.

"It's me." It's Katy. "As soon as I saw that article I knew what had happened." Katy says. "Marion Lacy is a madwoman. Oh sweetie, don't worry. It will blow over."

"I hope so," I tell her glumly, wondering when Jack is going to call, because after all, if Rachel, Katy and Tish have all seen the bloody newspaper, then he's *bound* to somehow get one, too . . . even though Tish and Rufus have bought up the entire Hoboken stock. I mean, I don't know if the *New Jersey Times* covers the whole of New Jersey, or if it just covers the whole of Hoboken . . .

"I can't believe I got lulled into such a false sense of security," I moan. "I mean, after your experiences with her I really should have known better."

"What's done is done," Tish says. She sounds a bit glum, too.

"Is everything okay?" I ask, because I've been so immersed in myself, I forgot to ask about her new job and Tom.

"Oh, the job's great. There's just so much potential—"

"But?" I prompt her when she pauses.

"It's Tom," she tells me. "He's taking this kinda hard."

"He just needs time," I say, wisely quoting Dr. Padvi to her. "He just needs to get to grips with the new reality, and to reach a positive level of tranquility."

"Yes, but I wish he'd load the dishes into the dishwasher, and make the beds, while he's moving toward his level of tranquility," she says. And then, "I'm sorry, Emma, I didn't mean to offload on you."

"But that's what friends are for," I soothe her. I'm sure they'll work it out . . .

And, of course, my day wouldn't be complete without a call from Sylvester. Because *of course* one of the lunch crowd left a copy of the newspaper in Chez Nous.

"Zis woman Marion, she is terrible," he says by way of greeting. "We are zinking of you, sweetie. Don't you worry, Emma, my lips are sealed. I put zis in ze trash where it belongs, and we will never speak of it again. At least, I will never speak of it again, but I can't talk for David because I am not speaking wiz him."

Oh dear. There must be Problems From Florida . . .

"She is calling all ze time, and David he is whispering down ze phone because he doesn't want me to hear, and she doesn't care if it's our busiest time, and I am doing most of ze work. And I have to go to start ze lunch menu. I speak wiz you later." Click.

3:30 P.M.

No one said it would be easy, I think, as yet another potential client evades my grasp and hangs up. But I am not defeated. After all, this is only Day One and one should give things a chance before admitting defeat . . .

Plus Rachel's just e-mailed the *New Jersey Times* to Mr. Stoat in London. It's true! I am just thanking my lucky stars that I haven't had more calls to report sightings of the bloody thing when Rachel calls me again. This is what happened.

"I've just had an idea," she says without any preamble. "I think you could turn it to your advantage."

"How? Everything about it is a lie."

"Yes, but it's still a published article in the media, although media isn't a word I'd use to describe such a trashy article. Fucking *propaganda* is the word I'd use to describe it. Christ, you should go see a lawyer and get a threatening letter sent to Marion fucking Lacy just to scare her—"

"But where are you going with this?" I interrupt, because she's wandering off topic again. And I really have to get back to my desk and start work at some point.

"Well, *technically* it could count for your inheritance, couldn't it?"

"But it's all a lie."

"Marion fucking Lacy and Matt fucking Jones have used you shamelessly—it's only fair that you get to capitalize on it, too."

Actually, she has a good point—out of the ashes the phoenix rises. I *like* that idea . . .

"I've just scanned it onto my computer," Rachel says. "Just give me the e-mail address for the London lawyer and I'll send it now."

What great friends I have!

See, they *understand* me. It never occurred to *any* of them for even a moment that I'd sanctioned that awful interview.

And just as I am about to start to do some actual work, my desk phone rings again, and it's Jack. Oh shit.

"Er, hi," I squeak, anxious that he, too, is calling about the terrible article. I cross my fingers.

"Hey, how're you doin'? You feeling any better?"

"Yes, much," I tell him, remembering to breathe again. How sweet is that, calling to check how I'm feeling. He's been all lovely and kind to me all week—all gentle and concerned about me.

"You sure? Cos I'm getting kinda worried about you."

"Positive." See what I mean?

"Okay—see you later. Look, I've got to work late, but if you feel worse, if you need me for anything—anything at all—I can skip out earlier—just call my bleeper and I'll come as quick as I can, okay?"

"I'll be fine," I tell him, a bit guilty for deceiving him.

Sunday, July 27

A whole week has gone by since the HUSSI article. And it's been three days since the *New Jersey Times* ran the story. So I think I'm safe . . . I think I can start breathing again.

When I say safe, I mean that I think it's time to stop worrying about someone outing me as a thankless daughter who casually slanders her dear father in such a scandalous fashion . . .

But Mr. Stoat wasn't too impressed. He called me at work on Friday . . .

"My dear Miss Taylor," he says, in his dry dusty voice. "I'm sorry, but this just won't do."

"But it's media coverage," I insist. "And small breasts are important things to make a stand about."

"And I'm sure you've suffered with them," he says, and I am sure I hear a note of amusement in his voice. "And it's true, the article does prove that you've carried out the courage of your convictions by not acquiring breast implants, but your aunt had something more proactive in mind."

"But what, Mr. Stoat? What can I do? Couldn't you give me a little hint?"

Although, it has to be said, I am kind of relieved, at the same time, because I don't really want to capitalize on the terrible things the article said . . .

"I wish I could, Miss Taylor, but your aunt's instructions are explicit. You have to work this out for yourself. But let me give you a small piece of advice. This article does not show commitment to others. And rather than triumph over adversity, it displays you as a *victim* rather than a *victor.*"

So that's that. I *must* think of something else, because I'm just not sure I'm cut out for this telemarketing thing.

Anyway, I haven't really seen Jack properly all week—despite the fact that I've spent every night at his place, he's home late and so tired he doesn't want to do anything more than veg out in front of the TV for a while before bedtime.

But Friday night was just like old times . . . apart from the fact that Jack is a bit quiet and preoccupied. I am a bit worried that Claire Palmer will show up at the gym and crash our Thai meal, but she doesn't. Because she's in Boston. Alone!

It's true! Yayhay!

She had to leave on Wednesday night and isn't expected back until tomorrow or Tuesday, which is fabulous! Jack, of course, couldn't go with her on account of having to work on several new proposals he's putting together.

For tonight's *traditional* Chez Nous dinner with only *true* friends, I am wearing a loose-fitting, form-hiding soft pink top, and drawstring combat pants. This is because these are the only things that currently fit me properly. I have lost three whole pounds, and this is not a good thing. This is *not* a good look for me . . .

Still, I don't think anyone will notice . . . after all, Jack hasn't noticed and he sees me naked practically every day.

This thought holds me until we reach Chez Nous.

"Honey, I missed you last week," David grabs me and kisses me the instant we walk through the door. "Hey, you've lost weight," he adds. "Hasn't she, Jack? Are you still drinking the body-enhancing shakes? How come you're getting so skinny?"

Thank you, David, for noticing, I think sourly.

"She's been ill this week," Jack says, closely scrutinizing me. "You *have* lost weight."

"I'm fine," I tell him. "Look," I say, grabbing one of the tuna tartlets from the table and biting into it. "Yummy."

"Eat ten of them," Jack says, kissing my cheek. "I'm just gonna see if Tom's doing okay, but I'll be counting," he tells me, as he heads over to Rufus and Tom at the bar. How lovely he is, worrying about how much I eat, and about Tom's lack of a job.

But I'm still a bit peeved with David for noticing my skinniness. "So how's your mother? All better now?" I ask, just a bit sarcastically.

"God, just don't mention my mother. Sylvester's already given me enough grief about it."

"But what are all the mysterious phone calls about?" David blushes, which is unusual for him because he's so outré and up front with everything. It takes a lot to embarrass him.

"Let's just leave that alone for now," he says mysteriously, and plies me with Shiraz.

"*Chérie*," Sylvester says with his usual dramatic flair, and I'm not sure if he's referring to me or to Betty as he picks her up and kisses the top of her head. "Come, at least *you* are loyal. Let me take you to Viggo." He flounces out of the room.

"He's right, you *are* looking rather scrawny," Rachel tells me, as I sit down next to her. "Stop fucking worrying. That article is behind you," she adds, for my ears only.

"I hope so," I say, as Tish passes me a plate of cream cheese pastries. I take one and nibble on it. Actually, my appetite's really coming back with a vengeance.

"You can't eat those," Hugh says, whisking the plate away from Rachel. "Risk of listeria. Or those," he says, moving the plate of tiny tuna tartlets. "Too much mercury."

"Who knew there were so many things pregnant women can't eat?" Rachel says rather darkly. "I'm sick all the time, I can barely contemplate food, but the only things that tempt me are things I can't have."

"I hope they can talk some sense into Tom," Katy says, glancing over at the bar, and I notice the dark shadows under her eyes.

"No luck yet in the hunt for a job?" Tish says, as she scribbles "tuna tartlets" on her note pad. She hardly goes anywhere without it these days, just in case a good wedding idea occurs to her.

"He got three rejections this week," Katy tells us.

"But at least that means he's making an effort," I say, soothingly. "You know, getting out there, and all."

"But he's not even getting interviews. He thinks it's his age."

"Maybe he should think of a life change," Rachel says. "Maybe he should retrain and do something he really likes."

She has a point—after all, we all know that Tom hated working on Wall Street.

"And maybe he should help out more around the house," Katy adds. "The minute I walk in the door after a hard day at work, he passes Alex to me and disappears into the den to commune with the Internet."

"I wish Hugh would spend more time communing with the Internet, instead of watching me like a hawk," Rachel scowls as she takes a sip of water.

"How hard is it to operate a washing machine? How difficult is it to make a bed? Jeez, I love the guy but many more weeks of this and I'll be certifiable."

"What does Tom like to do? What are his hobbies . . . apart from the Internet?" I ask encouragingly. Surely there's something that could ignite his imagination?

"He likes painting." Katy rolls her eyes, and sighs.

We all sigh with her. Because we all remember the time Tom decided to paint their house himself. They had to hire a professional painter to come and redo the job.

"Let's talk about something ungloomy," Rachel says. "All we seem to do at the moment is worry, and whine, and shake our heads."

"Yeah." Tish firmly puts down her pen. "Let's talk about happy stuff. Like the old days."

And as we are all trying to think of something positive, the door chimes tinkle.

"Hi, all," calls a happy voice from the door.

Claire Palmer.

"I made it back from Boston early," she says, breezing into the restaurant as if she owns it. "So I thought I'd come and hang with you guys."

And after she's made the round of my friends (who are all delighted to see her, naturally), barely even looking at me (on account of saving me for last) she sits down and reaches across the table to pat my hand in a faux-sympathetic way.

"Emma, sweetie, I'm so sorry about your troubles," she says in a stage whisper. A whisper should be quiet, and for the ears of the Whispered To only. But Claire is definitely not quiet. She has everyone's attention as she reaches into her bag, and I know. I just know.

She has a copy of the *New Jersey Times* in there . . .

"My God, I didn't realize what a terrible time you had growing up. And your father . . . you poor, poor thing . . ."

The whole of the restaurant is quiet. You could hear a pin drop. Because, of course, everyone knows what she's talking about. Everyone except Jack, of course . . .

"Sweetie, are you getting therapy for this?"

"What are you talking about?" Jack asks.

15

....

My Fifteen Minutes of Fame

TO DO

1. Figure out way of preventing Claire Palmer from hijacking my life (with help of only true friends Sylvester and Katy).
2. Work on image. Withered, emaciated sunflower does not project image of triumph in face of adversity.

My loyal friends all, of course, immediately start talking in a bid to explain the situation to Claire (and to Jack) as they protest my innocence, and Marion Lacy's vileness, and the skewed article.

Jack, I notice, does not add his opinion, and is conspicuous by his silence after reading Claire's copy of the article . . . surely he can't think I deliberately set out to hurt my father and Peri? He can't believe that I think he's dissatisfied with my boobs, especially after all the times he's told me that they're just right for me. *And* just right for him, too. This is not good . . .

But Claire, fake that she is, is immediately full of false contrition and even manages to force some crocodile tears.

"I'm so sorry, Emma," she tells me, prettily dabbing at her

eyes with a tissue. "I didn't mean to embarrass you. God, I feel so *bad* about it. You must all think I'm some kind of monster."

I absolutely do.

"Of course we don't. Don't beat yourself up, sweetie," Tish says soothingly as she pats Claire's hand. "Emma understands that it was a genuine mistake, don't you Emma?"

"Sure," I say, my favorite lie when I really mean no.

"That fucking woman is a public menace," Rachel jumps straight in. "I still think you should threaten to sue her for it, Emma. You should sue Matt Jones, too."

"Here, sweetie," David hands Claire a glass of wine. "This will make you feel better."

"Marion's such a bitch," Katy says. "I should know."

She is not the only bitch, I think, as I watch my friends fussing around Claire.

I am the hurt one, here. I am the one who has been blighted; yet Claire Palmer has to usurp me even on this.

"You should have seen the trouble Marion caused for us last year," Tom says. "But Katy really told her where to stick her ugly face," he adds, smiling briefly at Katy in his old-Tom way. His old-Tom-before-losing-his-job way. So at least that's a good sign, isn't it?

"I feel so bad about this," Claire says again, sprouting fresh tears. "Can you forgive me? I hope I haven't caused any friction between you and Jack. Your dad being married to his sister, and all."

Thank you for pointing that out, I want to say, but don't. "I'm sure you wouldn't *deliberately* set out to cause trouble between me and Jack," I say rather flippantly, flashing her a sickly sweet smile before I glance across at Jack. "Only someone really *nasty* and *vindictive* would do something so underhand." Jack closes his eyes briefly, and shakes his head, because he, for one, does not miss my meaning.

Claire's eyes narrow for a second, because she cannot mistake my meaning, either. But she doesn't say anything more about the article.

Instead, Claire recovers quickly and shifts the attention of all back to herself. All through dinner (which I barely pick at) she entertains us all with her tales of the ineptitude of the building team working on the Boston Crisis.

And during dessert, as she entertains us all even more with her sharp wit, I just want to escape home as soon as is politely decent. I want to scream that my friends are all taken in by her artificial sympathy and her synthetic regret.

All except Sylvester . . .

After a quick visit to Betty upstairs to check that she is okay (and, I have to say, I'd hoped that Jack would follow me so we could talk in privacy—but he didn't), I have elected not to sit back at the table where Claire is holding court with Tish, Rachel, Tom, and Katy. I have also elected not to join Jack, Hugh, and Rufus at the bar because let's face it, it's getting fairly obvious that Jack doesn't want to talk to me. Instead, I have elected to sit myself down on the overstuffed sofa in the corner, for five Claire-free minutes.

After hardly uttering a word all evening, on account of bustling back and forth to the kitchen muttering under his breath, Sylvester hands me a glass of brandy and sits down. I think he and David must have had a fight, earlier.

"I zink you need zis," he tells me. "Zis woman. Claire. I do not like her," he hisses to me *sotto voce*. "I zink zat maybe, just maybe, she talk about ze article to cause trouble wiz you and Jack. I zink zat maybe she likes Jack and wants to steal him away from you."

It's such a relief that it's not just me obsessing. At last, someone who won't think I'm paranoid about the whole thing. A voice of reason amidst Claire-adoration chaos.

"Thank *God* it's not just me." I feel some of my strain dissipate. And then, "What made you suspicious?"

"I am French," Sylvester shrugs his Gallic shrug, as if this explains everything. "We know about zese zings." And then, throwing Claire a dirty look, "She never speaks to you unless she has to. And *voilà*, tonight, she is all sympathy to you about ze article, and crying her false tears."

"I think she's trying to hijack my life," I say, taking a hefty gulp of my brandy. "No one would believe me if I told them—it just sounds so . . . so . . . improbable. Even to my ears. Even Jack thinks I'm imagining it."

"Jack, he is such a—such a *man*," Sylvester shakes his head. "He is straightforward and simple—he doesn't see her feminine wiles at work. *Dieu*, he is just like David!"

"What are you guys whispering about?" Katy asks, as she sits down next to Sylvester.

"We are plotting revenge," Sylvester tells her rather dramatically.

"Sounds good. Can I join you? Because if I have to listen to that women say one more word to Tom about how he should be supporting me, and how proud he should be of me, and how important it is for me to retain my independence, I'll throw up. Hell, it's okay for me to moan about Tom, but she hardly *knows* us."

"What?" I ask faintly, because I'm so amazed that she just said this, I'm practically speechless.

"I'm sorry, Emma, I know she's Jack's boss but I just don't like her. There's something mean about her eyes. And I don't mean to worry you, honey, but I think she'd like to steal Jack away from you."

"You see? You see?" Sylvester says. "Zis is what I have just said to Emma."

"But she's so sneaky," I say, so relieved that I'm no longer alone in this. "She's really careful and sly about how she tries to undermine me." And I launch into a brief account of Claire's doings.

"You can't let her get away with it," Katy says. "But I see

your point. She's got everyone thinking that the sun shines out of her ass."

"But what am I going to do?" It's just so frustrating. What is even more frustrating and annoying is that Jack is practically ignoring me. Anger, along with the brandy, is burning in my stomach.

"Zis is difficult. But let us zink on zis," Sylvester says.

"She'll slip up," Katy adds. "We just have to watch and listen, you know, give her enough rope and she'll hang herself."

This is a great idea! A glimmer of hope at the end of a dark tunnel! And then I remember Sylvester's earlier bad temper.

"So . . . how are things with you and David?" I ask, as I watch Jack leave the room. Probably to check on Betty. Wonder if I should pop upstairs and have a word with him?

My backbone stiffens. If he wants to be childish and ignore me, I am not going to make the first move.

"I do not want to zink about zat," Sylvester sighs, and Katy and me sigh with him. But we know that Sylvester will tell us, because Sylvester can't bear *not* to tell us.

"I zink he met someone in Florida," he says rather dramatically under his breath. "All zese phone calls, all zis whispering, I zink zey are not to his mozzer at all." He pauses for effect. "I zink he has anozzer lover."

"Not again," I say, insistently. "Remember the last time you thought he was having an affair and it was all harmless?"

"Zat is what I am zinking, too. So zere is a simple explanation and I just have to wait until he is ready to tell me."

And while we are trying to ingest the rather amazing idea of Sylvester being patient and waiting until the right moment, Jack reappears with Betty in his arms.

"Emma," Jack addresses me for the first time since Claire's announcement. "It's kinda late. We should be going."

Oh, so he's obviously not lost his voice then. Because it

will come in useful when we discuss why he's behaving so childishly. I swallow the rest of my brandy.

"Hey, guys." Claire immediately extricates herself from the middle of the conversation she is having with Rachel and Tish. "Is it okay if I walk home with you? I don't want to play third wheel," she says, laughing prettily, "but it's kinda dark out there."

Betty, oh wise dog, growls. Jack, oh foolish man, smiles at her. And me, what do I do?

I say nothing. I just seethe. Obviously.

This time as we walk home, Jack does not reach for my hand. Jack does not make extra room for me between him and Claire. Jack does not make an effort to include me in the conversation. And so I walk a few paces behind them, with Betty, and I might as well not *be* here.

Call me a bit unreasonable, if you like, but I kind of expected Jack to listen to what I had to say before he jumped to conclusions and began this silent treatment. Call me just a tad impatient, if you like, but I kind of expected he would just *trust* me.

"You want to come in for coffee?" Claire asks Jack as we reach her apartment.

Coffee? Do we want coffee? What gives her the impression that I want to waste even more torturous time with her? But of course, she's not asking *me*.

In that moment, I know that I've had it. I am not going to put up with one more second of her. *She* knows that *I* know that she is trying to steal my boyfriend, who doesn't believe me, and she's also fully aware of the fact that things are rather strained between Jack and me.

"Count. Me. Out," I say, rather curtly. "I've had as much as I can stomach tonight." And then, without slowing my pace, without bothering to tell her good night, "Coming Jack?"

I am holding my breath that he follows me.

I am halfway down the street before he catches up with me.

"I can't believe you were just so rude to Claire," is his opening gambit. Wrong choice of words.

"I can't bear her. She's horrible. And she can't stand me. I told you this, already."

"And I can't believe you could be so fucking stupid," Jack adds, as if I haven't spoken.

"And I can't believe you're talking to me like this, without even giving me a chance to explain. It was a mistake."

"You *know* what Marion Lacy's like." He picks up pace as we round the corner, and Betty whines.

"Yes. I've had that particular lecture several times. I don't need it again. Not from you. And can you slow down—Betty, if you remember, can't run fast."

"What if your dad sees it? Can you even imagine the kind of harm it could do to his reputation?" he asks, as he takes the front steps two at a time.

"I've worried about nothing else all week." Exasperated, I pause on the bottom step. "But I *can't* fix it. Why do you think I've lost weight? Because of the bloody article, that's why." And then another thought occurs to me.

"And *how* will my dad see it, Jack? Rachel checked—the paper has a wide distribution in Hudson county, but the chances of it reaching the deepest, darkest depths of New Jersey is highly unlikely. Are you going to send him a copy? Or should we just leave that one for good old Claire?" Betty whimpers and trot-hops up the steps, and rubs herself against Jack's legs. I think she's upset by this fight. She is not the only one

"What *is* this fixation with Claire? Don't be stupid."

"You already called me stupid," I say, smarting at his tone. "Do try to be a little more inventive."

"You want *me* to be more inventive? I think you got that covered."

"That's right, rub salt in the wound."

"But you know what hurts the most? What really hurts?" he says, lowering his voice as Betty whimpers again. "All of our friends knew about it, and I had no fucking clue. Why didn't you *tell* me?"

"Because, unless it's escaped your notice," I say, "we don't talk much these days, do we? Because you're always too tired and you don't have the time. When was the last time we talked—really talked? What about your ex-fiancée, Jack? Or is that subject still taboo? What are we doing here, Jack? You and me?"

"Enough." He glowers at me from the open doorway. "I'm too tired to do this now. I've had enough."

"Me, too," I tell him wearily. "Me, too." But I am not just talking about our fight.

For long seconds he just looks at me as the gulf widens even more deeply.

"You coming in, or what?" he asks me finally, as he turns and goes into the house.

"Or what!" I snap at his disappearing back.

I don't wait for his reply.

Instead, I turn on my heel and stride off into the darkness.

When I reach my apartment, I am too weary even for tears. Which is odd. Because here I am, not sure if I am actually part of A Couple anymore or if, in fact, I am once again a carefree atom.

And as I strip off my clothes and reach for a baggy old T-shirt, I don't feel particularly carefree. How could things go so wrong between us so quickly? At which moment in time did this gulf begin to yawn between us?

As I slip the T-shirt over my head, its scent hits me like a swift, sharp blow. My stomach lurches, my heart begins to pound, and a huge lump builds in my throat, spreading up behind my eyes. It's one of Jack's T-shirts and it smells of him. All clean, and male, and spicy. I abandon it in favor of one of my own.

And half an hour later, when I'm tossing and turning in bed, I miss him so badly, love him so much even my bones ache with it. But I still can't cry . . .

I nearly jump at the sound of the telephone. I check the Caller ID and grab it. Thank God!

"It's me."

"I know."

"I'm a jerk."

"I know that, too," I say, relieved.

"Ouch. Does that mean I'm too much of a jerk to come in?" he asks, and then I hear my doorbell ring.

And there he is. With a bunch of flowers that have seen better days. And Betty, of course.

"I brought you these," he says carefully, as he holds out his withered offering. "They remind me of you."

"I am a withered, emaciated sunflower, it seems."

"Well, I got them from the late-night store. It was the best I could do." And the expression on his face is so sad, so tired, so yearning, *I* yearn for *him*.

"It's the thought that counts," I tell him. I hold out my arms to him, and before I can think, I'm engulfed in his warmth.

"I should have listened," he says, kissing the top of my head. "I know you'd never do anything to deliberately hurt your dad. Or me. Emma, you are the sunshine of my life, and I—I don't want to lose you."

"I don't want to lose you, either," I croak against his chest, because my vocal cords refuse to work. That's one of the nicest things anyone's ever said to me.

"I've just had a lot on my mind recently."

"I know."

"And I take it for granted that you'll understand."

"I do, but—"

"And I *know* we need to talk," he says, his voice breaking. "But—not right now, I can't right now. I need some time. I just need to straighten out some stuff."

"I can do that, too," I tell him, as his heart pounds against my ear.

"I just—you do know I love you, right?"

He said it!

That's only the second time he's ever told me he loves me. This is a major breakthrough. This has got to be a good sign. And, after all, all relationships go through bad patches.

"I love you, too," I tell him, as I lead him upstairs.

Wednesday, July 30

I'm a local Hoboken celebrity!

It's true!

When I say celebrity, I mean that my article in HUSSI, and subsequently in the *New Jersey Times,* has generated *fan mail!*

"Like, everyone was so impressed with your article!!" Human Being Stacey tells me after I opened my front door ten minutes ago to find her and six other Human Beings on my doorstep.

And the reason I know that they are Human Beings is because they are all wearing the HUSSI uniform—black, shapeless T-shirts and khakis.

I feel a bit guilty, I think, as I wish for Scotty to beam me up, because Stacey has left several messages on my voicemail and I haven't gotten around to calling her back and breaking the bad news to her that I am no longer her acolyte. Or initiate.

What else can I do but invite them inside?

"You've got fifty-three letters so far," Human Being Jane tells me, brandishing a plastic bag as they all follow me up the stairs. "The *New Jersey Times* forwarded them to us."

"Yeah, but that article was a total misinterpretation," I say rather dryly. "You would not believe the grief it has caused."

"I know," Jane says, blushing. "I'm sorry—you don't know how hard it is to resist Chair Human Being Marion when she gets an idea in her head."

"Yeah, it was a lot better before she joined HUSSI," another Human Being adds as they all find places to sit down in my small living room, which is already overly cramped with my giant birthday presents.

"Look—can we stop being Human Beings for a while?" I ask them, because it's tiring remembering to say it all the time. "Only it gets on my nerves."

"That works for me," Jane says. "When you come to think about it, it sounds stupid."

"But Marion says—" Stacey pipes up.

"Please." I hold up my hand. "Do not mention that woman's name again. It gives me a headache."

And after I make them coffee, I find out why, other than to deliver fan mail, they are paying me this unexpected visit.

"We don't want you to leave HUSSI," one of the other women tells me. "You're so good at standing up to   the unmentionable woman."

"We want our organization back to the way it used to be," another woman tells me.

"We think you're just the catalyst we need to break her stranglehold on the other women," Jane tells me.

"But why doesn't anyone say anything? Why is Marion in charge, anyway, if you all dislike her so much?"

"Before Marion, there were just nine or ten of us. And when Marion came along, she brought twelve of her close, personal bulldogs with her. Our previous chairwoman got voted out, and Marion got voted in."

"They were the good old days."

"We did—you know—useful things. Like the fund-raiser to help raise awareness of disease and unwanted pregnancy among teenage girls. That was really good."

"I don't see how me being a member is going to change

the headcount, though," I say, scrambling my brain cells in a desperate bid to remember the rest of their names.

"Some of Marion's staunchest allies are losing it with her," Jane says. "She's bossy, she's difficult, and she's mean to people. The power has gone to her head. This article, even skewed as it is, has really raised a lot of respect for you. I think they're ready for a change."

"But I don't want to be in charge," I tell them, remembering Katy's coup over Marion when she took over the PPPTA. Marion was bossy and mean in those days, too.

"Oh, you don't have to be Chair Human Being."

"Please, Emma!!"

"We just want to use your connection to Emmeline Pankhurst to remind everyone why we formed in the first place. People will listen," Jane insists.

"Please, Emma, just come to tonight's meeting!!"

Well, what harm could it do?

"Okay."

"You won't regret it." Jane shakes my hand, handing me a membership form and a pen.

I sincerely hope not.

11 P.M.

Man, did I rock! I was great!

I think Marion was a bit surprised to see me, though. And she was even more surprised by the amount of friendly support I got when I told her how angry I was about the HUSSI newsletter, and the *New Jersey Times* thing, and how they skewed my point of view.

And when I said "I don't think that the shape of a Hershey's Kiss is something to get our knickers in a twist about. We should be concentrating on actually doing something *real* for the community, rather than wasting our mental resources on something as silly as a breast-shaped chocolate," Marion got quite huffy.

"Human Being Emma, you have no right to formulate an opinion. As you're not even a proper member—"

"Oh, but I am, Marion," I say, waving the document at her. It does not go unnoticed that I don't add her "Chair Human Being" prefix. "And I'm equal to everyone. Says right here, I'm allowed to table a discussion if I want to."

"Emma's right," Human Being Jane, or just Jane, gets to her feet. "We all have a right to be heard," several voices are raised in assent. "Please continue, Emma."

"Well," I say, because I've had a great idea. I've just had a mental image of Auntie Alice being Queen Boudicca. "I think we should adopt Emmeline Pankhurst's motto of 'Deeds not words'—you know, a deed which would really help the Hoboken community. But when I say deeds, I don't mean violent ones," I add, just to make it abundantly clear to everyone that I don't envisage any burned mailboxes or smashed windows. "Because even Mrs. Pankhurst realized that violent deeds only lost public respect."

And you know what? Everyone really liked that idea. So we've adopted the motto. We're all going to do some research and figure out what it is we want to do.

This is going to be great. We're going to do something for the community and triumph over adversity. I'm going to really give it my best shot! (Plus, I will really earn my inheritance.)

My euphoria holds me until I arrive back at my apartment.

There are four real messages for me on my voicemail. When I say "real," I mean apart from the telemarketer recorded messages.

One is from a local Hoboken radio station. They picked up on my *New Jersey Times* piece for their human interest section and want to interview me about my small breasts. My first public appearance. Me, Emma Taylor, radio star!

Of course, it's only a small AM station, but this could be my chance to officially set the record straight. It could be the beginning of something big! A media event in which I can prove my convictions, and prove to Mr. Stoat (and to myself, obviously) that I'm . . . that I'm what?

It's just not going to work. Mr. Stoat was clear that the small breasts issue just won't be enough.

Plus, after my first experience with the media, I am a bit hesitant to voluntarily get involved with another . . .

Any lingering images of fame instantly vanish when I listen to the remaining three messages.

They are from Peri.

"Like, I can't believe you could *do* this to your poor father," she shrieks down the telephone, and my heart sinks. She only refers to him as "your father" when she's pissed with him. But obviously she's not pissed with him this time. She's pissed with me. No prizes for guessing why . . .

"Do you know how much you've hurt him? Like, how could you, Emma? How *could* you?" Click.

What else can she be referring to but the dreaded article? With a heavy heart I listen to the next message, and wonder how Peri found out. Did Claire send her a copy? It's exactly the kind of thing she would do . . . Come to think of it, it's exactly the kind of stunt Marion would pull, too.

"It's like, a complete pack of lies. Your father would never try to force you to have surgery. I'm, like, so ashamed you said that. And Baby Britney's feeling the stress and she won't stop *crying.* And I'm so, like, stressed. And soon I'll have to *leave* Breast is Best. Because I'll have to feed Baby Britney formula, and the group is *strictly* for breastfeeding mothers." Click.

I hit my head with the base of my palm. And then I listen to the third message.

"Your father's business will be, like, ruined. And we'll be bankrupt and homeless."

16

....

Radio Star!

TO DO

1. Become fantastically hip, great-advice-giving Radio Goddess and help nation (Hoboken) with problems.

2. Commission own Web site . . . theradiogoddess.com would be a good domain name (must have a little chat with Tom when he's not so distracted—he knows all about that kind of thing). Will (obviously) have to have special e-mail (theradiogoddess@theradiogoddess.com?), so that fans can write to me.

3. Obviously, would be a good idea to actually purchase own computer, too . . .

"Peri just needs time," Jack tells me a week later, as he's leaving for work. "She knows in her heart of hearts you wouldn't deliberately set out to hurt your dad."

I spent last weekend with Dad and Peri. The sometimes-demonic antics of my four-year-old half brothers seemed a small price to pay to try and restore family harmony, although Mary, the nanny, has had a calming effect on them.

Fortunately, she managed to prize my car keys away from them before they fed them to the waste disposal . . .

"I wish I'd never given that bloody interview," I say to Jack, as I pour coffee into my mug.

Dad was his lovely old self, apart from being a bit subdued. But Peri, although I explained the whole thing, hasn't quite forgiven me. She was very quiet the whole weekend, which isn't like her at all . . . she barely mentioned her birth experience . . .

"Quit worrying," Jack hugs me and bends to kiss my forehead. "Peri doesn't hold grudges for long. Look, I gotta go. See you later."

"No you won't," I remind him. "I've got a HUSSI meeting and I need to catch up on some stuff at my place."

"I don't understand why you're still mixed up with that group," he says, shaking his head as he attaches Betty's lead to her ribbon-adorned collar. "Ever heard of the saying 'once bitten, twice shy?' You *know* Marion's a nightmare."

"Oh, that's all changing," I tell him. "Jane's in the process of staging a coup so that we can push Marion and her cronies to the background and concentrate on doing something worthwhile."

"Is this still about your auntie's will?" he sighs, and smiles at me indulgently.

"Well, partly," I tell him. I don't think he's taking it very seriously. "I mean, I want to earn my inheritance, but it's more than that. I need to have more interests, you know, and if I can do something positive at the same time, well, that's good then, isn't it?"

"Go conquer the telemarketing world, Human Being Emma." He pauses at the door. "And remember to eat. You can't afford to lose any more weight."

Jack, who is still working like a maniac, has been affectionate and attentive since our fight. I think he's reaching his plateau of tranquility . . . at least I think he's climbing the mountain toward it, which is a good sign . . .

I still haven't made any progress with my telemarketing, though, but it's still early days. See, I'm being positive.

Actually, I've just had a positive thought on the Peri and Dad front. I've had a couple more voicemail messages from Hoboken Happiness AM. I wonder if I should do the radio interview? Because it would be a prime opportunity to put that horrid article to rest . . .

Friday, August 8
6:30 A.M.

Hoboken Happiness AM radio station, Secaucus.

Gordon Smiley: "Rise and shine, Hoboken, this is Gordon Smiley and our wakeup song this morning was Led Zeppelin's 'What Is And What Should Never Be,' 'specially chosen for you by our guest, Emma Taylor.

"Emma's recent article in the *New Jersey Times* caused quite a commotion, and she's here today to talk to you about her small-breasted years of torment. Good morning, Emma."

Me: "Good morning, Gordon, thank you for inviting me. And I'd just like to say an especial good morning to my dad and to Peri, my stepmother. And to my boyfriend, Jack, of course."

Gordon: "It's interesting that you mention your dad, Emma, because the article suggests that your relationship with him has been very strained over the years. Does this mean that you've finally made your peace with him?"

Me: "Not at all, Gordon. Actually, when I say not at all, I mean that there was never any strain between us. My dad's a completely great guy. But that article was taken from a local newsletter. It was terribly skewed and all personal references were, well, not really relevant to me at all. So

it's actually the misrepresentation of me in that very article that's *caused* the trouble between me and my dad. And
I really, truly couldn't be more sorry for all the trouble it's
caused for him."

(God, I hope my dad and Peri are listening. I called last
night to remind them to tune in.)

Gordon: "So you didn't suffer years of small-breasted torment?"

Me: "Well, obviously I suffered from society's stereotypical
perceptions of the perfect female form, Gordon, on account of being practically flat chested. It's so hard in this
modern world to avoid it. But my dad was always really
supportive of me. He thinks I'm great just the way I am."

Gordon: "But Joseph Taylor's one of the area's top plastic
surgeons. Didn't he ever suggest that you should have implants?"

Me: "Absolutely not, Gordon. Not suggest. Just, you know,
offered me the opportunity if I *wanted* it. My dad is one
of the sweetest men alive, as well as being a top plastic
surgeon.

"And you wouldn't believe the amount of free recon-
structive surgery my dad does to help the victims of
accidents—quite a lot of burn victims, actually, who he
helps to return to as normal an appearance as he can. So
that they can get on with their lives.

"You see, Gordon, Dad believes in surgery only if it's
important to the individual. When someone goes to see
him, Dad discusses all the implications with them first,
and actively encourages them to speak to a therapist before deciding on drastic plastic-surgery options.

"It's all about ethics, see, and Dad is, well, highly ethical. They don't come any more ethical than Joseph Taylor,
hahaha."

Gordon: "Speaking of ethics, Emma, what prompted
HUSSI's editor to misrepresent you, do you think?"

Me: "Well, Gordon, I think it's a sad sign of the times. It's all about attracting readers, you see. Sensationalism to sell copies, instead of reporting the complete and absolute truth. I mean, adding pathos to my story is what got it noticed by many in the first place. Including you.

"And it's wrong, but sometimes the sad, pathos-ridden or glamorized untruth is more interesting than the happier, less sensational truth. I'm sure I don't have to point out to you that making up stories goes on at the most prestigious publications in the country."

(Actually, am rather pleased with that comparison to the national press—it's all that newspaper reading and self-enlightenment Dr. Padvi's book encourages me to do.)

Gordon: "So what is the true message of your article, Emma? Are you anti implants?"

Me: "Well, I'm glad you asked me that, Gordon. You see, it's all about accepting oneself. About making choices based on what the individual truly feels is important. And if implants are necessary to your personal happiness, then that's completely fine. But if you're having surgery to please someone else, or to conform to peer-group pressure, then I'm definitely against that."

(God, this is great. I think radio could really be my thing.)

Gordon: "Folks, we're taking a short break, and then Emma will be here to take your calls. Emma's second musical choice this morning is Led Zeppelin's 'Communication Breakdown.' "

(Seemed like an appropriate choice—hope Dad and Peri understand. Actually, hope that Jack gets the message, too.)

Gordon: "And now for our first caller. Tell us who you are and what is your question for Emma."

Caller #1: "Hi Gordon and Emma, this is Jack. I don't have a question for Emma, I just wanted to drop by with a male opinion—Emma, babe, it's great you're proud of your small breasts—don't change them an inch."

(He *is* listening! How lovely of him to call.)

Me: "Thanks Jack. I appreciate your support."

Gordon: "Caller, you're on the line to Emma."

Caller #2: "Hi, this is Rachel. I'd like to hear Emma's views on compromising within a relationship when the other person is being totally *unreasonable*. I'm a pregnant scientist and my fiancé's *insisting* that I avoid contact with all lab experiments and take a *desk job* until the baby's born. Don't you think that's completely fu—*unreasonable?*"

(Oh, this is a tricky one. But am glad Rachel remembered not to curse on air.)

Me: "Well, Rachel, on the one hand your fiancé may have a point. Maybe he's just worried about you coming into contact with specific substances that might injure your unborn child, and—"

Rachel (rather frostily): "I see. So you're saying that I should just do whatever he fu—whatever he says and hand over complete control of my life to him."

Me: "No, not at all. What I was going to say was on the other hand, I think you have a point, too. Is there any way that you could continue with your lab work, but only with safe projects? Hahaha, I mean, if I were pregnant, I wouldn't want to work with, you know, secret diseases or anything—not that I know what it is that you do, hahaha . . ."

Rachel: "Thanks, Emma. You're right. Before I give up lab work I shall *insist* that my fiancé produce *specific proof* that the experiments I'm working on could be potentially harmful. In fact, he's listening to the show so he knows *exactly* how I feel about it. That was very insightful of you."

(Oh, God. I hope I haven't caused trouble between Hugh and Rachel. I mean, I do see Hugh's point. But his fussing is getting a bit out of hand.)

Gordon: "And now for our next caller."

Caller #3: "Hi, this is Katy. I'd like to hear Emma's views on sharing the burden of domestic life. My husband recently lost his job and I've become the main breadwinner. He's now at home with our little boy full time. And okay, so he never *thinks* to fill the dishwasher or make the beds. He hasn't figured out yet how to work the washing machine. I totally *understand* this—he needs time to get into a routine. After all, I know how hard it is to look after a toddler."

Gordon: "Katy, I need to push you along here—we have other callers waiting. Can you give Emma your question?"

Katy: "I'm getting to it, Gordon. So my point is this. At a time when we're under a financial constraint because I don't make as much money as he did, do you think it's fair that he's spent over a *thousand dollars* of our savings on a new computer that we don't need?"

(I didn't know Tom had bought a new computer system . . . oh, God, what do I say? How do I avoid taking sides?)

Me: "Katy, I think you should definitely talk to T—, er, your husband. Tell him that you feel he should try to help out around the house, because after all, you're working a full-time job. And although taking care of a toddler *is*, obviously, a full-time job too, maybe he could—you know—load the dishwasher while you make the beds? And, er, on the question of the new computer system . . . er, well, I would find out why he needs it. I'm sure he has a very good reason."

(Whew. That one was close.)

Katy: "Thanks, Emma—that's great advice. You know, he's been on an economy drive recently so I guess that if we can afford a new computer system, we can definitely afford not to give up our weekly dinner with friends."

Me: "Thank you, Katy."

Gordon: "Caller, you're through to Emma."

Caller #4: "*Bonjour*, Emma, zis is Sylvester. My boyfriend's *mère*, she doesn't know he is gay. And now she says she is sick

and wants him to get married to a nice *girl*. *Merde,* she is not
sick. She is just trying to manipulate him. And now he has secret phone calls all ze time, and I zink he's having an affair."

Me: "Try to stay calm, Sylvester. I'm sure your boyfriend is
only trying to keep his mother happy. Which is very com-
mendable, and everything. But unfortunately we can't always please our parents with our life choices. I think your
boyfriend should definitely, *definitely* explain the situation
to his mother. No matter how hard it is. And I'm sure
there's a reasonable explanation for the secret phone calls."

Sylvester: "He is listening to you right now, and I hope zat
he takes zis advice. I am seriously zinking of leaving him."
   (Oh.)

Gordon: "Emma, we have more callers waiting to speak
with you, but we're also receiving a lot of messages on our
bulletin board. Julia, a Human Rights lawyer from London, England, wants to know your views on whether she
should take a minibreak with her husband, or spend the
weekend working on a very important political asylum
case."

   (Trust my mother to get this on the Internet. Trust her
to put me on the spot about the dratted minibreak, which
she and George are supposed to be leaving for today. Oh,
I wish I hadn't told her about my radio debut . . .)

Me (thinking hard): "Well, I think the asylum case is very
important, but as the courts will be closed over the weekend, I'm sure that Julia can delegate some of her work and
still go on the minibreak with her husband. Maybe she
could work today, then leave for the minibreak early this
evening, because it's all about compromise, and she
should spend time with her husband, too."

Gordon: "Thank you, Emma. Hello caller, who is this?"

Caller #5: "This is Tish. My fiancé's mother is coming for
a visit in October and she's bringing her best friend and
her best friend's daughter with her. The best friend's

daughter is my fiancé's old girlfriend and she's not married. Emma, do you think I'm being unreasonable for not wanting his ex-girlfriend staying in my home and coming to my wedding?"

Me: "We're certainly getting a lot of calls about difficult mothers today. Er, I would definitely tell Ru—your fiancé that the ex-girlfriend is a bad idea."

(God. Poor Tish. This is terrible. I'll find out more when we have our usual Friday coffee after work.)

Gordon: "We have time for one more caller. Who is this?"

Caller #6: "Emma, this is just so, like, awesome. You being on the radio—I called round and told all my friends and we're all tuned in. We just wanted to tell you how proud Daddy and me are. This is, like, great. Daddy's right here with me and he just wants to say a word."

Dad: "Emma, honey, we love you. I knew you'd find a way to set the record straight."

Peri: "And I just want to add that whoever, like, sent that copy of the *New Jersey Times* to me and Emma's dad, well, they should be really ashamed of themselves. Whoever you are, you are a mean, nasty, terrible person and I hope you have a miserable life."

I think my first radio appearance went rather well. Gordon Smiley, who also happens to be the Executive Producer, was really impressed.

"We've never had such a great response to an unknown guest. You did great, Emma."

"Thanks," I beam, as I shake his hand. "I really enjoyed it." I did, actually, but I just hope he doesn't realize that the callers were all my close, personal friends. Apart from Peri and Dad, because that was fairly obvious.

"Maybe we could get you to come in again to discuss something fairly similar. I'll get one of our guys to give you a call and maybe have a brainstorming session."

"That would be great." Just imagine. Me, a radio star . . . imagine working so close to the designer outlets . . . I could pop to Donna Karan during my lunch breaks. Heavenly!

Plus, Rachel has recorded the broadcast for me on her computer and she's going to send it to Mr. Stoat in London. (Well, it can't hurt, can it?)

My euphoric radio interview carries me all through my telemarketer day.

I think I'm becoming a hardened pro now, because the hang ups and being put on hold to piped music are just part of my daily routine and I don't get upset about them.

I still haven't generated any work, though . . .

And the radio interview didn't make the cut with Mr. Stoat . . . he called me as soon as I got to work.

"My dear Miss Taylor," Mr. Stoat tells me in his dry dusty voice. "Let me just say that I thoroughly enjoyed your radio debut, but I'm afraid that it won't do."

"But I made a stand for what I believe in," I say, grasping at straws.

"And I'm very happy that you've reunited with your father and stepmother," he says, his voice tinged with amusement, "but damage limitation to restore family harmony doesn't fulfill the terms of your aunt's will."

"But can't you, you know, just give me a little clue about what Auntie Alice wants me to do?"

"I wish I could, but her instructions specifically forbid me to do so," he sighs, and I get the feeling Mr. Stoat would really like to help me out here.

"I'll try to come up with something else," I tell him.

"I'm sure you will succeed. You are a very resourceful young woman, Miss Taylor. Have a good weekend."

"I'll try," I say happily, because I *am* resourceful. I think I *have* come up with something else.

HUSSI is planning a really good campaign. It was actually

Marion's idea, which was a bit of a shock, but she seems to be adapting to the new regime (i.e., we've gradually dropped the Human Being thing and more of our members are speaking out with their opinions, which is excellent).

And this campaign is really important. Apparently, there are plans for a new Internet café—Marion found out about it from a contact in the town's planning department, and let's face it, as Marion pointed out, Hoboken needs another new café like New Jersey needs another mall.

What we really need is a Human Being's center—you know, for moms and dads who stay at home with small children. They get so isolated. It could also double as a community center for the more mature, retired population of Hoboken—we could have tea dances, or chess and cards evenings. And the youth of Hoboken wouldn't be excluded, either, because we could include an after-school sports program, and have chaperoned dances and stuff.

Anyway, Human Bei—Jane's going to speak to the Town about it, to see if we can get some grants. And her sister's an architect, so she's asking her to draw up some plans. Which is good, because Jack's too busy at the moment to do pro bono designing for us.

Yes, I think, as I leave the office for the weekend. Things are looking up. Because despite not having made progress with my telemarketing, I've certainly made progress with other aspects of my life.

1. Dad and Peri are talking to me again.
2. My relationship with Jack is reaching its tranquility plane.
3. I have a bright (possibly) future (also possibly) as a radio star.

Plus Claire Palmer has gone to Boston for the weekend. Alone.

★   ★   ★

"I can't take it any fucking longer," Rachel announces a week later at our Friday-after-work coffee. "I'm a reasonable woman, I can compromise," Rachel says, building up to a rant. "Hugh's gone too fucking far this time."

"What's he done now?" I sigh.

"He's applied pressure to Human Resources. I am now officially an—an *administrator.*" The way Rachel says it makes it sound like he's sold her into bondage and she has to perform unmentionable sex acts every night. "I made it clear that I wasn't going to let this pregnancy change my life, but I didn't figure on Hugh trying to change it for me."

"He's not the only one," Tish says, glowering at her coffee. "I'm so sick of Rufus's mom and fucking Niamh."

If Tish is cursing, this is serious. God, that's terrible, though, isn't it? Dragging your son's old ex-girlfriend to visit with his fiancée.

"She's beautiful, she's a great cook, she'll make some lucky guy a great wife . . ."

"But if Rufus wanted Niamh, he'd have married her years ago when he had the chance," I point out.

"I understand why Hugh's done this," Rachel says, sipping her soda. "But what really pisses me off is the fact that he's forced my hand."

"I think I need to force *Rufus's* hand," Tish tells us.

"I agree that it makes *sense* for me to have a desk job for a while," Rachel says, doing a surprising about turn. "Because I'm tired a lot of the time."

"You know what Rufus is like—he never does anything without a push," Tish says.

We sip our drinks thoughtfully.

"I'm going to give him an ultimatum," Tish announces. "If he doesn't put his foot down with his mother, there will be no wedding."

"But sweetie, isn't that rather drastic?" I turn to Rachel. "Tell her she's being too drastic."

"Why?" Rachel says, unsurprisingly. "Drastic is sometimes the only answer to a problem."

"I knew I could count on you for support," Tish adds. "I'm giving Rufus two weeks, and then I'm moving out."

"Oh, I've already given Hugh his ultimatum," Rachel announces, looking straight at us. "As of this point in time there will be no wedding."

This is terrible. She's making a *huge* Hugh mistake. She loves Hugh. In fact, Hugh is the first person she's ever been in proper love with . . .

How to delicately, yet firmly tell her she's making the biggest mistake of her life?

"But you love Hugh," I tell her, once I've scooped my jaw up off the floor. Might as well just spit it out. "Couldn't you you know—couldn't you just talk it through with him?"

"And this, from the woman who's still not living with her partner. What is going on with you and Jack?" Rachel pins me to the spot, cunningly switching the attention away from herself.

But you can't just make life-altering statements like "the wedding's off" and then try to change the subject.

"We're just biding our time," I hedge. "And don't change the subject."

"I wish I'd bided *my* fucking time," Rachel jumps straight in. "Then I wouldn't be in this fucking mess. Pregnant, alone . . ." she sighs, then rolls her eyes rather pathetically. Which is odd.

If there is anything that Rachel is *not*, it's pathetic.

"Stop being fucking pathetic," Tish tells her, before I can open my mouth. "I'm sorry, sweetie, I don't mean to sound harsh but it's time for plain speaking, here," she continues. "Emma's right. You love him. You need to talk to Hugh and clear up this mess before it gets any worse."

"But what about you, Miss Tish?" Rachel wags her finger. "I'm not the only one talking ultimatums, here."

"Yes. But I'm not moving out straight away. I'm giving him time to mull it over and talk to his mom. And this is different. We don't have a baby to think about."

There is a silence as we await the flare of Rachel's temper. But it doesn't come.

"I've tried talking to him," she says, elbows on the table, face cradled between her hands. "He's not listening. He won't even fight with me anymore. I can't *stand* it."

This is not good. Rachel thrives on a good argument . . .

"But what will you tell your mother?" I ask, a few moments later. Because let's face it, her mom (or rather, her dad) is going to be stuck with a huge bill for her daughter's nonwedding. It's probably too late to cancel everything.

"I just want my old Hugh back. I want him to realize that he can't organize my life for me. So I'm not actually canceling the wedding," Rachel tells us. "Yet."

I am still pondering Rachel's situation as I head back to my apartment to collect my gym things, and clothes for the weekend, when my cell phone rings.

"It's me." It's Jack. "Do you mind if we skip the gym and the Thai meal tonight? I gotta work late and I don't know what time we'll be done. And I'm beat. I'll bring back takeout, later."

"Okay," I say happily. At least it means no Claire at the gym.

17

············

Wedding Bells?

TO DO

1. Hike up volume when Claire Palmer next complains about Led Zeppelin DVD. After all, Jack's house is more *my* house than *her* house.
2. Design fantastic campaign for Chrysanthemum Lingerie (thereby avoiding having to make telemarketer calls).

So when Jack and Betty arrive home at eight-thirty, with Claire still in tow because they need a food break before they do any more work, I am more than a little disappointed.

"Princess," he says, placing the takeout on the counter as Betty growls at Claire and trot-hops out of the kitchen. "I got your favorite spicy chicken. Oh, Claire and me just have to get a little further along with this blueprint, then I'm all yours." Jack flashes me his best "please understand, please be nice," look.

And because I *am* understanding and nice, but because I am also not giving Claire the satisfaction of causing more trouble between Jack and me, I smile back in a very confident, nonvictim kind of way.

Claire is watching me closely, and I want her to know that she's of such little worry to me, she might as well be a fly that I can't be bothered to swat.

I haven't seen her since Jack and me had the fight. Absence has not made my heart any fonder

"Lovely," I say brightly, because he *is* lovely. What is *not* lovely is the way that Claire frowned at me from behind Jack's back when he said, "then I'm all yours."

I smile even more widely, showing lots of teeth.

I haven't seen that much of Jack, either, recently. He says that he spends so many office hours with clients, he has to catch up on his actual work in the evenings in his own time. And I do understand, but I just wonder when this will settle down.

On the bright side, I think he really is reaching his plateau of tranquility—the nights I spend at my place, these days, are usually spent with Jack. He says he can't sleep without me . . .

"I'm sorry to wreck your plans for tonight," Claire tells me as we sit down to eat. She doesn't sound sorry at all.

"You haven't wrecked them," I say sweetly. "Jack's been working so hard, it will do us good to have an . . . early night."

She does not miss my meaning.

"Yes, it's so demanding, but *fulfilling* being an architect," she says, not missing a beat. "Tish told me about your recent, er, changes at work. Tish is such a talented interior designer, and job satisfaction is so important, don't you think?"

My heart sinks as I wait for the other boot to drop. Because how can being a telemarketer compare with a career in architecture?

"You should see some of the advertising campaigns Emma's worked on," Jack says, frowning slightly as he opens a carton of rice. "She has some fantastic ideas. She's really talented," he adds, leaning across the table to squeeze my arm.

How loyal is that?

"So, Jack," Claire quickly changes the subject. "The sooner we start, the sooner I'll be out of your way. Let's work while we eat."

They fill their plates and ensconce themselves in Jack's dining room because it doubles up as an office. I pick miserably at my spicy chicken and then give up. I'm not hungry, after all . . . So I take Betty for a trot-hop. Just long enough for her to do her business, because making myself scarce is not on my agenda. Claire would *love* that.

See, I need to emphasize to Claire at every opportunity that I am very much on the scene. And to remind Claire that Betty sees straight through her nefarious plans because this dog is no fool. And neither is *this* woman . . .

I am determined to have some time alone with Jack later.

When I arrive back at Jack's, however, Hugh is arriving at Jack's, too . . . complete with two suitcases. Oh. Rachel followed through with her plan, then. I hope she knows what she's doing.

But this is a bit awkward, because I don't know what to say to him.

"Hi, Emma," he says, and I think he might have been crying because his eyes are a bit red. But I don't mention this, obviously. "I guess you heard the news."

"Yeah. I'm sorry. It will sort itself out," I tell him to reassure him. "It's probably a combination of pregnancy and wedding nerves."

"You think?"

Poor man. "Completely," I say, because I know that Rachel loves him. "I think Rachel's just not used to, you know . . ." Now how to say this with diplomacy and tact? "Someone taking such good care of her." There. Very subtle, I think.

"You mean someone who overfusses, rearranges her work schedule without her consent and generally tries to take over her life." Hugh doesn't beat around the bush. "It's okay, Emma, you don't have to be subtle—I'm a scientist, I need plain speech."

"Well, er, I wouldn't have put it quite like that . . ."

"Rachel did."

I can imagine.

"In fact, there were quite a lot of fucks and bastards, along with what she and her black belt in karate would like to do to me if she weren't pregnant."

"I'm sure she didn't mean it all . . ."

"That's what I thought." Hugh attempts his old jovial smile, but it doesn't quite reach his eyes. "She just needs time. Jack told me I could stay here for a while—is that okay with you?"

How nice and considerate for asking, seeing as it's not even my house.

"Absolutely," I tell him, beaming encouragingly.

Anyway, after I get Hugh installed in the attic, and after I poke my head around the dining-room door, just to let them (i.e., Claire) know that I am here, and after Betty growls at Claire, just to let her know that *Betty* is here, too, I decide to watch my Led Zeppelin DVD in the living room.

See, it's next door to the dining room, and my presence will be felt by Claire.

Hugh appears two minutes later.

"Hey, do you mind watching this? Only we can change it if you like," I tell him.

"No—I love Led Zeppelin," he says, "if you don't mind the bad company."

"I'd love the company," I tell him, meaning it. "Let's crack open this bottle of Shiraz Special Reserve."

And you know what? Five minutes later Claire Palmer sticks her head around the side of the living-room door and glares at me. She doesn't see Hugh.

"Emma," she hisses under her breath so that the sound

doesn't carry to Jack. "Can you turn down that racket? We're doing important work here and we can't concentrate."

It's not *racket*. It's "The Immigrant Song." But I don't say this.

Instead, ignoring Claire, I say to Hugh (who *did* hear Claire hissing at me and is not terribly impressed judging by his scowl), "Is this too loud for you, Hugh?" and Claire almost jumps out of her skin as she sees him.

"Nope," Hugh says, his eyes narrowing behind his glasses. "It's perfect. Hello Claire," he says flatly.

"Er, Hugh. Hi." Claire is embarrassed, and I'm completely delighted to see her off balance and speechless for once. I think Sylvester was right. Give Claire enough rope and she'll hang herself with her own cleverness . . .

Thinking of being clever, I totally ignore Claire and pad into the hall. "Jack, is the music bothering you?" I call from the dining-room door, because I want Claire to hear me. "Is it too loud for you, too? Only if it's distracting you from work, I'll turn it down."

"It's great," Jack tells me, his chocolate brown eyes crinkling tiredly as he smiles at me. "You know what? I'm done for tonight." He puts down his pencil and stretches, then follows me into the hall. "Claire—I just want to chill out and hang with Emma and Led Zeppelin. Let's finish this tomorrow."

"Fine," Claire Palmer says, smiling sweetly at Jack. But her eyes are flashing fire at me (just like The One Ring).

A small victory. And yet it is mine! Y-e-s!

You know, apart from the night I flew back from England and Sylvester nearly got us arrested on the turnpike for dangerous driving, I can't remember the last time Sunday night at Chez Nous was cancelled . . .

Tonight, for a change, Sunday night features Hugh, Jack, Sylvester, Betty, and me in Jack's living room, along with

Chinese takeout and a couple of bottles of wine. Our DVD viewing of choice for tonight features the original French movie *La Cage Aux Folles*.

Despite having to squint at the subtitles, it is hilarious. It is fantastic. But the reason we are watching it is not because we want to improve our fantastically inadequate French-language skills, but because this is Sylvester's favorite movie.

It features Renato, gay nightclub owner, and his drag-queen boyfriend Albin. It also features Renato's son, Laurent (from a single heterosexual encounter because Renato believes that one should try everything at least once). Laurent is engaged to the daughter of a prim and proper politician.

Renato and Albin (in drag, pretending to be Laurent's mother) are trying to play the perfect couple to impress the prim and proper politician. It is not working . . .

"You see, you see?" Sylvester demands of us. "Zis is just like me and David—he will not tell his mozzer ze truth, and now he is engaged and we are in a mess. Just like ze movie."

Sylvester is here with us, rather than all of us being at Chez Nous with Sylvester and David because Sylvester left David today and moved into Jack's house . . .

I must admit, it was a bit of a shock to open the door at six-thirty this morning and find Sylvester there, complete with a suitcase, plus his personal pots and pans.

"You see?" Sylvester continues, pointing to the screen. "All zis deception is just making more problems."

I know what he means.

David, it seems, has told his mother that he is happily living with someone, just to get her off his back. His mother, who's made a miraculous recovery, is now planning a visit to meet "Sylvie," David's "fiancée."

And let me make one thing very clear. Although Sylvester's mannerisms may be camp, he is a six-foot Adonis, and even dressed in drag (and I *have* seen him in drag) there would be no way anyone could mistake him for a woman.

Monday morning
7:15 A.M.

"Hey, sleepyhead," Jack wakes me with a cup of tea the next morning. "Have you seen the time?"

I carefully open my eyes to slits to test the brightness of the room and wince. Nope, too bright. It hurts too much.

We were all up into the wee hours of the morning chewing the fat. Which consisted of (a) what Hugh should do about Rachel, i.e., back off with his fussing, treat her like he did in the old days (I helpfully mentioned that he should pick some fights with her to prove himself), and wait a while (I also helpfully told him that she hasn't yet canceled the wedding), and (b) what Sylvester should do about David, i.e., no, we didn't think it a very good idea if he, Sylvester, were to call David's mother, especially in the wee hours of the morning.

Of course, chewing the fat also involved the consumption of copious quantities of wine, and now a million tiny hammers are beating on my brain.

"You need to get up," Jack bends to plant a kiss on my forehead. "You'll be late for work."

"Like I care?" I groan, snuggling back under the comforter with Betty. How can he sound so cheerful? How can he not have the same hangover as me? After all, he drank too much of the same wine as me.

"I hate work," I tell him grumpily, as Betty starts licking my hand. "I'm considering taking the day off sick. Or better still, the year off sick."

"I thought things were going okay," Jack says, sitting down on the bed beside me. He takes hold of my hand and begins to caress it reassuringly.

"I hate my job. I hate telemarketing." Yes, this is pathetic. I should show more backbone but I feel too hungover. "I haven't pulled in any accounts yet. I think I might become natural wastage soon."

"Why didn't you say something sooner?"

"When?" I ask, peeling open an eyelid. He's already showered and dressed for work. How can he look so great after so little sleep and so much wine? "When is there ever time?" I ask him grumpily. "On Friday night when Claire and you were working, and then Hugh moved in? Or on Saturday when you and Claire were working and I was trying to cheer up Hugh? Or on Sunday, after Sylvester arrived?"

"I know, I know," Jack sighs, tugging me up into a sitting position so he can pull me into his arms, and I feel instantly better. "But I promise you, things will get less hectic soon. Maybe we could take a short vacation? You know, maybe a long weekend next month some time," he says, kissing me before disappearing through the door. "Think about it."

"The answer's yes," I call after him as Betty trot-hops at his heels. Who needs to think about it? Time away with Jack sounds lovely.

"Oh," Jack's head reappears around the bedroom door. "I've got dinner—"

"—with clients tonight," I finish for him. "You told me already. I'm having dinner with Katy and Tom, anyway."

"Great, send them my love."

I hope it *is* great, and not an evening of watching yet another relationship disintegrate . . .

"Are you coming back here, later?" Jack's head reappears around the side of the door again.

"Well, my place is closer."

"Me and Betty will come back to yours, then."

8:00 P.M.

"Sweetie, that advice you gave me on the radio was great," Katy kisses me as she opens the front door. "It *was* just a communication breakdown."

"Oh, good." She looks very happy. This is *great*. "So you and Tom have worked it all through, then?" I wonder how she managed that, because Tom, it has to be said, is a lot like Jack in terms of not opening up easily. I suppose it's because Katy and Tom have been married for so long. They've long since achieved their plateau of tranquility . . .

"Only after I got home from work on Friday, and he disappeared upstairs straight away. That was my breaking point, you know? The final straw."

"So what did you do? I should take notes for myself . . . and for Rachel, Tish and Sylvester."

"I know. What a mess." Katy shakes her head. "But things have a habit of resolving themselves—they just need to *understand their questions* and reach *their higher transcendental planes of togetherness.*"

"My God, so Dr. Padvi's book really worked for you and Tom, then?" I ask. I lent it to her last week.

"Not exactly," Katy laughs. "I decided I'd reached *my plateau of untranquility*, so I marched upstairs and demanded to know why he didn't help around the house, and why he was avoiding me, and if my job was really a threat to his masculinity then he should get over it."

"Wow," I say, impressed.

"Splitting up is very drastic," Katy sighs. "How's Claire?"

"Don't ask." I throw up my hands in disgust. "But I think Jack's starting to see the cracks. He kind of leaped to my defense the other night when she tried to get in one of her friendly digs. I don't know if he realized it was a dig, but it's a start. But back to you and Tom."

"After I said my piece, I burst into very undignified tears. I know, I know," Katy adds, "it wasn't a very empowered thing to do, but I couldn't help it. Obviously he could see how upset I was, so he told me about his new job. He just wanted to make sure it was more certain before he told me."

"Ohmigod! He's got a job? That's fantastic," I say, hugging her. Whew. "Tell me about it."

"You know, I think I'll let Tom tell you all about it over dinner," she whispers to me, as we reach the kitchen door. "Let him have his moment of glory."

"Here she is," Tom greets me and hands me a glass of Shiraz. "Our very own radio star."

"Well, I wouldn't put it quite like that," I say, pleased by his well-meaning support. Pleased at how cheerful Tom actually *looks*. And the kitchen is tidy, too . . .

"Come, sit down and eat," Tom tells me serving me a huge portion of lasagna (who knew he could cook?).

"So come on, I hear you have some good news."

"Well—" Tom pauses, then grins widely. "I got a job."

"That's fabulous," I say, but what will happen to Alex? Will they get a baby-sitter, or will Katy give up her new job, which she loves?

"I've sold my first freelance article to a financial magazine," Tom announces proudly. "I've already made back the money I spent on the new computer. And they've asked me to write two more articles for them based on the proposals I sent."

"Fantastic."

"But that's not the end of it," he says, taking a deep breath. "What I really want to do is become a Web site designer— I've been fooling with the idea for a while, and I thought— hey, why not make money out of my hobby? And I've already got my first commission—I'm creating a site for some accountant friends of mine."

"I'm so proud of you, Tom." Katy reaches across the table and touches his hand. "And you know what?" Katy turns to me. "We don't have to worry about a baby-sitter for Alex."

"No—I can take care of him during the day, and I can work at night and on weekends. So it's the best solution all around."

Friday, August 29
5:30 P.M.

Thank God it's Friday! I am on my way to meet Rachel and Tish for coffee. I wonder if Tish will be moving into my apartment this evening, because Rufus's ultimatum runs out today. It's odd, actually, because she hasn't called me today. At all. She hasn't answered her phone calls, either. Strange . . .

Rachel and David, on the other hand, have called me incessantly all week. Rachel, to find out if *Hugh* is suffering enough (because she barely catches sight of him at work anymore, since her move to her desk job), and David, to tell me how much *he* is suffering without Sylvester.

I'm spending far too much time in the restroom.

But yesterday afternoon, something rather wonderful yet curious happened at work . . . My phone rang . . . and for a change, it wasn't one of my friends. I've (possibly) landed a really lucrative account.

It's true!

This is what happened . . .

"Good afternoon, Cougan and Cray, Emma Taylor speaking. How may I help you?" Courtesy and efficiency personified, that's me. Plus, William Cougan is talking to Grady, and within earshot, so I have to sound like I'm, at least, trying to do my job.

"This is Hanko Matsushita of Chrysanthemum Lingerie," the Japanese woman (at least I think she's Japanese) on the other end of the phone tells me without any preamble. "I want you to put together a portfolio of ideas for our new American line. Are you interested?"

I nearly fall off my chair.

"Of course, er—"

"We want to break into the American market with our new, patented, odor-fighting underwear," she continues. "We want fresh, inventive ideas. Do you have a pen and paper?" she asks, politely. "I'll spell my name for you."

And after she gives me her name and phone number, and tells me that her assistant will send me all of the relevant blurb about the company, and sales figures in Japan, etc., I can hardly contain my excitement as I thank her, and forget to ask her how she came to me, Emma Taylor, in particular. Or was it just the luck of the telephone-directory draw? I must make a mental note to ask her . . .

Hanko Matsushita was quite vague, actually, about her vision for Chrysanthemum . . .

But this is great! This is fantastic!

"Not a personal call, I trust," William Cougan says rather unpleasantly as he passes my desk.

"Of course not, sir," I tell him, keeping my face straight. "I may have just landed a very important lingerie account," I add, just so that he knows how valuable I am to the company. "Chrysanthemum Lingerie. They're very big in Japan."

"I know who they are," William Cougan says, his manner warming slightly. "I want to be kept informed of progress."

I now have something to report for the Friday meeting!

This morning at the progress meeting, however, I'm a bit disgruntled when Grady assigns the new man, Paul Morgan, to oversee me. I don't *need* to be overseen. I can manage quite well on my own.

When I say new man, I mean our new senior account manager. Although the company is downsizing, Paul Morgan is an exception to the rule. He's Babette Cray's cousin (which Angie and me discovered from Tracey, obviously).

Later, Grady explains to me privately that this account could be worth serious money, because he's heard all about Chrysanthemum Lingerie, and they're a big deal. And if we don't land the account (which of course we will, because I've already received the company info—it was couriered to me earlier this morning and I already have the beginnings of a great idea), if anyone can afford to take the heat of not winning it, then Paul Morgan can. On account of being Babette

Cray's cousin. Grady's so good at the political game . . . and besides, Paul seems nice—I'm sure we'll work well together.

I can't wait to tell the girls my good news . . . but in a discreet kind of way, on account of them both having far more to worry about . . .

When I reach our regular café, Rachel is already there.

"Hi," she greets me enthusiastically. "I saw Hugh just now," she tells me.

"Hi, yourself," I say, and order a cappuccino. "Thank God. Finally."

"He came to see me just before the end of work. He wanted me to have dinner with him, tonight. To talk."

"You said yes, obviously." This is a very good sign.

"I told him that he'd had plenty of chances to talk to me in the past two weeks, and what had taken him so long? And that I'd think about it."

"What?" I don't believe I'm hearing this.

"Yeah, that's what he said, too," Rachel grins. "In exactly that same tone of voice. I think he's getting his fight back."

"Oh." The light dawns. Although why Rachel thrives on arguments I will never know.

"So don't worry, you and Jack won't be stuck with him forever. So about my bridal shower," she says, cunningly changing the subject. "Do you know what Tish has planned? Because I told her I just wanted a quiet dinner with you three girls and Sylvester. I can't face anything big and loud."

"Don't worry about it," I tell her. And then, "Speaking of Tish, have you heard from her today?"

"No, she hasn't returned any of my—" Rachel pauses. "Talk of the devil," she says nodding toward the entrance.

"Hi, sorry I'm late," Tish breezes through the door, a huge smiled pinned to her face. "And I know, I know, I haven't returned your calls, but there's a really good reason for it."

I am speechless. I am not the only one, because Rachel's mouth is also open in fly-catching mode . . .

Tish is completely radiant. The white, fitted skirt and jacket cling lovingly to her curves, and contrast with her stunning, olive complexion. Her rich brown hair is elegantly arranged in a chic knot at the back of her head, and she's wearing the diamond earrings that Rufus gave her for Christmas.

She is to die for.

"Look," she says, breathlessly holding out The One Ring. Nestled beneath it is a wedding band. "Rufus and I just got married."

18

....

Plateau of Tranquility

TO DO

1. Resign from job (if, in fact, am not already fired).
2. Never. Get. Involved. With. Marion. Lacy. Ever.
   Again. I should *know* by now that this path leads
   only to madness.

Well, knock me down with a feather!

"What!" Rachel recovers control of her mouth before I do.
"Without us? How could you *do* that?"

"I'm sorry, honey," Tish says, but she's smiling as she
sits down. "I know I've let down the side for female emancipation or something, but I couldn't leave things the way
they were. And I didn't want to split up with Rufus, because let's face it—it took me three years to get him in the
first place."

"But—but—" My mouth still won't work. I can't take this in.

"I know, but what about his mom and Niamh?" Tish has
the grace to blush. "When you think about it, it's so stupid.
How could I think Rufus would forget me the moment he set
eyes on Niamh?"

"Not stupid," I say, thinking about Claire Palmer. "We all worry about things like that."

"Rufus couldn't see the problem with his mom and Niamh," Tish continues. "He's not a weak man, just a quiet one—in his eyes, how could his old girlfriend change his feelings for me? But he came up with the perfect solution—get married straight away to show me his commitment, and give me the security."

"So his mom and the wonderful Niamh are still coming in October?" Rachel hits her head with the palm of her hand.

"Well, maybe, maybe not—" Tish pauses, then smiles a very sneaky, sly smile. "Let them come if they want. But as Rufus and me are already married, there won't be a wedding for his mom to attend. Or try to break up. So Niamh's presence as a potential bride would be superfluous."

"Sneaky," I say, filled with admiration.

"I'm impressed," Rachel shakes her head with disbelief. "I can't think why none of us thought this up. It's a win-win situation."

"Exactly," Tish's eyes light with triumph, and all three of us burst into laughter.

"Girl power," Rachel says, once we've stopped clutching our stomachs. "You should never underestimate the strength of feminine wiles."

"Anyway, I gotta go," Tish says, getting to her feet. "Rufus is parked on a yellow line—he's taking me away for a few days—I don't know where, it's a surprise."

And then we're hugging her, and all three of us have tears streaming down our faces.

After she leaves, Rachel turns to me. "You know, she really wanted that huge wedding—she's been planning one for years."

"But in the end it didn't matter to her. Rufus was more important."

"Exactly," Rachel tells me. "She compromised."

Wednesday
4:20 P.M.

William Cougan has spent the last half hour sequestered in Grady's office with my initial ideas for the Chrysanthemum Lingerie account.

Paul Morgan and me have been working on it all week, and I have to say, I think it's looking good . . . but William Cougan and Grady have spent the last ten minutes yelling at each other . . . I can't hear what it is they're actually saying, but judging from the volume of Grady's voice, he's giving as good as he's getting.

When my telephone rings, it is a welcome distraction.

"I hope he will be very happy wiz his *mère*, and an empty bed at night," is Sylvester's opening gambit.

David's mom arrived from Florida on Sunday, and Sylvester is even more miserable. He spent the weekend moping around the house, or following me and Betty around Hoboken.

Jack's house is stuffed with flowers on account of David sending floral "I love you" messages to Sylvester. Two bouquets per day for nearly two weeks is a loud message—I don't think I could hold out for this long but Sylvester is ignoring them.

Jack and Claire spent the weekend working at the office, rather than from Jack's dining room, because Claire says she's allergic to pollen . . . yeah, right. I just bet she is.

"Why does he send more flowers? Why doesn't he come to *see* me?"

"Well, that might be something to do with the fact that you won't speak to him on the phone, and disappear upstairs when he comes to call," I tell him, my eyes flashing nervously across to Grady's closed door. What's going on in there?

And then my phone beeps at me to indicate an incoming internal call. "Sylvester, honey, I have a call waiting. I'll call you back—I think the boss is summoning me. Bye." I feel a bit guilty for blowing him off, but I will see Sylvester later and will go though this at least ten times before I can get to my HUSSI meeting.

"Emma Taylor speaking," I say, with more confidence than I feel.

"Come through," William Cougan barks at me, then hangs up.

I do not have a very good feeling about this. And you know what? I don't deserve to get barked at.

I punch Angie's extension. "Angie, can I transfer my calls to you for a few minutes? William Cougan's on the warpath again."

"Sure, honey."

I square my shoulders, take some deep breaths, and straighten my jacket and skirt before going into the office.

Grady is staring out of the window. His shoulders are set in a way that suggests he is not happy.

William, who is pacing up and down with my Chrysanthemum Lingerie folder in his hands, looks plain angry. I know this, because his face is so red I half expect to see steam coming out of his ears.

"This," William tells us, without even bothering to say hello, "is terrible."

And then, before I can take in the nastiness in his voice, he *throws my dossier into the trash.*

What?

Hanko Matsushita hasn't even seen those ideas yet, so how can William Cougan decide that it's terrible?

"If you could explain what it is that you don't like about them, I'm sure we'll be able to come up with something else," I say in what I think is a very calm, reasonable voice.

I'm not sure what William Cougan is upset about, but I'm pretty damn sure that he has no right to treat me like this.

"They're obviously only an outline at this stage," I continue, "but—"

"I don't know what it *is* that you and Paul Morgan have been working on," he interrupts me, "but I'm quite certain it wasn't on this account."

"William, that's out of order," Grady leaps to my defense.

This is so despicable. Although William doesn't spell it out, he does not need to. He *knows* that I used to live with Bastard Adam, and I think he's trying to suggest that there's something between Paul and me. Which is ridiculous, because I've only known Paul for a short time.

"With all due respect, sir," I begin, my indignity flaring, "I don't think you have any right to—"

"Obviously you don't think at all," he interrupts. And is about to say more, when Angie knocks on the door and enters immediately.

"There's an urgent call for Emma," she says, without any preamble.

"She can call back. We haven't finished here yet," William Cougan barks at her.

"It's urgent," Angie stresses. Angie has absolutely no respect for William Cougan and ignores him completely. "It's Rachel," Angie says directly to me. "She's had an accident. She's fine, Hugh says not to worry, but she's in the hospital. I've taken the details for you."

Oh God. When Hugh said she's fine, does he mean that *she's fine,* or that *she and the baby are fine?*

I immediately head toward the door.

"Where do you think you're going?" William Cougan asks me. "You heard what she said. Your friend's okay."

"I *know* where I'm going. To the hospital, obviously," I throw over my shoulder.

"I am hereby removing both you and Paul Morgan from this account," William growls. "And I want to see some results from the telephone campaign."

I don't bother to look back.

*　　　*　　　*

"I wasn't looking," Rachel tells me, Tish and Katy an hour later. "I can't believe I just stepped out in front of that bicycle."

She's got a black eye, and is a bit bruised, but apart from that everything is fine. Whew. But she's got a saline drip attached to her arm, and the doctors want her to stay overnight, just to make sure.

"The main thing is that you and the baby are okay," I say reassuringly.

"That's all that matters," Tish pipes up.

"It's probably your pregnancy hormones, sweetie." Katy pats her arm. "I was a nightmare when I was pregnant with Alex."

"And at least it was only a bicycle and not a car," Hugh tells her. "It could have been much worse."

"Yes, I know," Rachel snaps at him. "You don't need to ram it down my throat. I could have lost the baby . . . God, *I could have lost the baby,*" she says, bursting into tears.

"Hey, now," Hugh says, putting his arms around her and holding her close. "I didn't mean to ram anything down your throat, I meant simply that I don't know what I'd do if something happened to you."

Katy, Tish, and me glance at each other. I think it would be diplomatic of us to leave Rachel with Hugh.

And as we walk out into the summer evening, I don't give a damn about my impending unemployment. I can't bring myself to worry about a stupid job. And although part of me really wants a shot at the Chrysanthemum account, I feel free. I really do. I take a deep breath and smile at Katy and Tish.

"I think the wedding's back on," I say to them. Whew.

"How is she?" Jack pulls me into his arms the minute I get back to his place. We're staying here all the time, at the moment, to keep Sylvester and Hugh company.

"She and the baby are fine. She's got a lovely black eye, though."

"I take it Hugh's not coming back here?" Jack smiles down at me, as Betty snuffles around my feet in welcome.

"Only to collect his stuff," I smile back at him.

"We were so worried," Sylvester says, bustling into the hallway. "First you do not call me back, like you promise, and zen you don't come home, and we don't know what's happened, and zen David he call to tell Jack about Rachel's accident—"

"Try to remember to breathe, Sylvester," I say gently. "I'm sorry, I should have called but I forgot."

"I miss my David," he wails, wafting up the stairs. "I am going to lie down. All zis stress, it is bad for my nerves."

He is not alone.

"He got two more bouquets today. And you got two calls," Jack tells me as he takes my hand and leads me into the kitchen. "One from Human Being Stacey!! to find out why you weren't at the meeting—"

"She's probably panicking because we're doing our march on Saturday." I sit down at the kitchen table, glad to take my weight off my feet, meager though it is.

"Ah, Auntie Alice's inheritance—I hope it's as interesting as your finial," Jack teases me, pouring me a glass of Shiraz. "Here, I have a feeling you might need this."

"I do," I say, "I've had a terrible day."

"I know." He sits down beside me. "You also got a call from Grady. He says to tell you to come to work tomorrow."

"Oh, I don't know if I'm relieved or pissed about that," I laugh, as I recount my afternoon William Cougan experience to Jack.

"Don't worry," Jack tells me, putting an arm around me. "If you get fired, I won't let you sleep in your car."

A major breakthrough, I feel.

Friday night

All in all, it's been a very busy week, I think, as I get ready
for tonight's surprise dinner . . .

When I arrived at work yesterday morning (half an hour
late, because I didn't feel inclined to rush) Grady was waiting for me. With my dossier in his hand.

"Babette loved your ideas, you're back on the project," he
tells me straight away. And before I can ask him more, my
telephone rings. "Ah, the Emma Taylor hotline," he says,
with a wink. "I hope Sylvester and David manage to work
out their problems."

Honestly, Sylvester is so indiscreet about, well, everything.

"What color panties are you . . . wearing?" Jack's voice
makes *me* flush indiscreetly, and I glance anxiously
around the office. We haven't done this for a while . . . actually, we haven't had any other kind of sex for a while, either . . .

"They're . . . all white . . . but—"

"Not in a virginal kind of way," Jack laughs as he finishes my
sentence for me. "I can't stay on long, I'm due in a meeting in
two minutes—I called to see if you're still gainfully employed."

Oddly, I am a bit disappointed (and a bit hot) from the
fading possibility of a repeat of our cell-phone naughtiness,
but I do have work to do.

"I am a very busy account manager with a lingerie account to plan," I tell him.

"Don't take any crap."

And I don't. Because William Cougan hasn't been anywhere near me . . . he has enough on his plate with Babette.

I got it from Tracey in Human Resources, obviously.

It's all political. William Cougan's temper wasn't aimed
at me, at all. It was aimed at Paul Morgan. Or rather at his
cousin, Babette . . . apparently Babette's called in an independent team of accountants to audit the company

books, and William Cougan is thinking of taking early retirement.

And that's completely fabulous, isn't it?

Talking of completely fabulous, I check out my appearance one last time. I am wearing a simple, black shift dress, which swirls just above my knees. It is elegant, yet not in a too-dressy way. It also looks expensive—but it wasn't because I got it for ten bucks on one of our outletting trips, but who's going to guess? (Apart from Rachel and Tish, who were with me at the time.)

"That's a gorgeous look for you." Jack's arms enfold me from behind, and he plants a kiss on my neck.

"You look pretty hot, yourself," I tell him, and Betty woofs in appreciation. "And you, sweetie," I add, because her silver bow and ribbon are adorable.

We're ready. All we have to do now is get Sylvester to Chez Nous for his surprise dinner with David and David's mom.

It's true!

David, spurred on by Tish and Rufus's "elopement," and Rachel's near-death experience, and his mother's excellent health, decided it was time to make the great romantic gesture to Sylvester tonight.

David's mom took the news that "Sylvie" was really Sylvester quite well, apparently . . . Her main point of concern was would they be able to adopt a baby? Because all of her friends have grandchildren and she doesn't . . .

"Taxi's here," Jack tells me. "Time to go."

It's our job to get Sylvester to Chez Nous without *telling* him we are actually taking him to Chez Nous. Sylvester thinks we are taking him out for a nice, posh dinner to cheer him up.

"It's so nice you are doing zis for me," Sylvester says, as we climb into the cab, and I can't help but smile. If only he knew. "At least I know who my *real* friends are," he adds, sighing dramatically. "At least you love me, unlike zat—zat good for nozzing David."

Jack catches my eye and smiles wryly at me as we ready ourselves for another diatribe from Sylvester. But it will keep him occupied and he won't notice where we are going.

"Why are we here?" Sylvester demands five minutes later as we pull up outside the restaurant. "David, he does not want me here wiz his precious *mère*. He is ashamed of his true identity. He is ashamed of—of *me*."

"Don't be a baby." I tug at his sleeve to get him out of the taxi. "David is definitely not ashamed of you. He loves you. Why else would we be here?"

The last thing we need now is an uncooperative Sylvester.

"David has something special to tell you," Jack says nonchalantly as he climbs back into the cab. "He asked us to get you here, but if you want to go home, fine. We'll all go home together, and you and David will never be reunited."

"Okay, I come."

Jack said just the right thing. I *knew* Sylvester wouldn't be able to resist.

As we push open the door, the lights come on to the shouts of "Surprise."

Everyone is here. Rachel and Hugh, Tish and Rufus, Katy and Tom, David and his mom . . . But not Claire Palmer, because David isn't too keen on her any more. I must find out why . . . besides, this is just for *old* friends.

The whole restaurant is bedecked with garlands of red roses, and candlelight. Expectation fills the room and is almost a physical entity as we wait for David to speak.

David and Sylvester's eyes meet across the crowded room, and I feel an emotional lump building in my throat.

"Sylvester," David says rather nervously. "I'd like you to come up here for a few minutes because I have something I want to say to you."

Oh God, this is so romantic. I can see that Katy and Tish already have their tissues at the ready.

"Go on, honey," I give Sylvester a little push. "You know you want to." He hasn't uttered a word since we walked in the door.

As Sylvester walks slowly toward the front of the room, I feel my eyes filling with tears, too.

"Here," Jack whispers in my ear as he puts a tissue in my hand. "I brought you this."

"I should have done this years ago, and I just hope you can forgive me—" David pauses as his voice cracks, and I can see that his eyes are glistening, too.

"This is so cute," Rachel whispers to me, and her voice is a bit squeaky.

"Here, in front of all of our friends," David takes a small box out of his pocket, and opens it. "And especially in front of my mother, I want to give you this ring as . . ." David's voice cracks even more, and he clears his throat. "As a sign of my love and commitment to you, I want you to wear this commitment ring. Please, please come home to me," he finishes in a rush.

"I will," Sylvester manages to say, because for once he is speechless. And as David slides the ring onto his finger, we all cheer and clap wildly.

"She broke my heart," Jack tells me later, much later, as we lie quiet in bed, after love.

We are tangled in the sheet, entwined, and I can hear his heart beating against my ear. His arm tightens around my body as he pulls me closer. I hardly dare to breathe as I await his next words.

"Her name was Laura. I was twenty-four and new to Hong Kong. I fell in love with her the instant I laid eyes on her my first day at work. She was my boss, you know that already, and—eight years older—so self-assured, and sophisticated, and confident."

So not like me . . .

"We dated, we got engaged within a month—God I was so

young—and then three months later Chip came for a visit," he continues. "This part you already know, because I told you last year."

I nod my head against his chest, not wanting to interrupt his flow.

"There isn't much more to tell. Chip always wanted what everyone else had. He took one look at Laura, and decided to sleep with her. I found them in bed together—I *had* to find them in bed together, because Chip needed his victory and planned it that way. Fuck, the oldest cliché in the book. Can you believe it? I should've seen it coming, but I didn't. And that was the end."

"What happened?" I ask quietly.

"We broke up. Laura got transferred to another project, and Chip moved on, as he always did."

"I mean to you."

"You know the rest," Jack says. "I was scared to risk getting hurt so badly again. I couldn't get past Laura and move on, so I didn't allow anyone to get close to me. *Couldn't* allow them to, because that part of my heart was a frozen wasteland. And so I became an ionic bonder for a while—" he pauses, shifting position so that he can look into my face. "Until you," he grins, lightening the mood.

"It's my irresistible electron," I tease him, following suit.

"Irresistible is the right word," he says, running his hand from my breast to my hip. "You know, I was also wary because I worried that we got together so soon after your breakup with Bastard Adam. I just thought that it was too good to be true, you know, and that I'd gotten you on the rebound."

"I felt the same way about your mysterious Laura," I tell him, loving him so much I could explode with it. "I thought I was just for now instead of for keeps."

"Emma, will you—" he pauses, and my breath catches in my throat.

Ohmigod he's going to propose to me. All this time I've wanted it. I can't believe it's about to happen.

But what about Auntie Alice's inheritance? What about that little clause right at the end of her letter instructing me not to marry Jack?

Auntie Alice's inheritance versus marrying Jack.

There is no choice . . . I'd give up everything in a heartbeat to be with Jack.

"Will you live with me?"

"Yes."

And as he kisses me, I can't help a tiny pang of disappointment. On the other hand, maybe I can have Jack and my inheritance. This is, after all, a great move in the right direction!

Saturday
10:30 A.M.

This HUSSI march is going to be a triumph! I just know it!

Euphoric and filled with boundless enthusiastic energy after last night, I'm ready to fight. But only in a metaphorical, nonviolent kind of way, of course . . .

Jack is *so* adorable. And wonderful. And amazing . . . All it took to melt the iceberg in his heart was the love and patience of the right woman. As Dr. Padvi says, we just had to reach our plateau of tranquility . . .

Jack had to go to work this morning . . . something to do with a contract for a chain of buildings, but I don't care about him spending time with Claire. Because I, Emma Taylor, am the love of Jack's life.

This afternoon I'm going to start moving my stuff to Jack's place, and tonight Jack's taking me on a date. It will be the first time we've been out together, just the two of us, for ages. We're going to the new seafood restaurant so we can have a nice, romantic dinner and talk some more.

Anyway, I am wearing cargo pants, plus a skimpy black tank, plus black sneakers. Not because this is a great look for me. Not because this is a conformist look for me, either, on account of everyone else wearing cargo pants and black tops. No, it is just for comfort. Plus, if we all wear something similar then we can spot each other easily in a crowd.

"Remember fellow Human Beings, we are fighting for the sake of the community," Chair Human Being Marion tells us, as we all stand outside her house with our banners ready. She still clings rather obsessively to that silly title, but if it makes her feel better then why not?

Two dozen HUSSI voices (mine included) shout "yes."

This is going to be great. I have my job and the Chrysanthemum account, I have Jack, and now I'm going to show my commitment and triumph in the face of plutocratic adversity!

I hold up my phallic finial. I've brought it with me, because it seems appropriate that a small part of Auntie Alice should be here to see me standing up for my convictions. I am totally committed to fighting for a community center for Hoboken!

Human Being Kim has her tape recorder and camera to record our stand for community rights in the HUSSI newsletter.

"After today, HUSSI will no longer be an insignificant blip on the map of Hoboken. We will have a real voice! Come," Marion says, punching her fist in the air. "Deeds not words."

And we're off!

I'm totally ready for action, but of the nonviolent kind, because "deeds not words" isn't about wanton destruction, but about peacefully yet pointedly making our stand. At least I hope it does . . . Marion looks a bit too cheerful about this.

"I think Marion looks *too* happy," Jane says as we stride

down the sidewalk. "Maybe I'm just being overly suspicious, but she's just too—you know—enthusiastic."

"This is going to be great!!" Stacey squeaks, waving her banner rather excitedly as she just misses hitting a hapless passerby.

And as we walk along, I think Jane's wrong. We're all happy and enthusiastic as we hand out leaflets that Jane prepared listing the reasons why we're making our stand. We need a community center—not an Internet café!

People smile and say hello to us as we pass. Children wave to us. This is great, this is just how I imagined it should be.

But when we reach the site, just as we see the workmen excavating the foundations, things take a nasty turn for the worse.

As if someone has just flipped the sanity switch, Marion and her followers begin to run toward the site screaming their obviously prearranged war cry. "Power to the people! Down with bastard plutocrats!"

Marion and her followers begin to pelt obviously prearranged paint-filled balloons at the workmen.

And then Marion and her followers break through the protective barrier and make a beeline for the poor guys who are, after all, only doing their jobs. Within moments, the scene is one of mayhem and madness, with only Jane, Stacey, myself, and a handful of rational HUSSI members left standing on the perimeter.

"Shit," Jane says, as a squad car squeals around the corner and pulls up to the curb.

"This is like, awful!!" Stacey exclaims as two more squad cars pull up and several large police officers jump out and leap to the rescue of the workmen.

As Human Being Kim snaps her camera to capture the whole sorry episode on film, I realize that Marion Lacy has sabotaged us again. I should have known she'd do something like this.

And, in the midst of the mayhem on the building site, as

angry, shouting women hurl abuse and blue paint, I see Jack in the midst of the fray, as a HUSSI radical leaps at him. Claire Palmer is fending off another banner-waving HUSSI radical.

Fuck.

19

....

Jail Bird

TO DO
1. Swear off men. Forever.
2. Reach own personal, individual plateau of tranquility by upsetting Claire Palmer.

This is not how I imagined the first day of my new triumphant life would unfold . . .

I have spent the last two hours in police custody explaining that (a) Auntie Alice's finial is a family heirloom and not an iron vibrator, (b) that I definitely haven't, nor was I intending, to use it as a lethal weapon, and (c) I had no idea about the blue paint or attacking the workmen.

Finally, they let us go.

And as I step out of the doors with a group of quietly simmering HUSSI members, and into the bright September sunshine, I squint, blinded by the light.

Marion Lacy is not among us. Which is a good thing at this moment in time because I might otherwise be tempted to do something I would regret. I just hope she gets charged, convicted, and made to do some awful community service job.

Like assisting Public Works with the maintenance of the sewer pipes for ten years or so . . . she'd be good at shit shoveling . . .

I still can't believe the chaos our peaceful march became. All my plans for making a triumphant stand ruined, poof, just like that. On the bright side, I still have another six weeks left to win Auntie Alice's inheritance. I'm sure I'll think of something . . .

I'm trying to distract myself. Because I'm trying not to think about Jack.

I still can't believe the look on Jack's paint-covered face when he saw me standing there with the mad, crazy women attacking *his* project . . . Well, that's the only logical explanation, isn't it? Why else would he *be* there? I tried to go over to him to explain, but I was being detained by a police officer and a pair of handcuffs at the time, so it was a bit difficult . . .

Claire Palmer was hilarious, though. She was furious. Her long, blond hair streaked with blue paint is an image I will hold dear for a long time.

"What a mess," Stacey says angrily to Jane and me.

"I know," I agree, shaking my head. And although I am sad that she's lost her exclamation points again, I am completely gratified that the mood of our group is definitely not one of defeat. We are all suffused with angry determination.

"Marion will suffer for this," Jane tells us. "This is totally not what HUSSI is about, and I've had enough of her."

"Think of the negative publicity this could cause for us," another Human Being says. "This could really damage us."

"You should stage that coup soon," I say, my hand tightening around my finial.

And as they immediately begin to plot ways to get rid of Marion, I see Jack outside the cinema, just across the road from the police station. I freeze.

Even though his face is still covered in now-dry paint, he is glowering at me. I can almost see the tension vibrating in his shoulders as he bunches his fists in his pants' pockets.

Slowly, he crosses the road and begins to climb the steps, one foot in front of the other, until finally he is looming over me.

"What the hell do you think you were playing at?" he says, now glowering down at me. "Do you *know* what you've done?"

"We weren't playing, it was serious. It was our march for the Human Beings Center," I tell him indignantly. "It was supposed to be peaceful, but it went wrong."

"Yeah," he laughs, looking up at the sky. But it is not a nice laugh. "You could say it went wrong. Do you know how much damage your fucking group's caused?"

"But *I* didn't cause any damage," I tell him. I don't think I've ever seen him so angry. "I didn't *know* that Marion and her militant crowd were going to start throwing blue paint everywhere, and generally launching themselves in front of bulldozers and stuff. I didn't think they—"

"No, that's the trouble. You didn't think. It's just like the HUSSI newsletter all over again."

"That's right, throw that in my face," I tell him, my temper flaring.

"Yeah, well at least it wasn't blue paint."

"Jack, what *is* this? I didn't know this was one of your projects—"

"This could ruin *everything*," he says, pushing his blue hair off his forehead. I think he's overreacting just a bit. And let's face it, what's a bit of blue paint compared to losing my inheritance?

"I know the blue paint is a pain, but it's a building site, and it's not like the paint ended up on your precious building because it hasn't even been built yet," I say, without drawing breath.

"That is so not the point, you—"

"And don't you forget that I've lost out here, too," I leap straight back in, because my temper is really up and running now. "I've lost the chance to prove myself to Mr. Stoat and get Auntie Alice's inheritance."

"Ah, the infamous inheritance," he says, tipping his head up to the sky. "Emma, there's far more at stake here than some crackpot relic from your mad auntie."

I gasp.

"Auntie Alice was most certainly *not* mad, she was—"

"You just don't get what you've done, do you? This isn't any old project, this is a *big* deal."

"But I didn't know. You never tell me what you're working on, you—"

"Larry Stenton's planning a chain of these Internet cafés across the East Coast area. And if it gets out that my live-in girlfriend was part of the . . . screaming group of *lunatics* attacking the first one, then Larry might decide not to use us for the rest of the chain."

This is the final straw. It's obvious that Jack cares more about work, and his reputation, than about me. I see red as my tongue slides into overdrive.

"How will Larry find out? Who's going to tell him? Let's face it, the HUSSI newsletter isn't exactly a national paper."

"No, but Matt Jones of the *New Jersey Times* wasn't too thrilled when his cameraman's equipment got covered in blue paint. Hell, for all I know he'll be sending Larry the bill for repairs."

Matt Jones was there this morning? God, this is much worse than I thought . . .

"That's not something you need to worry about," I tell him, furious with him. Furious with myself, ashamed of myself, too. How could I have been so stupid? "I'm not moving in with a man who cares more about his work than about me," I say, bravado and guilt pushing my tongue into overdrive. "So it won't be a problem for you, will it?"

"Don't be ridiculous—"

"I'll be as ridiculous as I like," I leap right back in, because I'm going to say my piece whether he likes it or not. "You're always at work, you compartmentalize me, you only see me when it suits you, and even then you don't really share your whole self with me. And then, in fact, when your nasty boss makes snide digs at me, and generally tries to cause disruption between us, you don't even *see* it."

"Oh, I'm just loving this," Jack drawls, folding his arms across his chest. "We're doing the Claire thing again. What is it with you and your obsession with Claire?"

"Funny how quite a few of our friends see through her, isn't it Jack? In fact, it's odd that you won't take anything I say about her seriously, isn't it, Jack? But then maybe you do—maybe you just like having two women fawning over you. You know, Jack, I've had enough of this. Enough of you."

"Fine."

He turns on his heel and strides off down the steps without another word. I burst into tears.

Friday, September 12
8:00 P.M.

"He's totally out of fucking order," Rachel rants, as we sit around her dining-room table.

When I say we, I mean Rachel, Katy, Tish, Sylvester, and me. It is Rachel's bridal shower, and I am trying not to cry. But not sad tears. Angry tears. Ashamed-with-myself tears . . .

My first thought when I awake each morning is that I am no longer with Jack, but before the threatened tears and excruciating pain can rise to overwhelm me, my second thought is how angry I am with him.

If I can focus on my anger, I can get though the day.

Work is surprisingly unimportant to me. Although I've put my energy and willingness into the Chrysanthemum account, I just cannot raise my old enthusiasm.

And although Paul Morgan is easy and enthusiastic to

work with, I cannot get enthusiastic about his attempts to
date me, either. Wonder how he found out that I'd split with
Jack? Probably from Tracey in human resources . . . Charming and handsome, Paul has the whole of the female work-
force at his feet and Tracey (despite being married) often
calls down to see him under the guise of seeing me.

I do think it's a bit insensitive of Paul to imagine I'm over
Jack so easily, though . . .

But I'm not going to date my boss again. I did that once and
look where it got me. I'll tell you where it got me—sleeping in
my car and involved with Jack is where it got me . . .

Actually, I'm seriously considering giving up on dating
forever.

And although Paul would make a charming addition to
Rachel's wedding party tomorrow, and although it would
mean that I had a date, instead of turning up like some sad
spinster, I've decided that I rather like the *content* spinster
option.

Besides, Auntie Alice wouldn't worry about going alone.
She reveled in her independence, and I'm going to revel in
mine. I'm going to be Queen Boudicca, rising to the challenge. Definitely. Despite the fact that Jack is attending the
wedding with Claire . . .

Rachel was a bit worried about Jack and Claire's presence,
but she can't go uninviting people just because I've either
fallen out with them or can't stand them.

It will be fine.

Auntie Alice will sustain me . . .

My anger will sustain me . . .

"He's just a—a guy," Katy tells me, refilling my glass. "We
all know they're not that great about saying how they feel—
except you Sylvester, darling. Here, Emma, drink this."

In the week since the march, since my fight with Jack, I
have had plenty of time to think about what I said, and to regret some of it. And to cry a whole ocean of tears.

Although I do feel that Jack *did* compartmentalize me, and he *did* push me to one side too many times, I was just as guilty of not talking to him and telling him how I felt.

Our fight is a prime example. Why didn't he fight back harder? Or, indeed, at all? Why didn't he argue me into living with him? The night before was so gentle, so tender, so . . . God, I *can't* think about that now . . .

At least the *New Jersey Times* hasn't mentioned the HUSSI incident . . . And I should know. I have been waiting on Mr. Patel's doorstep at the crack of dawn every morning this week for the papers to be delivered. I think Mr. Patel suspects that I am some kind of nutcase.

But although I also think that Jack was more concerned about losing his contract than losing me, I have been agonizing over the speech I made about Claire. Because even *I* have to admit that Jack never once really gave me that much cause for concern about her. It was Claire I was concerned about.

At least that's what I thought until tonight.

Claire Palmer has moved in with Jack.

It's completely true!

Talk about leaping into my bed before it's cold . . .

"It is a disgrace, zat woman moving in wiz Jack before ze dust has settled," Sylvester says.

"But it's not *like* that," Tish says. "She's just moved in temporarily because her apartment is being painted." Tish is now heavily into the work on Claire's apartment. "Although"— Tish pauses—"she's very—demanding. To tell the truth, I'll be relieved when her apartment's finished."

Somehow, I don't think that Tish is quite so fond of Claire now that she's working for her.

"Her apartment's décor *is* important," Rachel defends Claire. "*I'm* demanding about that kind of stuff. Fuck—" she grins around the table, "I'm demanding about everything."

"But only in a good way, sweetie," Sylvester says. "Zis

Claire, I zink she is trying to steal Emma's life. *Non,*" he says, holding up his hands. "I know zat I am sometimes too dramatic, but zis time I am right. I zink zat woman's up to no good."

"I just can't see it," Rachel says.

Actually, Claire is a lot like Rachel, but without Rachel's good bits. And I wonder if that is part of the reason she gets on with Claire so well. But let's face it, her pregnancy hormones are still playing havoc with her.

"And I stand by what I said about Jack," Rachel continues, "He is a complete fucking idiot—but he loves you, Emma. *You.*" Rachel leans across the table and pats my arm. "He is a covalent bonder, and he bonded with you."

"It's written all over his face," Katy tells me. "Tom saw him in the deli on Monday and he looked like shit."

"Well, good. I'm sure it's because of his precious project and not because of me," I insist, and my lovely friends look at each other and shake their heads.

"She's still in denial," Rachel announces.

"I think she just needs time," Tish says, and my heart contracts with pain.

"Look," I say, with more cheer than I feel, because I just don't want to talk about this anymore. "This is a fucking Bridal Shower. Let's have some fucking fun."

Saturday, September 13
Rachel's wedding day

Today is going to be wonderful.

Nothing is going to ruin it, and I am going to enjoy myself (or at least pretend to enjoy myself) if it kills me (which it might, but have to put on a brave face for Rachel).

In a couple of hours' time I will be at Rachel's apartment, along with Rachel, Tish, and Katy. I will be upbeat and happy as I help my best friend ready herself for what is, after all, the happiest day of her life . . . or will be, if her mother doesn't fuss too much . . .

These thoughts hold me until I check my mailbox and find the latest edition of the HUSSI newsletter.

There is a rather grainy picture of Jack and me outside the police station as we had our last fight. Underneath, the caption reads:

HUSSI member Emma Taylor breaks up with long-term lover, architect Jack Brown, over proposed plans for new Hoboken Internet café.

The article is completely awful, and although doesn't quote me, is slanted toward the fact that I felt so stongly about my boyfriend's involvement in the project that I publicly humiliated him and broke up with him. Which is kind of true . . .

I immediately throw it into the trash. Human Being Kim must have been lurking outside the police station . . .

And although I try to convince myself that it's all Jack's fault for not telling me about it in the first place, I cannot. I should have made more effort to talk to him. I should have been more strident in my efforts to save our relationship, but I wasn't. And now it's too late to fix it.

And then another thought occurs to me . . .

Jack was right, I think to myself ten minutes later after another early-morning visit to Mr. Patel's store. Mr. Patel had a copy of the *New Jersey Times* in his hand, and was already ringing it up on the register when I opened the door to his store . . .

Matt Jones saved his article for today for the special weekly features section. There is a whole article about HUSSI (interview given by Marion Lacy) complete with the grainy picture of Jack and me breaking up. I wonder how much Human Being Kim got for selling that photo, and whether or not I can sue her.

This is a disaster, and could really cause trouble for him at work . . .

"Honey, how are you doing," Tish asks me six hours later, her face a picture of concern.

"I'm great," I say, trying not to glance across the huge banquet room to Jack and Claire. They really do make a striking couple.

"Zis is terrible," Sylvester tells me, as he scowls across at Claire. "I cannot believe he brings zis woman."

"Sylvester, it's fine. Rachel invited her," I say soothingly. The last thing I want is for Rachel's wedding to be ruined. I think wrecking Jack's career is enough trouble making for one year.

"How are you holding up?" Katy asks me, as Tom takes Alex to the bathroom.

"I'm great," I say, smiling brightly.

It has been like this all through the day. My lovely friends, concerned for my welfare, have all taken turns to fuss, and ask me how I'm doing. Because apart from my split with Jack, they have all, obviously, found time to purchase and read their own copies of the *New Jersey Times*.

How lovely that they've all been following the newspaper in their quest to support me. Matt Jones will be a hero because I expect it's increased sales to no end.

But I'm doing crap, because every time I catch sight of Jack's beloved face my anger dissipates and the pain in my chest is so tight, I can barely breathe. So I'm not looking at him at all.

"Stop it," Rachel, a vision in a simple, clean, elegant white dress, tells me. "Your English half is worrying about that fucking newspaper, isn't it?"

Until now I didn't think that Rachel knew about today's

article. I have been especially careful not to mention it in front of her, because I want today to be perfect for her.

"You read the newspaper on your wedding day? Didn't you have enough to keep you occupied?" I ask, but she can see that I'm smiling. Or trying to.

"I know you, Emma Taylor," she adds, a steely glint in her eye. "Now will you just go talk to that man?"

"No. I'm going to get some more of this lovely wine," I tell her.

Yes, I am a coward. My backbone is definitely crumbling.

As the bartender fills my glass with Chardonnay, instead of my usual Shiraz (because I don't want to get any stains on this lovely, pale cream bridesmaid dress) a small, furry body whines pitifully and snuffles against my feet.

"Betty, sweetheart," I say, squatting as elegantly as I can in this dress to pet her, and I can't help a smile at the sunflower yellow bow that Jack has fastened to her collar. "I missed you, honey," I croon as she licks my hand, and I wonder how Jack persuaded the posh maître d' to allow a dog in the banquet hall.

And as I worry if our breakup has damaged her forever, I see a pair of masculine legs in front of me. And I forget to breathe . . .

But I can't squat forever, so I get to my feet, and Jack is there in front of me. I can't bring myself to look into his face, so I focus on Betty, instead.

"Emma," he says by way of greeting, and I feel several pairs of eyes watching us.

"Jack," I nod briefly, and try not to notice how lovely he looks in his dark suit.

"How—how are you?" Why is he attempting to make conversation with me? He can't be the only one who didn't see that bloody newspaper this morning.

"Oh, I'm, you know, good." I can do this, I tell myself. The first time is always the hardest, and besides, we'll have to see each other in the future, because apart from the fact that his sister is married to my father, we have a lot of friends in common. It's unfair to make them choose between us, after all.

"Good. How's—how's work? How's the new lingerie account?"

God, this is awful. We're like two strangers. And I wish he hadn't mentioned work.

"It's going well," I say, trying to stop my hand from shaking as I gulp at my Chardonnay. "I've managed not to sabotage any one else's career, anyway," I add, gulping more Chardonnay. And I can't bear it, I have to ask him. "Er, speaking of—work—" I take another gulp of wine. "Did—did you see the *New Jersey Times* this morning?" I ask in a rush. Might as well get it out into the open.

"Yeah." I risk looking at his face. And my stomach begins to churn. "It was terrible," he says, smiling one of his wry smiles and my pulse kicks up speed.

"I'm sorry," I tell him, meaning it. "I hope it's not going to cause you any trouble—"

"It's fine," he says. But I know it can't be fine. Even if Larry Stenton doesn't hear about it, I'm sure it will make Jack a laughing stock at work . . .

"So—how's the lovely Claire?" I ask sarcastically, because I can't resist. Call me a masochist if you like . . .

"Emma—" he says, touching my arm. "I—" he breaks off, and whatever he was going to say is lost as Betty begins to growl.

"Jack, there you are," Claire Palmer is beautiful, yet ice cool in a pastel suit. "And Emma. How *are* you dear?" she asks with false sympathy as she touches my arm. "That article in the paper this morning was so . . . so terrible," she says, her hair falling around her shoulders as she shakes her head.

I am not giving her any hint that I am upset, because that

is what she wants. I try to conjure up the picture of Claire covered in blue paint.

"Really, dear, you should be more careful what you get involved in. It could have serious repercussions for Jack," she laughs her tinkly little laugh. "Although I'm sure we can manage the damage limitation. After all, it's not as if you and Jack are together any more, so that should help things considerably," she adds, smiling slyly at me as she tucks her hand possessively in the crook of Jack's arm. "Jack, did I tell you that Larry Stenton's coming for a visit next week—we should invite him for dinner."

She has not seen Rachel standing behind her. She does not see Rachel freeze and scowl as she hears Claire callously dismissing my relationship with Jack.

Betty, who has so far only been growling, leaps forward and bares her teeth at Claire. Although Betty cannot understand English, she is obviously sensitive to tones of voice and gets the general gist of Claire's words.

"Really, Jack, you'll really have to do something about that mangy dog," Claire says, taking a step backward. "It's a public menace."

"She's not the only one," I say, before Rachel jumps in to defend me, because the last thing she needs today is trouble at her own wedding.

I don't wait to hear Claire's reply, because although Betty is a wonderful, sweet thing and is an excellent judge of character, Claire is right about *one* thing.

Jack is better off without a ditz like me to ruin his career.

So I grab Rachel's arm and steer her to the ladies' room before she can explode and ruin her own wedding.

"That bitch," Rachel says through clenched teeth, as I hustle her through the door.

"I know," I say.

"Sylvester's so right about her stealing your life," she says.

"I know."

"Katy saw it. So did David, Hugh, and Tish. Fuck, I've been so blind. I just couldn't see what a bitch she is," she hits her forehead with the base of her hand.

"I know."

"Why couldn't I see it? I'm usually like Betty on character assessments."

"I know," I sigh.

"Can't you say anything else other than 'I know?' Why didn't you fight back just then? Why didn't you let *me* fight back *for* you?"

"Because . . . Look, sweetie," I sigh, placing a hand on her arm. "Apart from the fact that she has a point, that I could have ruined Jack's career with my stupid HUSSI demonstration—"

"Jack's as much to blame. If he'd told you about the fucking Internet café in the first place, you wouldn't be in this mess now. In fact I'm gonna go out there and—"

"No," I interrupt her before she can build up to a Rachel rant. She's a lot more like her old self these days. And it's lovely that she wants to leap in and fight my battles for me, but I have to do this my way.

"—tell Jack what a jerk—" she continues, and I place my hand on her arm and leap back in.

"I told Jack about Claire weeks ago and he didn't believe me," I say. I don't point out the obvious—that Rachel didn't believe me, either, until just now. "Jack has to figure this out for himself. And then he has to make his own decisions."

"Honey, I'm so sorry," Rachel says, her face a picture of remorse. "*I* didn't believe you about Claire, either. What kind of callous, hardhearted friend am I?"

"You're the best friend I could ever wish for," I tell her. "Now let's go finish your party With Style."

The rest of the wedding banquet passes in kind of a blur, and I stick to my friends at my end of the head table. I don't want to risk any more Claire encounters. Rachel, true to her promise, resists all temptation and leaves Claire well alone.

Greater love hath no woman than Rachel for her friends.

And when it's time for Rachel to throw her bouquet, *I* resist all attempts from my friends to stand with the other unmarried women.

"Come on," Katy tells me.

"It's tradition," Tish adds.

"Exactly," I say, "I'm making a new one."

"She's fucking right," Rachel tells me. And then she kisses me on the cheek. "You stay right there, honey."

And as Rachel stands on the balcony, her back to the throng of women below, I see Claire Palmer among them. God, I hope she doesn't get it. Anyone but her . . .

And as Rachel takes aim, and throws the bouquet over her shoulder . . . it flies completely over the women and lands on one of the tables. On Jack's table. In front of Jack.

The crowd cheers, and Claire Palmer beams at him as she walks back to her seat. And as she takes her place, her hand is on his arm, and she's whispering in his ear.

It's obviously a sign that Jack is going to marry Claire!

6:30 P.M.

Thank God this wedding is nearly over, is all I can say.

"My mother completely loves him," David tells me and Rachel. "I mean, it was a complete shock at first, but after she got used to the idea, she's really taken him under her wing. He spends more time with her on the telephone than I do."

"I told you it would work out," Claire Palmer says, as she joins our group. "Really, David, you could have saved yourself all this angst if only you'd listened to my advice and been honest with your mother."

I think Claire's had a bit too much to drink. I hope she

wakes up with a stinking hangover. But I can't help but glance around for Jack, because where Jack goes, Claire is bound to follow . . .

"Thank you, Claire," David says caustically, and I can see him backing off from her a bit. "But Emma was right. We just had to wait until we reached our mutual planes of tranquility."

"That book's great, Emma," Tish says from my elbow. "Rufus and me have been working on our positivity."

"I must read it," Rachel tells us, glaring at Claire. "I think I may need to focus on my tranquility in the coming months."

"At least you're not feeling sick all the time," I tell her.

"What book are you talking about?" Claire asks, and I wish she'd just go away. "I'm very widely read myself."

"It's Emma's self-help book. *Living Together: How to Transcendentally Compromise with Your Loved One* by Dr. Padvi Choyne," David tells her. "It's completely fantastic, just like Emma."

"Oh, I've heard about that," Claire laughs, and it is not a pleasant sound. "There was a big scandal about it in the publishing world about two years ago. My, my, Emma, that's too funny . . ."

"Maybe you'd like to share the joke with the rest of us?" David asks her silkily.

"What joke?" Jack asks, as he joins us.

"Really, Emma, that's just so . . . you," Claire snorts. "Padvi Choyne doesn't exist," she explains very helpfully. "It was a scam self-help book written by a phony psychologist— hence the name Padvi Choyne—it's an anagram for phony advice."

What does this woman want from me? Blood? What is this "Humiliate Emma" thing she's got going on?

"Really, dear, you are so silly. But we all know that after your recent behavior. God, I'd love to have seen your father's face when he read that article."

In that moment it is clear how Dad and Peri got their copy of the article. Thank you, Claire, I think, for hanging yourself on too much rope . . .

And as she crumples into a fit of giggles, I see red.

And in that instant I know what I am going to do. Tipping my elbow slightly forward, I empty my glass of Shiraz (because I switched to my favorite wine after the throwing-of-the-flowers incident) down her suit.

Claire shrieks as it hits her, and I think the red wine suits her even better than the blue paint.

"Oops," I say, to her. "I wish I could say sorry. But I'm not."

20

....

Communication Countdown

TO DO

1. Show courage of convictions.
2. Show commitment to others, world or otherwise.
3. Show triumph in face of adversity.

Reasons to achieve all of the above: no, not to qualify for Auntie Alice's inheritance . . . to qualify for Jack.

Sunday, October 5

Where else would we all be on a Sunday night except at Chez Nous?

When I say all, I mean Rachel and Hugh (newly back from honeymoon), Tish and Rufus, Katy and Tom, and, of course, Sylvester and David. And me.

Claire Palmer, fortunately, is no longer on the guest list.

No one's seen her since I poured my wine down her three

weeks ago at Rachel and Hugh's wedding, and abruptly departed. Good riddance to bad rubbish.

Jack isn't here, either. He is avoiding me, and who could blame him?

I felt a bit bad about the wine episode, actually. Not because of Claire Palmer's suit being ruined, but because I hadn't meant to cause a scene on Rachel's special day. I wanted it to be perfect for her. It was a very childish thing for me to do, but I'd really had enough of Claire and her snide remarks.

And I don't care if Dr. Padvi Choyne is a phony . . . I, personally, think a lot of the advice within the book's pages is very good . . .

Actually, I haven't seen Rachel since the wedding, either, because she and Hugh only arrived back from Aruba this afternoon.

Of course, I *have* spoken to her on a daily basis . . . we've all spoken to her on a daily basis. After all, it is vital to have access to telephone communication with friends at all times of the day and night, from all corners of the globe, even on honeymoon . . . even at the airport on the way to the honeymoon . . .

Rachel called me from the airport to ask (a) was I all right, because she was fucking worried about me, and (b) to tell me that I hadn't ruined her fucking wedding. I'd *made* her fucking wedding . . . she hadn't had such a good laugh for ages. And, of course, she had a bit of a rant about Claire (because there's nothing Rachel loves more than a good rant, thank God).

"I never actually *liked* her" she tells me, hastily rewriting history as she and Hugh wait for their outward-bound flight. "Not exactly *liked*. I just needed time to come to a decision about her, because you should never make a snap decision about someone."

I let that pass.

"I'm sure it was just my pregnancy hormones," she says.

But anyway, since the wedding I have moved past my anger with Jack and am now in the missing, grieving, regret-what-I-said, regret-what-I-did, love-you-so-much-it's-killing-me phase. A year ago, when we broke up before we actually got together, I had Jack-itus, and I couldn't imagine ever feeling worse.

It is nothing to how I feel now.

Because now I know what I am missing.

And I do miss him, terribly. I am trying to figure out what to do, because what if he's glad to be rid of me?

But while I have been pining for him, I have discovered something very interesting . . . several interesting some-things, actually . . .

I got a call from Mr. Stoat a few days after the wedding to talk about my horrible HUSSI escapade. I must say, I was *very* surprised to hear from him.

"My dear Miss Taylor," Mr. Stoat tells me in his dry dusty voice when I pick up. "Let me just say that I was very sorry to read in the *New Jersey Times* about your rather dramatic separation from Mr. Brown."

"I'm not following you, Mr. Stoat," I say, because I didn't send him a copy of that particular article. I was too busy seething about Claire and missing Jack.

I bet it was Rachel . . . knowing her, she probably scanned and e-mailed it to him about five minutes after she received it, despite it being her wedding day. It was so lovely of her to try this . . .

"And sad though it is, I'm afraid it just won't do in terms of qualifying for your aunt's terms and conditions."

"Don't stress over it Mr. Stoat," I tell him, because I have ceased to care about the bloody inheritance. "Rachel's a bit forthright. She probably thought it was worth a shot sending it to you."

"I didn't receive it from your friend Rachel," Mr. Stoat tells me. "I got it from Mr. Brown."

After Mr. Stoat hangs up it takes me quite a while to scoop my jaw up off the floor . . .

Jack sent it to him? Jack tried to help me qualify for my inheritance. How lovely of him to do that! And how much I ache for him . . . I don't know what to do . . . I ought to, at least, pick up the telephone and thank him.

But every time I start to dial his number, I get cold feet. What if Claire answers the phone?

But there's more . . .

On Wednesday Paul Morgan and I met with Hanko Matsushita to discuss the Chrysanthemum campaign. She completely *loved* our ideas and Cougan and Cray have the contract. It's true!

Picture this: One day in the life of the Chrysanthemum girl (have suggested actress such as Kate Hudson or Reese Witherspoon to give young, fun-loving ambience).

Chrysanthemum girl leaps excitedly out of bed, showers, and then puts on her Chrysanthemum underwear before selecting marvelous designer outfit. Chrysanthemum girl on way to work in crowded subway. Chrysanthemum girl in meetings, Chrysanthemum girl at lunch. Chrysanthemum girl rushing around for busy afternoon of work. Chrysanthemum girl goes out to dinner, and because her underwear is so fresh and odor fighting, she doesn't need to change first. Her slogan: Odor of Chrysanthemums—end the day smelling as sweetly as you began (okay, have borrowed a bit from D. H. Lawrence—I just knew my English degree would come in handy one day).

My other idea featured Crown Princess Masako look-alike and following her around on her busy day as a diplomat and new mother (have always admired her, but it might be a bit insensitive to the Japanese Royal Family).

Anyway, Hanko completely loved Chrysanthemum girl, so that's great, isn't it?

Another great thing is that William Cougan, like Elvis, has

left the building. It's true! According (naturally) to Tracey, Babette offered him either early retirement (plus she insisted on purchasing ten percent of his shares so he no longer was a voice) or early retirement to prison.

Things around Cougan & Cray will be very different from now on, I feel.

But after the meeting with Ms. Matsushita, just as she was getting ready to leave, I remember that I've been intending to ask her something . . .

"Ms. Matsushita, I've been meaning to ask you. Why did you approach me, in particular, about this account?"

"You were highly recommended by Jack Brown," she tells me. "He worked on our new office building."

I must do *something* . . .

And tonight, Tish told me something *else* very interesting about Jack.

"Claire Palmer's moved back to her own apartment and Jack's not working with her anymore," she tells me the minute I arrive at Chez Nous. "In fact, he hasn't got a job. Claire fired him. Rufus saw him walking Betty earlier, didn't you Rufus?"

"Aye," Rufus agrees with her. A man of few words, Rufus. "He looked really tired and washed out," Rufus adds, so I know he must really mean it. Actually, poor Rufus is looking very tired and washed out himself, these days, I think, as I try to absorb the startling news about Jack.

Although Rufus and Tish are deliriously happy, and although he's managed to deflect his pushy mother from visiting for a bit, Rufus has other fish to fry. Tish fish to fry . . .

See, in view of her impending (according to Tish) decrepitude, she wants to start a family as soon as possible, and has purchased even more magazines, all of the necessary books on pregnancy, and all the necessary equipment to determine when she is most fertile.

We just don't mention folic acid around her because she

knows all about the benefits of folic acid in great depth. But on her fertile days, Rufus doesn't get a great deal of rest, and Tish has taken to wearing loose-fitting clothes, just for practice . . .

"Oh," I say, my mind clicking and whirring with the Jack news as Sylvester pushes me into the nearest seat and hands me a glass of Shiraz.

Jack lost his job? Oh, God, this is all *my* fault. Me and the stupid HUSSI demonstration . . .

"Poor Jack, you must do somezing about him," Sylvester wails. "Zis is stupid, you are meant for each ozzer. Poor Betty, she needs her *mère.*"

"I know," I say.

"Someone to love and cherish her. Forever," Sylvester stresses. Sylvester, it seems, also has babies on the mind these days. He turned forty-one two weeks ago and David says it's just a broody phrase he's going through . . .

"I know," I say again.

"Darling," Rachel tells me, "we've been talking about your situation and we're all agreed." Rachel is completely back to her old self, now, and has her finger back on the pulse of everyone's business (particularly mine) and what she feels would be right for them (particularly me).

Hugh, it seems, has got the hang of fighting with her again and starts at least two arguments a day to keep her happy. He is a wise man . . .

"And on the practical side you have a small apartment full of huge birthday gifts," Katy informs me. "They'd look so great in Jack's house." Katy, ever of the logistical mind, has to go to Africa on business to check that the money her charity raises for children is being spent wisely. She hasn't told Tom, yet, because he's still getting used to being a stay-at-home dad. But I think he'll be okay with it. And he has landed several more Web sites to design, which is great.

"I know," I say yet again.

"You were made for each other," David adds his weight to the conversation. "Sweetie, what's taking you two so long—you're worse than me and Sylvester. And yes, Sylvester, it was all my fault before you remind me of it."

"I know." I'm wondering if I should even bother opening my mouth.

At least I *think* I know Jack and me are made for each other . . . I have to take a chance. I have to find out for once and all. I can't live my life in this miserable limbo . . .

"And you can't let your insecure English half worry," Tish adds. "Jack needs a push. In his eyes, the disaster with Claire was all his fault and he didn't believe you."

"I know." Honestly, is anyone actually listening to me here? But actually, Tish has a point. My English half . . .

"Sweetie, you can't just keep saying 'I know'—you have to have a plan," Rachel starts another rant. "You have to make a list. Remember what Mrs. Pankhurst said—Deeds not words."

"Actually, I *do* have a plan . . ." I know, in that moment, exactly what I am going to do. Since the last article in the *New Jersey Times,* Matt Jones has left repeated messages on my voicemail. It seems he wants to interview me . . . But after my brushes with his newspaper, I don't feel very warm toward the media in general. Except for Hoboken Happiness AM, of course. Actually, Gordon Smiley's team has been trying to reach me, too . . .

"After all, if Mohammed won't come to the mountain, the mountain will have to go to Mohammed," Rachel tells me.

"Yes, I know," I say. "As I was saying, I have a plan."

Rachel pins me to my seat with her gimlet eyes. "Spill," she commands me. So I do.

Friday, October 10
10:30 A.M.
Hoboken Happiness AM radio station, Secaucus

Gordon Smiley: "Rise and shine, Hoboken, this is Gordon Smiley and our wakeup song this morning was Led Zeppelin's 'Since I've Been Loving You,' specially chosen for you by our guest, Emma Taylor.

"Emma made her first appearance on this show several weeks ago following an article in the *New Jersey Times,* when she talked about a rather small feature of her anatomy.

"By popular demand, we've managed to persuade her to come back to visit us again. Emma recently made the *New Jersey Times* again, but this time it featured the very public split between Emma and her boyfriend, Jack Brown.

"The main thrust of the article was that Emma and Jack were on two opposing sides of the construction of a new Internet café. Emma was protesting against construction. But Jack is, or was, one of the architects working on the project. Good morning, Emma."

Me: "Good morning Gordon, thanks for inviting me back. And yes, you're absolutely right. We were on opposing sides of the dispute. But that wasn't really the problem. You see, I didn't know Jack was working on that project. He didn't know that I was planning to protest that particular project site."

Gordon: "So it's a case of communication breakdown?"

Me: "That's the absolute crux of our problem. And you know, the repercussions were terrible. Apart from the fact that we had a terrible fight and we split up, Jack lost his job. And I really want to make it up to him. So if there are any listeners out there looking for a completely fantastic architect, please call the radio station and leave your details."

Gordon: "Emma, that's a really nice thing do. But I under-stand that you have something to say to Jack. Do you know if he's listening?"

Me: "I hope so. I truly hope so . . ."

(God, I hope he's listening. But I'm also petrified that he *is*. What if he doesn't come?)

Gordon: "Folks, because of the communication break-down between them, Emma is here today to open up the lines of communication between her and Jack. Go ahead, Emma."

Me: "Er . . ."

(Okay, I have to do this. I *want* to do this.)

Gordon: "Emma?"

Me: "Jack . . . if you're out there, I just want you to know that I miss you terribly. We should have talked . . . but we didn't . . . and so I'm going to say my piece right now.

"One hundred years ago today Emmeline Pankhurst created the Women's Social and Political Union to further the Suffrage Movement and votes for women.

"Among other things, the suffragettes fought for female emancipation—the right to choose. Today I'm making my own stand for the one thing that will truly emancipate *me*.

"In court, Emmeline Pankhurst once said, 'We are here, not because we are lawbreakers; we are here in our efforts to become lawmakers.'

"Here, on the radio, in front of all the people listening this morning I, Emmeline Beaufort Taylor say to you, Jack Brown, 'I am here, not because I am a lawbreaker; I am here in my effort to become a . . . a . . . a lovemaker.' "

(Small pause as my voice breaks.)

"You're my extra electron, Jack, and I'll never be fully charged, never be complete without you. I love you . . . I've never loved anyone more. I want to spend the rest of my life with you. I want to have children with you.

"Jack Brown, will . . . will . . . you marry me?"

(God, I did it. My voice wobbled, my legs are wobbling, *all* of me is wobbling, but I *did it.*)

Gordon: "I don't know about you folks out there, but there isn't a dry eye in the studio here. Emma, that was beautiful. And if Jack says no after that, I'll be happy to step into his shoes. Now, you have something more to say to Jack, don't you Emma?"

Me: "I'm making my stand for you, Jack. If the answer is yes, come to the radio station parking lot. I'll be there until midday. If you don't show, then I . . . I guess it's over between us. But I hope that you *do* come. *Please* come . . ."

11:00 A.M.

I'm a complete bag of nerves when I step out of the radio station and into the parking lot. This is not helped by the fact that it is filled with people. But I couldn't technically make a stand if there was no one to witness it.

Even Julia is with me in spirit. Well she's listening on the Internet, so it's almost the same thing. At least I hope she's listening . . . I called her yesterday to tell her to tune in, but I got George instead.

"She's gone to some beauty salon shindig," George tells me rather dourly.

"What's she suing them for?" I laugh, because it's nice to hear she's getting back to normal—she's been so concerned with her age since Auntie Alice died. But it's always about causes with Julia, thank God.

"Oh, she's not suing them," George tells me. "She's having her hair touched up and her free radicals liberated, or some such nonsense. I tell you, Emma, she's not getting all this 'stay young forever' rubbish from me."

"I'm sure it will be okay, George," I sigh, and George sighs with me. "After all, it's entirely normal for a woman to want to make the most of herself," I add, because it's true, isn't it? I mean, I don't think using wrinkle cream twice a day makes one a slave to preserving youth and beauty. Although Julia has never concerned herself with beauty treatments before . . .

"Aye, that's what I thought. I'll tell her about the radio show—give me the particulars and I'll make sure we're online."

Anyway, as well as George and Julia in spirit, a radio crew is out here with me, and will be feeding information to Gordon Smiley on the air so that the listeners can be kept up-to-date with my progress . . .

Or my lack of it . . .

"Good luck, Emma," Jane says, giving me the thumbs up.

"This is so romantic!!" Stacey clasps her hands together.

There are quite a lot of HUSSI members here today to watch me make a fool of myself . . . but not Marion, obviously.

Shortly after the debacle with the blue paint, Marion and the more extreme members of the group departed under a cloud . . .

Apart from the fact that she was trying to plan an extremely unpopular campaign (picture this: a blockade of all the streets in central Hoboken to promote child safety—can't you just imagine the chaos and dangerous accidents that would cause?), there were rather a lot of questions about just *what* the Anthropoid Allotments, Homo Sapiens Handouts and Creature Contributions were being spent on.

I suppose Marion has more to worry about these days, with her court case coming up and all . . .

Fortunately, Jane is now running the group, and you know what? We eat Hershey's kisses at the meetings, just to spite Marion's legacy. And we're currently arranging a fund-raiser to raise money to help Native American children get shoes and blankets. You wouldn't believe in this day and age that so many children in this nation don't have a blanket to keep them warm at night, would you? But it's completely true . . .

Anyway, all of my friends are here, of course, because it wouldn't be the same without them . . . God, *what if Jack doesn't come?*

"He'll come," Tish, looking all fecund and Mother Earthish in a loose-fitting dress, tells me. Rufus, who looks bleary-eyed, just nods agreement. I hope they get pregnant soon.

"He'd better fucking come," Rachel says with a steely glint in her eye. "Hugh called him this morning to make sure he'd be listening to your broadcast. Have you got everything?"

"Yes," I tell her, and take a deep breath.

I have: a pair of handcuffs, my gel bra, a fire extinguisher (just in case) . . . and Auntie Alice's phallic finial. I know this isn't what she had in mind when she left me her bequest, but I can only hope that she will forgive me for choosing Jack, instead.

"Right. I'm ready," I tell David, and he handcuffs me to the iron railings surrounding the parking lot.

Now we wait . . .

11:20 A.M.

"Zere is plenty of time," Sylvester tells me, squinting toward the road for signs of Jack's car. "He will come, because he is a romantic at heart just like me, and he cannot resist you, Emma. And I called him zis morning to remind him to listen."

I wish I were as sure.

"Also, David, he called Jack zis morning. Rufus called, too, so zere is no chance he can miss it."

11:45 A.M.

There is still no sign of Jack, and with only fifteen minutes to go, my stomach is churning and I feel sick. My legs are rubber, and I'm leaning against the railings for support. It just doesn't *take* this long to get here from Hoboken.

"Here, drink this," Katy tells me, handing me a bottle of water. "Tom's gone to the car to check the traffic news on the radio. I bet Jack's stuck in traffic on Route 3."

"Relax," Rachel orders me, but I can see that she's not quite so confident any more.

"Hey, Emma," Sid, one of the radio crew tells me. "We just got a message on the bulletin board from your mother. She said she and George will be over on the next plane to sue the pants off Jack for broken promises, or something, if he doesn't show."

How lovely is that?

"And she also said to remind you to wear sunscreen on account of the skin-damaging properties of the sun."

11:50 A.M.

"Maybe he's had an accident," Katy frets.

"Well thanks, that's very reassuring," Rachel scowls at her. "And no, Hugh, I don't want to sit down, before you ask."

"I wasn't going to say a word," Hugh holds up his hands. "But if you want to end up with varicose veins then hey, I'm fine with that."

And so they start a halfhearted argument. But at least it passes the slowly dragging time.

But what if Jack *has* had an accident, what if he was speeding to get here and . . . No. I am not going to obsess.

"He'll be grand, so don't yer worry," Rufus tells me quietly. "He'll be here."

11:57 A.M.

My well-wishers are now completely silent.

They are exchanging solemn, disappointed headshakes, and are then glancing back at me with pitying expressions.

But you know what? I don't regret doing this for a minute. I went all out for what I wanted, and I knew that failure was a possibility. A strong one, it seems.

"David, can you unlock me? I think it's a bit pointless to continue with this," I say, my heart in my shoes.

"Just three more minutes, honey," David wheedles. "You've been here this long, you might as well finish in style."

"A Frenchwoman, she always does everyzing wiz style," Sylvester tells me. "You are an honorary Frenchwoman to me, *chérie.*" He pats my arm, and I stiffen my backbone. That's one of the nicest things anyone has ever said to me.

And he's right. Always do everything With Style.

Even abject humiliation . . .

11:59:45 P.M.

Countdown has begun on the air, and the crowd is counting down with the radio. I think they are trying to make me feel better, because people keep calling out things like "You go girl," which is nice . . .

"Come on, sweetie," Rachel says, putting her arm around my shoulders. "Let's get you out of here."

"*Non.*" Sylvester is adamant. "We wait fifteen seconds. Jack, he will be here."

11:59:58 P.M.

That's it then. Time's up. I have my answer.

"He's here!"

A loud roar emanates from the crowd, and I can't believe my eyes. To cheers and whistles, Jack drives my daffodil yellow, flower-painted Beetle into the parking lot. The crowd parts like the proverbial Red Sea as Jack pulls up right next to where I am chained.

And as Jack opens the car door, and as Betty (resplendent in yellow bows) trot-hops across the tarmac and woofs excitedly at my heels, and as Jack climbs out of the car, his eyes are firmly fastened on mine. He is smiling. It is the sweetest sight I have ever seen, and it does not escape my attention that his eyes are glistening with tears. In his hand is a bunch of flowers.

I am a withered, emaciated sunflower again, it seems.

And as he reaches me and raises my free hand to his lips, the crowd goes wild.

"What took you so long?" I say, but my voice comes out as a squeak because I have absolutely no control over my vocal chords.

"Because I stopped for these," he says, placing my sunflowers on the wall. "And this," he says, as he releases my hand and reaches into his pants' pocket.

It is a small, velvet box.

And as he opens it, my heart pounds in my chest and tears stream down my face.

Inside is a completely perfect diamond ring, and a sob catches in my throat.

"I wanted to arrive With Style." His hand trembles as he slides the ring onto my finger. It's a perfect fit.

"The answer is yes," he says.

And as he takes me into his arms and kisses me, I forget the crowds, I forget my friends, I forget everything. Except for Jack.

I even forget to burn the gel bra.

....

Epilogue

Saturday, October 11
7:15 A.M.

When I open my eyes my first thought of the day is *thank God I'm in Jack's bed. With Jack!*

And my second thought is *I'm getting married! I'm going to be Mrs. Emma Brown! Y-e-s!*

Although we'll have to wait a little while on account of Jack not being gainfully employed at the moment . . . see, Jack wants us to have a proper wedding with all the bells and whistles, and everything. And let's face it, my three thousand dollar savings won't go very far—not nearly enough for even a new roof!

But after everything I went through to get him back, he says I deserve only the best.

Oh, my lovely man was so embarrassed about Claire, and about not seeing through her before. We had a long chat about things when we got home (home is such a lovely word) yesterday afternoon . . . see, Jack didn't get fired. He quit!

This is what happened . . .

"I can't believe I didn't see though Claire Palmer sooner," Jack tells me, as he leads me into the bedroom and takes me into his arms. "She was so terrible at Rachel's wedding. Why didn't I see it?"

"Don't worry," I say, snuggling into his warmth. I'm feeling too good to think about Claire right now, and can afford to be magnanimous. "Rachel didn't see through Claire until the wedding, either, and you know how good she is at character assessment—well, under normal circumstances."

"I'm a *guy*," he says as we sit on the bed. "I'm not good at this feminine wiles stuff."

"I know," I say, as I stroke his cheek with my finger.

"After your stylish exit from the wedding, she really showed her true colors. And you were right about another thing, too—she really thought, you know—me and her . . . And nothing happened, I swear. I made her move into a hotel the next day."

"I know," I say again, loving him even more. "At least she has great taste in men." See, I've let go of my anger, as per Dr. Padvi's instructions . . . I still think that's a very good book, despite being a phony.

"And then I was too ashamed of myself to come after you. I should have listened to you. I shouldn't have compartmentalized you."

"I made a mess of things, too," I say, as I tug at his T-shirt. See, we're really reaching our transcendental planes of tranquility, here. "But it doesn't seem right that you lost your job and she kept hers."

And then Jack tells me some very interesting Claire news . . . apparently, some big shot firm in Boston has made her an offer and she's already left! As far as I'm concerned, Boston can have her. And, it seems, she left under a bit of a dark cloud—apparently, just after her sudden departure there was talk in the office about her bad treatment of more junior staff . . . complaints had been made to senior management.

So Jack didn't really need to hand in his notice at all. Except he did. Need to, I mean.

"Even with Claire gone, I'd still be working the same crazy hours—more, in fact. And you know what? After I lost you I realized that all those long hours at work were meaningless."

How lovely is he!

"No one goes to their grave wishing they'd spent more time at work," I tell him wisely. Auntie Alice used to say this a lot. A very smart woman, Auntie Alice.

"I mean, I'll still need to get a job—but I was thinking of something less crazy. Maybe going it alone?"

"Absolutely," I say, tugging at his zipper. "Money isn't everything. As long as we have enough for what we need, we'll be fine."

Jack takes my face in his hands. "Whatever did I do to deserve you, Emma Taylor? How did I nearly throw you away?"

"Let's not start apportioning blame," I tell him. "It's all in the past, now."

"Like your inheritance."

I told him about that marriage clause in Auntie Alice's letter, too. We're not going to keep things from each other from now onward. Because that's what got us into trouble in the first place.

"I don't care about any old inheritance, I just want to marry you."

"You sure?"

"Absolutely," I tell him, snuggling closer. "What would I do with the whole railing, anyway?"

So since then, we've pretty well spent the last seventeen hours in bed . . . Oh, telephone . . .

I mean, it's not like I don't want to chat with my friends, but it is important to cement one's engagement with a lot of uninterrupted togetherness, isn't it?

"Go on," Jack rumbles in my ear as he spoons me closer, and I can hear the smile in his voice. "You know you want to pick up. It's probably for you—one of your multitude of friends, desperate for your advice. Or your mother."

See—Jack totally understands me! Well, most of the time . . .

As I reach for the phone, Jack moves with me and nuzzles my neck, and his hands are doing wicked things to—certain parts of my anatomy. I can barely breathe.

"Hello," I burble down the phone. At least the person on the other end can't see what we're doing!

"My dear Miss Taylor," Mr. Stoat tells me in his dry dusty voice. "I do hope I'm not calling at an inconvenient time."

"Not at all," I say, trying not to gasp. I'm going to miss my little chats with Mr. Stoat, but I have to wonder why he's calling.

"Get rid of whoever it is real quick," Jack whispers, nuzzling my ear. "I have plans for you Emma Taylor."

"I thought it might be appropriate to call on a Saturday, rather than to wait until Monday morning," Mr. Stoat continues, as I try to focus on him rather than on Jack's hands. "Because I would like to congratulate you on demonstrating all three qualities required by your late aunt's will."

I *have?* I sit up and Jack stops nuzzling my neck, and removes his hands from my person.

"What? But I *can't* have. And besides, I'm getting married. Auntie Alice said definitely no marriage," I say, as Betty trot-hops across the bedroom and bounces onto the bed.

"That was entirely her point," Mr. Stoat tells me. "She wanted you to disobey that clause."

At this point I'm totally confused. I slide out of bed, and begin pacing the room.

"But what about the rest of the terms? I haven't done—"
The light is finally beginning to dawn.

"Yes, Miss Taylor, I have a recorded copy of yesterday's transmission from your very good friend Mrs. Peters."

Aha. Rachel. It's still odd hearing her called by Hugh's name, though.

"Point one. You have shown the courage of your convictions by making your stand for Mr. Brown, yesterday. Point two. You have shown commitment to Mr. Brown. Point three. You triumphed in the face of adversity. Your aunt would be very proud of you, my dear. But now for the most important part of your inheritance—"

As Mr. Stoat tells me about my inheritance, I let out a squeal of excitement and I'm jumping up and down buck naked on the bedroom floor.

Jack and Betty are watching me from the bed. Jack is grinning, and I could swear that Betty is, too (and yes, I do realize that she is a dog, but who knows?).

"I have already entrusted it to the hands of a reputable courier and you should receive it early in the week."

"Thank you, thank you, thank you, Mr. Stoat." I'm so excited I can barely breathe.

"And Miss Taylor, may I just say that it has been a pleasure dealing with you. Many congratulations to both yourself and Mr. Brown on your forthcoming nuptials."

When I hang up the telephone, I leap onto the bed and onto Jack.

"Jack," I tell him. "You are not going to *believe* this."

"I take it you've earned your inheritance?" he asks, as I plant kisses all over his face.

"I get an embroidered E. P. handkerchief," I tell him, still kissing his face.

And then I tell him something else.

"Plus a check for two hundred and fifty thousand pounds."

I think it's safe to say that two hundred and fifty thousand pounds will pay for a *very* nice wedding!

And a new roof, obviously . . .

AVON TRADE... because every great bag deserves a great book!

ALISA KWITNEY
Author of *The Dominant Blonde* and *Does She or Doesn't She*

Sometimes you've got to get him...

On the Couch

"Alisa, charming, funny, and sexy."
—Carly Phillips, *New York Times* bestselling author

Paperback $10.95
($16.95 Can.)
ISBN 0-06-053079-0

SONIA SINGH

Goddess for Hire

Paperback $13.95
($21.95 Can.)
ISBN 0-06-059036-X

CAROLE MATTHEWS
USA Today bestselling author of *For Better, for Worse* and *Bare Necessity*

THE Sweetest TABOO

Is nothing sacred?

Paperback $10.95
ISBN 0-06-059562-0

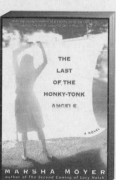

THE
LAST
OF THE
HONKY-TONK
ANGELS

A NOVEL

MARSHA MOYER
author of *The Second Coming of Lucy Hatch*

Paperback $13.95
($21.95 Can.)
ISBN 0-06-008164-3

Temporary
Insanity
a novel

LESLIE CARROLL

Paperback $13.95 ($21.95 Can.)
ISBN 0-06-056337-0

MICHELLE CUNNAH
author of *32AA*

CALL WAITING

A NOVEL

Paperback $10.95
($16.95 Can.)
ISBN 0-06-056036-3

Don't miss the next book by your favorite author.
Sign up for AuthorTracker by visiting *www.AuthorTracker.com*.

Available wherever books are sold, or call 1-800-331-3761 to order.

ATP 0804